PRAISE FOR DONNA GRANT'S BEST-SELLING ROMANCE NOVELS

"Grant's ability to quickly convey complicated backstory makes this jam-packed love story accessible even to new or periodic readers." –*Publishers' Weekly*

"Donna Grant has given the paranormal genre a burst of fresh air…" –*San Francisco Book Review*

"The premise is dramatic and heartbreaking; the characters are colorful and engaging; the romance is spirited and seductive." –*The Reading Cafe*

"The central romance, fueled by a hostage drama, plays out in glorious detail against a backdrop of multiple ongoing issues in the "Dark Kings" books. This seemingly penultimate installment creates a nice segue to a climactic end." –*Library Journal*

"…intense romance amid the growing war between the Dragons and the Dark Fae is scorching hot." –*Booklist*

**DON'T MISS THESE OTHER NOVELS BY
NYT & USA Today bestselling author DONNA GRANT**

CONTEMPORARY PARANORMAL

ELVEN KINGDOMS
Rising Sun ~ Dark Heart ~ Storm Wood
Mountain Fire ~ Burning Sea

THE BASTARD DUOLOGY
The Bastard King ~ The Uncrowned King

DRAGON KINGS® SERIES
Dragon Revealed ~ Dragon Mine ~ Dragon Unbound
Dragon Eternal ~ Dragon Lover ~ Dragon Arisen
Dragon Frost ~ Dragon Kiss ~ Dragon Born
Dragon Marked ~ Dragon Forged ~ Dragon Sieged

REAPER SERIES
Dark Alpha's Claim ~ Dark Alpha's Embrace
Dark Alpha's Demand ~ Books 1-3: Tall Dark Deadly Alpha
Dark Alpha's Lover ~ Dark Alpha's Night
Dark Alpha's Hunger ~ Dark Alpha's Awakening
Dark Alpha's Redemption ~ Dark Alpha's Temptation
Dark Alpha's Caress ~ Dark Alpha's Obsession
Dark Alpha's Need ~ Dark Alpha's Silent Night
Dark Alpha's Passion ~ Dark Alpha's Command
Dark Alpha's Fury

SKYE DRUIDS SERIES
Iron Ember ~ Shoulder the Skye ~ Heart of Glass
Endless Skye ~ Still of the Night ~ Blood Skye
After Midnight ~ Kiss of Skye ~ Between Twilight

DARK KINGS SERIES
Dark Heat ~ Darkest Flame ~ Fire Rising ~ Burning Desire
Hot Blooded ~ Night's Blaze ~ Soul Scorched ~ Dragon King
Passion Ignites ~ Smoldering Hunger ~ Smoke and Fire
Dragon Fever ~ Firestorm ~ Blaze ~ Dragon Burn
Constantine: A History, Parts 1-3 ~ Heat ~ Torched
Dragon Night ~ Dragonfire ~ Dragon Claimed
Ignite ~ Fever ~ Dragon Lost ~ Flame ~ Inferno
A Dragon's Tale (Whisky and Wishes: *A Holiday Novella*,
Heart of Gold: *A Valentine's Novella*, & Of Fire and Flame)
My Fiery Valentine ~ The Dragon King Coloring Book
Dragon King Special Edition Character Coloring Book: Rhi

DARK WARRIORS SERIES
Midnight's Master ~ Midnight's Lover ~ Midnight's Seduction
Midnight's Warrior ~ Midnight's Kiss ~ Midnight's Captive
Midnight's Temptation ~ Midnight's Promise
Midnight's Surrender ~ A Warrior for Christmas

CHIASSON SERIES
Wild Fever ~ Wild Dream ~ Wild Need
Wild Flame ~ Wild Rapture

LARUE SERIES
Moon Kissed ~ Moon Thrall ~ Moon Struck ~ Moon Bound

WICKED TREASURES
Seized by Passion ~ Enticed by Ecstasy ~ Captured by Desire
Books 1-3: Wicked Treasures Box Set

HISTORICAL PARANORMAL

THE KINDRED SERIES
Everkin ~ Eversong ~ Everwylde ~ Everbound
Evernight ~ Everspell

KINDRED: THE FATED SERIES
Rage ~ Ruin ~ Reign

DARK SWORD SERIES
Dangerous Highlander ~ Forbidden Highlander
Wicked Highlander ~ Untamed Highlander
Shadow Highlander ~ Darkest Highlander

ROGUES OF SCOTLAND SERIES
The Craving ~ The Hunger ~ The Tempted ~ The Seduced
Books 1-4: Rogues of Scotland Box Set

THE SHIELDS SERIES
A Dark Guardian ~ A Kind of Magic ~ A Dark Seduction
A Forbidden Temptation ~ A Warrior's Heart
Mystic Trinity (a series connecting novel)

DRUIDS GLEN SERIES
Highland Mist ~ Highland Nights ~ Highland Dawn
Highland Fires ~ Highland Magic
Mystic Trinity (a series connecting novel)

SISTERS OF MAGIC TRILOGY
Shadow Magic ~ Echoes of Magic ~ Dangerous Magic
Books 1-3: Sisters of Magic Box Set

THE ROYAL CHRONICLES NOVELLA SERIES
Prince of Desire ~ Prince of Seduction
Prince of Love ~ Prince of Passion
Books 1-4: The Royal Chronicles Box Set
Mystic Trinity (a series connecting novel)

DARK BEGINNINGS: A FIRST IN SERIES BOXSET
Chiasson Series, Book 1: Wild Fever
LaRue Series, Book 1: Moon Kissed
The Royal Chronicles Series, Book 1: Prince of Desire

MILITARY ROMANCE / ROMANTIC SUSPENSE

SONS OF TEXAS SERIES
The Hero ~ The Protector ~ The Legend
The Defender ~ The Guardian

COWBOY / CONTEMPORARY

HEART OF TEXAS SERIES
The Christmas Cowboy Hero ~ Cowboy, Cross My Heart
My Favorite Cowboy ~ A Cowboy Like You
Looking for a Cowboy ~ A Cowboy Kind of Love

STAND ALONE BOOKS
That Cowboy of Mine ~ Home for a Cowboy Christmas
Mutual Desire ~ Forever Mine ~ Savage Moon

* * *

Check out Donna Grant's Online Store at
www.DonnaGrant.com/shop
for autographed books, character
themed goodies, and more!

Kiss of Skye

SKYE DRUIDS

EIGHT

NEW YORK TIMES & USA TODAY BESTSELLING AUTHOR

DONNA GRANT

KISS OF SKYE
© 2026 by DL Grant, LLC
Cover Design © 2026 by Hang Le
ISBN 13: 978-1-958353-69-1
Available in ebook, print, and audio.
All rights reserved.

Glimpse at BURNING SEA
© 2026 by DL Grant, LLC

All rights reserved, including the right to reproduce or transmit this book, or a portion thereof, in any form or by any means, electronic or mechanical, without permission in writing from the author. No part of this book may be used to create, feed, or refine artificial intelligence models, for any purpose, without written permission from the author. This book may not be resold or uploaded for distribution to others. Thank you for respecting the hard work of this author.

This is a work of fiction created without use of AI technology (Human Authored™ — Reg #: 2622975, https://authorsguild.org/human). Any names, characters, places or incidents portrayed in this novel are either products of the author's imagination or are used fictitiously. Any resemblance to actual people, places, or events is purely coincidental or fictional.

No AI Training: Without in any way limiting the author's exclusive rights under copyright, any use of this publication to "train" generative artificial intelligence (AI) technologies to generate text is expressly prohibited.

www.DonnaGrant.com
www.MotherofDragonsBooks.com

Kiss of Skye

SKYE DRUIDS

EIGHT

CHAPTER ONE

SKYE DRUIDS

London

The soft, steady drizzle painted the air in a gauzy gray, as if the entire city had been placed under a damp veil. Light clung to the slick pavement in long, silvery streaks while headlights blurred into ghostly halos as traffic crept past. This wasn't the downpours she was used to back home. This rain seemed almost indifferent.

Rowen didn't bother to open her umbrella as she walked out of the hotel doors and into the shower to the cab waiting alongside the curb. It wasn't exactly cold, but the dampness had teeth, crawling against her bare legs and curling into her toes, making her wish she had worn the pants instead of the dress.

She hurriedly slid into the back seat and gave the driver directions before trying to get comfortable in a vehicle that had held dozens of people that day alone. Her gaze moved to the windows and the unbroken sheet of pewter sky. In the twenty-six hours she had been in the city, she hadn't seen a speck of blue. It was as if London had forgotten the color.

Revulsion rose quickly. The cobblestone streets, traditional pubs, and medieval architecture didn't impress her. She couldn't care less about the city's long history and royal landmarks. It was loud, dirty, and crowded. And if she heard "*You're from across the pond*" one more time, she was going to scream.

Rowen loosened fingers that clutched her purse too tightly. She only had a little more time in the UK before she could return home. She missed her family. She missed her routine. She missed her life, though some might call it dull. It was hers. The quiet, sedate setting was much more her pace, proving once more that she had been the wrong choice for this trip.

Finally, the cab slowed and pulled to the curb. She climbed out into the rain and tightened the belt of her trench coat before adjusting the strap of her purse on her shoulder. It was when she thought to open her umbrella that she realized she had left it in the cab, which was now long gone. But she didn't care that she would likely look like a drowned rat.

"Two umbrellas in just over a day. That's a personal record. Yay, me," she mumbled to herself.

Rowen turned her attention to the surroundings. There were many similarities between the UK and America, but there were just as many differences. For one, the parking lots. Or rather, car parks. Similar, but different. She sighed and stared at the striking, ancient structure before her. The white-gray stone matched the other prominent architecture around the city. One talkative cab driver had explained that it was called *Portland stone* and had been quarried from the Isle of Portland in Dorset. She'd learned that it had been used as far back as the Roman era, which made it difficult to determine just how old the construction was.

Rowen sighed as she made for the prominent—and intimidating—building. She spotted others making their way to a grand entry, complete with a covered portico. There were no guards stationed outside. Druids didn't need them to keep those without magic away. She quickened her steps as much as she dared on the slick sidewalk.

It wasn't that she was in a hurry to get inside. It was more about getting out of the rain and finding warmth. All she had to do was get through this last night in London, and then she could go home and deliver her report on the London Druids to her group, the Salish Druids.

From the moment Rowen had read the email invite, she had wanted to ignore it. There had been open communication between the London and Salish Druids going back decades, but no one from the San Juan Islands had ever been invited over. Granted, they had never invited anyone from London to them either. Every Druid knew the power London had. They had always been respected.

That respect had gradually turned to fear, though. At first, it was the small things London did that were overlooked or explained away. Then the incidents became larger and more frequent, making the Salish Druids sit up and notice. Others had wanted to travel to the UK, but for some reason, Brenna—the leader of the Salish Druids—had chosen her. Rowen had attempted to politely refuse, but Brenna wouldn't take *no* for an answer. So, here Rowen was, in a city she loathed, about to enter a viper's nest.

The heels of Rowen's boots clicked softly on the pavement as she approached the portico. She had expected there to be a grand edifice, but the double-domed front doors looked like so many others, going so far as to have a stained-glass fanlight window above the door. The likenesses ended with the ornate cast-iron knocker and handles, which held a touch of mysticism in the design.

As she got closer, she could see that the stained glass wasn't exactly like the others. It was actually a tree of life, with its limbs extending outward and upward, and its roots mimicking the branches. Once before the closed entrance, she stared at the raven's head protruding from the door, holding the knocker in its beak.

Ravens were powerful symbols and messengers to Druids. The birds were linked to wisdom, prophecy, and the connection between the living and the Otherworld. Moreover, ravens were associated with death and transformation. Her gaze dropped to the handle that resembled a root. If she had any doubts about where she was, they vanished. Rowen grasped the door knocker and quickly rapped twice.

Almost instantly, both doors swung open, and a petite brunette in her early forties greeted her with a toothy smile and eyes just a little too wide-set. "Rowen," the woman said, smiling, the corners of her soft brown eyes crinkling. "We're so excited to finally have you here. Please, come in. I'm Ella, and I'll be showing you around."

For a second, Rowen almost turned and bolted. She didn't want to go inside. She didn't want to talk to any of the London Druids. And she certainly didn't want to mingle among them, acting as if she liked them. It would be so easy to turn away, but she couldn't. The Salish Druids were counting on her. Returning home without the information they needed would only mean that a replacement would have to come. How could she do that to someone else?

Rowen took a deep breath and, against her better judgment, stepped across the threshold. She paused, almost expecting there to be a loud boom or some kind of response to her entering the building. But maybe she just watched too much TV.

Ella waited expectantly, her smile never wavering. Rowen's hands were clenched so tightly into fists that she had to forcibly loosen her fingers. She tried to smile, but by the quick furrow of Ella's brow, Rowen knew she'd missed the mark by a mile. Instead, she turned her attention to the décor.

While the outside of the London Druids' stately headquarters looked like many other buildings in the city, the inside was something else altogether. A black and white marble floor lay beneath her feet, and glossy wood paneling covered the walls while a glittering chandelier hung above her. It all likely cost more than her entire house.

"I can take your coat," Ella offered after shutting the doors behind her.

Rowen didn't want to hand it over, in case she wanted to make a hasty exit, but that would be rude. So, she reluctantly shrugged out of the garment and passed it to the Druid. That gave her time to look at her new acquaintance. Ella was on the shorter side, though her four-inch black stilettos brought her to Rowen's five-foot-six-inch height. The knee-length, black pencil skirt highlighted Ella's thin frame, while the royal purple satin shirt with a bow tied at her neck gave her small chest some definition.

"Isn't that better?" Ella asked with another too-bright smile as she draped Rowen's trench over an arm. "Do you have any questions before we go in?"

Rowen shook her head and slipped her purse strap over her shoulder. There was still time for her to grab her coat and leave. The urge was strong, but once more, she pushed it aside. "I'm good."

"I hope your flight yesterday was good. We could've made arrangements for someone to show you around the city last night."

She had assumed they were keeping an eye out for her, but that didn't lessen her unease. "I found my way around all right."

"Of course, you did." Ella laughed, the sound high-pitched and grating.

Rowen suspected they had followed her. She could ask, but what would be the point? The London Druids were used to getting their way. No one refused them. At least, no one who was around to talk about it. She didn't want them to know how much they unsettled her.

Ella handed Rowen's coat to someone. "Why don't we go in? There's still a little time for me to introduce you to some of the more prominent members before the meeting begins."

Rowen grudgingly followed her deeper into the foyer. Then, they went through another set of doors. She caught a glimpse of more chandeliers. No bright fluorescents that seared the eyes for these Druids. Along the walls were paintings in various sizes that looked as if they'd come from multiple time periods. Along with the wall art were pieces on tables and columns that looked as if they belonged in a museum.

Ella began introductions immediately, dragging Rowen's attention from the artwork to the people. There were so many names that it didn't matter if she repeated them; they were lost in a sea of faces and words in the next breath. Everyone was dressed impeccably. It made her glad that she had decided to change out of her jeans and follow instructions by wearing a nice dress. It wasn't as grand as most of the other women's attire, but Rowen had never much cared about such things.

"And here is Roger Hughes," Ella said. "He's one of…"

Rowen smiled and nodded, but tuned Ella out. The woman kept giving her more information than she needed. It was overcrowding her brain. Rowen couldn't figure out if it was just Ella's nature or if there was another reason for it.

Thirty minutes later, they hadn't made it another two feet when a gong sounded. Instantly, the crowd began to disperse, and conversation dimmed.

"It's time for the meeting," Ella said excitedly.

Her reaction was near cult-like, and yet another mark against the organization in Rowen's eyes. The group moved as one, slowly making their way through a set of doors into a larger room that was more like an amphitheater filled with rows of chairs. The ceiling soared so high above her that Rowen couldn't make out what was painted upon it. Mammoth columns the color of old bone lined the sides, standing like tall, unmovable guardians. She saw etchings on them. From afar, they looked like hieroglyphs.

She moved toward the nearest column to get a closer look and saw spirals, knots, and jagged sigils. She ran her finger along them, tracing a knot. It wasn't hieroglyphs. This was the language of the Druids, passed down through the generations. It didn't matter where a Druid's home was. They all knew this language.

Suddenly, Ella gripped Rowen's arm. She followed Ella's gaze to see more people streaming in. She was about to turn away when she saw one man apart from the others. Tall, distinguished, and drawing the eye of those around him. Just one more reason to get out quickly.

"Did you see him?" Ella asked breathlessly.

It was the kind of enthusiasm she expected from someone seeing a movie star or a royal. Rowen stopped short of rolling her eyes. "Sorry, no."

Ella absently touched her hair and adjusted her shirt. "You wouldn't be so flippant about it if you saw him. He's the most eligible bachelor in the organization. *Everyone* wants him."

Rowen ignored the comment. She didn't care who had caught Ella's attention. She was too busy ogling the artwork. The more she saw, the more she was sure some of it had come from a museum.

"Rowen."

She once more followed Ella as they walked to take their seats. Rowen was beginning to wonder if this was some special ceremony for something only the London Druids celebrated, because it was starting to cross the line from meeting into something else entirely.

Three Druids, two men and a woman, walked onto a stage, and their presence silenced the room in a heartbeat. Rowen wanted to roll her eyes again. It seemed these Druids really leaned into the fanfare of their power. The trio was all in the later stages of their lives, and one held an uncanny resemblance to an actor who usually played a villain.

Ella leaned over and whispered, "Those are the elders. I'm sure you'll wish to speak with them."

"That won't be necessary."

"Few get that honor. If they agree, you must," Ella stated sharply, her smile disappearing as displeasure flared in her eyes.

Rowen soon forgot Ella as the elders began to speak. At first, it was nothing more than talking about the strides the Druids were making around the world. It was obvious that the three led the organization. She had heard rumors that London had moved to such a consortium. Perhaps they had no choice with so many members, but it was unusual not to have a single leader.

More unusual was the sheer size of the assembly. Druids didn't typically gather in such numbers, so as not to bring attention to themselves. If society were losing its mind over the idea that there might be alien life in the universe, how would it react to learning that magic was real?

Witch hunts, anyone? It was better to keep those without magic in the dark so as not to upset the balance. Because it would. There would be a divide. Those with magic against those without. And there was a lot more of those without.

Suddenly, the elders finished and moved aside. Rowen looked between heads to see the stage as a woman walked up. She stood in silence for a moment and simply smiled.

"I know many of you are anxious for an update about the Skye Druids," the woman said. "I'm happy to report that our enemies will soon be vanquished."

Rowen's blood went cold as Ella clapped happily beside her.

CHAPTER TWO

SKYE DRUIDS

Mason Crawford, the Earl of Brannelly, stayed at the fringes of the assembly as he always did. Most assumed he was a pompous arse by remaining off to the side, and he let them believe that. It kept most—though not all—at a distance.

He gave a halfhearted clap as the rest of the ballroom erupted into cheers when Melody Brown finished speaking. She had served under his mother, who had held the position of elder for a handful of years. It felt like a lifetime ago that his world had changed in the blink of an eye. Melody had always had her eye on an elder position, and she was the type to do whatever it took to secure the role. He wondered if she would covet it so desperately if she knew the truth.

Every decision Mason made, every word that fell from his lips, had been carefully and methodically planned. He shared nothing with a single soul. If anything was written down, he burned it. There was no digital or analog documentation. It was all in his head. And it was getting harder to keep track of everything.

The lengths he had gone to in order to keep his plans hidden were extreme, to be sure. But they had to be. A couple of times, it had almost gotten to be too much, and he had reached out to his sister. As soon as he heard Ferne's voice, he was reminded of what he was doing and why he had to withdraw from everyone.

If he made it out of this, he had a lot of explaining and apologizing to do. At least Ferne was too far away for London to hurt her anymore. She was with the Druids on the Isle of Skye. And contrary to what Melody had just announced, those on the isle weren't about to fall.

And if they did, it wouldn't be to London.

Movement out of the corner of his eye caught his attention. Mason glanced to the side to find Thomas Oliver motioning him over. He could ignore Thomas, and a part of him wanted to, but the other part—the one that had shoved everyone out of his life—knew he couldn't. Mason put his hands on his thighs and rose to his feet before heading to Thomas. Mason had known the elder for his entire life. Their families had been close. To the point where Carlyle, Thomas's only child, had been his best friend.

Had been.

Mason quickly squashed the pain that flared when he remembered the last words he and Carlyle had exchanged. He had wanted to tell Carlyle and Ferne everything, but he knew they would've rushed to his side to help. The only way he could finish his plan was by knowing that both were on Skye, where London couldn't touch them.

The elder Oliver wore a smile as Mason approached. Thomas was fit and looked a decade younger than his fifty-three years, with gray just beginning to show at the temples of his blond hair. It hid the truth, just as his grin did. But Mason had learned to play the same game. He was no longer the fool Thomas believed him to be.

"Thomas," Mason said by way of greeting when he reached him.

"Good to see you, Mason. You could be at the front. Why do you sit back here, off to the side?" Thomas chided gently.

One day, Mason would get to say everything he wanted. But today wasn't that day. He shrugged and shifted sideways to look at the crowd, his gaze moving over faces he knew, and others he didn't. "I'd rather not be mobbed by those trying to catch my eye."

"Sitting over here isn't stopping that. You're an unmarried earl. That puts you in high demand, my friend." Thomas chuckled and slapped his back. "Come with me."

This was the fourth time Thomas had asked Mason to leave a meeting. They slipped unseen into the darkened recesses of the ballroom and then out a door into the back of the building that only a portion of the organization knew about—and even fewer saw. It was meant for those rising through the ranks. He and Ferne hadn't been allowed back there, even though their mum had been an elder. There were strict rules.

Which was a load of shite. Thomas bent every one of them. He was one of those people who lied about everything. There wasn't a single word that fell from his lips that was truthful. Mason had discovered that shortly before London kicked Ferne out of the organization—and the city.

It had been a blessing. They had always been close, and he missed her terribly, but the only thing that mattered now was her safety. And *safe* was something she wouldn't have been, had she remained. He knew what he was getting into, and he did it because his parents needed justice.

He needed justice *for* them.

"There has to be someone who has managed to catch your eye," Thomas said as he glanced back at Mason.

His eyes were the same blue as Carlyle's. It was difficult for Mason to meet Thomas's gaze, but he made himself. "Running the estate is taking up too much time to think about dating."

Thomas shook his head. "Don't be like me and wait too long. Find a woman and have children. You need an heir for your title." Fake concern lined the elder's face as he said, "It all falls to you now."

It didn't. The title would pass to Ferne's children, but Mason didn't say that. Ferne was dead to the organization, banished and forever forgotten by them for daring to go to Skye. It was a cardinal rule for the London Druids, and all because, ages ago, the Druids of Skye had kicked out a group of people. Those Druids had eventually found their way to London, and their hatred had permeated through the generations with a vengeful, bitter gripe that never loosened.

"It's difficult, I know," Thomas continued. "I have no idea where Carlyle is, and the longer he goes without answering my calls, the more worried I become. What if he's…there?"

Carlyle was on Skye, and Mason would bet his family's title and estate that Thomas knew that. Just one more lie to add to the mountain. One day, he would tell Thomas what he knew, but it wasn't quite time yet. He still had to play this game for the time being.

Mason drew in a deep breath and jumped in with both feet. "Carlyle wouldn't do that. He'll come home. He always returns."

They turned a corner and came to a stop outside a closed door. It was a room Mason hadn't seen before. A frisson of unease curled through him. Thomas had been pulling him aside lately for a reason, but Mason was always on guard for the unexpected. There was no telling what the elder wanted with him, and he needed to find out. He had been playing his part perfectly, but he was tired of being watched, tired of having his phone conversations listened to.

"I hope you're right. I miss my son." Thomas lowered his gaze to the floor. When he looked up, his brow was furrowed, and his lips pinched. "Let's keep this conversation between us. Please. You know what will happen if…" Thomas shrugged helplessly.

"Of course. You can trust me. You were always like a second father to me." Mason knew he was laying it on thick, but the event called for it.

Maybe Thomas had done the same to his parents. Led them to believe they were friends and then had them murdered. That was the type of person Thomas was, and Mason hated that he hadn't seen it until now. He hadn't been able to save his parents, but he *would* save Ferne and countless others.

Thomas swallowed loudly and ran a hand over his face. "Thank you." He cleared his throat and pushed aside the false pain. "You know we've had our eye on you for some time."

"Is this when you finally tell me who that *we* is?"

Thomas chuckled. "You'll learn everything eventually. This is just another step of many."

"Wait," Mason said when Thomas reached for the knob.

"What is it? I thought you'd want to follow in your mother's footsteps."

Mason leaned a shoulder against the corridor wall, his disquiet mounting as warning bells went off in his head. "You know I do.

This organization meant everything to my parents. I want to honor Mum and all she contributed."

"That's why you're here, son."

Mason barely stopped himself from flinching at the endearment.

"Now, come. It's time you begin your road to being an elder," Thomas replied with a smile and opened the door.

Mason called to his magic and felt it zing through his body, rolling heavy and fierce beneath his skin. He could hold his own against Thomas. His father had spent years training both him and Carlyle. Mason knew what he was doing, but that didn't mean he was reckless enough to believe himself invincible. There was no telling how many Thomas had recruited to follow him.

Thomas, or one of his pawns, would end his life. It was just a matter of time. Ferne would be alerted, as would a select few others. But he had left explicit instructions on what to do if he were killed or disappeared.

Magic filled both his palms as Mason turned the corner and followed Thomas inside the room. Two men played billiards while another stood off to the side, watching the game with a tumbler of alcohol in hand. Mason shot a quick look over his shoulder to make sure no one came up behind him from the hallway.

Meanwhile, Thomas greeted the occupants as Mason evaluated the room. He knew all three inside. The two playing pool were a handful of years younger than Thomas and highly respected in the organization. The other man, James, was Mason's age. They moved in different social circles, though. James had had to prove himself, as those who came from families with lesser magic always had to within the London Druids.

Thomas turned to face him with a smile and spread his arms wide. "Welcome. You've earned your way here."

Mason didn't move a step farther inside. The warning bells in his head began to toll even louder as he realized that he no longer felt his magic. His heart started to thud like a drum against his ribs as he became hyperaware of everything around him.

"We're going to ensure you get everything you deserve. Aren't we, lads?" Thomas asked, his voice taking on a deadly note.

Suddenly, James cut his eyes to Mason's left. It was the only warning he got before all hell broke loose. A hidden door to the left flew open, and a man ran out. Adrenaline rushed through Mason as he raised his hands to call to his magic, but there was no answer. The man rammed a shoulder into his stomach, knocking the breath from him and shoving him backward into the doorway. Mason drove his elbow into his assailant's neck to loosen his hold, then grabbed the man and held him down before jamming his knee into the man's face, knocking him out.

Mason shot a look toward Thomas to find all four men watching him intently. If he didn't know better, he might think this was some kind of test. There was nothing friendly about this. He had been brought here to be killed.

The *snick* of a door unlatching to his right caused Mason to swing around to find another concealed door opening. This time, a woman rushed him. Once more, he tried his magic. And once again, it didn't answer. He wasn't in the habit of hitting women, but he wouldn't stand there and wait to be struck either. This was life or death.

She was on him in an instant, knocking into him with the force of a battering ram. Her knee drove viciously into his side. He gasped, and almost immediately, another strike clipped his temple. The room spun as he tried to pivot. She looped her arm around his neck to drag him back, but he had been trained for worse. He twisted sharply to his left and slammed his elbow into her ribs. She gasped, loosening her hold just enough.

Mason used his momentum and dropped low, throwing his weight forward and flipping her over his shoulder. She hit the floor with a hard thud. He whirled around, chest heaving and blood pounding in his ears. He tried to back out of the room, but the first attacker came at him again. Mason heard footsteps behind him, seconds before the woman and another man were on him.

The weight of all three sent him stumbling forward. He felt pressure at his side and was taken to the ground. Someone landed a hard blow to his thigh as he struggled to shake off his adversaries, throwing punches, kicking, and elbowing anything near him.

He backhanded the woman, but it took more effort than it should have. Mason then leveled the man nearest him with a solid punch. His attacker grunted before staggering to the side and falling against the wall, sliding to the floor.

The last man smiled excitedly while wiping blood from his lip. Mason dodged a sharp jab to his head and landed what should have been a solid hit to the man's stomach, but it barely registered. Mason knew something was very wrong. He wasn't going to be able to last much longer at this rate. Thinking quickly, he grabbed his attacker, and they rolled until he was on top. Mason pulled up every ounce of energy he had and struck him in the throat. His assailant started coughing and choking as he wheezed for breath.

"Kill him," Thomas demanded.

Before Mason could stand, the woman plowed into him. They

rolled into the hall, where the walls prevented either of them from moving freely. The moment he was outside the room, his magic surged, fluid and radiant, into his palms. He directed it at her head as she pulled out a small revolver. The force of his strike caused her skull to bounce off the side of the wall with a sickening thud before she slumped over, eyes open and empty.

There was no time for rest as the sound of quick footsteps came from within the room. Mason looked toward the door to realize he and the woman had traveled several feet down the corridor in their fight—and it just might have given him an advantage. Right now, he needed everything he could get.

Mason pulled himself to his feet with shaky arms and unsteady legs, far weaker than he should have been. He took a step toward the room to confront Thomas when he felt a pull on his left side. He looked down to find his shirt soaked in blood. Pain exploded through him then, and every breath was like fire singeing his veins.

"Fuck," he murmured.

"Oh, Maaaaaason."

Thomas's voice floated to him, soft and lilting like a friend beckoning to another. But beneath the placid tone was something colder, sharper. It made Mason's skin crawl. If he didn't get out now, he never would, and he was losing too much blood to withstand another fight.

His mum might not have allowed him into the corridors, but she had drawn him a map and forced him to memorize the locations to go to, should he ever have a need to leave swiftly. He took off running to the left, only to crash to his knees when his right leg crumpled beneath him. Mason looked down to find his black dress pants drenched in blood.

Panic thrummed through him, beating like a chaotic drum. He took a steadying breath and braced his hand on the wall before hauling himself to his feet, fighting through the agony and his rapidly weakening muscles. His fingers, covered in blood, fumbled to unbuckle his belt as he considered his location and where to go. The nearest place was a room just to the right. Thomas would look there first, but if Mason could get inside before another attack, he might be able to slip into the secret tunnel.

He lurched awkwardly forward as he glanced behind him, every millisecond counting. Thomas called for him again, his voice louder as it drew nearer. Mason quickly slipped into the room and hurriedly tightened his belt around his upper thigh above the wound to stem the flow of blood.

Adrenaline kept him going as he hastily scanned the space for the brick. There was no time to make a mistake. If Thomas found him now, he was dead. Sweat trickled down Mason's brow as he hobbled to the left and reached across the copier. Just before he laid his hand on the brick, he paused. He didn't want to leave a trail of evidence behind him.

Mason gritted his teeth against the pain and leaned over farther to press his elbow against the brick instead. But nothing happened. He sucked in air through clenched teeth, each breath carving its way into his lungs like a blade. His throat was raw, chest heaving, the rhythm of survival savage and feral. He shifted over another brick and pressed his elbow into it.

A soft click filled the room, barely audible, before a portion of the back wall shifted. Stone scraped against stone in a slow, gritty grind, the sound muffled by age and dust. The bricks moved, exhaling to reveal a narrow gap and the cold breath of darkness beyond. He wasted no time moving to it. Once inside, the door closed behind him. Mason drew out his mobile and turned on the light to illuminate his way.

There were numerous turn-offs, but there was only one he needed.

CHAPTER THREE

SKYE DRUIDS

The longer Rowen remained in the building, the more she felt as if she needed a shower. There was something wrong with the London Druids, but she couldn't lay her finger on what it was. The meeting was part sermon, part social gathering. And all ick.

"I need the restroom," Rowen whispered to Ella, who hadn't let her out of her sight.

"The toilet is down the hall to the right."

Rowen bristled at the subtle correction. She bit off a curt response and turned away. Three steps later, she whirled around when she noticed the woman behind her. "I can find it on my own, thanks."

"You could get lost."

"I don't need my hand held," she stated plainly.

Ella's lips, stained red with lipstick, pinched slightly. "This is a large building, and you aren't allowed in some areas."

"Perhaps I'll pee right here, then," Rowen snapped.

Ella jerked back as if slapped. "I'm merely trying to be civil."

"You're hovering, and it's rude."

"Fine," Ella stated and lifted her nose. "I'll wait here."

Rowen turned on her heel and found her way to the bathroom. Twice, she looked over her shoulder to make sure Ella hadn't followed. Once inside, she closed and locked the door and rested her forehead against it. Then she walked to the sink and splashed water on her face. It was only when she looked up that she saw her mascara running.

"Great job, Rowen," she mumbled while cleaning under her eyes.

She paced the small room, thankful she had it all to herself. Ella was superglued to her side, and that would make sneaking out difficult. It would be in her best interest to stay until the end. That way, she wouldn't draw more attention to herself. But she hadn't gotten through the first hour. How in the world could she get through the rest? Especially since she didn't know how long the meetings lasted or if they would *let* her leave.

They had to, though. If she didn't get on her return flight, her mom would know. But what could her family or any of the Salish Druids do against a group the size of London? Nothing. And London knew it. It had been a mistake to accept the invitation, and an even bigger one to attend the so-called meeting.

"Fuckfuckfuckfuckfuck," she whispered.

Rowen's head whipped around as someone jiggled the door handle. It was a reminder that she couldn't remain in the *toilet* forever. She could fake an upset stomach and say she ate something that didn't agree with her. That was plausible.

There would likely be Healers around to handle that, though.

Her lips twisted. That meant the migraine idea wouldn't work either. Ella probably had an answer to every excuse Rowen might conjure. So, her only option was to go with her original plan and sneak out. She had gotten past her mom and aunt many times. She'd get past Ella.

Rowen flushed the toilet for anyone who might be listening, and checked her reflection in the mirror as she looped the strap of her purse over her head so it lay across her body. Then she opened the door to find two girls, no older than ten or eleven, standing with their heads together, talking. They didn't spare her a look as they shoved past her into the room.

She stepped into the hall, expecting to find Ella waiting. Others stood clumped together in the short passage, talking. She slowly wove her way through them while keeping her eye out for Ella. When she saw a doorway leading to another room on her left, she took it, hoping it would get her back to the front.

It wasn't that her group of Druids didn't mingle, because they did. And they did it after meetings. But this seemed to be more about who you knew and what you could gain from that connection than forging bonds that strengthened and nurtured magic. A gathering of Druids was much like a coven of witches. A single Druid could be powerful, but a cluster that joined their magic could be invincible.

Thankfully, Rowen was barely noticed as she worked her way through the room and found another doorway. To her delight, it led her closer to the front door. A cautious glance proved Ella wasn't around. Rowen knew getting out of the building would take every devious and crafty tactic she had—without using magic. No sense in turning the attention of every Druid in the building on her.

As she moved about the building, she walked with purpose, as if she had every right to go wherever she wanted. The crowds hid her from Ella, but it also made it more difficult for her to find her way to the front. She meandered casually while keeping an eye out for any hint of Ella's purple shirt.

Elation soared through Rowen when she caught a glimpse of the entryway straight ahead. She had to keep herself from sprinting toward it. She had made it this far. She would make it the rest of the way.

Believe it, and it will be.

Her mother's words whispered into her mind. Rowen kept moving forward. A burst of euphoria filled her chest when she finally stood in the foyer. She was about to grab her coat when she spotted purple out of the corner of her eye. Rowen decided to leave her favorite trench and hurried to the door instead. She opened it only wide enough to slip through.

The cool evening air hit her heated skin, and a smile split her face. Relief zinged through her as she paused. The drizzle from earlier had stopped, and dusk was fully upon them, with the streetlights and business lights reflected in the puddles and beads of water everywhere. It was only once she was outside that she let herself be thankful that the door hadn't been locked.

Rowen eyed the cabs passing in front of her. She could race out and flag one down, but what if someone came out and saw her? What if Ella checked outside? No, she couldn't chance that. She didn't want a confrontation. All she wanted was to get to her hotel, grab her belongings, and go to the airport. She'd sleep there if she had to. Because she wouldn't take the chance that Ella or anyone else from London might come to her room.

She hurried away from the door and headed to the side of the building toward the River Thames. Twice, she looked back, but she didn't see anyone coming after her. The smile she wore faded when she remembered the CCTV cameras everywhere that would be able to track her. She could use her magic to disable certain cameras, which might buy her a little time, but not much, since she'd never get all of them. Better to take her chances for now. If she were backed into a corner, she would turn to her magic. Because no one was going to force her to remain in the city.

Her steps slowed as the river loomed ahead of her. She looked to the right, then to the left. Her instincts told her to go right, even though that would take her along the backside of the building she had just escaped from. It didn't make sense. Nor was it safe. She tried to go left, but only got a few steps before her intuition had her looking to the right again.

Rowen shook her head in defeat and turned in that direction. She was jogging along the sidewalk when she saw a door open about fifteen feet in front of her. Her heart seized as she thought someone might be coming for her, but then a man staggered out before falling to his hands and knees. She started to hurry past him, but the agonized groan of pain brought her up short.

She stood there, telling herself to keep going, to forget him or whatever trouble he might be in. She had her own problems. Yet his labored breathing reached her over the sounds of the city. Rowen reluctantly turned her head toward him in time to see him struggling to use the side of the building to pull himself up. The light above the door cast his face in shadow, but not the dark, wet stain against the left side of his shirt.

Blood. She dug her nails into her palms as she lowered her gaze, spotting the belt tightened around his thigh as a tourniquet. He managed to get to his feet and kept his shoulder pressed against the building as he clumsily hobbled forward an inch at a time. Rowen didn't know who he was or what had happened, but he was obviously trying to flee the organization. Someone would come after him, just as they would her. If she were smart, she'd forget all about him and worry about getting home. Then she remembered how her instincts had led her right to him.

"Shit," she murmured and pivoted to head to him.

Suddenly, his leg gave out, and he crumpled to the ground with a laborious grunt. Rowen ran the last few feet to him as he attempted to get to his feet again. She dropped down to one knee. "I can help," she told him.

He looked up at her and blinked twice as if not really sure she was there. Only half his face was illuminated by the light, but she recognized him from the meeting. He was the same man Ella had been oohing over.

He shook his head as he drew in a labored breath, sweat beading his brow. "You shouldn't get involved."

"If I don't, you'll bleed out before you get to wherever you're headed. Trust me, it'd be better if I did. But…I can't leave you."

Indecision creased his face. When he didn't reply, she made the decision for him. He didn't pull his arm back when she wrapped it around her shoulders. She wasn't tall—and she was in heels—but she used everything she had to get him to his feet. It took them three tries before he was upright. He had at least seven inches on her. She hadn't realized he was that tall. She settled his right arm more comfortably around her, thinking he wasn't that heavy. Then, he leaned his full weight on her. Rowen nearly buckled under him, but she widened her stance and waited to move until they were both ready. Then they began their measured and uncoordinated journey.

"They'll be after you now," he said between heavy breaths.

"Let me worry about that." He was leaning more and more on

her with every step, yet he fought to keep himself standing. She wouldn't be able to get him far before she collapsed under his weight. They needed a ride. And quick. "Tell me you have a vehicle."

His breath rasped in the silence—harsh, uneven, and laced with pain. "Can't…take…it."

"Do you have another option? Because I sure as hell don't." She began to wheeze under the strain. Thank god for yoga, or she'd be flat on the ground.

"They'll track," he huffed.

She bit back a cry of pain when the heel of her shoe slid into a crack in the pavement and twisted her ankle. "They'll find us regardless with all the CCTV. We need to get you to a doctor."

"No," he barked.

She glanced down at his leg to see it drenched in blood. "Look, I have enough shit to deal with. I can't have you dying on me."

"I have…a place…to go."

There was no way he'd be getting there on his own, though. What was the English saying? In for a penny and all that? "Great. Let's get in your car." She spotted cars lined along the road. "Which one is yours?"

Please, please *let it be close.*

He tripped then, pitching them forward. She lunged with one leg and took the brunt of his weight as both arms went around his waist to hold him. His sharp inhale of pain—along with a warm, sticky wetness on her arm—told her he had another injury. But she kept him semi-upright with only his left knee on the ground. His lungs worked in ragged gasps. She chanced a look at him and saw the effort etched into every line of his face—and it wrecked her.

"I've got you," she told him. "We can do this."

She wasn't sure if he'd heard her or if he was too lost in the pain.

"Come on. Get up. I'm not going to ruin a perfectly good dress for nothing."

To her surprise, she thought she heard him chuckle before he attempted to stand. She held steady, waiting as he got his foot under him. She winced as he dug his fingers into her shoulder.

"Car…across," he panted.

Rowen looked across the road. "You're kidding."

He shook his head, unable to produce any more words. She used her shoulder to swipe away some hair sticking to her sweat-streaked face and glared at the crosswalk signal, willing it to change.

Step by step, they drew closer, and just as they reached it, it turned white so they could cross. She kept one arm around him and the other braced against his chest. His right foot was dragging, but he kept moving. Both of them were breathing heavily from the exertion, but they reached the other side.

"Where to?" she asked, adjusting his arm so it wasn't pulling her hair.

He swallowed, the sound loud even above the noise of the city. "Around…corner."

It was just her luck that he'd parked on the opposite end of the city. Passersby looked at them, but no one offered to help. He nearly went down twice, but she kept him erect. Her muscles were shaking from the strain, and her heels made it more difficult. She thought about kicking off her shoes, but she wasn't going barefoot.

Neither said another word as they gradually made their way to the next corner. It felt like a thousand miles away. She was losing him fast, though. She had all his weight and nearly dragged him down the street.

As they turned the corner, he jerked his chin toward a vehicle. "There."

She eyed the cars, trying to figure out which one he meant. It could've been any one of them, so she kept walking until he pointed to the sleek black Aston Martin. It wasn't until they got closer that she realized it wasn't black but a green so dark it appeared black.

"You…drive," he wheezed.

His voice was barely a whisper now. There was no time to argue about driving on streets she didn't know. "Fine, but you'll have to stay awake to tell me where to go. Otherwise, I'm driving your ass to a hospital."

He nodded. At least, she hoped it was a nod.

Rowen brought him to the passenger side and was about to ask for keys when he touched the door. Lights flashed as it unlocked. She leaned him against the vehicle as she opened the door. He practically fell into the seat before she had a chance to help him. She lifted his legs in, one at a time, then shut the door.

As she raced around the front of the sports car, she glanced toward the Druid headquarters and spotted several individuals who appeared to be searching for someone. It could've been her or her new friend, but she wasn't going to wait around to find out. She quickly slipped into the driver's seat. They lost precious time as she figured out how to adjust the seat so she could reach the pedals.

Rowen blew out a calming breath. This was her first time driving on the *wrong* side of a car as well as the road, all while at night with a man hanging around death's door. She was usually good under pressure, but this might be the time when she folded.

"Which way?" she demanded as she looked at her passenger.

He had his head back against the seat but opened his eyes and shot her a quick look. "Last chance to leave me."

"That ship has sailed. Which way?" she asked again.

He struggled to pull in a breath. "Go up two blocks and take a right."

She looked for the ignition switch. Just as she was about to dig out her cell phone for a light, he reached over and pushed a button. Like a predator waking, the engine roared to life in a low growl that turned into a throaty purr. The sound beneath her wasn't as loud as she had expected, but there was precision and the promise of controlled power in the deep rumble. Like something wild barely held in check.

She felt the roaring engine in her chest as the vehicle vibrated, waiting for her command. She wrapped her fingers around the steering wheel and put the car into drive. Once she checked to make sure the road was clear, she pressed the accelerator. The Aston Martin lunged forward smoothly and effortlessly, but too fast. Instantly, she pulled her foot back.

"Don't stop," the man whispered.

Rowen accelerated again. This time, she was ready for the aggressive machine. She rolled through the intersection—thankful for the green light—and past the headquarters, but she didn't dare take her eyes off the road. It took everything she had to keep the car on the correct side of the street. Even at a sedate speed, the Aston Martin was less vehicle and more coiled snake, ready to strike.

"Hey," she said after she took the right turn and glanced at him. His eyes were closed again, and she feared he was dead. "Where to?"

"Three blocks…then…another right," he replied without opening his eyes.

She kept a lookout in the rearview mirror, but anyone could be following them, and she wouldn't know it with all the traffic. Each time she thought he was unconscious or dead, he answered her, leading her street by street…somewhere—all with his eyes closed. Without lighting, it was hard to tell just how bad off he was. And with each second that ticked by, she worried that he wouldn't survive.

Soon enough, they were headed out of the city. She opened up the car once she reached the highway. The gauge told her she was going ninety, but it didn't feel like it. After passing several vehicles, she slowed and moved into the right lane.

"Now where?" she asked.

He didn't answer. Terror gripped her as she cast a furtive glance his way.

"Hey," she said louder, giving his right arm a slight shove.

He groaned as he opened his eyes. "I'm…here."

"You scared the hell out of me. Don't do that again," she snapped.

"Sorry."

Rowen shook her head. "We need to stop the bleeding soon. You've already lost too much blood."

"Exit."

"Where?" she asked, looking ahead.

"Now."

She realized he was referring to the exit they were passing. Rowen slammed on the brakes and jerked the wheel to take the ramp at the last second. He grunted and jolted in the seat as a car honked behind them. His eyes remained open after that. He kept a hand on the dashboard as he directed her to a storage unit. She had to punch in a code to get in. Once the large iron gate rolled open, he guided her to the back, where the largest units were.

"Last…one," he murmured.

She pulled up to the unit and put the car in park. She thought of his earlier comment about being tracked, but it wasn't as if the vehicle could blend in. It would be better if she hid the car, but that wasn't her priority right now, he was. Rowen spotted a digital lock unlike any she had seen before. "What's the combination?"

"I…have…to."

The light hanging off the storage unit shone into the car, spotlighting his ashen face. Apprehension knotted in her stomach. "I don't think you can stand."

"Retinal…scan."

"Of course, it is," she murmured as she unbuckled her seat belt.

Rowen ran around to his side and opened the door. Getting him in had been fairly easy. Getting him out was something else altogether. He tried to help, but it was clear that he had used the last of his reserves just to make it to the car. She was on his wounded side, but he didn't seem to care. After his feet were on the ground, she tugged him out of the vehicle. He then used the car to balance himself as they walked to the building.

She did her best to hold him up when he leaned over to unlock the unit, but they lost that battle within seconds. He fell hard—and took her with him. His groan of pain cut right through her, but he didn't lie there in agony as she might have. They worked together to get him up and, with a little finagling and some luck, handled the lock. She had to prop him up against the side of the building to raise the door, and as she did, a light clicked on, making her gasp.

This was no mere storage unit. It had been turned into a hidden, utilitarian base. The outside looked like any other unremarkable, oversized, climate-controlled unit. The inside, however? It was clear that he had not only thought this through but had spent considerable time and money. The walls were reinforced and insulated. One side was for sleeping, the other for gear and living.

A narrow cot rested against the left wall, neatly made. A small kitchenette sat on the right, with a mini fridge, a kettle, and a hot plate, giving it a bunker-like feel. A single, locked cabinet in the corner glinted with reinforced hinges. A row of hooks held coats, weapons, and keys. There was even a narrow, stainless-steel shower tucked behind a sliding panel, as well as a toilet—sleek, composting, and expensive.

He was *very* prepared. And if he had gone to these lengths, then he had a first-aid kit somewhere.

"All right," she said as she reached for him. "Time to get you fixed up."

CHAPTER FOUR

SKYE DRUIDS

Mason should tell her to leave, to run as far from him as she could. But he didn't, because he needed her. That had become crystal clear on their journey to his car. He never would've made it on his own. He would, in fact, have bled out somewhere on the street, likely with Thomas and his pawns standing over him.

He wasn't afraid to die, but he also wasn't ready to depart the world. At least not before he could talk to Ferne and explain things. Then there was justice for his parents. Those two things kept him going when all he wanted to do was lie down and give up. Yet he was the one who had begun this ploy with Thomas, and he intended to finish it.

Ferne's face kept flashing in his mind. Her voice, along with the tremor of hurt and anger from their last conversation, replayed in his head on repeat. The storage door was open, and the light within blinded him. Bloody hell, he was tired. So very tired. It was taking all he had to keep his eyes open.

"Hey. Stay with me. I can't do this alone."

The American's voice was coaxing but firm as she looped his arm around her thin, narrow shoulders once more. She was a lot stronger than she seemed, and she had gotten him this far. It was only a little more to the bed. Then he could lie down and finally rest.

He reached for the last bit of energy as she tugged him upward. His legs were jelly, the muscles refusing to obey his commands, but to his surprise, he got to his feet. If it weren't for the woman, he likely would've toppled right over. He was so unsteady. He spotted a set of discarded black heels near them. How had he not known she was in heels before? He started to lean and jerked back. Agony cut through him, snatching his breath. That's right. The pain kept him focused solely on his body.

"One step at a time," she told him.

He would've smiled if he had the energy, but he was concentrating on shuffling forward. The woman was a complete stranger, yet she was risking her life to help him. She could've left him at any time. He didn't know why she stayed. Hell, he didn't even know her name or her face. He tried to look down at her but only saw a wealth of strawberry blond hair.

"Nearly to the bed." Her voice was strained as she tried to keep him upright, made worse each time he tilted. "Let's not fa—"

His right leg gave out, causing him to crash onto the edge of the cot, sending fire racing through his veins as fresh blood poured from the injury on his left side. Dots edged his vision. He would pass out soon. She got one leg onto the cot, then the other. He reached for her as she rolled him onto his back.

"Under…bed," he rasped.

She said something, but he couldn't make it out. He shut his eyes against the too-bright lights above him. The loud clanging of the door being lowered echoed around him. Then there was silence. Maybe she had finally left. She could take the car or contact the organization and tell them where he was.

He should care, but he didn't. All he could think about was the mistakes he had made. And there had been many. There were a few regrets, too. Was it easier to face death slowly, knowing it was coming? Or to have a quick ending where someone didn't expect it? He could now definitively say that quicker was better.

Lingering allowed him to relive his blunders and turn over his regrets again and again, with no way to rectify them. He didn't have a chance to say goodbye to Ferne. There was no last look at his family's estate or a visit to his parents' graves one last time.

A cool cloth touched his brow, and then the American said, "Stay with me."

He tried to answer her, but the words wouldn't form on his lips. He remained conscious as she cut away his clothes. Her quick intake of breath told him the wounds were as bad as he feared. The time to take him to a hospital or a Healer was long past, and he wouldn't have allowed it anyway. There was no one in the city he trusted.

And yet, here sat the American.

Mason had brought her to his safe house. She now had access to nearly everything. Maybe letting her help him was his greatest mistake. But maybe, just maybe, she was the one who could save him.

He pried open his eyelids and got his first good look at her. She knelt next to him, her pale skin a stark contrast to the black dress she wore. Strawberry blond hair had been hastily pulled away from her face. Blood streaked her cheek and forehead. He attempted to focus on her features, but his eyesight went fuzzy. It was only then that he realized she was softly singing.

It was easier to focus on her words as his lids drifted closed. He winced when she began to stitch his thigh, but it didn't hurt as much as it should. The more he concentrated on the words of the song, the less pain he felt.

Mason's body became light, as if he were drifting upon the sea —or maybe a cloud. He felt fingers in his hair, stroking his scalp, the way his mum used to do when he was ill. He let go then. It was only as he drifted away that he realized the American sang *Songbird* from Fleetwood Mac.

CHAPTER FIVE

SKYE DRUIDS

Rowen lost track of time and everything around her as she hurried to stanch the flow of blood from the man's wounds. She focused on his leg first since the injury was dangerously close to an artery. She had become adept with a needle and thread out of necessity, since her cousins constantly got into some form of mischief or another. They had hidden many an injury from their moms.

Not once had she thought she would ever call upon those skills to save the life of a man in London, though. She tied off the last knot and sat up. After a quick check to ensure that he still breathed, she got to work on the wound along his left side. She winced once she got a look at the long slice that ran from just under his arm and curved downward toward his waist.

The cut was almost a foot long and much deeper than she had thought. It hadn't bled as freely as his leg, so she hadn't paid it as much attention. Rowen moved his arm so she could get a better view of the laceration. After she'd cleaned it, she got to work stitching it. Her hands were steady, the spacing even, as she worked as quickly as she dared.

Only when she finished and secured the last piece of tape did she inspect the rest of him for more injuries. Thankfully, there were none. She sat back on her haunches and closed her eyes, allowing herself a breather. There wasn't time for rest yet, however. There was still too much to do. She rubbed the back of her wrist across her forehead to push away some strands of hair before getting to her feet.

The man had lost a lot of blood, and she had done all she could without any herbs or being a Healer. The rest was up to him. But she could get him comfortable in the meantime. She removed his expensive shoes, now scuffed and splattered with blood, and set them aside. Then she gently finished cutting his clothes so she could toss them aside. Once she found a towel, she wet it and began to clean the blood from his body.

She started at his neck, the cloth moving softly down his muscular chest and the light dusting of dark hair. His skin was a warm brown that contrasted nicely with the silver-gray eyes she had glimpsed. It was a mix that she imagined made people look twice, then stare. She was certainly intrigued. Now she understood what had made Ella so giddy.

Rowen followed the path of her hands down his flat stomach and ripped abs. Her gaze lingered for a moment before she moved the cloth to his shoulders, rippling with sinew. Dark markings on his upper right arm caught her attention. She leaned forward to get a better look at the complex and elaborate tattoo of a large triskele that started at his shoulder and unfurled into a band of Celtic knotwork that twisted down his powerful biceps.

The knotwork wasn't clean. In fact, it was flawed in

appearance, but upon closer inspection, she realized it was a maze that looped in on itself. Interwoven in the knotwork were ogham runes. She recognized the ones for shadow, mist, and misdirection. At his elbow was a warding sigil she didn't recognize.

She smoothed the cloth down his right arm, finding more details the longer she stared at the tattoo. Curious, she carefully moved his left arm and saw that it was also tattooed. This design was different. Centered at his shoulder was a Celtic hound in mid-leap, with its mouth closed. She knew it represented silent guardianship and fierce loyalty. The detail in the design was staggering, but flowing from the hound was a band of interlocking shields that ran down his arm to the elbow, each marked with a spiral sun motif. Nestled within the spirals were knot-formed sigils, resembling closed eyes. Lastly, there was a binding knot wrapped around that elbow.

Rowen had seen many Druid tats, but this was unlike anything she had ever come across before. There was meaning in each design. She knew some. Others, she didn't. But she *wanted* to know. Hopefully, he would live and be able to tell her.

She wrung out the cloth in clean water and went back to her task, stopping along the waist of his boxers before shifting to his legs. They were corded with thick muscles, matching the rest of his impressive body. This was a man in his prime, but someone within the London Druids had wanted him dead. They hadn't used magic, though. Which surprised her.

All too soon, she'd finished her task. She was about to move away when she paused and looked at his face. His black hair was trimmed close on the sides and back. The top portion was slightly longer, allowing the wavy strands to fall attractively. People might have looked twice at his build and coloring, but it was his face that truly captivated.

He had the kind of jaw sculpted by gods and envied by mortals—sharp, uncompromising. Utterly commanding. His lips were full and sensual, the sort that might have looked too soft on another man. But on him? They hinted at danger and decadence in equal measure. Deep furrows lined his brow, carved by years of intensity, while thick, midnight-dark brows slashed above his eyes like twin blades.

Her breath caught. He wasn't just handsome. He was arresting. Had the kind of splendor that could stop time and defy reason. And a face that made a person forget their name and purpose… everything but him.

She shook herself out of her stare and tenderly wiped his face, wishing his eyes would open so she could look closer at their color. The eyes told the story of a person's soul, and if one dared to look deeply enough, they could see the many lifetimes the individual had lived.

When she was done, Rowen covered him with a blanket. He was resting now, and the blood flow had been stanched. It gave him a fighting chance. Now, all she could do was wait. She got to her feet and opened the mini fridge to find bottles of water, juice, and even a few beers. She grabbed some water and downed it quickly to soothe her parched throat.

The adrenaline was wearing off. Soon, she would want to sleep, but she still had a couple of things to see to first. She dug the key fob to the Aston Martin out of the man's discarded pants pocket, grabbed a roll of paper towels and a garbage bag, and lifted the rolling door enough that she could bend at the waist to get out. She shut it partway and made her way to the side of the storage, noticing there was a place to park. It would be better to completely hide the flashy car, but at least it wouldn't be sitting in front of his unit in case someone came looking for him.

The moment she opened the vehicle door, the sharp, metallic stench of blood hit her: hot, coppery, and suffocating. She cleaned up as much as she could, but there was so much of it. She had no idea how the man was still alive with the sheer amount of blood she was getting up. Most of it had soaked into the carpet and floormat, but there was still quite a bit along the door and even more on the seat.

It began to sprinkle as she knelt on the concrete and scrubbed harder and faster, worry about the stranger living through the next few hours weighing heavily on her. She had thrown caution to the wind and helped him, despite not knowing anything about him. He could be a killer. He could be…well, anything. And she had helped him. What would she do if he died? Just leave him there? She shook her head, unable to answer that.

The security light above her caught on something along the passenger door. She peered closer, moving her head until she spotted it again. There! It was some type of marking that was difficult to see in the night. She ran the pad of her finger over it to feel the roughened section of distinct ridges and grooves. She shifted the door so the light caught on it just right and was able to see the protection ward clearly.

This, like the tattoos, had been done with purpose. The stranger must have known he was in danger to go to such extremes. She took another look along the outside edge of the door and found two more—one she recognized as a cloaking ward.

Now that she had found them, it was easy for her to uncover the others scattered throughout the vehicle, all in places most would never look or notice. Some were similar to those she knew, but different enough that she wasn't sure of their meaning. They could be more protection wards or sigils to hide him.

Her dress was soaked by the time she climbed into the driver's seat to move the car around to the side of the building in an effort to hide it. She had to back up and adjust a few times to get the vehicle just where she wanted it. Then, she braved the rapidly increasing rain shower to race back to the storage door. As she ducked inside, she glanced at the frame and found more wards. They covered the entire side, from floor to ceiling. A look over her shoulder confirmed that others were on the opposite side.

Whoever the man was, he moved with deliberate caution, though whether to shield himself from danger or to stay a step ahead of the law was anyone's guess. She wouldn't know anything about him until he woke. She lowered the door and nodded approvingly when she found a digital lock inside. A chill ran through her from her dress sticking to her as she slid the bolt into place. She wanted to curl up somewhere and sleep for at least two days, but unless she was fine atop the rug over the concrete floor, she wasn't lying down anywhere.

Rowen debated taking the car to her hotel, but given how she'd left the organization—even before she'd encountered the injured man—she wasn't sure that was a good idea. Staying in her wet dress, however, wasn't an option. She shot the still unconscious man a look of regret before digging through the cabinet for something to change into. When she found nothing but food, she turned to a chest. Inside, she discovered clothes. She grabbed a gray tee, the material thin from frequent wear. Beneath it was a pair of thick sweatpants with a store tag still on them. She snatched a set of socks for her cold feet before closing the lid and changing.

She ripped off the tag and put on the too-large sweats, rolling the waist and the bottoms just so she could walk. Once the shirt and socks were on, she slowly warmed up as she paced in front of the cot. When she stopped shivering, Rowen checked his bandages. She was happy with how they looked, so she grabbed the second blanket and curled up in the chair.

The sound of rain hitting the metal roof filled the silence. She stared at the man, watching his chest rise and fall in a steady rhythm. As fatigue set in, her thoughts ran over the events of the night, from her arrival at the headquarters to them driving away. She sat up frantically as she thought about her purse. Just as she was about to rise, her gaze landed on it near the cot. She hadn't remembered letting it drop to the floor. Truth be told, she didn't remember several things about that night amid their frantic dash to leave the city.

It was funny how the mind skipped over things when a person's life was hanging in the balance. She should call home. Her mom needed to know what she had discovered. At the very least, she should tell her family that she was okay. They would want to hear her plan, but right now, she didn't have one.

She had no idea what the man's name was, his connection to the London Druids, or why they'd tried to kill him. Which, of course, meant she had no way of knowing just how deeply she had stepped in it this time. Usually, one of her cousins was getting into something or another. It seemed it was Rowen's turn.

Her momma always said she did best in crises, but she didn't feel that way now, being so far from home. There was no one to turn to. No family or friends to help her. But that wasn't exactly true. There was Senna.

The last time Rowen spoke to her cousin, Senna was in Spain, but that was over four months ago. Senna, who was two years older, had left home in the dead of night eleven years ago, and she hadn't stopped running since. Rowen didn't know the whole story, but she knew enough to know that Senna had tangled with the wrong family.

Aunt Rhea was still upset that Senna hadn't turned to the family for help. Rowen had thought the same thing for a long time. Right up until she had overheard her mother and aunts whispering one night about their magic not working like it used to. There had been fear in their voices, a kind of dread she had never heard in any of their tones before.

Things had changed after that. It was subtle, but Rowen had been watching for them. From then on, she observed and took note of everything from the Druids who came and went from the islands to how everyone acted at meetings.

It was only after Brenna had tapped her to go to London that she'd confronted her mother with everything.

Maris Thornevale had gripped her arms, a sad look in her light blue eyes. "I know you don't want to go, sweetheart, but you must. Don't worry about us. We'll be fine."

"What aren't you telling me, Momma?"

Maris's light blue eyes lowered to the floor for two beats. When she met Rowen's gaze, she wore a smile. "A lot, I'm sure."

"Don't do that. I need to know."

Maris sighed and dropped her arms to her sides. "We aren't as safe here as we thought. Some of us have noticed our magic waning. We need more Druids to strengthen the islands. London could give us that."

"There are other Druids in the States. We should go to them first."

"We have. A few answered our call, but they either don't stay or they can't help. We need those from the original source."

Rowen swallowed. "You mean the Skye Druids?"

"I do," Maris said with a firm nod. "Word has reached us that they are attacking others, so I don't dare reach out to them. London, however, has given us a lifeline. We have to take it."

The memory faded as Rowen sighed. Her news about London would be yet another devastating blow to the Salish Druids.

CHAPTER SIX

SKYE DRUIDS

Mason opened his eyes, more than a little surprised to discover he hadn't passed on to the other side. His mouth was dry, and his attempts to swallow only made his tongue stick to the roof of his mouth. The steady drone of rain beat upon the roof, but everything inside the unit was still. The American had probably taken his car and left. He couldn't blame her. She'd done more than others would have.

He needed to get up and find water. The simple act seemed as insurmountable as sprouting wings and flying. He turned his head, and that small movement sent pain rolling through him, sharp and relentless like broken glass. The harsh, fractured sound of his strained breathing was loud to his ears. Each time he thought the agony would relent, it doubled until it consumed him. He squeezed his eyes closed, caught in the vicious cycle of pain.

"Easy," came a soft, feminine voice near his ear.

She laid a hand near his wrist while her other gently stroked his forehead with a cool cloth. Her touch eased him, allowing him some much-needed time to get a handle on the worst of the discomfort.

"Drink," she urged.

He met eyes a blue so pale they seemed ethereal. Streaks of silver and white within the blue only added to the otherworldly appearance, while a darker blue like faded denim circled her irises. The gaze drew him in until he was drowning in the hues.

Something touched his lips. He parted them and felt a straw against his lips. Immediately, Mason began to drink. The sweet, satisfying taste of the water filled his mouth before sliding down his parched throat and into his stomach. All the while, he held her gaze, transfixed.

"Not too much," she said, breaking eye contact as she withdrew the water and twisted to set it aside.

That's when he took in the wealth of strawberry blond hair that fell just past her shoulders. She turned back to him and pressed a wet cloth to his forehead again. He was at once thankful that she was there and wary of why she'd stayed.

He followed her finger as she tucked a strand of hair behind her ear. She watched him as cautiously as he watched her. He had been too hurt when they met to really see her. But he saw her now. An oval face framed by waves of fire-kissed hair, freckles scattered like stardust across pale skin. Her chin lifted in quiet defiance, lips full and lush—temptation in their curve. And her eyes…bloody hell, those eyes. They locked on his, piercing straight through to his soul.

There was an air of steel around her, as if she were ready to take on whatever came her way. Those like her were survivors. Whether they wanted to be or not. Fate had bestowed that upon her, and it appeared as if she carried it uneasily.

He knew the feeling well.

"I stitched you," she said into the silence. "I can't say it's my best job, but time was of the essence."

Her accent wasn't strong. At least, not in the obvious way. It had a calm, measured pace. A slightly laid-back tone. Words stretched a little longer, and the vowels curled at the edges. Every word was easy on his ears.

"Thank you," he croaked.

She shook her head. "Please, don't try to talk." She licked her lips and shifted from her knees to sit on the rug next to him, cross-legged. "You lost a considerable amount of blood. You've been out for eight hours. I, ah," she paused and glanced toward the mini fridge, "I helped myself to some food and clothes."

He flashed her a quick smile and grunted.

"I also moved your car," she added. "I didn't think it would be good sitting out front. Though I just moved it to the side of the building. Not sure it's going to stay hidden for long, but it's something. I did my best to clean the blood from the car."

He mouthed *thank you*.

"I'm Rowen, by the way. Rowen Thornevale."

Before he could try to tell her his name, she lifted his wallet.

"I got bored," she said, wrinkling her nose by way of apology.

He chuckled, which set off another round of pain. She was back immediately with the cloth. He shut his eyes as she bathed his heated face.

"Mason," she called.

The sound of his name pulled him back to consciousness. He blinked open his eyes to find her face above his, her brow furrowed, and worry etched in her pale orbs.

"I found your first-aid bag." She turned away for a moment

and returned with the water once more. "You seem very prepared, and I'm glad you were, since you've been getting hotter to the touch each time I checked." She pushed out two pills from a blister pack. "Take these antibiotics."

He opened his mouth as she dropped the pills onto his tongue. Then the straw was there again. He drank deeply, letting the capsules slide to the back of his mouth and then down his throat.

"Is there someone I can call?" she asked, taking the water away again.

He grabbed her wrist, gripping it too tightly by her pained expression. "No one," he stated.

"All right," she said. "I can see from this setup that you were expecting something to happen. I saw the wards on the car and this unit. The door is bolted. My phone ran out of battery hours ago. I might have stitched your wounds, but by the look of things, you really need a Healer or a doctor."

"Can't," he said and felt his eyes closing.

He wanted to tell her how important it was that he remain hidden. He wanted to tell her to get out while she could. But his body had other ideas as he slid into unconsciousness again.

When Mason next woke, he still felt like shite, but at least he could swallow. He rolled his head on the pillow to look for Rowen and found her across from him in the chair, asleep, her head at an awkward angle.

How long had he been out this time? She was right, though. He needed a Healer, but he couldn't trust reaching out to anyone. He had one other option: Skye. If he could get to the isle, Ferne would help him. The problem was, Thomas and London would be looking for him, and he was in no condition to drive himself.

The wards he had inscribed in various places in the unit would only shield him for so long. Thomas wouldn't stop until they found him. Mason didn't know how Thomas had figured out that he'd been playing him. He had been careful, but obviously not careful enough if the elder had figured things out. Mason had been prepared for an attack, but one with magic, not weapons. And he'd nearly died from that mistake.

He *would be* dead if it weren't for Rowen.

Strands of her straight, strawberry blond locks fell against her face, and her mouth was parted slightly as she breathed deeply and evenly. He ran his eyes down the long, pale column of her throat. The blanket had fallen, revealing his gray tee. It hung on her smaller frame so the short sleeves fell to the middle of her upper arms.

Mason lifted the blanket covering him and peered down to see the bandages along his side. He steeled himself and lifted his head from the pillow. There was a fresh onslaught of pain, but he was ready for it this time. It took his breath away once again, but he was able to get it under control more quickly.

He moved the blanket to get a better look at his right leg. The wound was on his upper leg, more toward his inner thigh area. As if his attacker had been trying to hit his femoral artery. She had missed, thankfully.

"What are you doing?" Rowen asked sleepily as she squatted beside the cot.

"I needed to see."

She raised her brows as his head fell back onto the pillow. "See what? That you were injured?"

He grunted at her sarcasm. He probably deserved it, though. Then, he stilled when her hand covered his forehead.

"You're no longer warm. That's a good sign."

She put the straw to his lips again, and he drank greedily. She then rattled the blister pack of pills. He gave her a nod and accepted two more before washing them down.

"Who are you?" he asked.

She cut him a look before rising to settle into the chair across from him. "I already told you my name."

"But not who you are or what you were doing at the London headquarters."

"I'll answer if you will," she retorted.

There were a great many things he could tell her that would give the illusion that he was being open. Yet even as the thought went through his mind, he recognized that she could—and likely would—do the same.

"Deal," he said.

She brought her knees up to her chest. "I'm from Orcas Island. It's a part of the San Juan Islands of Washington state. Brenna, our leader, has received numerous requests from London for us to visit."

She didn't sound as if she had been keen on the idea, which was interesting. Perhaps she saw London for what it really was.

"I was chosen to make the trip. Last night was my first meeting," she told him.

"What did you think?" he asked.

She studied him for a long moment. Finally, she said, "It was peculiar."

A chuckle rose up before he could stop it. The pain silenced it a heartbeat later. He blew out a breath. "Is that all?"

"What would you say if I told you that I had to sneak away from the woman who was showing me around? That I bolted before the meeting was even finished?"

He met her gaze. "I'd say you were smart and did the right thing."

She dropped her socked feet to the floor and leaned forward to prop her elbows on her knees. "And you?"

There was far more to her story, but she was keeping that to herself. He respected that, and he hoped she did the same for him. "I was at the meeting."

"I saw you."

He quirked a brow. "Did you?"

"Ella, the woman with me, was quite enamored with you and took great pains to point you out to me."

"I take it I didn't make much of an impression on you."

Rowen shook her head. "It was more that I was already trying to find a way out and had just gotten there."

Smart girl if she figured that out so soon. He wished others would. "What was it that didn't sit right with you?"

"Everything," she answered immediately. "It should've felt welcoming. Instead, it was too polished, too rehearsed. Like a façade built to dazzle and distract. And underneath it all, something was wrong."

"That's because it is." Either Rowen was true to her word, or she was one of Thomas's spies. Mason had yet to figure out which. She had saved him, which gave her a little leeway, but not a lot.

She glanced down at her hands. "I saw you enter the meeting without blood covering you. Then I saw you, well,"—she nodded toward him—"like I found you."

An image of Thomas smiling triumphantly flashed in his head. "I ran into a bit of trouble."

"You ran into a whole lot more than *a bit*. Do you know who attacked you?"

Mason nodded as he raised his gaze to the roof. "I do."

"Do you know why they did it?"

"Yes."

There was a brief pause, and then she asked, "Are you going after them?"

CHAPTER SEVEN

SKYE DRUIDS

Emotions played over his face—anger, resentment, resolve—as Rowen waited for his answer. She had her own affairs to worry about. The last thing she needed was to get involved in something that didn't concern her. And while she hadn't asked to get embroiled in Mason's troubles, here she was. Smack-dab in the middle of a world of shit.

She could leave. She'd had ample opportunity while he slept. It wasn't as if he could stop her now, even if he wanted. Yet, she remained. And for the life of her, she couldn't say why. Maybe she felt responsible for him. Maybe she thought he could give her more information on the London Druids. Maybe she was just foolish.

"I am going after them," he said, pulling her out of her thoughts. "I have been for some time."

The shiver that went through her had nothing to do with a chill and everything to do with the intent of his words. But it was his voice that captured her. His accent spoke of old bloodlines and an expensive education—all calm dictation and cold restraint. But beneath the aristocratic surface, she heard it: something darker. It was the kind of voice that could recite Shakespeare or undress you with a single word. Smooth. Measured.

Quietly devastating.

Her cousins had *oohed* and *ahhed* over her making the trip. They had talked about how wonderful the British accent was. She hadn't understood until she heard Mason. He was much like his voice. Controlled. Crisp. Dangerous. She imagined that if and when he released that restraint in the bedroom, it would be a wild, sensual ride that left his bedpartners forever changed.

Stormy gray eyes slid to her. She had been close enough to perceive the silver streaks in them that looked like lightning. He was a building storm waiting to unleash upon his enemies. And god help anyone who got in the way. She wished she were still beside him. She wanted another look at those mystical, mesmerizing eyes, to try and pinpoint the exact color of the gray.

"No more questions?" he asked, his voice rising slightly in surprise.

Rowen swallowed and returned her attention to their conversation. "I was trying to figure out why you're going after your own. Because that is what you're doing, isn't it?"

He hesitated, his eyes narrowing slightly.

That's when it dawned on her. He didn't trust her. She hadn't divulged everything to him, either. But she *had* risked her life to save him. If she were in his shoes, she'd be wondering if his enemies hadn't sent her in to gain his trust.

"You're right. It's none of my business," she said. "You made it out this time. You might not, the next. I don't think I need to tell you to prepare better when you face them again."

"Why did you stay here with me? You could've taken my car and left."

Rowen looked at the door, her thoughts drifting to lazy days on the island. She missed the smell of her mom's freshly baked sourdough bread, the call of the bald eagles, and the slam of the screen door as her family rushed in and out of the house. The steady waves rolling onto the shore and the moon reflecting off the water. It felt as if she had left a lifetime ago, instead of just days.

"I didn't want to leave home. I was against any kind of association with London." She drew in a breath and looked at Mason. "And before you ask, I didn't have a specific reason. Only a gut feeling."

"Sometimes, that's all we have to go on."

She shrugged one shoulder. "Others felt differently. Some thought London could help us. So, here I am. In a city that's too loud and crowded." Rowen closed her eyes as she remembered standing outside the Druid headquarters. "I didn't want to attend the meeting, but I promised our leader, Brenna. Even before I entered, things felt…"

Rowen paused and held back a shiver as she opened her eyes. Mason's gaze was steady as he returned her stare. She brought the blanket up around her shoulders. "Things felt oily. As if a residue covered everything and everyone, some more than others."

"Everyone?" he asked, his brows raised.

She parted her lips to answer, then paused. After a moment, she shook her head as she raised her shoulders again. "I didn't pay too much attention to others. Ella introduced me to so many that their faces and names soon blurred. I was overwhelmed. I was more concerned about getting away from her and out of the building than paying attention to specific individuals. However, one speaker did garner my attention."

"And who might that be?"

"I think his name was Thomas Oliver."

A seething storm of indignation crossed Mason's face as he chuckled humorously.

"Do you know him?" she asked.

Mason snorted. "You could say that."

When he didn't elaborate, Rowen continued. "The way Ella acted made me think they weren't going to take *no* for an answer about anything. They assumed my being there was confirmation that we would be joining them. It didn't matter that I was only sent to check things out. Ella knew where I was staying. She even knew what flight I came in on. They were tracking me, which meant they were aware of my flight out. I was just trying to get away when I stumbled upon you. And I stayed for several reasons."

He stared, waiting for her to list them.

"I couldn't leave you. There is also the fact that this place is heavily warded. Yes, I found the one under the rug," she added. "I want to go home, but I don't want to chance them waiting for me at the airport."

"How will you get home, then?"

Good question—one she had been asking herself. "I've not figured that out yet."

"Every problem has a solution. You just have to find it."

"You sound like my mom," she said with a small smile.

Mason's eyes were growing heavy. "Have you called them?"

"Phone ran out of battery, remember?"

He mumbled something she didn't understand before he fell

asleep again. She sighed and tried to get comfortable, but she was tired of being in the chair. Her ass was numb, her hips kept cramping, and she was desperate to stretch out and get some actual sleep.

Rowen eyed the rug for a long moment before giving up and dropping onto it, extending her legs as she yawned. The long, exaggerated stretch felt amazing. She used her arm as a pillow when she curled onto her side and pulled the blanket up to her shoulder. Now that she was relatively sure Mason's fever wouldn't return, she could let herself succumb fully to sleep. He was getting stronger each time he woke. She would need answers to her problems soon.

A loud noise yanked Rowen from sleep. She immediately rose onto her elbow and looked at the cot to find it empty. A quick scan of the storage unit showed Mason leaning a shoulder against a wall, gasping for breath. He had on sweatshorts and clutched a shirt in one hand.

Rowen jumped to her feet and rushed to him. "What are you doing? You should be in bed."

He briefly met her gaze and tried to smile, but it came out more like a grimace. "Need to get moving."

"I don't think you popped any stitches. I need to see your leg."

"Then look," he told her.

She wanted him lying down, or at least sitting, but she didn't think she would get either. The quicker she looked at his bandage, the faster she could help him dress and get something in his stomach.

Rowen slipped her fingers into the elastic waist of his shorts and tried not to think about his warm skin against hers. She tugged them down to his knees and dropped to her haunches to inspect the bandage, very aware of how close her face was to his body.

"No bleeding," she told him as she quickly pulled up his sweats.

He was staring at her when she straightened. A dark shadow of whiskers covered his jaw. His breathing had slowed slightly, but she still needed to get him off that leg.

"Please sit," she begged.

When he nodded, she wrapped his arm around her shoulders and helped him to the chair. He moved better than when she'd first met him, and he didn't put nearly as much weight on her this time. That didn't mean it was easy to get him the few feet to the chair, though.

"Are you hungry?" she asked after he was seated.

He leaned back after putting on his shirt and nodded. "I could eat."

She opened the metal cabinet to inspect its contents. "Why didn't you wake me? I could've gotten you anything you needed."

"You were asleep."

"So?" She pulled out a few options and set them on the table for him, then got out a bottle of water.

He wrinkled his nose at the selection. "Could you boil some water?"

"Of course." She set about filling the electric kettle and glanced at him. He had opened a carton of chocolate-covered cookies and was nibbling at one. It must have tasted good because he put the entire next one in his mouth.

Rowen found the paper cups and set out two before digging out the tea. He only had the traditional breakfast tea, but she quite liked it. It didn't take long for the water to boil, and then she poured it over the tea bags and sat on the edge of the cot as they steeped.

"You need more time to heal," she stated.

Mason stuffed another cookie into his mouth and shrugged. "I'll heal while I drive."

She glanced at his right leg, wondering how that would feel as he pressed the accelerator. It was none of her business. She needed to let it go. They each had things they needed to deal with. He wasn't part of her problem, and she wasn't part of his.

"Come with me."

He seemed as shocked by his statement as she was. Rowen stared at him for a long minute. She didn't know whether he had offered because he needed assistance, or because he was trying to help her. In the end, it didn't really matter.

"Look," he said and cleared his throat. "You were seen helping me. They won't ask why, and they won't allow you time to give them a reason."

"You make it sound as if I should be worried about my life."

He wiped his mouth with his hand. "You should be. They want me dead, and they'll likely kill you for preventing that."

That put a whole new spin on the situation. "What did you do?"

"It isn't what I did. It's what *they* did. I was merely responding."

"That didn't answer my question."

He looked down at the cup of tea. "No, it didn't. If you come with me, I'll tell you." His gray eyes swung back to her. "But if you choose not to, the less you know about the situation, the better."

That sounded ominous. "How good are my chances of getting out of the country?"

"On a plane, by changing your flight? None. You won't even get into the airport. They'll have every entry watched."

"I suppose renting a car is out of the question."

He gave her a flat look.

Yep. Just what she thought. "I could take yours. It's warded."

"It is, but it won't matter. They'll be looking for it. The London Druids are a vast organization. They've been recruiting members from outside the city for years. They have Druids of every level of government and police. Trains and ferries will also be watched."

The more he spoke, the more anxious she became. Was she trapped in England forever? "How are you getting out?"

"Driving."

"You just said your car would be spotted."

He flashed her a sexy smile. "I won't be driving the Aston."

Of course, he'd have another vehicle. She should've thought of that.

"You don't have to decide anything now, but you need to know the facts," he told her before taking a drink.

Could she believe him? It wasn't as if she had many options. She would have to trust her gut. It had led her to him. Maybe she should see what his plan was. "Where are you going?"

"Skye."

Her mouth fell open. Of all the places, she hadn't anticipated him saying that. "As in the Isle of Skye?"

"The very one."
"You can't."
He quirked a black brow. "And why not?"
"It isn't safe."

CHAPTER EIGHT

SKYE DRUIDS

The pain was a constant, low pulsing that drummed through Mason's body. Sitting up had sapped most of his strength, but getting his shirt on had nearly undid him. He would've been on his arse if Rowen hadn't woken when she did.

She intrigued him. He shouldn't trust her, but her coming to his aid and caring for him had overshadowed that. Her warmth and authenticity drew him to her without him even realizing it. It was why the flash of fear in her gaze when he mentioned Skye took him aback.

"What do you mean Skye isn't safe?" he asked.

Her brow wrinkled as she became absorbed in discarding her tea bag and adding sugar to the brew. He waited patiently. A few times now, she had paused before replying. It was no doubt her way of coming up with a way to tell him what she wished to convey while also keeping something to herself.

There was a quiet, methodical way about her. And yet, in a stressful situation like getting them out of the city, she hadn't stumbled even once. He was beginning to think there wasn't anything she couldn't do. Case in point: her exit from headquarters. The fact that she had gotten out of there at all was surprising.

"You're so close to Skye. Surely, you know," she said.

Mason ate another cookie while watching her. The sugar was giving him a burst of energy and would help fight off any infections. They also gave him the calorie intake he needed. The caffeine in the tea also went a long way to making him feel better.

He finished swallowing the cookie before he said, "I know Skye well. What is it you think I should know?"

"The Druids there are dangerous."

She issued the statement as if he were a simpleton. "Any Druid can be dangerous. The Skye Druids are the strongest of us all."

"It has nothing to do with strength and everything to do with them attacking other groups."

Mason's gut twisted in fear. He kept it from his face as he asked calmly, "Where, perchance, did you get such information?"

"I don't remember where I first heard it. Maybe one of my aunts. I think it spread through word of mouth first, but I did see it on one of the message boards. Everyone in the States knows to stay away from the isle." Rowen walked back to the cot and sat upon the edge, tea held between her hands.

Was this Thomas's work? Or was it another Druid group? The Skye Druids were risking their lives for the entire world, and someone was actively working against them. He should've known about this. Mason squeezed his eyes shut. He had to learn everything so he could pass it on to Ferne. He opened his eyes and tried to recall the name of the hacker who worked with Carlyle.

"You're wrong about Skye," Mason told her. "They aren't

attacking other groups. It's the other Druids attacking *them*. Specifically, London and Edinburgh. Skye is merely trying to stay alive while also battling an ancient evil bent on domination."

"I'm sorry. What did you say?" Rowen asked, eyes wide.

Mason blew out a breath. "I'd rather tell you on the way. It's a long drive. If you're coming, that is."

She didn't reply.

He ran a hand over his jaw. "My sister and best friend live on Skye. I know what's happening there. Whatever you're being told is a lie that most likely originated within the London branch."

"Why would they lie about Skye?"

"You were in their headquarters. You saw them. But the real answer is anger. Ages ago, Skye Druids banished a faction from their land for corruption. Those few put the reputations of the Skye Druids at risk, so they were forced out. Those Druids traveled to London and set up their own organization. Anger and resentment have been passed down year after year, generation after generation, directed at the Skye Druids and all who call the isle home."

Rowen blinked, uncertainty in her pale blue eyes. "I've never heard this."

"I'm not surprised. London doesn't like it to get out. They want the world to believe they are bigger and stronger than Skye. They might have more members, but they will never best the Skye Druids. London goes so far as to spell every child within their ranks so they're alerted should one of them go to Skye."

"You just said your sister is there."

Mason nodded slowly. "Yes, Ferne is there. So is Carlyle. My best friend, who is also Thomas's son."

"Who cares if someone goes to Skye, then? And why waste the energy on a spell?"

"Control. Anyone who goes to Skye is automatically banished. Not just from the London organization, but also from their families. They're cut off forever."

Rowen blew out a breath. "That's harsh. And totally barbaric. No organization should have the right to dictate what a person does or doesn't do. Definitely not what their family does. Is that why you're going after them?"

"It's part of it."

"You didn't banish Ferne, did you?"

Mason hesitated. "No, but I had to make Thomas believe I did."

"Don't you mean the elders?"

"The elders aren't ruling London. They're nothing but a show for the others. The real one in charge is Thomas."

Rowen's eyebrows rose on her forehead. "And his son is on Skye. I bet that didn't go over well."

"No one knows."

"Does Thomas?"

His side was beginning to throb. Mason attempted to adjust in his chair, but there was no escaping the pain. "I don't know. I think maybe he does."

"That's a lot to take in."

He had only told her a portion of it. If she couldn't handle this part, then she shouldn't be going with him. Perhaps he shouldn't have invited her to begin with. The opportunity to share what had happened with another person had been too great. However, he should've thought it out more carefully.

"If you want to get home, there might be a way across the

border in Scotland. London loses a lot of control there. It would be easy to get you across to Ireland, and from there, you could board a plane to America."

Intelligent eyes studied him. "Have you changed your mind about me going with you?"

"I'm giving you a way out. You had no idea what you stepped into by coming to London, and certainly not by helping me. You saved my life. The least I can do is get you home."

"I knew coming to the UK would change things, but I couldn't have imagined it would reveal so much deception. I came to take answers back to my group. If I leave now, I won't have the full picture. Besides, you can't drive yourself."

He took offense to her words. "I'd get myself there."

"And do how much damage to your wounds in the process? We have to get to Scotland, whether I'm staying with you or not. So, the decision has been made. I'll drive. When do we leave?"

"Now."

She rolled her eyes. "I knew you were going to say that."

"We need to grab whatever you want from here. It's going to be about a twelve-hour drive. I'd like to limit our stops to keep from being seen."

Rowen jumped to her feet and finished off the last of her tea. "I'd better grab some food and drinks, then."

"If you look in the bottom of my trunk, some of Ferne's clothes are in there. She's a little taller than you, but there might be something that fits."

"Thanks," Rowen said as she glanced down at her attire.

He waved away her words. "There should be some boots and a pair of trainers of Ferne's in there, as well."

Mason's gaze ate up the sight of Rowen shoving aside her hair as she bent over to look in the chest. Her back was to him, giving him a view of her firm ass.

"Shall I grab a few things for you?" she asked, her voice muffled.

"Please."

"Anything in particular?"

He made himself look away. "Whatever you want."

While Rowen moved about gathering items and putting them into bags, he worked to scoot to the edge of the chair. He was still much too weak for his liking. At least he could stay awake now. If only the pain would lessen.

"Here you go," she said and set a pair of Adidas slides at his feet.

She flashed him a grin and spun around, her strawberry tresses fanning out around her. Rowen was right. Druids needed to know the truth about what was happening on Skye, but they also needed to learn about the real London. It was easier nowadays to get the word out about something, but that didn't mean everyone would believe it. Oh, some would. Readily, in fact. But there would always be others who dismissed it.

Or worse, went to London to seek answers.

By the time he got his right foot into the slide, sweat beaded his forehead. Bloody hell, this was rough. Getting to the car would be an adventure.

One by one, Rowen set bags on the small table. He tried to stop her when he thought she was making up the bed, but she folded the blanket she had used and added it to the rest of the things they were taking.

"How far is the car?" she asked.

He nodded to the hooks on the wall. "You'll need the second

set of keys." Once she grabbed them, he said, "If you look behind the metal cabinet, you'll find a latch."

When Mason had put all of this together, he had done things hoping that Ferne might be with him. He hadn't anticipated a pretty American with grit and determination—and entirely too much bravery.

There was a soft click, and a passage between his unit and the one next door popped open. Rowen wore a wide smile as she moved toward the opening. He couldn't take his eyes off her as she peered into the other side and then looked back at him in shock. Mason grinned, knowing she had seen not only the car, but also the boxes within.

"Well, I think it's safe to say you prepared," she replied with a soft chuckle. She moved into the other unit. "This isn't the kind of vehicle I expected to be in here."

"That's the point," he replied, raising his voice so she heard him.

Mason used the table and the back of the chair to push to his feet. He didn't attempt to put any weight on his injured leg this time. The few cookies and caffeine had given his body some energy that should allow him to hobble to the car.

"I can't leave you for a second," Rowen muttered as she rushed to his side and slipped his arm around her shoulders. Hers wrapped around his waist, careful not to get near the bandages on his left side.

She fit against him nicely, and the more she put herself there, the more he found he liked it. Once more, he leaned on her for help. He tried to hop and immediately regretted it. After that, he dragged his right leg. He was shaking and sweating by the time they reached the vehicle, the caffeine and sugar had been used up immediately.

She got the door open without releasing him and then helped him to sit down slowly. She gently lifted his right leg and set it inside. He moved his left to join the other while she brought in the bags.

Mason reclined the seat to relieve the ache in his side. He fastened his seat belt and then waited. It wasn't long before Rowen raised the door to the unit and slid behind the wheel.

CHAPTER NINE

SKYE DRUIDS

The hum of the road beneath the tires soon filled the car as they merged into the evening, five o'clock traffic. Rowen hated to drive without some kind of music. The silence grated on her nerves, and they were still frayed from having to get back on the freeway. She relaxed her fingers so they no longer had a death grip on the steering wheel and glanced at the radio.

Why hadn't she taken a few moments to get acquainted with the car before driving off? The strange roads and becoming adjusted to driving on the opposite side of the car took all her attention. She didn't dare try to split her awareness. Mason was no longer wheezing as heavily as he had been once he got more comfortable, so she wasn't about to ask him. It looked like she would be driving in silence for a few hours. She glanced down to find the gas gauge. As she had expected, the tank was full. It would be miles and miles yet.

She had been surprised to see that Mason's second vehicle was a Ford Focus. The five-door hatchback wasn't flashy, and the silver was ordinary. If the UK were anything like the States, the color would blend in with thousands of others on the road. Which was precisely why he had chosen it.

Rowen shifted in her seat. She was getting to see much more of England than she had expected. It might be fun if Mason weren't injured, and they weren't worried about Druids catching them. Then again, without the people after them, they wouldn't have met, and she wouldn't be sitting in the car with a handsome Brit. She chuckled, imagining what her family might say when she got home and told them this story.

"What is it?" Mason asked.

She glanced at him and shrugged. "This isn't how I imagined my time in London would go."

"And that made you laugh?" he asked incredulously.

Rowen grinned as she shook her head. "I was thinking about what my family's reaction will be when I share the story."

"Do you have a big family?"

"It's just Mom and me," she admitted. "But I have a large extended family, with my four aunts and cousins—only a handful left over the generations. Most chose to remain on the San Juan Islands."

Mason grunted. "I've never heard of the islands. Are they pretty?"

"They're stunning."

"I saw you pack a couple of the burner phones. You could use one to call home."

She adjusted her grip on the wheel. "I will eventually. I want to make sure I'm safe first. Because if I can't assure them of that, my mom will likely jump on a plane."

"So, that's where you get your fierceness from."

Rowen jerked her head to him, surprised by his words. "I'm not fierce."

It was his turn to chuckle. "I beg to differ. Tell me about your family."

"Nope. You promised me an explanation about Skye when we got on the road, and we are headed north. So, start talking."

"See? Fierce." Mason sighed and went silent.

Rowen looked over to see him staring out his window. She regretted pushing and was about to tell him to forget it when he began talking.

"Every London Druid is raised on tales about Skye. They always paint the Skye Druids as evil and conniving. It's done to strike fear in the young and make everyone else distrust them enough to stay away."

"The threat of banishment doesn't do that?"

"Most times, but some are curious, and others need to see and experience something for themselves to know if it's all true."

Rowen shot him another look. His face was turned away so she couldn't see his expression, but his voice was tinged with what sounded like regret.

Mason braced his elbow on the door and rested his forehead against his hand. "When I learned my sister had reached out with her magic to someone on Skye, I urged her to go."

"Even though you knew she would be banished?"

"Yes. I wanted us to go together, but she couldn't wait. She was needed there. London had already kicked her out of the organization for talking to the Skye Druids. We knew they would keep coming after her, and I had to get her away to keep her safe."

Rowen frowned. Something about the way he'd said the last part niggled at her. "She wouldn't be safe with you?"

"My mum was one of the elders. My father was high-ranking in the hierarchy of the organization, as well."

Her brows shot up on her forehead at the news. Mason wasn't just a part of the London Druids. He and his family had been in deep. He must have stumbled upon something someone didn't want him to know.

Mason's head rolled to her. "They died in a plane crash."

"Oh, I'm so sorry. What a horrible thing to happen."

"There were things about the crash, and events after, that didn't make sense. The more my questions were deflected or ignored, the more suspicious I became. That's when I decided to look into it."

"Let me guess, if London found out, they'd go straight for Ferne?"

He nodded. "And I couldn't have that. I feared what might happen to her on Skye, but I knew she was safer there than anywhere else. Turns out I was right. She fell in love with one of their Druids."

"I take that to mean she isn't coming home."

Mason looked out the windshield. "She's found her place. She was always powerful, but now, she has the backing of Druids who will ensure that no one from London who means her harm ever gets to her."

"Is she your only sibling?" Rowen asked softly.

"She is."

That meant he was alone. No parents, no sister. Rowen sometimes got annoyed with her family for always being up in her business, but she couldn't imagine it any other way. "Does Ferne know you're looking into the crash?"

"She suspected it before she left, but I didn't tell her much. I kept it from everyone. I was careful and diligent in hiding what I uncovered."

Rowen had always been a sucker for a mystery. She was dying to know what he had uncovered, but none of that told her what she wanted to know about the Skye Druids. She was ready to shift gears when she suddenly put two and two together. "Wait. Is that why you were attacked?"

"I believe it is."

"You found something, then?"

His lips flattened briefly. "I looked into something they had deemed an accident. I was questioning them, and that doesn't happen. But, yes, I found a link to a newly hired mechanic at the air strip and Thomas. A little more digging, and I found that fifty thousand pounds was wired to the mechanic's bank account the day after my parents' crash."

"Did you confront Thomas?"

"I wanted more information, but I was getting close. I knew he was playing me, but he must have discovered what I was doing. He's made it clear he wants me dead. He'll keep coming until he finds me."

"He won't set foot on Skye. Good move to head there," Rowen told him.

"I'm more concerned about Ferne and Carlyle."

Rowen frowned as she cut a quick look at him. "I don't understand. You said they were safe on Skye."

"To make Thomas and those watching me believe I had banished her, I…"

Rowen grimaced as she realized what he had done. "She believes you cut her off."

"I told myself it was the right thing to do for her, that I'd be able to fix it once I had answers. Now, though, I'm not so sure."

Rowen moved into the other lane and drove around a slower car. The silence between them lengthened. She had so many questions, but she left him to his thoughts. There was plenty of time for him to answer them.

"The Druid Ferne reached out to on Skye was a woman named Kirsi," Mason continued. "Ferne saw her battling an ancient evil and wanted to warn her. Turns out, the Skye Druids already knew that something was happening on the isle. It began slowly. Minor things that few paid much attention to. Then Druids began losing their magic."

Rowen's stomach dropped to her feet. She thought about her family and the Salish Druids experiencing the same thing. But she kept it to herself for the time being.

Mason blew out a breath. "Then a mist started killing people. It targeted Druids, specifically. I don't know all the details, but I do know that it's one of the reasons Carlyle and his friends went to Skye. He and a small group travel the world, providing justice for Druids who either can't get it themselves or won't. They call themselves Knights. It had been years since I'd last spoken to Carlyle. We were as close as brothers once." Mason paused and lowered his arm to his side. "My father spent hours training us. He created an obstacle course of magic so we could hone our skills."

Rowen had grown up with magic, but Mason's upbringing was vastly different. She could wield magic, and if need be, shield herself and others from it, but to use it in battle? That was something new.

"I see by your face that isn't something you do," Mason said.

She shot him a quick glance and shook her head. "Can't say we've ever needed it."

"I often used to ask Dad why it was so important that Carlyle and I knew what to do in battle. His response was always the same. *You never know what could happen, son.* Since his death, I've wondered if he and Mum challenged Thomas's control of London. That perhaps that's why Dad took so much time training us. Maybe he knew Carlyle and I would have to fight."

"Did Ferne not join you?"

Mason shook his head. "And she's the one in the middle of a war zone right now. The irony isn't lost on me."

"What kind of war? I've not heard anything about it."

"You wouldn't. The Skye Druids have been careful about keeping it contained. I don't know what it is they're fighting, but it's a formidable foe. I know it's going to take all of them to pull it off. Ferne made it clear that if Skye falls, the rest of the world will, too. She originally wanted London to join Skye to help."

Rowen twisted her lips. "I bet that went over well."

"She's tried to talk to me about it the few times she called. I wanted to ask her more, but I knew the phones were bugged. I even caved and called her once. It was a mistake, but I didn't learn my lesson. I called Carlyle. He was furious at me, and he let me know it."

Rowen had the urge to reach over and cover his hand with hers, but she resisted the need to comfort him. "You've been doing all of this on your own. Once you explain it to them, they'll understand."

"If they let me explain. The point is, the Druids of Skye are at war, but they're fighting something sinister. Meanwhile, London has aligned with Edinburgh to kill those on Skye and wrest power from them. Ferne and the others have been up against an ancient evil, as well as other Druids invading their home."

"The more you talk, the more I'm beginning to hate London."

Mason twisted his lips. "I know how you feel. I've had to pretend to be a part of them."

"You don't anymore."

"True. I'm not sure I've convinced you about Skye, though, have I?"

She shrugged. "I only have your word to go on. I've not met a Skye Druid—at least not that I'm aware of. But the ones creeping me out are the London Druids. So, I think it's best if I reserve judgment until I meet those on Skye."

"Does that mean you're coming to the isle with me instead of going home?"

"It does." She shot him a grin. "My family likes details, and they're going to need to know all of this."

CHAPTER TEN

SKYE DRUIDS

Mason jolted awake with a start. He stared out the windscreen, his gaze on the tree in front of him. Rowen had pulled over, and he hadn't even realized it. He swung his head toward her, but found her seat empty.

He used his hands to push himself up in the seat to ease the ache in his hips, and instantly regretted the small movement as pain rose up and sent fingers of agony streaking through him like lightning. It robbed him of breath and made sweat break out on his forehead. Whatever strength he might have managed to reclaim during the last few hours evaporated in an instant.

It took several moments for the deep beat and searing sting to diminish to a burning discomfort. He would've laughed had he been able. Each breath felt like jagged nails along his left side. He couldn't twist, bend, or reach for anything, since it tugged at the edge of the wound. And if he made the mistake of laughing or breathing deeply? The strike of pain was sharp and biting. Sitting was torture enough. And nothing eased the pulsing of the injury.

Then there was his thigh. The burning there had subsided, at least, but it had been replaced by a dull throbbing and a constant pressure, as if the wound remembered every inch of the blade. There was a tightness that alternated between the bandage and the stitches.

He was frustrated with the limits of his mortal body and irritated that he had allowed himself to be injured in the first place. Mason had been keenly aware of how little sleep Rowen had gotten, and he had been determined to stay awake. If he couldn't drive, then he figured he would at least keep her company and make sure she didn't fall asleep at the wheel. Yet he hadn't even managed that.

A glance at the clock on the dash told him that he had only been asleep for about thirty minutes. Still, that was thirty minutes too long. He got his bearings and tried to determine where they were. Rowen had pulled into a narrow lay-by, curved into the edge of the motorway. Before him lay an expansive view of moorland with patches of mist clinging to the hills. Blue-gray clouds hung in the silvery sky, and the rising sun caressed the tops of the tall pines in a streak of brilliant light. The place looked and felt remote. It was quiet. The kind of location where time paused.

Mason's magic swelled and swirled, tugging at him from somewhere far ahead. It slid just beneath his skin as if awakened, as if the land itself was calling to him. He didn't need a map to know they were getting close to Skye. Even from hours away, the air hummed differently. He could *feel* it. The island's magic had reach. For a heartbeat, he forgot the ache of his wounds and the threat that hovered over them.

But where was Rowen?

Doubts entered his head then. Maybe she'd finally had enough of taking care of him. Perhaps she was working with London, and they would arrive at any moment to finish him off.

Even as those thoughts worked their way through him, he knew they were ridiculous. Yet the suspicions lingered in her absence.

Movement outside caught his attention. He turned his head toward a cluster of trees. Beyond them, he spotted more peaks rising in the distance. Then he saw her. She exited the woods as if they reluctantly allowed her to depart. Her steps were slow and unhurried. She still wore his gray shirt and a pair of Ferne's white sweats, but it wasn't her attire he saw. It was her.

Wonderment and awe filled her beautiful face as she gazed about her, clutching a cluster of flowers and bits of greenery in one hand. She bent, then straightened, adding another bloom to her collection. At one point, she paused and lifted her face, her eyes closed. A soft breeze caused strands of her hair to lift softly.

It was as if her appearance alone called to the magic and created an enchanted space just for her. He could have sat there watching her forever. Her beauty, her elegance…it was mesmerizing.

Then she stepped into the sunlight. The beam struck her strawberry blond locks, and his breath seized in his lungs. Her hair caught the light, glowing with hints of fire. The soft, coppery gold appeared as if it had been steeped in the sun. It was the kind of color that looked otherworldly, as if touched by magic. She stood there, lit by the Highland morning, and he couldn't look away. She transfixed him.

As did the land.

Her gaze suddenly met his, and a soft smile curved her lips. There was nothing sexual in it, but heat curled low in his gut just the same, slow and undeniable. Mason pushed the flicker of desire away as she drew nearer.

She opened the passenger door, and cool, damp air brushed his skin. The sound of birds waking to meet the day filled the still morning. Rowen knelt on the pavement next to him and laid out the flowers. Annoyance swelled in his chest. His life was on the line, and she had stopped for flowers? He tried to tell himself that she probably needed the break, but couldn't it have waited until they got petrol? She could've stretched her legs then.

Harsh words were ready to fall from his lips when she began plucking the petals from one of the flowers to stack in her lap. Mason watched her do that to the other flowers before she turned her attention to the leaves of yet another plant.

"Can you hand me that cup of hot water?" she asked without looking up.

For a beat, he debated whether or not to release the words gathering in his throat. Then, he glanced at the center console and saw two paper cups. One was empty, but the other was filled with steaming water. She had stopped already, and he had slept through it.

All his anger dissolved instantly. Mason carefully lifted the beverage with his right hand. He was ready to switch to his left when her fingers brushed his. He released his hold as she took it with another of her sweet smiles. It was fleeting, though, as she returned her attention to the flora in her lap.

With quiet focus, she took several white petals and crushed them in her palm before smelling them. Then she dropped them into the still-steaming water. Next, Rowen crushed yellow petals before adding them to the cup.

"What are you doing?" Mason asked curiously.

Her pale blue eyes briefly met his before she turned her attention to the small, bluish purple petals. "The tea will help with your pain."

"What's in it?"

"Yarrow, which will promote wound healing," she said, pointing to the white petals. "It has astringent and antibacterial properties. The yellow flower is calendula, an anti-inflammatory, and also has healing properties."

He nodded to the flower she was handling. "And those?"

"This is comfrey. It's used to speed healing," she answered as she ground the petals between the heels of her hands.

When she separated them, he saw the oils from the petals coating her palms. She added more to the grouping and repeated the steps. Then, to his surprise, she stuffed some of the green leaves into her mouth and chewed them before mixing them with the other petals and looking his way. He glanced at the concoction resting in her palm.

"The plantain leaves are known as nature's Band-Aid. They're great at soothing irritated skin, reducing inflammation, and promoting wound healing."

"Are you putting that in the tea?" he asked dubiously.

She chuckled softly. "This is a poultice."

Before he could reply, she lifted the hem of his shirt with her free hand and gently began to peel away the bandage that ran the length of the cut on his side. He held his breath when she spread the poultice on his wound. There was a little pain, but the moment the compress met his skin, he felt the slow unraveling of discomfort. Then he heard her whispered words. A Druid chant he didn't know. Still, he recognized the magic.

Once fresh bandages were set, she lifted the edge of his shorts and carefully removed the dressing there. He watched her deliberate movements as she made more of the poultice and applied it to the knife wound.

A kind of tranquility came over him as he sat there. Without the constant pain, his muscles were able to relax, and he released a long sigh. His eyes closed as her finger moved softly over his skin, drawing him deeper into a state of peace.

He wanted to keep her hand on him when she smoothed the pad of her finger along the edge of a fresh bandage and repeated the chant, but he didn't. Instead, he opened his eyes and watched her carefully—and lightly—wrap up the rest of the leaves into a napkin. Her movements were slow, purposeful. There was nothing hurried or harried about her. She seemed to run on a different clock than the rest of the world. Or maybe it was just him and those around him.

Rowen then lifted her face to the sun and closed her eyes, simply sitting there for a heartbeat. He had the overwhelming urge to touch her face. Her earthy beauty called to something deep inside him that was fiercely male. And intensely carnal.

"I thought you said you weren't a Healer," he stated softly.

"I'm not."

He quirked a brow. "I beg to differ."

She pressed her lips together as she looked away. He waited for her answer, but she grasped the cup, along with the napkin of herbs, and climbed to her feet. Mason didn't take his eyes off her as she closed his door and walked around the front of the car before climbing into the driver's seat. He waited for her to respond.

Rowen placed the cup in the center console and sighed. "I'm

not a Healer. Some might mistake what I do for that, but there's a difference."

"What do you do?"

"I hear the plants. They tell me which of them will help, and how to administer them."

He nodded, his amazement for her growing. "I'm very glad they do. It's the first time I can breathe easier."

"This is just a brief lull. The pain will return," she cautioned, looking at him. Then she handed him the tea. "Drink all of it."

"Thank you. For everything."

She tucked her hair behind her ear and started the engine. "We're about four hours from Skye."

"I can feel it." He sipped the tea. The initial sip wasn't bad, but it left a bitter aftertaste on his tongue.

"Me, too," she replied softly. After a long beat of silence, she asked, "Do you think that's why London didn't want anyone coming?"

Mason shrugged and took another, longer drink, wanting to get it finished quickly. "I'm wondering the same thing. Ferne never said anything about it, but I didn't give her a chance."

"You'll get it sorted with her."

"You don't know my sister. And I...well, I went to extremes to make her think I had cut her out of my life."

Rowen checked the road before she put the car in drive and pulled into the lane. "She'll listen to what you have to say, if for no other reason than to try and understand."

"She might be too angry."

"Probably, but you're family. She'll listen."

Mason tried to forget their last conversation. "You sound sure of that."

"Family can be complicated. We take a lot of shit, but we also forgive a lot. Just be prepared to do a bunch of begging for forgiveness. And answer any question she poses, even if it's the same one a hundred times."

"Are you speaking from experience?" He probably shouldn't have asked, but he was dying to know more about her.

Rowen grinned. "It comes from having a large family."

"How large?"

"Sometimes, too large." She laughed softly. "The island only has a population of six thousand. Tourists come all year, but it's still small. Everyone knows everyone, and that, of course, means we're all in each other's business. I've learned not to even try to keep a secret."

He needed to look up the San Juan Islands so he could picture them as she talked. He went to take a drink and realized the only thing left were the herbs. He set the cup aside. "Do you have siblings?"

"No, but I never noticed with my cousins. We're a pretty tight-knit group. They're more like siblings to me."

"And they let you come by yourself? I'm surprised your entire family didn't travel with you."

Her fingers tightened on the steering wheel. "Mom wanted to come, and then it was supposed to be one of my cousins joining me."

"What happened?"

"Aunt Maelin. She proclaimed I had to come alone."

Mason pulled his gaze from the magnificent loch they were passing to look at her. "Is she a seer?"

"She's a dream weaver. She didn't tell me what she saw. All she would tell us was that I had to come alone."

Her words began to sound as if they were coming from a far distance, and Mason's eyes suddenly grew heavy. He fought against the pull of sleep, but he was no match for it.

CHAPTER ELEVEN

SKYE DRUIDS

Rowen shot Mason a quick look to make sure her magic had taken effect so he could rest. That's when the herbs did their best work. His wounds worried her. The bleeding might have stopped, but he was still much too weak. The quicker she got him to his sister, the quicker Ferne would be able to talk him into a hospital. Or, if luck were on their side, Skye would have a Healer. What Rowen knew for certain was that Mason couldn't continue much longer as he was.

She settled more comfortably in the seat and continued north. It was difficult to temper her need to speed down the road and reach the isle quicker. She kept glancing at the screen on the dash, hoping the estimated time of arrival would change. At least the scenery was stunning and made up for it. There were so many places she would've liked to stop and explore, but that was for another time.

After driving for so many hours, she had gotten used to the roads and the car. They had made it out of England without incident, but the disquiet that had gripped her since the meeting hadn't released her yet. There had been a shift the moment they drove into Scotland, though that might have been her imagination. Their talk of Skye and the history between them and London had been fascinating—and disturbing. Yet she yearned to know more.

Soft music played in the background as Mason slept. She was glad to be on a quieter stretch of road now, only passing a few cars every now and again. It was almost as if she had entered another time. History was all around her. And so was magic.

Magic was spoken about often in the Salish community, at least among the Druids. Much of their past had been lost from her ancestors, who had come to the New World in the 1600s. Or maybe that account had been intentionally removed. Regardless, there was a wealth of history to learn and pass on to her family and the other Salish Druids. Hell, *all* the Druids in America. She truly believed that knowledge was power. She also didn't want to see history repeating itself, and it would unless *all* Druids knew that history.

There was a wealth of difference in the magic of the Salish Druids, and she knew the same applied to Skye. While she hadn't cared much about the London Druids while there, she knew she had missed an opportunity to gather information. She hadn't gotten to see Mason's magic, but hopefully, she would get the chance. Maybe one of the Skye Druids would allow her to compare their magic. She was curious to discover all the differences and even the similarities, because if all Druids originated from Skye, there had to be parallels.

For the next few hours, she drove through the gorgeous Scottish countryside and gasped—repeatedly—at the stunning landscape while taking mental pictures. She had never been one to pull out her phone for pictures, since none she took ever truly captured the essence of anything. She would rather hold those images in a special place that she alone could revisit.

"You drugged me."

She briefly met Mason's gaze. "I gave you a little urging through my magic. You needed it to heal."

"That isn't fair to you," he said groggily and then yawned. "You've not slept."

Rowen found herself yawning with him. She was tired, but they were close. She could make it the rest of the way. "I'm doing okay."

"I don't know how I'll ever repay you."

She felt his eyes on her. They pulled at her, urging her to look his way again. Each time she did, she found herself drowning in pools of molten mercury—volatile, magnetic. And impossible to look away from.

"That's good, because you don't need to," she answered.

Before she left, her mom had claimed she was in a rut. That a trip was just what she needed to find her way out. Rowen preferred to think of her life as structured. She had a routine, and she kept to it. She was as far from spontaneous as it got. And that's how she liked it.

Yet this trip had been anything but routine. She had made impromptu decisions time and again without hesitation. Maybe her mom had been right about that rut, because Rowen felt more alive than she had in years.

His voice was pitched low when he said, "I want to."

"Let's talk about this later," she suggested, though she had no intention of changing her mind.

A sign on the side of the road read that the bridge to the Isle of

Skye was 24 miles. She was about to point it out when she heard Mason's sigh. Rowen followed his gaze to the body of water that stretched around the curve of the land. The calm water rippled silver in the morning light. Seabirds soared in the wind around fishing boats. Beyond, Skye rose dramatically on the other side of the sea, green and rugged in the early morning sun.

Excitement mixed with nervousness as she followed the road toward the Skye Bridge. There was no more talk between her and Mason. They were each lost in their own thoughts as the isle drew near. She tried to memorize everything she looked at, but she knew she would never be able to do it justice while describing this striking land. It was something that had to be experienced firsthand. No matter how or why Rowen found herself here, she was glad of it.

As she drove the Focus onto the bridge, she noticed Mason's breaths quickening. His hands were clenched on his legs as he stared silently out the windshield to the isle before them. Somewhere out there were his sister and his best friend—and the Skye Druids.

He had spoken about a war being waged there, but nothing she saw hinted at anything. Then again, with magic involved, nothing was ever cut and dried. Did everyone who lived on Skye know about the Druids and magic? What about the tourists? If the isle was anything like the San Juan Islands, the magic was kept secret.

Her attention swung to Mason when he shifted in his seat and hissed in pain. The herbs and her magic were wearing off, but they had lasted longer than she had expected.

"I need to see to your wounds. We'll find a place to rest once we're on Skye," she told him.

He grunted. "I'd like to change, too."

She raised a brow but kept her thoughts to herself. Rowen could feel Mason's tension as they crested the bridge and began the curving descent. Their tires thudded off the bridge onto the isle's soil. Ahead, the road split. To the left was Kyleakin village, and to the right, the wild unknown of Skye.

Rowen turned left and headed into the small, coastal village. It had a quaint harbor and views toward the mainland. She saw a few places that might be good to stop, but something told her to keep driving. Mason stared out the window without uttering a word. She wished she knew what was going through his head. It must be difficult for him to be somewhere that he'd learned went against everything he had been taught.

She continued along the winding, scenic road with the water on one side and the rugged land on the other. Her magic screamed to be let loose, for her to get out of the car and touch the ground. The land pulsed with power, its magic in every blade of grass and tree leaf. She saw it in the oodles of waterfalls—some nothing more than a trickle from rocks to massive cascades—the striking lochs, and exquisite beaches.

Everything about Skye was dramatic and astonishing. She hadn't thought anywhere on Earth could compare to Orcas. She had been wrong. Skye wasn't steeped in magic. It *was* magic.

They drove slowly, passing homes and cars pulled over at lay-bys and pull-outs, as visitors attempted to get the perfect picture. Rowen had no idea how large the isle was, or how long it would take to circle it, but she was prepared to find out. Until she remembered that Mason needed tending.

Rowen planned to stop at the next village she came upon, no matter what she found. Mason had remained quiet, but his anxiety had only grown. The village appeared out of nowhere. She eyed various shops, but she slowed when she spotted a black and white awning over a door with a sign proclaiming: *Tea Talker*.

She glanced at Mason as she pulled into the small lot and parked. Rowen shut off the engine and turned to him. "How bad is the pain?"

"I'm fine." Then he softened his words by swiveling his head toward her. "I half-expected Druids to arrive the moment we reached the isle to force me to leave."

"They didn't."

He shook his head, his lips twisting. "No, they did not."

"I'm guessing by the name of this place that they sell tea," she said with a grin.

Mason chuckled. "Should we give it a try?"

"If you're up for it. If not, I can get it to go, and we can get back on the road."

"I have no idea where Ferne is."

"Ah." She'd thought that might be the case. "Changing in here will be difficult, but I bet they have a restroom, er, toilet, for you to use. The herbs can remain if you'd prefer."

He nodded. "Let's leave them for now. The pain is manageable."

It likely wouldn't stay that way when he tried to walk, but he knew that. There was no need for her to point it out. "All right. What would you like me to grab out of your bag?"

"Anything besides these shorts."

"What? Don't like how we Americans dress so casually?" she teased.

His gaze slowly moved over her T-shirt and sweats that she'd had to roll up because they were too long. Those steel-hued eyes shifted with every unspoken thought. Then he blinked, and the emotion was gone.

"I'd rather no one see the bandages," he explained.

Rowen swallowed, suddenly too warm. "Got it. I'd advise against jeans."

"Agreed."

"I did pack some sweats. Will that work?"

He nodded, still staring at her.

Rowen licked her lips and hastily looked away. "Be right back."

She hopped out of the car and opened the back hatch to rummage in the bag she had packed for him. The sweats were on top, but she paused there and took a deep breath to steady herself. Then she closed the trunk and walked to the passenger side. He had already unlatched the door for her. She swung it wide and gave him an encouraging smile.

"I parked close to the door. Hopefully, the toilets won't be that far," she said as she helped him get his feet on the ground.

"Bloody hell," he murmured, out of breath.

She moved to his side and gripped his arm to help him stand. She expected him to tip to the side, which is why she planted her feet and caught him before he could fall.

"Fuck."

Rowen swallowed a smile. "You're doing good."

"Liar," he said, but he chuckled.

They reached the door and got inside better than she had hoped. A red-haired waitress walked toward them, smiling.

"Excuse me," Rowen said, stopping her. "Do you happen to have a toilet?"

"Sure do," the woman said. She turned and pointed to an area adjacent to the counter in the back. "It's to the left, just beyond that wall."

Rowen shot her a smile. "Thanks."

"I got it," Mason mumbled.

"Mm-hmm." But Rowen didn't release him as they headed to the back.

It wasn't until they turned the corner that he removed his arm from her shoulders. "I don't know how long I'll be."

"You have ten minutes before I come looking for you," she warned.

There was a crooked grin on his face as he hobbled away. She watched him for a few seconds before walking back around the corner. There, she stopped and gawked in awe at the place. The ceiling was glass, allowing light to filter in for the numerous plants that were everywhere. Tables in various sizes were set with an eclectic array of chairs. At the back was the wooden counter with an antique cash register, but it was the shelves lined with glass jars behind the kiosk that had her attention.

"Can I help you?" asked a woman with a Scottish accent.

Rowen looked toward the voice to find a pretty brunette, who took boho to a whole new standard and worked it in stunning fashion. "Hi. Yes, I think I'd like one of everything."

The woman's smile grew. "I can make that happen." Her brow furrowed. "I saw the man you came in with. He looked injured. Is he all right?"

"He's…" What did she say? She couldn't exactly blurt out that she needed a Healer. Skye might be home to Druids, but that didn't mean everyone here was one. Yet as she looked into the woman's golden brown eyes, she found herself saying, "He ran into some trouble recently."

"Hmm. Let me put something together for him. My name is Ariah, by the way."

Rowen sighed, not realizing until then that she had been tense. "Thank you. I'm Rowen."

"What would you like to drink?" Ariah asked.

Rowen shrugged. "You pick."

"I can do that," Ariah said with a smile. "Find a seat, and I'll bring the tea out."

Rowen turned to pick out a table, wishing Orcas had a tea house like this. She'd be in it every day.

The bell over the door chimed, and she looked toward it to see a pair of women enter. The one with long, black curls and stunning green eyes caught her attention by the stark similarities between her and Mason. It was there in the line of her face, her nose, and the way she smiled.

The woman had the kind of beauty that turned heads, just like Mason.

On a hunch, she walked over to the pair. "Excuse me," Rowen said, looking up into brilliant and arresting green eyes. They were the olive green but had a sharp, cutting band of dark olive, set against the contrast of her dark features. "Apologies for interrupting, but does your name happen to be Ferne?"

The woman's smile slipped as those green eyes narrowed slightly in wariness. "Who wants to know?"

It was the way Ferne held her head that reminded her so much of Mason. Rowen glanced over her shoulder to see if he had come out of the restroom yet. "It is you, isn't it? I'm Rowen. I'm here with your brother."

"Mason?" Ferne repeated, doubt in her voice.

"He's in the restr—toilet, changing. We were stopping here before he called you."

Ferne's friend walked away, leaving the two of them alone. Ferne didn't seem to notice. All her attention was focused on Rowen. "Wow. London has sunk to a new low. Or is it Edinburgh? I don't care where you hail from, or which of them sent you, but you should leave before I make you."

"I'm tel—" Rowen began.

"Ferne," Ariah said, interrupting them as she walked up. "I think you and Rowen should sit."

The two women exchanged a long, silent look. Then, with a frown furrowing her brow, Ferne headed to a table. Rowen followed her, and they each sank into a chair.

"What's going on?" Ferne demanded, her voice tight with barely controlled anger—and a hint of worry.

Rowen ran her fingers through her tangled hair. Maybe she should've gone to the restroom, too. She probably looked an absolute fright. "My name is Rowen Thornevale. I'm a Salish Druid from the States. London invited someone from my group to visit. While there, I encountered your brother, who had been attacked."

"Attacked?" Shock widened Ferne's eyes and slackened her lips.

Rowen nodded. "He needs a Healer. And quickly. He'll tell you he's fine, but trust me, he isn't. I stitched him to stop the bleeding, but he's in a bad way."

"How bad?"

Rowen took a deep breath and laid out everything quickly and succinctly.

CHAPTER TWELVE

SKYE DRUIDS

Ten steps. That's all it was for Mason to get from Rowen to the bathroom. It had seemed simple enough. Easy, even. He had been so very wrong.

Those ten steps had felt like ten million. He'd gotten to the door of the toilet without falling on his face. Though once inside, he had stumbled against the wall, bounced off it, and barely caught himself on the edge of the sink to remain upright.

During that, he had managed to pull his side. Whatever Rowen's herbs had done to ease his pain vanished in the blink of an eye. He was breathless, drenched in sweat, and riddled with agony as he made his way to the toilet. There was no dignified sitting. His legs shook so badly from the exertion that he collapsed onto the seat.

The room spun, causing him to hold on to the wall and the sink. Splashing cool water on his face sounded like heaven, but that would require him getting up. He could stay there and wait for Rowen, but she had already done so much. Too much, actually.

Mason didn't know how long he sat there before he finally regulated his breathing. He slowly and carefully removed his shorts, which was far easier than getting his feet into the sweats. That wore him out again, and he had to rest once more before pulling the pants over his knees. Next came the hard part.

He drew in a deep breath and slowly released it. Then he used the wall next to him and stood, keeping his weight on his good leg. He had to be vigilant, so he didn't overcompensate and pull the stitches in his side again. His fingers were weak and wouldn't work properly, so he made several attempts before he got the sweats up. Just as he was ready to cheer, he realized his shorts had fallen to the floor. There was no way he was bending over, and he wasn't sure he could get back up if he sat down again. He decided to leave them and pivoted to the sink.

He leaned against the structure and ran his hands under the faucet. Cool water spilled over his skin, easing the heat in his palms and wrists. He gathered a handful and splashed his face. Most of it soaked his shirt, but the chill felt so good, he did it again—twice.

That's when he dared to look at himself in the oval mirror. His hair was a mess, he had two days' worth of stubble, and his skin was drawn tight, as if every ounce of strength had been sucked from it.

The man staring back at him was nearly unrecognizable. Not because he looked knackered, but because everything he had feared was true. The people he had trusted were immoral. Evil. He wasn't sure there was a safe place for Ferne—or anyone, for that matter.

The smell of tea reached him, and his mouth watered at the thought of some caffeine. He slowly turned and limped to the door, using the wall for support. Once outside, he stayed against the wall as he slowly, agonizingly, made his way around the corner of the wall to find Rowen. He owed her everything. He would've bled out on the sidewalk if not for her. She hadn't just gotten him out of there and stitched him up. She had brought him to Skye.

Mason was sweating again. He scanned the shop and found Rowen immediately. Her hair drew his attention like a parched man to water. She had her back to him as she talked to a brunette beside her, and he was thankful that she couldn't see the state he was in. He was determined to make it to her without help. Hopefully, he wouldn't make a fool of himself and fall into the chair.

He put the toe of his right foot against the floor. It was only then that he realized he was only in his socks. Where were his shoes? The toilet, perhaps? He should care, but right now, he didn't. His gaze moved around him, but if anyone noticed that he was shoeless, they didn't say anything. Mason steadied himself on his left leg and then put the barest amount of weight on his right toes as he inched forward. Two more like that, and he was past the corner.

There were chairs he could grab hold of, but they likely wouldn't keep him upright. He'd fall, making all kinds of racket, while also hurting himself and drawing every eye to him. And the place was busy. Every table was taken, and three people were queued at the counter to order.

Inch by inch, Mason moved toward Rowen. He hated the weakness that had taken hold of his body, and he wanted to push himself. At the same time, he hoped she would turn to look for him. He needed her to lean on. And…he wanted her against him again. Not just to hold him up, but so he could feel her.

Pain pulsed in his leg with every shuffle, unforgiving and sharp as glass. His side felt like fire threaded with needles shooting up and down his body. He was close enough to Rowen that he could call out to her. He parted his lips to do just that when the brunette moved, and he saw the second person sitting with Rowen. His gaze connected with his sister's, and shock ran through him.

"Mason," Ferne said, her green eyes large as she hastily stood.

Rowen twisted in her chair before jumping up and running to him. She looped his right arm around her shoulders. "You should've called out to me."

He heard her, but he couldn't answer. He was too busy staring at his sister.

"Uh, yeah," Rowen said sheepishly. "I'll explain, but let's get you to a chair first."

The brunette who had been talking to Rowen came up on his other side and lent a hand. They got him to the chair, and he had never been so grateful to sit down as in that moment. He closed his eyes, the pain swelling and threatening to swallow him.

Someone pressed a cool, wet towel to his forehead. He recognized Rowen's touch as she stood behind him to hold up his head and wipe his brow. She was talking, but he couldn't make out the words. He felt himself drifting. Not quite asleep, but not awake either. It would be so easy to slip into unconsciousness. Then he remembered that Ferne was here.

Mason focused on Rowen's movements and then her words. Slowly, he was able to make out what she was saying.

"...I shouldn't have let him go alone," she said.

Ferne's voice was tight as she said, "He was always stubborn."

"We'll see to him."

He didn't recognize the woman's voice. Was it the brunette?

Mason opened heavy lids and blinked several times until everything came into focus.

"There he is," the brunette said, a slight smile on her lips. "You need to drink this."

She held a cup of tea to his mouth. Mason took an obligatory sip, not sure he wanted anything. As the hot liquid ran down his throat and into his stomach, it spread like a soothing wave, easing tight muscles and calming his breath. When she bade him to drink more, he eagerly obliged. Again and again. By the time he'd drained the cup, he could hold his head up.

Rowen returned to her chair, her pale blue eyes filled with worry. He gave her a nod, letting her know that he was okay. For now.

"Some of your color has returned," she said as her gaze swept over him.

He shot a glance at the empty teacup. "I hate to tell you, but that tasted better than your brew."

That got him the smile he had hoped for.

"I'll make another cup," the woman said before walking away.

Mason swung his gaze to his sister. She sat stiffly, staring at him as if he were a complete stranger. He wanted to reach over and embrace her, but he could tell she would refuse it. "You look good."

"You look like shit," she replied.

"That's good, because I feel like death."

Rowen got to her feet and grabbed her tea. "I think it's best if I leave you two alone."

"Please stay," Mason urged. "There are parts in the story I won't be able to tell."

A look passed between Rowen and Ferne that made him frown.

"Stay," Ferne told her.

A long minute ticked by before Rowen lowered herself into the chair. Another cup of tea was set in front of him, but the woman was gone before Mason could thank her.

"Ariah knows what she's doing," Ferne said. "She's one of us. Drink whatever she puts in front of you."

Mason intended to do just that. His pain was still there, but it no longer felt as if it were controlling him. He took another drink. All the while, Ferne's gaze was locked on him, the look in her eyes suspicious, guarded. He set down the fragile cup. "Before you left to come to Skye, you guessed that I was looking into Mum and Dad's accident."

"I swear to all that is green that if you acted like the absolute wanker you are to keep me safe, I'm going to wallop you," she bit out angrily.

Mason understood her ire, and he didn't blame her for it. "You're all I have left, sis. If London had gotten to you, I never would've forgiven myself."

"Did it ever enter your mind that I was thinking the same thing?" she retorted, green eyes flashing.

Ferne was one of the gentlest souls he had ever known. His sister was loyal and true—a rare combination in today's chaotic world. She was powerful in her own right, but he knew he had a duty to protect her. "I did."

"And you proceeded anyway? You're a right bastard, Mas."

"You were safe here. The moment I learned that Carlyle was with you, I knew he would look after you should anything happen."

Ferne's nostrils flared as she shook her head, but she remained silent.

"I had to know the truth about Mum and Dad." Mason sighed. "If our parents were murdered, then others were at risk. *You* were at risk. More than that, I wanted to know who killed them so I could bring them to justice."

Ferne rolled her eyes and crossed her arms over her chest. "How's all that going for you?"

"Badly, actually."

Ferne snorted. "You don't say."

"I found something," Mason stated. "I was digging a little deeper to tie everything together when I was attacked, instigated by Thomas Oliver. He isn't missing at all."

Ferne released a long sigh and dropped her arms. "We know. Were you aware that he tried to kill Carlyle?"

Shock slammed into Mason. "What? When?"

"When Carlyle was in London, looking for him. Thomas's supposed disappearance was all a ruse to get Carlyle to come home. When he refused to join Thomas in ruling London, his father made an attempt on his life."

Mason couldn't believe the words, but then he'd had a difficult time reconciling all the things he thought he knew with what he had uncovered. "Is Carlyle all right?"

"He is, and he's here. There's a lot going on that you aren't aware of," his sister said.

Mason straightened in his chair, only to grunt in pain. He'd temporarily forgotten about his injuries.

Rowen took his hand. "This can wait. He needs a Healer."

"They're on the way," Ariah said as she strode up to the table.

"For now, let's get Mason in the back and on the sofa so he can lie down."

CHAPTER THIRTEEN

Scott & Elodie's cottage

"Do you have any idea how worried we were?"

From his position on the sofa, Luke stared across the room at his daughter, Willa, who paced agitatedly before him. He opened his mouth to reply, but she kept talking.

"You couldn't have gotten word to me or Scott?" she demanded, her blue eyes flashing in fury as she jabbed a finger at her brother, who sat in a chair to Luke's left. "I thought you were dead!"

Luke ran a hand through his dark hair that was getting grayer each time he looked in the mirror. Willa had been ranting like this for ten minutes. He didn't have the heart to tell her that if he hadn't witnessed Diana Barclay being stabbed by her youngest son, they still wouldn't know where he was.

Jasper stepped in front of Willa and folded her into his arms. She clung to him, her fingers curling tightly in Jasper's shirt sleeves.

Luke had had a wee bit of time to watch his baby girl and her beau together. Willa had found love. And more importantly, that love was returned. Luke studied Jasper as the man bent his dark head and whispered something in Willa's ear. His daughter wound her arms around Jasper, her shoulders shaking as she cried.

It tore him up to see his daughter cry. And knowing he was responsible for her anguish only made it harder to bear. There was no manual for becoming a parent. No one had ever warned Luke that the older a child got, the more a parent worried. And no matter how many times he thought he was doing the right thing, it never seemed to work out as he had hoped.

He drew in a deep breath and slid his gaze to his son, finding Scott's blue eyes leveled on him. Scott hadn't said much after their embrace at being together again, but Luke knew he had questions. They all did.

Whether he could—or *should*—answer them was something else.

When someone touched his arm, Luke swiveled his head to find Elodie setting a steaming mug of tea on the coffee table in front of him. She gave him a quick smile full of sadness and shoved her long, blond hair over her shoulder as she straightened to take the other chair in the living room. The five of them had decided to have this gathering at Scott and Elodie's instead of at Carwood Manor, where everyone would hear. Luke would eventually have to talk to the rest of the group, but this was for family only.

Luke scooted to the edge of the cushion and propped his forearms on his knees, clasping his hands together. He cleared his throat and said into the silence, "You may no' agree, lass, but I did what I had to do to keep you alive." He looked from Jasper to Scott and then to Elodie. "All of you."

"We've been handling things here. Which you would know if we had spoken," Scott stated.

His voice was calm, but resentment tinged every syllable. Luke didn't know what was worse: Willa's outburst or Scott's muted restraint. Both were as biting as blades. Best he started at the beginning, where everything had gone sideways. All for an ancient book with generations of Druid spells and who knew what else.

"After Willa and I figured out Beth's routine and made a play for the book, we went after it," Luke began after taking a sip of tea. He would've preferred a dram of whisky, but he would save that for later. "Beth was waiting for us. Before I knew it, her two guards were in the room with us. That's when I shouted for Willa to leave. We had a plan should anything go wrong. We were to split up and meet back at the flat. We both got out, but that's when I realized how easy it had all been."

Scott's blue eyes narrowed in confusion. "What do you mean?"

Luke glanced at Willa to find her watching him. He would rather go to his grave *not* revealing the next part, but there was no getting around it. His children wouldn't relent until they knew every detail. Better to rip off the Band-Aid now. "Beth didna lift a finger against us. She held the book to her chest, observing Willa and me fighting her bodyguards, smiling all the while."

"She didn't strike you at all?" Elodie asked, her brow furrowed in puzzlement.

Luke shook his head. "We got into her place too easily, and..." He paused and ran a hand over his jaw. "We got out too easily. I saw Willa leave, and a bodyguard followed. I knocked out the guard coming after me with the intention of catching up to Willa, but I only got two steps away when something took over my body."

He tried not to think about how effortlessly Beth had used the magic—or how helpless he had been. Those ninety-three minutes were the worst of his life. And they still haunted him. Delving into the story and the memories took him back to that night, and the terror that had wrapped its frosty, gaunt hands around him.

And squeezed.

He closed his eyes, hearing the screams as if from a distance, all the while knowing it was *his* hands hurting others, his body attacking. His eyes watching it all.

"Dad?"

Willa's soft voice penetrated the memories, making them scatter. Luke met her gaze as she untangled from Jasper's arms and came to sit beside him. She took one of his hands, and he gratefully threaded his fingers with hers. It had been him and the kids for a long time after his wife died. Willa and Scott had been his whole life. Now, Elodie and Jasper were his kids, too. He would die for the four of them. And in some ways, he wished he had.

Jasper leaned a shoulder against the hearth. "I've found it's just easier to let it out."

Luke squeezed the bridge of his nose with the thumb and forefinger of his free hand. Jasper was right. It'd be better to get it over with. He dropped his hand and paused for another heartbeat before saying, "Beth wanted us to enter her residence because she wished to try a spell she found in the book."

"What kind of spell?" Elodie asked, her voice barely above a whisper.

Luke couldn't look any of them in the eye. "One to take over another's body."

Willa squeezed his hand, but Luke still couldn't meet her gaze. He'd break if he did. He was barely holding it together as it was.

He focused on the mug of tea that was growing cold on the table. "She gained control of me. I never saw it coming. It happened before I even realized it. Then she made me do…terrible things," he rasped, the weight of the words crashing into him. "I saw it all—*heard* it all—but I couldna stop it, no matter how hard I tried. For a little over an hour and a half, I was forced to do her bidding."

His hand shook as he ran it down his face. If he lived a thousand years, he would never forget the sight of the bodies around him. "I feared I might run into Willa. I kept praying that she'd made it out and got away. I did everything I could think of to regain control of my body, but it was like I was a fly trying to knock over a mountain. Her control was absolute, her power undeniable. And then, it just suddenly stopped." He snapped his fingers. "Just like that."

Scott asked, "How did you finally break away?"

Luke slid his gaze to his oldest child. "I didna. Something happened to her. She doubled over and dropped the book. The moment the link between us was severed, I ran back to the flat for Willa." He looked at her. "You were no' there."

"They chased me through the city. I managed to get out and came here," she said.

Luke nodded. "I know."

"How did you know?" Jasper asked coolly.

Scott grunted. "I was wondering the same thing."

"It took some doing," Luke explained. "But after I scoured the city and spent days watching both Beth and George, I realized that Willa had managed to leave the city. I was being hunted, which made it difficult for me to reach out. I didna know what was happening on Skye, and I couldna take the chance that someone would be harmed just because I rang my children."

Willa wiped at her wet cheeks. "You got out of Edinburgh, though. Where did you go? Why not come to Scott and me?"

"I didna leave at once. In my surveillance of George, I discovered that she was taking meetings with the London Druids." Luke blew out a breath. "I knew something was going on, and I wanted to find out what it was."

Elodie asked, "Did you?"

"I know George had dozens of meetings with London that no one knew about. There were other meetings with Beth, but not even she knew what George was doing behind everyone's back. One night, I followed George to the docks and saw her board a yacht. Ten people got off while she talked to someone on the ship for thirty minutes. She left with a smile, and those who disembarked followed her into the city, where she set them up in flats. I tried to follow them, but they were good at going undetected. Better than most, actually."

Elodie crossed one long leg over the other. "We've known George's connection to London for a bit. We wondered how long it had been going on, and you've now given us a timeframe."

"I'm no' sure what good that does. George and the Edinburgh Druids can cause trouble, but London is after much more," Luke said.

Willa leaned back against the cushion. "And Beth still has the book."

"Until London tries to get it from her," Scott said.

Luke shook his head. "They willna be able to. She was toying with me. I doona care to ever get close enough for that to happen again, and all of you should feel the same."

"We need to figure out how to counteract such a spell," Jasper said.

Willa twisted her lips. "That'll be difficult since we don't know what the spell is. It's like trying to write a word when you don't know the alphabet."

"We have to start somewhere," Jasper argued.

Elodie propped her chin on her fist. "I agree that we need to have something in place for such a spell. We need to share this with Bronwyn since she's Beth's cousin," Elodie told Luke.

"How long have you been on the isle?" Scott asked him.

Luke had hoped that question wouldn't be posed, but he had known it was wishful thinking. "Four weeks or so."

"Four?" Willa repeated, shock raising her voice.

He covered her hand with his. "A couple of the London Druids caught me trailing them. There was an encounter. One of them got away, but I took care of the other. My time in the city was over, but I couldna head straight to Skye. I detoured to a few other places to see if anyone followed me."

"Did they?" Jasper asked.

Luke nodded. "The first time they attempted to take me back to Edinburgh. The next three, they wanted to end my life. I got away, but no' without some wounds. I laid low and eventually made my way to Skye. From there, I set about finding you two," he said, looking from Willa to Scott.

"Where did you stay?" Scott asked.

Luke shrugged. "Anywhere. Everywhere. Mostly, I took refuge in caves."

Elodie lowered her arm and rested it on the arm of the chair. "Mom said you knew who she was, and that you knew Diana Barclay, as well as her husband's name."

"You'd be amazed at the things a person can learn when hiding and listening. One of the London Druids mentioned Diana's name when I first trailed them in Edinburgh. They also talked about her husband, Reginald. And both her sons."

"Kurt and Parker," Jasper said.

Luke dipped his head in acknowledgment. "I slipped into the local library and used their computers to do a little research to discover more."

"How much more did you find out?" Willa asked.

"Well," Luke said, "I learned about Scott and Elodie, which led me to the MacLean family."

Elodie's lips tightened slightly. "And my mum."

"Aye. I also learned about Willa and Jasper, as well as his mother, and the fact that he was kidnapped from Skye as a baby." Luke looked each of them in the eye. "Whether you believe it or no', I didna stay away because I wanted to. I kept my distance to watch over you."

CHAPTER FOURTEEN

SKYE DRUIDS

Tea Talker

Everything happened quickly once Ariah announced that Mason was going to the back to await the Healer. Rowen had watched the brief exchange between Mason and Ferne, feeling awkward and intrusive, even though they had asked her to remain. That didn't change as she helped Ferne get him to the back of the shop.

His breath rasped in the silence—harsh, uneven, and laced with pain. Sweat covered him by the time they sat him on the sofa. Rowen started to back away, but he grabbed her hand. The beseeching look in his eyes took her aback.

He held her gaze for a long moment. "Don't leave."

"She'll be right here," Ariah told him.

Rowen squeezed his hand and nodded reassuringly. His fingers slowly slipped from hers as Ariah and Ferne laid him on his back. Rowen scanned the room, taking in the shelves of tea, the long table where Ariah evidently mixed the brews, and the small desk off to the side. She backed away another few steps and fought not to rush to Mason's side when she caught his wince of pain.

He didn't need her now. He was in Ferne's and Ariah's capable hands, with a Healer on the way. Rowen fidgeted, crossing her arms over her chest before letting them fall to her sides and then crossing them again. She bit her lip as Ariah lifted Mason's shirt and saw the bandages along his left side covering the laceration.

Ariah dropped to her knees and removed the bandages, along with Rowen's poultice. The Druid lifted the herbs to her nose and sniffed. She slid her golden brown eyes to Rowen. "You did this?"

Rowen nodded.

"It helped," Mason said, his voice tight.

Ariah set aside the compress. "Of course, it did. Smart thinking, Rowen."

"Bloody hell," Ferne murmured when she saw the long, jagged wound curving down Mason's side.

Mason swallowed loudly. "Looks worse than it is."

"I was in a hurry," Rowen explained about the stitching. "The bleeding was severe, and I had to get the wounds closed."

Mason rolled his head, his gaze meeting hers. "You saved my life. That's all that matters."

Concern deepened the frown on Ferne's brow as she turned to Rowen. "Thank you for taking care of him. You told me he was hurt, but I didn't think..."

She trailed off, unable to finish. Rowen flashed her a quick smile in understanding. The sight of Mason's wounds had startled her, as well.

Ariah studied the laceration for a long minute before climbing to her feet and gazing at his leg.

"Cut the bloody pants," Mason stated. His eyes were closed now, one arm thrown over them as if being awake was too much.

Rowen imagined that it was. She quickly looked around and found a pair of scissors before grabbing them and heading to the sofa. "Let me," she urged.

Both Ariah and Ferne stepped back to give her room. Rowen grabbed the material and lifted it. Just as she was about to cut into the fabric, she glanced at Mason to find his eyes slitted, watching her.

His lips quirked in a grin. "I think I should've left the shorts on."

"I was just thinking that," she replied, then she cut into the pants, opening a hole large enough to encompass the bandage on his thigh.

Rowen had no idea how Mason could tease now. Then she caught sight of Ferne and understood. His sister was witnessing just how close to death he had come. It had to be hard to reconcile that with the anger she had carried for weeks.

Once again, Rowen moved away so Ariah could get to the wound. The silence in the room was broken only by the customers' voices in the shop drifting to them.

"A single stab wound," Ariah stated.

An image of the interior of the Aston Martin flashed in Rowen's mind. A single stab that had bled profusely.

"What the hell was Thomas doing, attacking you with weapons?" Ferne demanded.

Mason's lips flattened. "I wasn't prepared for it."

"Why would you be?" Ariah asked. "We're Druids. We fight with magic."

Ferne's lips twisted. "Carlyle will go nuts when he finds out."

Ariah moved to the jars of tea and herbs and started taking several off the shelves to place on the table. Rowen switched from studying Ariah to Mason. His breathing had evened out, and she thought he might have fallen asleep. Minutes ticked by as they anxiously awaited the Healer.

Suddenly, Ariah was beside her. In a soft voice, she said, "Drink this."

Rowen looked down to find a cup of tea. She was tired, anxious, and worried. She didn't bother asking what it was, she simply drank. There was a soft floral note that lingered on her tongue. Lavender, perhaps? There was no jolt, just a quiet settling. A warmth that curled in her chest and spread low, like an exhale after a held breath. After each sip, the taste deepened. The hum of herbs, a whisper of spice, and something else she couldn't name. All of it smoothed the edges of her thoughts and calmed her anxiety like the comfiest blanket.

She was still tired, but not as restless or on edge now. Ariah had also given Ferne a cup of something. Rowen wanted to know what had been put into hers and made a mental note to ask Ariah later. She didn't want to interrupt her as she was mixing more blends. That's when Rowen saw her adding magic to one batch. She knew without a doubt that Ariah had added some to hers, and she was thankful.

"Ferne?" called a deep, Scottish voice.

Rowen turned toward the doorway to see a tall, handsome man in a suit enter. He had dark, wavy hair trimmed short and deep brown eyes. He opened his arms, and Ferne eagerly walked into them. The affection between them told Rowen he must be the man Ferne had fallen in love with. They shared a few quiet words, then the man looked up at her. Rowen smiled at being caught staring, hoping she hid her embarrassment.

The man and Ariah exchanged a nod in greeting before his dark eyes swung to the sofa. Mason was finally sleeping. She could tell by the way the lines around his mouth had smoothed. When Rowen thought the man might wake Mason, she stepped closer to the couch, ready to stop him.

The newcomer's dark gaze studied her for a long minute before he dipped his head. "I wouldna disturb him," the man whispered. "I merely wished to look at his injuries."

Rowen reluctantly stepped away, but stayed close enough to… do what, exactly? She was outnumbered if those three turned on her. She had gotten used to looking after Mason in their short time together, but it was clear that he didn't need her anymore.

When the man finished studying Mason's wounds, he held out his hand to Rowen. "I'm DI Theo Frasier."

"Rowen Thornevale. What's a DI?"

"Detective Inspector," Theo explained, keeping his voice low. "His injuries are grave."

Before she could answer, there was a commotion at the door. Rowen spotted two women and a man standing at the threshold, eyeing Mason. Ariah hurried to them.

"We might need to move to the side," Theo urged Rowen.

She backed up with Theo as Ferne approached them. Ariah stayed with the trio lined up along the edge of the couch. A heartbeat later, the three held their hands over Mason and began chanting. The words sounded foreign and familiar at the same time, and a strange stillness fell over the room as the Healers' magic swelled.

Rowen wished she had a phone to record the words so she could play them back later to decipher them. Magic filled the room, swirling around them like unseen fingers stretching out from the trio. If she could feel the periphery of their power, she couldn't imagine what it felt like to have the full force directed at her like it was with Mason.

The trio blocked her view of him and made it impossible for her to witness any healing, though she tried. She had a partial view of his face, where his arm was thrown over his eyes. He hadn't moved, at least not that she had seen. She didn't know if he was awake or still asleep, or if it even mattered. There were no Healers on the San Juan Islands. This was her first encounter with any, and she was intrigued by the process. Healers in the States were hard to come by, and any community that found one did whatever they could to keep them. And Skye had three.

It was unimaginable.

As soon as it had begun, it ended with the Healers lowering their arms. The woman in the middle turned to them and said, "There was some damage to his muscles, but we got it all repaired."

"Thank you, Lucy," Theo said. "Thanks everyone."

Ferne nodded, smiling. "Yes. Thank you all."

The Healers left without any fanfare. Rowen didn't see any payment involved, but that might have been taken care of beforehand. That was how it was back home.

"What now?" she asked.

Ariah's head cocked to the side. "Do you not have Healers?"

"Not where I'm from. They're rare, difficult to come by, and expensive," Rowen answered.

Theo's brows snapped together. "You pay yours?"

Rowen looked between the three. "You don't?"

"We did sometimes in London," Ferne said. "It depended on

many factors. Most times, the payment was some form of trade or favor."

Ariah shook her head. "We don't pay here. Our Healers are here to help the Druid community when we need it."

"You're lucky," Rowen murmured.

Theo grunted before he looked at the sofa. "Rhona will want to talk to him. I'd like to question him myself."

Protectiveness shot up in Rowen as she walked to the couch. "You act like he's the villain here."

"We're being cautious," Theo said.

Ferne touched his arm and walked toward Rowen. "The London and Edinburgh Druids have tried to infiltrate our group for weeks now. We need details."

"Then you'll need them from me, too," she stated.

Theo dipped his head and put his hands in his pockets. "Aye. We will."

"Let's allow Mason to recover here," Ariah said. "We can figure out if he and Rowen will go to the manor or elsewhere."

"You don't get to decide where we go," Rowen stated. "London tried to order me around, and I refused to take it from them. I'm not going to take it from you."

Ferne's green eyes filled with unease. "We're not London."

"Then don't act like it. Look what they did to Mason," Rowen said, motioning to him.

Ariah held up her hands. "I understand your concern, Rowen, but we're not the enemy."

"That's not what my people have been told." Her words brought a quick halt to the conversation.

Finally, Theo chuckled, the sound dry and humorless. "Let me guess. You heard that from London."

Rowen glanced at Mason to see if he was still asleep. "The news has traveled around, and it's been on message boards. I can't tell you who posted it or where it came from."

"When?" Ariah asked.

Rowen shrugged. "About a year or so ago. I don't really remember. From there, stories of how the Skye Druids attack other groups continued to spread."

"Bloody unbelievable," Theo murmured, raking a hand through his hair.

Ferne shook her head in denial. "That isn't us. We're fighting, but only the Druids like London and Edinburgh who come here to hurt us."

"That's what Mason told me." Rowen made her own decisions. Period. If any Skye Druid tried something, she was gone. Even if she had to load Mason into the car herself.

Ariah leaned her hip against the table. "If you think we're so vicious, why are you here?"

"I wanted to see for myself. And,"—she paused, drawing out the word—"Mason needed medical attention. He wouldn't take it in England. All he wanted was to get to Ferne. He has been adamant that you are the good guys. I came to England to discover the truth about London. I did. Now, I'm here to learn about Skye."

CHAPTER FIFTEEN

SKYE DRUIDS

The voices were muffled, as if he were underwater, but it was Rowen's voice that snapped Mason into awareness. He opened his eyes and rolled his head to the side to find her talking to Ariah, Ferne, and an unknown man. The need to protect Rowen rocketed through him with the force of a tidal wave. Just as he was about to jump up, he remembered his injuries.

He hesitated before moving, waiting for the pain. To his surprise, there was none. Mason listened to the conversation as he took a deep breath to test his side. He bit back a smile when he was able to fill his lungs with air and not wince in agony. Next, he tried to move his leg and, once more, found no tenderness.

The Healers must have already come. He forgot about that and soundlessly sat up to stare at the group. They were so focused on each other that none of them noticed that he was awake.

The unknown man said, "The best place for you and Mason is Carwood Manor."

"I already told you that you don't get to decide where we go," Rowen stated firmly.

Mason rose to his feet. "I agree with Rowen."

All four heads turned to him. Rowen's pale blue eyes lit up at the sight of him, and her lips curved into a smile. She took a step toward him, but Ferne had already crossed the distance.

"How are you feeling?" his sister asked worriedly.

He looked down at his thigh to see pink skin where the stitches had been. He then ran a hand along his left side, grazing the tender skin that also held no remnants of a cut or stitches. Mason licked his lips and said, "Hungry."

"That can be remedied," Ariah said with a smile and walked out.

Ferne waved over to the man in the gray suit. Mason looked into his brown eyes, watching the way Ferne looked at him with such love that he could only stare in amazement at his sister. He had never seen her so happy. It was there in her smile and the way she held herself. In her very being. He'd known before coming to Skye that she had found a place on the isle, but seeing her and witnessing it himself confirmed it.

"This is Theo," Ferne said proudly as she took her lover's hand and brought him closer. "Theo, this is my brother."

Mason studied Theo, waiting to see anything that hinted that he might not love his sister as deeply as she did him, but it was for naught. Theo was utterly besotted. He wore a look that said he would give Ferne the very moon if she asked for it.

"Mason," Theo said and held out his hand.

Mason took it, and they shook firmly. "Theo."

"I've been wanting you two to meet since Theo and I got together," Ferne said, smiling.

Mason grinned at his sister. "I'm happy for you. The only way I was able to keep going was knowing that Carlyle was with you, and that you had found someone."

"We have questions," Theo said.

Mason slid his gaze to Rowen. They looked at each other for a minute before he turned to his sister and Theo. "That's understandable. Rowen and I have had a rather difficult few days. She's not slept in close to forty-eight hours. I'd like to get us both some food and be allowed to rest before we proceed."

"There are plenty of rooms at the manor, and I know Bronwyn will open her home to you. Many of our group live there," Ferne said.

Before Mason could reply, Theo added, "The manor is safe and secure. It's the best place for you."

"We'll find other accommodations," Mason said evenly.

Hurt flashed in Ferne's eyes. "If you insist."

"I'm not sure you'll find much available," Theo warned.

Rowen said, "We'll make do."

"I know a place," Ariah said from the doorway. She had one hand on the doorjamb as she peered into the room. "I heard one of my customers this morning complaining that some tourists canceled their stay just this morning."

Mason dipped his head to her. "Can you get me in touch with them?"

"Let me get her number," Ariah said and walked away.

Ferne cleared her throat, her face tight with uncertainty and more than a little doubt about his decision. "Will you call when you two get settled?"

"Why don't you stay and talk to her?" Rowen told Mason. "I

can find my way to wherever we're staying and get some sleep in the meantime."

It was nice to be able to stand without being assaulted by the weakness that had plagued him since the attack. He was refreshed and renewed. A part of him wanted to run out and down the street, just to prove he could. But the dark circles under Rowen's eyes kept him in place. "You drove straight through last night and stayed up the previous night to tend to me. It's time you rest. I'll drive you."

"I can take Rowen," Theo offered.

There was the barest stiffening of Rowen's back at Theo's words, but Mason saw it just the same. She didn't trust Ferne or Theo. They could tell her they were trustworthy, but she wouldn't believe it. They had to earn it. Just as both he and Rowen had to prove to Ferne and the others that they were honest.

"We'll talk soon," Mason promised his sister. "I'd like a shower, some food, and a few hours to myself."

"But…" Ferne began.

Theo wrapped an arm around her. "Of course. Ariah will get you directions. We'll see both of you later."

Mason watched the couple walk away. Ferne looked over her shoulder at him before they disappeared around the corner. Their reunion could've gone many different ways. It hadn't played out as he had hoped, but it hadn't been as bad as it could have been either.

"You okay?" Rowen asked.

"She didn't hug me." Mason shook his head as he turned to face her. "I guess I hurt her too deeply."

Rowen gave him a rueful smile as she closed the distance

between them. "She was shocked to find you here, and then you came out looking close to death. There wasn't time after. And then…" She gave a swirl with her hand. "All of that."

It did make him wonder if Ferne would've embraced him had they gone to the manor. It was a silly thing to focus on, but they had always been close. Even when they were younger and fought constantly.

"You two will get back to the way things were. It's just going to take some time," Rowen said as if reading his mind.

Ariah walked into the room with a sticky note and a landline phone. "Here's her name and number. I just gave her a call to tell her about the situation. She's waiting on you for specifics."

"Thank you," Mason told her.

She shook her head, smiling and causing the long, silver moon earrings she wore to move. "This is what we do here. I also ordered you some food. It should be here shortly, or you can pick it up on your way out. It's just down the street. The holiday cottage is about ten minutes from here, and in a nice location."

"Come sit," he told Rowen after Ariah had walked away, and he lowered himself to the couch.

He dialed the number and watched Rowen make her way to the sofa. She yawned behind her hand and crossed one leg over the other. It didn't take long to give his payment information to the owner of the holiday let. They set up a time to meet so Mason could sign the agreement, and then he ended the call.

Rowen sat with her eyes closed and her arms crossed over her chest. The sooner he got her to a bed, the better. He was amazed that she had remained awake this entire time. Mason thought about leaving her there while he went to get the food and sign the contract, but if she woke to find him gone, she might think he'd left her.

He gently touched her arm, and her eyes flew open. "I'm awake," she said quickly.

Mason bit back a smile. "I need to make a few stops. I could come back to pick you up."

"I'll go with you."

She got to her feet, and they both walked to the front. He made a quick detour to grab his shorts, which were still on the toilet floor. Ariah stopped Rowen and handed her a bag of tea. After a wave to the Druid, they left and climbed into the Focus.

Rowen took the passenger seat, buckled in, and closed her eyes as Mason started the car and drove to the restaurant. He left the engine running when he ran in to get the food. When he came out, Rowen's head had lolled to the side, and her lips were parted in sleep. She didn't stir when he drove to meet the cottage owner. Once more, Mason left the car running. It didn't take long to sign the contract and get directions to the rental. Then, he was on the road.

Skye was a good-sized island, and it was surprisingly easy to get lost. Twice, he had to turn around after taking wrong turns, but he eventually found the cottage sitting on a hill with spectacular views of the mountains.

He parked and entered the combination to the lockbox to get the keys. Mason went through the cottage to check it out before returning for Rowen. She roused, bleary-eyed, when he opened her door. He had to help her into the house as she was still half-asleep and unsteady on her feet. He directed her to a room, and she fell onto her stomach on the bed.

Mason removed the too-big sneakers and socks she wore before tugging the corner of the comforter over her. He took one last look at her before closing the door behind him. It didn't take him long to get their few items out of the trunk and into the house. Only then did he eat. He scarfed the deli sandwich and ate every last crisp included.

He could have easily eaten Rowen's sandwich, too, but then there wouldn't have been anything for her when she woke. Mason put her sandwich in the fridge and heated some water for tea. He was no longer consumed by pain, which gave him time to think about Thomas's attack. Mason had put things in place for just such an event, but he still worried that something might happen to his staff—especially his butler, Billings.

It had killed Mason to keep Billings out of everything. The man had been more of a friend and second father than a staff member. Billings had been there for him and Ferne through everything. It wasn't that Mason doubted his loyalty. He had kept his plans from Billings so that when London interrogated him, Billings wouldn't know anything.

It was meant to keep Billings and the other staff protected, but that was before Mason realized just how far Thomas would go to get what he wanted. No one was safe. And he feared that not even the distance to Skye would keep him or Rowen out of London's grasp. By now, they would know she'd helped him, which meant the full force of Thomas's lackeys would be descending upon them.

And if they couldn't get to Rowen on Skye, they would strike elsewhere. She needed to alert her family. He should've thought about that before. She'd had time to reach out to them. Now, it might already be too late.

He rubbed his forehead. He didn't know how to reach her family, but he knew someone who could. Mason pulled out the burner phone and rang Ferne. She picked up immediately.

"I need a favor. It's for Rowen's family," he said.

Ferne didn't hesitate. "Tell me."

CHAPTER SIXTEEN

SKYE DRUIDS

"Did you find anything?" Ferne asked as she and Theo walked into the command center on the second floor of Carwood Manor.

Kurt nodded as he finished typing before mirroring his laptop screen on the huge monitor he had just hung on the wall the day before. "I did, indeed. I have all you'd want to know about the Thornevales of the San Juan Islands."

Behind him, a chair squeaked as Rhona, the leader of the Skye Druids, shifted in her seat. "They're called the Salish Druids."

Kurt glanced over his shoulder at Rhona before meeting Sabryn's gaze. His lover gave him a wink, which made him smile. On her left were Carlyle and Song. To Sabryn's right was Finn. On the other side of the room sat Elias and the manor's owner, Bronwyn. The others in their group were off doing different things, but Kurt was recording everything to send to them later so everyone could get caught up.

He pointed to the top right and a picture of a pretty woman in her fifties with light brown hair and blue eyes. "At the top is Maris

Thornevale, Rowen's mom. She's an only child, and it appears her father left before she turned one. Maris has four sisters—Talia, Sela, Rhea, and Maelin. I've traced the Thornevale line from the islands, across the US to Boston, up to Canada, and straight to Skye."

"You sound surprised," Finn said.

Kurt shrugged and leaned back in his chair. "More astonished at how simple it was to trace those roots, not that her ancestors are from the isle. All our ancestors are from here, but for most families, connecting those lines isn't nearly as easy."

"Are they powerful?" Carlyle asked.

Kurt leaned forward and hit a key, displaying all five sisters and their children. "The Thornevale line is what I would call strong, in magic as well as extending the line. As you can see here."

Theo scratched his head. "Are all those Rowen's cousins?"

"Looks like it," Bronwyn replied.

Rhona blew out a breath. "Then why send only her to London?"

"That's something she should be able to tell us," Ferne said.

Kurt swiveled his head to Ferne. Her lips were pinched, and her brow furrowed as she stared at the screen with all the pictures. "You all know I take what I do seriously, and every time I hack something or someone, it's to ensure our safety."

"We know," Elias said. "What did you find?"

Kurt pressed his lips together, his hands on the arms of his chair as he rocked back twice before hitting another button on the keyboard. The screen changed, showing incoming messages to the Salish Druids, sent by the London Druids. "As you can see, the emails go to Brenna Tidewell, who is the leader of the Salish

Druids. London has been sending requests for someone from their group to visit for over two years."

"Is London's interest in just these Druids? Or is it others?" Rhona asked.

Ferne made a sound at the back of her throat. "I bet it's others, too."

"You'd be right." Kurt swiped his screen to the side, where dozens of emails from London popped up, addressed to Druid communities around the world.

Carlyle shoved his chair back as he lurched to his feet. "What the bloody hell is Thomas up to?"

Song wrapped her hand around his wrist and gently pulled him back down to the chair. Everyone in the room shared in Carlyle's animosity toward Thomas, but it went much deeper for him since Thomas was his father. Kurt could relate after his younger brother had tried to kill him and *had* murdered their mother. Things like that ripped families apart.

"The sooner we talk to Mason and Rowen, the better," Rhona said.

"Thomas tried to end Mason's life," Ferne said. "He would be dead now if Rowen hadn't been there."

Kurt punched a few more buttons. "You're right, and I have proof. I found footage of Rowen hesitantly entering London HQ at 6:56. I'll start things an hour and a half later, when she comes rushing out the front."

Four smaller screens filled the larger one as he played the footage from all of them to show different perspectives. An image from a traffic camera across the street showed Rowen leaving the building. She looked both ways, in obvious distress, before going around the side. They watched her head in one direction before backtracking to go the opposite way.

As she walked, the screen on the lower left showed Mason stumbling out of the back door and collapsing. Ferne's gasp made it hard to watch. No one spoke as they watched Rowen hurry to Mason, then struggle to help him to his feet and, eventually, to his car before driving off.

Kurt quickly shifted the cameras to follow Mason's Aston Martin through London and down the highway to a storage facility. The sight of Mason falling while trying to open the unit was particularly difficult to watch. Kurt kept it playing, right up until Rowen moved the car and disappeared back into the unit.

"Is that all you have?" Elias asked.

Kurt shook his head and clicked another button. "I got them leaving."

It was a short clip of the unit next to the one where Mason and Rowen had disappeared. It opened, and a car pulled out. Rowen shut the rolling door before climbing into the driver's seat and driving away.

"I've not tracked them all the way to Skye, but I can if it would help," Kurt said, pausing the screen to show Mason leaning back in the seat, his face filled with pain.

Theo cleared his throat as he glanced at Ferne, who had yet to tear her gaze away from the screen. "Mason said Rowen drove all night. Based on the CCTV footage timestamp, it seems she did. She's wary of us, though. She said something about hearing rumors that we'd been attacking other Druids."

"We know that isn't true," Rhona said.

Sabryn stretched her back as she said, "But Rowen doesn't. And it's likely the other Salish Druids won't either."

"They need to know where she is and that she's safe," Ferne said. "Give me the number. I'll call them. I owe her that for what she's done for Mason."

Kurt sent the number to Ferne's mobile. "That's to her mum."

The room was quiet as Ferne dialed the number, but she kept it on speaker so everyone could hear.

"Hello?" answered a female.

Ferne licked her lips. "May I speak to Maris Thornevale, please?"

There was a slight pause, and then, voice tight with worry, Maris said, "This is she. How can I help you?"

Ferne hesitated, and Theo put his arm around her. "My name is Ferne Crawford. I wanted to let you know that Rowen is safe, but she is no longer in London."

"Where is she?" Maris demanded.

"She's resting right now. She was up all night driving," Ferne began.

"She could've called, then. Why didn't she? Where is she? And why isn't my daughter in London anymore?"

Ferne winced at the growing anger in the woman's tone. "I'm sure Rowen will explain everything as soon as she's up. She was exhausted and asked us to reach out so you wouldn't worry."

A loud snort came through the line. "I'm beyond worried. I've called and texted her, but she hasn't answered. None of the London Druids will tell me anything. You certainly sound British, though. I might be thousands of miles away, but trust me when I say, you don't want me and mine as an enemy."

"Rowen saved my brother's life," Ferne replied softly. "I still don't have the entire story, but I do know that if she hadn't been there, he would have died. They came to the Isle of Skye, where I am."

Open air met her words. Ferne looked around the room as the silence on the other end of the connection stretched on.

Finally, Ferne said, "I know what you may have heard about the Skye Druids, but it's a lie."

"So you say," Maris retorted.

"You're welcome to come and see for yourself."

Kurt shook his head and pulled up flight information from the Pacific Northwest and the flights to get to Skye.

Maris made an indistinct sound. "One of my sisters is at the airport now, trying to get a flight, but it'll take us well over a day to reach Rowen."

Kurt suddenly had an idea. He messaged Mason and asked for a picture of Rowen to reassure her mother. Within seconds, Mason sent over a short video. Kurt forwarded it to Maris's mobile and put it on the screen for Ferne to see.

"You should have gotten a video of Rowen," Ferne said. "You can see for yourself, she's sleeping."

When Maris next spoke, it was clear she was crying. "If I find out any of this is a lie—"

"I would expect nothing less. Rowen was a hero in saving my brother. I owe her everything, and we'll make sure she remains safe."

"From who?" Maris asked with a sniff.

Ferne licked her lips. "London."

CHAPTER SEVENTEEN

SKYE DRUIDS

Rowen rolled onto her back and did a full body stretch, then promptly winced at the soreness in her lower back and shoulders from the car ride and stress. She yawned as her eyes blinked open and focused on the ceiling, her gaze drawn to the beam of soft amber light coming from a small lamp on the bedside table, offering just enough brightness to see without hurting her eyes.

She rubbed her eyes and yawned again before sitting up. Only to frown when she became aware of the comforter pulled over her and that she was still in her clothes. She vaguely remembered walking into the house and entering the bedroom, but nothing after that. She must have crashed. Rowen raised her feet to see that someone had removed her shoes.

A glance at the bed showed she hadn't haphazardly kicked them off during sleep. She found them placed neatly side by side against the wall next to a white suede chair, where her bag of clothes sat. She scooted toward the edge of the mattress and noticed the water on the bedside table. She grabbed it and drained it in a few gulps while eyeing the rest of the room.

The walls had been painted a cross between mauve and beige, lending the room an understated luxury while the crisp, white furniture stood out like sculpted art, drawing the eye with effortless elegance. The bed linens and comforter were all shades of white, but each carried its own texture—cotton, quilted velvet, soft matte—layered to create richness and dimension. Throw pillows in muted mauve, deep plum, light gray, and warm sand added subtle color without disturbing the tranquil palette. Sparkle came in the form of a sequined mauve pillow situated on the chair. Delicate floral artwork lent the walls an air of quiet sophistication, with a whisper of nature's harmony. Sheer mauve curtains swathed the window frames, their gentle drape softening the white blinds behind them.

The room was calming and lavish yet comfortable and opulent. She sat in the space for several minutes, taking it all in. She would have no problem relaxing in this room. And that wasn't always the case—some places just had a weird vibe. But here, she could get cozy.

Rowen placed the empty water bottle on the table and got to her feet. Her toes sank into the plush, silver-gray rug that covered the majority of the room's wooden-planked floor. After she'd straightened the bed, she made her way around to the two tall windows. It took her a moment to figure out which lever raised the blinds. Once she did, light flooded the room, blinding her.

She turned her head to the side and raised a hand to shield her face until her eyes grew accustomed to the light. Her breath caught at the first glimpse of the wild, windswept mountains dominating her view. There was nothing gentle about the range. Their jagged, weatherworn spines were shrouded in mist and memory, shaped by centuries of storms. They weren't just a backdrop. They were a challenge, fierce and apologetic. Primal and brooding.

And they called to her soul.

Her gaze leisurely wandered across the mountains, taking note of the water cascading down the slopes, hollowing into rocks over millions of years and bequeathing an awe-inspiring panorama of unyielding defiance and untamed grandeur. The dark, craggy peaks stood in stark contrast to the rolling green hills she was eager to explore.

When she was finally able to pull herself away from the scene, she tried to find the sun in the sky to gauge the time, but eventually gave up and turned back to the room. The sight of a bright yellow sticky note on a door drew her attention. She walked to it and read: *Bathroom.*

Rowen grinned at the care Mason had taken. It would be easy to fall for someone like him. Not that she would let herself, but damn. The accent, the way he protected her, and now the way he took care of her? It was a lot for anyone to dismiss. But it wasn't a road she would venture down, no matter how tempting it might be.

She opened the door, expecting to find a toilet and perhaps a sink. Instead, she found a full bathroom with a shower and a claw-foot tub.

"I'm in heaven," she murmured as she looked around at colors that mimicked the bedroom.

She eyed the tub, imagining a long soak, but right now, she craved a shower. She turned back to the door to get clothes, when her hand knocked something on the sink vanity. She righted a small bottle of shampoo and noticed the rest of the options set out.

There was conditioner, two different bars of soap, hair gel, a comb, a blow-dryer, a toothbrush and paste, deodorant, eye cream, and face moisturizer. There was even a small bottle of mouth rinse.

Next to all of it was another sticky note that said: *It's all for you. M.*

Had Mason gotten all of this for her? She twisted her lips as she looked out the door to her bed. Rowen hastily stripped out of her clothes, grabbed items from the counter, and got into the shower. She scrubbed her skin until it was pink and washed her hair three times. After sliding the conditioner through the length, she let it sit for a few minutes as she stood facing the spray, the hot water rushing over her skin. She felt like a new person by the time she rinsed and dried off.

She wrapped the towel around herself and washed her panties in the sink before going to the bag for clothes. It would've been nice to have her luggage, but even she had to admit that she hadn't packed appropriately. She didn't travel often, and she had only left the US once to go to Mexico. Reading weather reports and comparing them to the weather she was used to hadn't adequately prepared her for London's weather. Now, she was much farther north and chilled, despite it being May.

Rowen dug into the bag and found some sweats. It would have to do while her panties dried. She moved the bag from the chair so she could sit and discovered two piles of clothes and another note.

We took a guess at sizes.

How long had she been asleep? Rowen sorted through the options and spotted a set of panties still in the plastic and ripped them open. She would have to wash her bra tonight, but she wasn't going without. Since she had no idea what the day held, she wanted to be at least semi-appropriate. Sweats wouldn't cut it. Ferne's jeans from the storage unit were too long, but there were three others to try. One pair, she couldn't get over her hips. The other was too tight in the thighs, but the third gave her the relaxed fit she preferred.

A soft gray sweater caught her eye. She put on a black Henley as a base layer, then slipped the sweater over her head. Once socks covered her chilly toes, she returned to the bathroom to brush her teeth and finish with her toiletries. Then she combed out her hair and added a little gel before drying.

Rowen studied herself in the mirror and bit back a yawn. She could sleep for another few hours, but wanted to get an idea of where they were and what was happening. Not to mention, she needed to call her mom soon. Oh, and they would be going to the manor. At least now, she was rested, showered, and looked presentable.

She put on Ferne's too-big sneakers from the storage unit and opened the door to her room. She looked to the right and found a couple of doors along the hallway that ended. Then she looked left. After a small hesitation, she stepped out onto a white-on-beige runner that ran the length of the corridor and covered more of the pretty wooden floor.

Within steps, she found herself in a cozy, well-appointed kitchen with a breakfast bar. Behind the barstools was a large window, revealing more of the breathtaking scenery. There was still no sign of Mason, though.

She continued her search in the living area, where she found an L-shaped sofa against the wall opposite a fireplace. A generous TV hung above the mantel while three chairs filled the space. There were board games and cards in a glass-door cabinet, along with fiction and puzzle books. Something to occupy everyone, it seemed.

Rowen walked to the windows to look for Mason. She found him outside, staring toward a body of water that reflected the mountains and rippled with the wind. His pensive expression kept her from immediately going to him. He looked good against the wild, unyielding land.

She had seen him at headquarters, but only briefly. The rest of her interaction with him had been while he was injured and weak. Now, he stood tall and commanding—and more handsome than ever. Imposing, even. A man who strode through life with his back straight and head held high. He was a fighter, a person of action who sought justice for his parents. But who was Mason Crawford, really?

There were multiple layers to him, and she had only peeled back a few. A part of her wished to learn more, but it would be foolish of her to even try. She tore her eyes from him and returned her gaze to the scenic wonders of Skye.

The house had stunning views, and she guessed it was rented more often than not. She couldn't wait to tell her family about everything. At the thought of them, Rowen wrinkled her nose. They would undoubtedly be losing their minds, wondering where she was, especially since she didn't get on her flight home. She should've taken a moment to call them once she reached Skye. Calming her mom down would be a feat in itself, and she'd likely be apologizing for weeks. Not to mention, her mom would use this against her forever.

She was about to go look for one of the burner phones when Mason suddenly turned toward the cottage. He jerked in surprise when their eyes met. A small smile curved his lips. A flare of excitement quivered in her stomach. She returned the grin as he continued walking and disappeared around the side of the cottage. Rowen adjusted her sweater and the shirt beneath and then touched her hair before the door opened. She had just lowered her arms and turned around when Mason came around the corner.

He brought the scent of the isle with him, as if the land itself clung to him. Rain on stone, windswept cliffs, and something green and ancient. Her magic stirred in recognition—an ache that felt familiar and foreign at once. She didn't know if it was in response to him or the scents that assaulted her, and she was afraid to find out.

"I thought you'd still be sleeping," he said.

She gave a halfhearted shrug, even as his deep, rich voice filled her ears. Just looking at him made her knees weak. "I'm rested enough. How long was I out?"

"Almost five hours. There's no rush," he told her. "If I woke you, I apologize."

"You didn't. Promise," she assured him with a grin.

He studied her with his piercing gaze—cool metal heated by fire. His expression was unreadable, yet warmth spread over her at his look. He dipped his chin and asked, "Are you hungry?"

"Famished."

He chuckled, the sound cutting through her and turning her insides to mush. Thankfully, he didn't notice her wobble as he turned away and motioned for her to follow.

"About forty minutes after we arrived, Ferne and Theo dropped by with groceries and some other items," he said.

Rowen took an unsteady step after him. "I took full advantage of the goodies in the bathroom. As well as the clothes."

He turned, his gaze lingering on her a moment. "Good."

"Thank you," she said as he opened the fridge. "For taking off my shoes and covering me."

"It was the least I could do after all you did for me."

She rubbed her lips together and moved deeper into the kitchen. It wasn't that she felt awkward now, but things were different. He was no longer on death's doorstep, and they weren't running from London. Though that didn't mean they were safe. It just meant that things had calmed a bit.

"I, ah, don't know what you like," he said as he leaned out of the refrigerator to look at her. "Perhaps you should come see what's here. Ferne brought a little of everything."

She nodded and came around the island. They were inches apart as he moved away, and she had the illogical thought to reach out for him. How many times had she slid against him, his arm around her? And now, she didn't dare get too close. "I'm not a picky eater. I can usually find something."

Rowen ended up grabbing a couple of eggs and some butter and set them aside. Mason sat on a barstool, watching as she readied to scramble the eggs.

"Want some?" she asked.

He shook his head. "I'm good for now, thanks."

It didn't take her long to cook the eggs and toast the bread. She joined him at the island to butter her bread and dive into the eggs. They had eaten on the drive, or at least she had, but it hadn't exactly been great food. It had been enough to keep her going, but she had been craving something tasty.

"Would you like some coffee or tea?" Mason asked.

She swallowed. "Tea would be great."

He filled up the electric kettle and got two mugs. Rowen polished off the eggs before the water finished boiling. It wasn't long before Mason set a cup in front of her. Instead of immediately sitting, he went into the cupboard and drew out two different kinds of cookies.

"I will never say no to cookies," she told him as she took one of each.

They sat in companionable silence, munching on the sweets. She noticed that his gaze kept going out the window over the sink.

"Did something happen while I was asleep?" she asked.

"Ferne and Theo dropped off everything and left almost immediately." Mason's lips twisted. "I could tell she wanted to talk, but she decided against it."

"Maybe she wished it to be just the two of you."

He lifted a shoulder in a shrug. "Perhaps. I explored a little around the cottage. There are a couple of other places around the loch, but it's pretty private."

"From what I've seen, this place is stunning."

"Wait until you get outside."

She grinned. "I'm game."

The light in his eyes dimmed a little. "I want to take you, but I'd like to get things taken care of with the others first."

"That makes sense. I need to check in with my mom."

He glanced her way. "I had Ferne contact your mum to let her know you were all right."

"How did that go?"

"She didn't calm down until I sent her a video of you asleep."

Rowen chuckled. "That sounds like her. I need to call them soon."

"I promised her you'd ring when you woke." Mason placed a mobile on the bar. "This one is for you. It came from Kurt's stash. He's been in charge of the Knights' security for some time."

It took her a moment to remember what Mason had told her about the Knights. "Oh, right. I remember you mentioning them now. Carlyle's involved."

"That's right. Carlyle, along with Elias, Finn, Sabryn, and Kurt. They've traveled the world, though they mostly stay in Europe. Elias is Scottish, Finn is Irish, Sabryn is from Washington, DC, and Kurt and Carlyle are both ex-London Druids."

Rowen nodded as she listened. "That's quite a group."

"It is. I didn't know about them until Ferne came to Skye. I was aware that Carlyle had taken up with a group, but I didn't know what they did. They came to the isle when Elias returned to help his sister, Elodie. That's all I've gotten so far, but I wanted to fill you in."

"I appreciate that. I also wanted to thank you for standing with me at the tea store. I might have overreacted about being told where to go."

Mason shook his head. "I felt the same. Had you not said something, I would have."

She found herself staring into his eyes again. Rowen cleared her throat and swiped up the phone. "Give me a few minutes to chat with my family, and then we can go."

"Take your time," he told her.

Rowen slipped off the stool and returned to her bedroom. Once she'd taken her seat on the bed, she drew in a long breath and released it. Then called home.

CHAPTER EIGHTEEN

SKYE DRUIDS

A light pattering of rain dotted the windscreen, obstructing Mason's view as he drove to Carwood Manor, so he turned on the wipers. Rowen's conversation with her mother had lasted over forty minutes, but he didn't begrudge her that time. He wished *he* could have another forty minutes with his parents.

He hadn't eavesdropped on her call. His mind had been too preoccupied with Skye. It was difficult for him to put into words what he felt being on the isle. Its wild beauty and untamed spirit took a back seat to the transcendent power that seemed to be everywhere he turned. Being here, experiencing it for himself, made him begin to understand why the Skye Druids were so protective of their home.

He also understood why those forced to leave were consumed with such hatred that it passed down through the generations. Mason had only been on Skye for a few hours, but already, he couldn't imagine leaving the isle behind. It would feel akin to removing a limb when he did. Was it his ancestral roots? Was it the magic? Was it something else entirely?

One could argue that he should've been contemplating his upcoming meeting with Rhona and the others, but he wasn't. He had nothing to hide. If they chose not to believe him, then so be it. He would leave, but only after he made sure Rowen got home—even if he had to take her there himself.

Which, now that he thought about it, he probably should. It would give him a chance to get to know some American Druids while ensuring that London didn't get their hands on Rowen.

"I don't think I have words to describe this place," she murmured, her face nearly pressed against the glass of the passenger window as she gazed out.

Mason glanced over to see the reverence brightening her face. "Rugged and stunning just doesn't cut it."

"Not in the least. How could I possibly explain how seeing this land touches my soul and makes me whole?" she whispered. "It's like…"

"You're home."

Her head swung to him. "Exactly. Like I was missing a place I didn't even know existed." She returned her attention to the landscape. "Every Druid should make a pilgrimage to Skye."

"Everyone around the globe feels some form of pull to the island. Most don't even realize what's calling to them. Others hear it loud and clear."

"Did you ever hear it?" she asked without looking at him.

Mason slowed as he came upon a car that had stopped to turn. "Skye was always forbidden. If I heard it, I ignored it."

Rowen sat back to look at him. "You sound troubled by that."

"I am. More with every minute I'm here. I'm upset that so many Druids listen to others spewing hateful rhetoric that only serves their interests. It's been like that for eons, and it'll continue."

"Unless you do something."

He snorted and glanced at her. "Me?"

"Why not you?"

"I'm one man."

She twisted her lips and shrugged. "Everything starts with one person."

"I'd like nothing more than to rid the organization of Thomas and everyone who follows him, but there's no way we'd get them all out. The seeds of loathing that were planted by our ancestors are too big and unwieldy to contain now. The hatred will continue to fester. It won't matter how many times we cut it down or try to yank it out, it won't go away."

"Then what's the solution? Start a new group?"

Mason sighed. "I don't know if there *is* a solution."

"Change is hard, no matter what it is. If you take on that battle, it's going to be an uphill climb. But I think it needs to be done."

"They murdered my parents. They'll come for me."

She pointed to the road they were supposed to turn onto. "Right here. And what makes you think you'll be alone?"

"Few will stand against the power of London."

"I'll stand with you."

Her statement was such a surprise that he jerked his head to her, only remembering at the last minute that he was driving and returned his attention to the road. "This isn't your fight."

"It became mine when they invited me here."

"I doubt your mum will feel the same."

Rowen laughed. "You'd be wrong. She asked if we wanted her and a few of my other family members to make the trip to help us."

Us. She bloody well meant it. Mason was excited that she was staying, but on the heels of that came the anxiety that something might happen to her.

"Don't," she warned. "I see that frown you always get when you've thought of something that upsets you. I can take care of myself."

"You don't know these Druids."

Rowen shrugged. "And they don't know me."

Mason was coming up with an argument when he saw the drive and turned down it. He peered through the trees and was rewarded with a glimpse of the weathered stone walls of a manor house, streaked with moss and time. The slate roof glinted dully, and chimneys jutted like sentinels against the brooding sky. It stood quiet and enduring. A house that had seen generations come and go and yet remained as steadfast as the isle itself. The tires rolled onto gravel as he pulled in next to a black Range Rover.

"Holy shit," Rowen murmured, her voice soft with awe as she stared out the windscreen. "Look at this place."

He grinned, wondering what her reaction would be to the Crawford Estate. She had no idea he was an earl. He hadn't told her. Not because he was trying to keep it a secret, but because there had been other things to deal with. Now, it seemed almost vulgar to tell her.

She hurried out of the car, uncaring about the drizzle, her wide eyes sweeping across every stone. "How old is this place? I can't put my finger on it, but it feels ancient yet young at the same time."

Mason came around the vehicle to stand next to her. "We'll ask when we get inside."

"Okay."

Except Rowen didn't head toward the door. She walked across the drive to a copse of trees where some wildflowers bloomed. He couldn't tear his eyes away from her. He was as taken by her in that instant as he had been when he saw her on the side of the road. She was stubborn, unwavering, and stalwart. She was also kind, generous, and compassionate. She knew her worth, and she didn't let anyone get in her way.

If he knew nothing else about her, he would still be impressed.

But he *did* know more. Rowen possessed a rare kind of magic that had nothing to do with spells. There was a quiet brilliance about her. A light that outshone everything else. She moved through the world with wonder in her eyes, seeing things others couldn't. Maybe it was the way she heard the plants, or perhaps it was just her soul. Whatever it was, he felt it every time he was near her.

And the more time he spent with her, the harder it became to imagine walking away.

She squatted beside a flower and leaned close to smell it, her touch upon the petal gentle. Then, she stroked her hand down the stem as if petting it. She straightened and wandered through the trees and the other flower beds, lost in her own world. And damn if it wasn't one he wished to be a part of.

He didn't know how long he stood there, simply watching her, before he became aware of someone beside him. Mason looked to his right and spotted Carlyle. The sight of his oldest friend sent a wave of emotion rocketing through him. He was about to embrace him when he recalled the last time they had met.

Carlyle's turquoise eyes were hard as they regarded him, and rain dampened his wavy auburn hair. He glanced toward Rowen. "So, she's the one who saved your life?"

"Yeah. Helped me to the car and drove with the London Druids chasing us."

"Ferne says she did more than that."

Mason swung his gaze to Rowen. He'd been in a lot of pain that night, but he had been ultra vigilant about everything, including noticing how calm she remained through it all. "I owe her everything."

"The rain is about to unleash on us. You should get her inside."

"Wait," Mason called as Carlyle started to turn. His friend paused and then slowly swiveled his head to him. "I'm sorry for what happened between us recently. It was all an act done to keep those I cared about out of harm's way."

For a long time, Carlyle didn't react. Finally, he said, "If you could have trusted anyone, it was me and Ferne. You chose to go it alone."

"For good reason."

Carlyle walked away, and Mason couldn't shake the feeling that he had damaged the relationships that meant the most to him beyond repair. It hurt deeply, but if it meant they lived, then it was worth it. Mason looked toward Rowen to find her scrutinizing him.

She made her way over. "Who was that?"

"Carlyle."

She shot a quick look at his friend's retreating back. "He upset you."

"My decision to undertake things on my own has hurt others, and that upsets me."

"If they care about you, they'll understand."

He put a hand on her back and guided her toward the front door. "I hope so."

"If they don't, then it's their loss."

Rowen's words softened the ache in his chest. It was like having his own personal support section, and it felt good to have her by his side. "You don't know me or what I've done."

She twisted her lips. "I did a bit of snooping in the storage unit when you were unconscious. That, plus what you've told me, paints a pretty good picture."

"You didn't find much there." He knew that for certain.

"Then tell me what I'm missing," she stated, pausing as they reached the open door.

He liked how the water droplets clung to the strands of her hair, begging him to touch it. So, he did. He would spill every secret he had if she asked. "I'll tell you anything you want to know."

"I want to know everything."

Bloody hell, she was beautiful. He wanted to count the freckles across her nose. More than that, he wanted to pull her against him and feel her softness alongside his body again. "Then you'll know it all. I don't think I'll ever be able to fully repay you for what you've done for me."

"I think coming to Skye is payment enough. But I want you to tell me who you are because you wish to share it, not as payment for something."

She didn't understand that he had already bared himself to her. He hadn't understood it until that moment, but it didn't alarm him. With her, he had nothing to hide.

Mason found himself sinking into the blue of her eyes, the

paleness tempting him to come closer, as if reaching for his soul. Fate had delivered her to him, and the more he got to know her, the more he liked.

Wanted.

Craved.

CHAPTER NINETEEN

SKYE DRUIDS

Each time Rowen looked into Mason's eyes, the world slowed. Her breath caught, her pulse tripped. While something raw and undeniable called to her, lured her. It was a pull that went deeper. Was dangerous. Irresistible. She knew she should guard herself, wrap her heart in steel. Instead, she leaned in, drawn closer each time…aching for something she couldn't afford to want.

She had seen him at his most vulnerable—the fear, the anger, and the rigid determination. His blood had coated her hands and arms. She had stripped him and seen his remarkable, mouth-watering body. She had felt the heat of his gaze when she used her magic on him. It was a level of closeness that she hadn't shared with another before, and it connected them in ways that could never be severed.

His injuries had exposed him, giving her a glimpse of his true self. It was a time when few could hold up the masks they wore. She knew nothing about Mason, and maybe because of that, she went in without preconceived notions. Over the years, she had seen people act in every way imaginable while wounded. Mason's unyielding and unwavering resolve to get to Ferne had shown Rowen the man he was.

Someone cleared their throat. Mason's gaze darted to the side. She dropped hers to the ground in an attempt to get a hold of her rioting emotions. When she looked up, Carlyle was at the door, studying them.

Mason gave her a nod, letting her know it was okay to enter. She eyed the structure. There was something different about it. She swallowed and stepped over the threshold, her wet sneakers sinking into an expensive-looking rug in the entrance. A quick look confirmed that others still had their shoes on, but she would feel better if she had someplace to wipe off any dirt. The place was immaculate. It held an old-world feel that hinted at generations of families, magic, and untold happenings within its walls.

The decor was a curious but beautiful mix of modern and old. The wood paneling gleamed, and the hanging art was breathtaking. She caught sight of a grand staircase that switch-backed up to the floors above, and Rowen had the urge to race up it to explore. If she were a child, she would've been up those stairs quicker than anyone could've grabbed her.

Suddenly, a woman in light gray sweats, fuzzy pink socks, and a navy sweatshirt hanging off one shoulder that read *Namaste* appeared. Her brunette hair was piled in a messy bun atop her head, and she rubbed her eyes. "I'm finally finished with the design."

"Just in time for our guests," said a male voice with a thick Scottish brogue.

Rowen looked to her right to see the man in question heading toward the stairs. He lowered his head of dark blond hair and greeted the woman with a quick kiss before she turned to them.

A smile split her face, her hazel eyes crinkling at the corners. "Mason," she said as she walked to them. "You and Ferne share a striking resemblance." Then those hazel eyes slid to Rowen. "And you must be Rowen. It's good to finally meet you both. I'm Bronwyn. This is my home. Please, make yourselves comfortable."

Mason dipped his head. "Thank you for the hospitality."

"Yes, thank you," Rowen replied.

"Finally, another American," came a voice behind Bronwyn.

Bronwyn chuckled. "Get ready. You're about to be inundated with a lot of names and faces."

She wasn't wrong. Rowen did a better job of keeping track of everyone here than she had in London. She met Sabryn from DC, and her partner, Kurt, the hacker. Bronwyn was quick to tug Elias to them. An Asian beauty introduced herself as Song, Carlyle's partner. Then there was Elias's sister, Elodie, and Scott. Willa, Scott's sister, and Jasper were next. Ariah was there with someone Rowen thought was Finn because of the Irish accent, but it turned out to be Killian. Finn popped in next. There was also Kirsi, Filip, and Callum, but what threw her for a loop was Willa and Scott's father, Luke, as well as Elias and Elodie's mother, Emily.

"Rowen's eyes have glazed over," Kurt said, getting a laugh from everyone.

Song grinned. "I still have the spreadsheet I made with everyone on it. I'll lend it to you if you need it."

"I think *I* might need it," Mason said.

Rowen heard the lightness in his voice, but he stood rigid beside her. She tipped her lips into a grin and nodded. Carlyle, she noticed, hadn't said anything to Mason since their encounter outside. Ferne wore her worry on her brow, and Theo stayed near her, offering comfort.

There were many Druids around Rowen, the ages ranging from a handful of years younger than her to several decades older. Everyone was jovial, but there was also an undercurrent of unease that no amount of lighthearted talk could hide.

It was Mason and her against everyone else. They may not say that, but everyone knew it for what it was. Rowen fought against the need to inch closer to Mason. She would be a fool not to be a little fearful of those around her. But what amped up that worry was the way Ferne looked at her brother.

"Let's go somewhere more comfortable," Bronwyn said as she started to the side.

No one followed her. Rowen glanced at Mason. He gave her a barely discernible dip of his chin, so Rowen swallowed her disquiet and trailed after Bronwyn into what she supposed was a parlor. The room was spacious with ample seating for all.

The mix of modern and old continued in this room, as well. The large windows let in natural light while giant pictures hung on the walls. Rowen chose a settee with room enough for one other person. To her relief, Mason sat beside her. The others filed into the room. Despite her initial thought that there was enough seating for everyone, a few had to stand. One chair was left vacant. The answer to who it had been saved for came a second later when a pretty woman with long, red hair entered the house and walked into the room.

Mason got to his feet as the woman approached. Rowen guessed she was around her age and reached for her magic as she observed Mason and the woman.

"Rhona," he said.

She stared at Mason for a long time before inclining her head. "Mason. Thank you for agreeing to speak with us."

Rowen tensed when the Druid leader's green eyes turned to her. She waited, unsure of what to expect from Rhona.

"I'm eager to hear about your journey, as well, Rowen," Rhona said.

Once Rhona sank into the chair, Mason lowered himself back onto the cushion beside Rowen. He sat close enough that his thigh brushed against hers. Some of the tension left her at having him near.

"Where would you like me to begin?" Mason asked.

Rhona crossed one leg over the other. "The beginning is always best."

Rowen sat silently as Mason gave them the same brief overview that he had given her about growing up training alongside Carlyle with his father. He touched on his mother being an elder, his father's high rank within the London Druids, and how life had been good.

"Then came the plane crash," Mason stated.

Rowen's gaze instinctively went to Ferne in time to see her flinch. It wouldn't matter how much time passed. That pain would linger for both of the siblings.

"I wasn't suspicious at first," Mason continued. "I was too shocked at losing both my parents, and my main concern was Ferne. We went through the motions and got through the burial, and then we grieved."

His gaze moved to Ferne, and the two shared a long look. Theo covered Ferne's hand with his and brought it to his lips to kiss her knuckles as Mason drew in a deep breath. Every eye in the room was on him, but he didn't seem fazed by it.

"My father served as a pilot in the Royal Air Force. He knew planes, and he knew *his* like the back of his hand. He never would have taken it up if there had even been a hint of something being wrong. I had resigned myself to it being a freak accident, right up until the report from the Air Accidents Investigation Branch concluded that it was pilot error, claiming improper pre-flight procedure."

Rowen could feel the anger radiating from Mason. He kept his hands resting casually on his legs, but the more he spoke, the lower his voice pitched. She wanted to reach out and touch him, offer comfort. She would have if they had been alone.

Mason paused. "The report wrote off their deaths—and the wreckage that followed—on Dad, but he was obsessive and precise about that plane. I knew the report for the lie it was, but when I questioned it, I was ignored. I leaned hard on the AAIB, using my influence and even my title, to no avail."

Title? Had he just said *title*? Rowen frowned, wanting to ask what he had meant, but there wasn't time to interrupt his story.

"I even turned to our family's closest friend." Mason slid his gaze to Carlyle. "Thomas. Your father promised to look into it, and when he didn't get anything, we both went to the elders." He shook his head, his nostrils flaring as his face hardened. "The elders studiously read over the report, and even took notes as I spoke. I honestly thought they would be able to do something. But there was nothing but silence in the weeks and months that followed. I can't tell you the exact moment I began to suspect a cover-up within the organization, but once the thought took root, I couldn't let it go. If they could kill an elder without consequences, then they could take out anyone."

A shiver ran down Rowen's spine. She had seen the London

Druids for herself. Had felt how off everything had been. And she would be happy to never see any of them again.

"What did you do?" Elias asked.

Mason blinked, his mouth relaxing as if he were shaking free of the memories. "I began to dig into the days and weeks leading up to the crash. I needed to know my parents' movements down to the minute. They went to London for a usual gathering and stayed in the city for a couple of meetings since Mum was an elder. It wasn't until I scoured my father's texts that I found one written in some sort of code. I couldn't decipher it and was loath to reach out for help. I didn't know who I could trust and who I couldn't. So, I dove into everything I could find about coding and decoding messages. Months later, I was still stumped. It was only after Ferne and I finally cleaned out their room that I found a small notebook tucked away in Dad's closet. Inside, I found everything I needed to decode the message."

"Why didn't you tell me?" Ferne demanded, hurt furrowing her brow.

It was Theo who said, in a soft voice, "You know why, love."

Rowen moved her hand over so that it rested half on Mason's leg and half on hers. He hadn't opened up completely, but he had done enough for everyone in the room to understand just how deep his outrage and pain went. He had stood alone against the behemoth that was the London Druids, shouldering everything on his own—and he was still standing.

She had meant it earlier when she told him that he could make a difference. He was the kind of individual who could inspire others to join a cause and continue when there was no hope. He was the kind of man who could bring about the type of change that so desperately needed to happen. And finally get to the truth of his parents' murders.

Rowen didn't know why she had been granted a front-row seat to all of this, but she had. It would be easy to return home and let things fall where they would in the UK, and she doubted anyone would blame her if she left. And while it might be safer for her now, what about in the long run? She had always followed her heart, and it had led her to Mason that night. It had urged her to help him get away and brought her to Skye.

She was meant to be here. With the Skye Druids.

With Mason.

So, she would stay. Even though she still didn't know the entirety of what she was getting involved in.

CHAPTER TWENTY

SKYE DRUIDS

Mason was all too aware of the silence in the room and the eyes on him. He should be worried about how the others were taking his story so far, but all he kept thinking about was Rowen. He had given her a quick accounting of things, but she had no way of knowing if he spoke the truth or not. All the documents he needed to prove everything had been digitized and were stored safely, where no one could find them.

The feel of her fingers against his leg nearly undid him. He had been so wrapped up in the memories of uncovering the crime against his parents that the tangled, cloying jumble of emotions tied to it had threatened to consume him once again. It was only her touch that had pulled him from its clutches.

He pinched the bridge of his nose with his thumb and forefinger and closed his eyes for a heartbeat. Then he lowered his hand and looked at Rhona. "Dad met with someone in London. I don't know who it was, or for what purpose. He and Mum extended their time in the city by a week. Ferne was at uni, and I was taking care of estate business. I didn't think anything of them staying. I checked with the staff at the townhome, but there were no visitors. My parents, however, went out once during the day and returned just after midnight. Both the butler and one of the maids mentioned how both of them were quiet and seemed troubled when they got home."

"Where did they go?" Ferne asked.

He shrugged as he looked at his sister. "I don't know. None of the texts or emails pointed to a location. They must have been communicating with someone another way."

"Someone in the organization, you mean," Carlyle said.

Mason gave a small nod of his head. "It's my guess. With Mum being an elder, she was privy to a lot of information. They must have stumbled upon something."

"Something Thomas didn't want getting out," Rhona murmured. She turned her head to Song, who sat near her. "Do you know anything?"

Mason frowned as he stared at Carlyle's lover, confused as to why Rhona would ask her.

Song shifted uneasily and looked at Mason when she said, "Thomas took me as a child and forced me to work for him."

"Exactly what did you do?" Mason asked.

Carlyle's lips flattened as anger flashed across his face. "You know the truth about Thomas now. Use your imagination."

"Did you know about my parents?" Mason asked Song, his stomach tightening with dread. "Were you the one who sabotaged the plane?"

Carlyle took a step around the sofa where Song sat, but she put a hand on his arm, halting him. Mason watched them exchange a silent look. After a heartbeat, Carlyle returned to his place beside the couch.

"You have every right to ask that," Song told Mason. "I would, too. I did many things I can never take back, but I swear, I never did anything to your parents' plane or your parents. I knew of them, of course, but the work Thomas sent me to do was usually away from headquarters and the elders."

"Do you know who might have been involved?" Rhona asked her.

A deep sadness came over Song's features as her shoulders drooped. "It could have been my sister. She and Thomas are together."

Mason leaned forward, bracing his forearms on his thighs, searching through his memories for all the times he had been with Thomas over the years to see if he remembered anyone who stood out.

"Can you ask her if she was part of it?" Rowen asked.

Song shook her head. "I didn't know where she was until a few weeks ago when Thomas tried to kill Carlyle."

"I'm sorry. Did you just say that Thomas attempted to end his own son's life?" Rowen glanced about the room.

"That she did," Carlyle replied.

Mason rubbed his hands on his thighs as he sat back. "Song showed up at the estate, pretending to be with me. I knew the instant she arrived that someone from London had sent her, but I wasn't sure why or for what. I played along while also hoping I could figure out why she was there."

"While that was happening, Finn and I went to London

because I hadn't heard from my father," Carlyle said. "I believed he had gone missing, and since I was on Skye, I feared what London might do to him. I was unaware of his true position within the organization. He kept it all from me. So, I went looking for Thomas at our place in the city. I found Song instead."

"Thomas ordered me to go there but told me I couldn't let Carlyle or anyone know where he was," Song explained.

Carlyle placed his hand on her shoulder and squeezed. "Finn and I followed her to Mason's estate. The four of us had a brief exchange, and I left, knowing that something had changed with Mason. I thought if I could get Song away from him that he would return to who he used to be, and Song could give me information on my father. Our plan was to kidnap both of them from the estate."

"Everything went to hell," Song murmured. "I went to Mason's office to retrieve something out of the desk I was instructed to obtain."

Mason interrupted her to ask, "What were you looking for?"

"I don't know," she replied with a shrug. "They didn't tell me that."

Carlyle stroked her hair. "She was attempting to get into the locked drawer. I could've opened it since it was the magical lock your father taught us, but I didn't."

"What was in the drawer?" Ferne asked.

Mason sat back as he grinned. "Estate records."

"Nothing to do with London and your parents' crash?" Theo asked.

Mason shook his head. "I never left a trail to be found. Everything I had was encrypted. It's safely hidden away and will only be released to Ferne should I die. I knew a hacker would be able to decode it, and she would then have all the information I'd gathered."

Song nodded, seemingly impressed. "While I was in your office, Carlyle showed up. Then, the next thing I knew, we were both being shot."

"We ran for our lives," Carlyle added.

Mason thought about the gun that had been pointed at him. "Why use guns on you? Why did Thomas have individuals use guns and knives with me? It doesn't make sense."

"They weren't ordinary guns," Carlyle said.

Song grimaced. "London has developed bullets that can render a Druid incapable of drawing on their magic, and there is a second kind that turns a Druid's magic on them."

"Fucking hell," Rowen murmured.

Mason agreed completely. "This is the first I'm hearing about these kinds of weapons."

"It has been kept quiet from all but a few," Song explained. "Thomas has been amassing an army for some time now."

A deep frown marred Rowen's brow. "For what?"

"To use against us," Rhona answered. "Against anyone who stands against him."

Carlyle blew out a breath. "I got Song away from the estate, but we were tracked. Eventually, she told me how she had been taken from her parents as a young child. She was raised with her sister at a manor house and kept there by the elders, who had her trained better than most of MI6."

Song twisted her lips. "As long as I did what they asked of me, my sister was allowed to live. We both thought the elders had my sister and Thomas somewhere at headquarters, so we decided to go to them."

"I found Thomas," Carlyle said bitterly. "I thought he'd be in some cell, possibly being tortured. It never dawned on me that *he* was leading London. He has been pulling the strings for some time now. He was the one who took Song and her sister. He was the one who set it up to look like he had gone missing so he could get me to London."

Mason narrowed his eyes suspiciously. "He hated you coming to Skye so badly that he brought you there to kill you?"

Song looked at the floor. Carlyle crossed his arms over his chest. "Actually, the bastard expected me to join him. He threatened Song to force my hand, but when that didn't work, he tried to take us both out."

"Fuck." Mason ran a hand down his face. "I had no idea any of that happened. I only discovered that Thomas was leading the London Druids a few weeks ago. I've been watched, the phones bugged, my car tracked, ever since I pushed to know more about the plane crash. Everything I did was under a microscope. It's why I became such a wanker. You were both safe here. And that's where I needed you to remain." He looked from Ferne to Carlyle. "Then you showed up, and I had to get you away before it was too late."

Finn tilted his head to the side. "Did you know your home would be attacked? Did you know Thomas was looking for Carlyle?"

"I knew nothing," Mason stated. "If I had, I would've alerted you."

Ferne asked, "What happened after the attack?"

Mason had dreaded this part. He knew it was going to look and sound bad, but desperate people did desperate things. "Once I learned Thomas's true role, I leaned heavily into how close our families were. I used the fact that Ferne and Carlyle were on Skye and how they had betrayed us to get close to him."

"You said what you needed to say to ingratiate yourself," Theo said with a nod. "That was smart."

Ferne glared at Theo. "It was stupid. He nearly got killed."

"He needed answers. Each of us would have done the same in his shoes, and we all know it." Rhona nodded at Mason. "Continue."

He glanced down at Rowen's fingers on his leg. "I never missed a meeting. I did everything he asked of me, no matter how trivial. And I was always on guard. I knew he could turn on me at any moment. I kept my findings from everyone, and I stopped talking about the crash. I outfitted a storage unit in case I had to lie low. I was prepared. Or so I thought."

He paused and thought about the assault. It was bad enough that Ferne had seen his wounds. He didn't want her to know just how frightening the ordeal had been. "It was a regular meeting. I hadn't been there long before Thomas found me. He asked me to follow him to the back. It wasn't the first time, and I had my magic at the ready, just in case. He was chitchatting about nothing in particular. I had never been to the room he took me to before. There were two men playing billiards and another standing off to the side when we walked in. Instantly, my magic vanished. The next thing I knew, a man attacked. I fought him off, but I didn't feel right. Then a woman came at me with a knife. I thought I knocked her out, but the next thing I knew, there was a third person, and all three came after me. Somehow, the woman and I fell into the hall as we fought, and my magic returned. I quickly ended her, but when I tried to get up, I felt my side. A step later, and I discovered my leg injury."

"How did you get away?" Song asked.

Mason glanced at Ferne. "Mum made me memorize a map of escape routes, and I used one. It took all of my energy, though. By the time I found myself outside, I couldn't get my legs to work anymore. Just when I was about to give up, Rowen found me."

CHAPTER TWENTY-ONE

SKYE DRUIDS

Rowen was transfixed by Mason's story, unable to look away from him as she imagined what he had gone through. He glossed over the fight, but she could imagine how brutal it had been. Maybe that's why she was unprepared when he looked over at her as he spoke the last sentence.

"I was running," she said into the quiet that followed, staring into his eyes. "I still don't know why I turned your way instead of the other. It didn't make sense to remain so close to headquarters, yet I did."

"Fate," someone said.

She pressed her lips together and remembered the others in the room as she tore her gaze from his. "For months, Brenna—the leader of Salish Druids—has been receiving invitations from London to visit. She ignored them for a while, but then we began seeing things in the chat rooms. There were discussions among our group about what we should do. It was decided that we needed more information."

"And that meant sending someone," Rhona said.

Rowen nodded. "Some volunteered, but my aunt said I should go."

"Why you, in particular?" Sabryn asked.

Rowen shrugged. "Aunt Maelin is a dream weaver. I don't know if someone visited her, or whether she visited someone. She never told me. All she said was that I had to come, and that I had to travel alone. I balked at first. Something about London reaching out bothered me. It isn't as if Druid groups don't talk to each other, but it was just…"—she shrugged—"off."

"Because *they're* off," Carlyle murmured.

Rowen shot him a fleeting smile. "London offered to buy a ticket and arrange where I would stay, and that's where I put my foot down, as did Brenna and my mom. We booked my trip, and before I knew it, I was on my way." She clasped her hands in her lap. "Things were fine until I was to meet the London Druids."

"At a meeting?" Carlyle asked with a shake of his head. "Why not before, with only a few Druids? Maybe even an elder or two?"

Mason grunted. "It was done strategically. They wanted to show her their numbers and strength."

"That was my thought," she told Mason. "Dread filled me the entire day leading up to the meeting. Even when I arrived and was greeted by a woman named Ella, I wanted to flee."

Ferne rolled her eyes. "Ella Howard? If that's who they sent to greet you, I would've run, too." She looked at Mason. "She was the brunette with the high-pitched voice, flitting about all the time, trying to be everyone's best friend."

"She wouldn't have been my first choice," Mason said with a wrinkle of his nose.

Rowen scratched her cheek before she tucked her hair behind her ear. "Ella took me around and introduced me. I just wanted to observe, but they acted like I was already a part of the organization. It made me incredibly uneasy. On top of that, Ella wouldn't leave my side."

"I wonder how many others they've done this to," Rhona questioned.

Theo sighed. "There's no telling."

"How long did you stay?" Ferne asked.

Rowen picked at her fingernail, noticing it had a slight chip in it. There was suddenly a soft pressure against the top of her thigh, and she glanced down to see that Mason had moved his hand so his pinky and ring finger were against her leg. Just as she had done to him. At his calming gesture, warmth spread from her chest outward.

"Long enough to hear Thomas speak." She darted her gaze to Carlyle. "The more he spoke, the more I knew I had to get out. When I rose from my seat, Ella started to follow. I said I needed to use the restroom, but she still practically walked me to the door. Had it been anything but a single toilet, I believe she would've come in with me."

Distaste distorted Elias's face. "They didna want you getting away."

"That's what concerns me," Bronwyn stated.

Rhona sighed. "There are a great many things about London that worry me, but this certainly stands out."

"How did you get away?" Carlyle asked.

Rowen chuckled. "I used to sneak out of my house, and my mom was ruthless about trying to stop me. She never caught me, and though it's been a long time since I had to call upon those resources, I did it. When I finally came out of the bathroom, I saw that people were milling about again. I hid behind some others and worked my way from room to room until I found my way back to the front door. I left my coat and ran."

She paused and swallowed. "Ella had hinted at knowing my flight times, as well as where I was staying, so I didn't feel comfortable returning to the hotel. I was considering my next move and how to get home as I went around the building. That's when I saw Mason stumble out of a door and crumple. Then I saw the blood. He had been hurt by the people I wanted no part of, so I went to help him."

"Not many would've done that. Thank you," Ferne said.

Carlyle dipped his head. "It was very brave of you."

"The brave part came after she got me on my feet," Mason said.

"We saw that. Actually, we saw everything from the time Rowen ran out of headquarters," Ferne said.

Rowen frowned in confusion before realizing that Kurt had likely hacked the cameras. "You were testing us to see if we would tell you the truth."

"We were being cautious," Rhona corrected her. "The fact is, you didn't have to help Mason, but you did."

Mason grinned. "You got us to the storage unit and got me stitched up."

Rowen only had to close her eyes to picture him lying on the narrow cot, soaked in blood, his skin ashen. He had skirted death. Sidled right up to it and danced with it, only to walk away. She still didn't know how he had done it.

"On top of all of that," Mason continued, "you drove through the night and got us here."

There was something in his voice, a kind of awe that she had never heard before. She turned her head to him and got caught in those mesmerizing gray eyes of his.

"Thomas will know you've come to the isle," Carlyle said.

Mason looked away, breaking the spell. Rowen tried to get a hold of herself. He felt beholden to her because she saved his life. There was nothing more to it than that. The sooner she acknowledged that, the better.

"We had nowhere else to go that London couldn't get to," Mason said.

Concern deepened the lines on Ferne's face. "What about the estate? What about Billings?"

"I kept him out of it," Mason told her.

Carlyle snorted. "Billings knows more than you think he does. But I also know he'll die before he gives up anything on you or Ferne."

"It'd better not come to that," Ferne murmured.

Mason's hands curled into fists on his legs. "If Billings or any of the staff is harmed in any way, I'll track down everyone who had a part in it."

"I'll join you," Carlyle stated.

Finn said, "We all will."

Everyone in the room nodded their heads in agreement. Rowen wasn't sure if that meant they believed Mason or if they still doubted his intentions. It was hard to get a read on things, especially when friendships dated back decades. She decided it would be in her best interest to stay vigilant. There was none of the unease she'd felt in London, but that didn't mean these people were her friends. She wasn't even sure what her relationship with Mason was.

"You should know that London has reached Skye," Rhona replied.

Mason tensed beside Rowen. "How?" he asked.

"That would be my fault," Kurt admitted reluctantly.

Sabryn put her hand on his arm from their spots on the sofa across from Rowen. "It isn't your fault." Sabryn looked at her and Mason. "As you know, London has been seeking out other Druids for years. They wanted my family, specifically my father, who was a senator. They sent Kurt and his brother so one of them could seduce me in hopes of swaying Dad if he didn't readily agree."

"Which he didn't," Kurt pointed out.

Sabryn shook her head. "No, he didn't. I fell for Kurt, but things went south with us when I discovered that his family had played a part in my father's death."

"Oh, my god," Rowen murmured.

"I was meant to be with my father that day, but I didn't go." A flash of pain contorted Sabryn's face. Kurt took her hand and covered it with his as she said, "I then went to England in search of Kurt."

Kurt nodded, and they shared a quick look. "I wanted distance from my family. Mum was high up in the organization, and at the time, I believed everything she did was to propel her upward. I made a pact with her that if they stopped trying to kill Sabryn, I'd have nothing to do with Sabryn. I had no intention of doing that. When I learned that she and Carlyle had become friends and were helping Druids, I made myself indispensable to them as a hacker."

"It wasna until recently that we discovered the person we knew as Sabertooth was actually Kurt," Elias said.

Finn grinned. "As you can imagine, that didn't go over too well."

"My brother, Parker, was after me," Kurt explained. "I thought Mum had sent him to find me, but he was trying to kill me. I came to Skye to warn the others, and Parker followed."

Sabryn's face filled with sadness. "Diana, his mother, eventually made her way here. That's how we learned that Parker was no longer following her instructions."

"He's taking orders from Thomas?" Mason asked.

Kurt shrugged. "Maybe. I didn't get a chance to ask him before he tried to kill me by using some kind of spell. I found out later that he'd murdered Mum."

Rowen realized that Mason had been right. The Skye Druids were fighting other Druids, but not for power. They were fighting to live.

"Is Parker still on the isle?" Mason asked.

Kurt shook his head. "The facial recognition program I've been running has put him in Edinburgh."

"That's only part of our problem." Rhona handed Mason her phone.

He read it before passing it on to Rowen. The screen was a news story with the caption:

ANCIENT MAGIC AWAKENS: ISLE OF SKYE'S DRUIDS UNLEASH GLOBAL DEBATE.

A quick read detailed a battle that had taken place on the isle. Rowen's gut clenched as she raised her gaze to Rhona. "What does this mean?"

"It means that while we've done our best to keep the things happening here a secret, it has been leaked," the leader said.

Bronwyn crossed her arms over her chest. "We think it could be Parker."

"There's a spotlight on us now," Rhona continued. "And it's going to make fighting the evil even harder."

Rowen steeled herself. "What kind of evil?"

CHAPTER TWENTY-TWO

SKYE DRUIDS

Edie

There was peace in the in-between place, a kind of harmony Edie hadn't realized could be so calming. Her recent encounter with the sky pillar, Sabryn, had set her back. If Sabryn's strike had hit a little more to the side, Edie wouldn't be here now. But the Ancients were looking out for her. Here, in this special dwelling, she was healing far quicker than she would have anywhere else.

She had sought out the invisible cottage once she got away from the Fairy Glen. That battle had been hers to win. She'd seen the outcome, had felt it in her bones. Sabryn had been weakening. Edie was ready to crush her—and the hopes of the other Druids—with one final blow. Then Kurt joined Sabryn. Together, they had been unstoppable. Even with the added power the Ancients had given her, Edie had come up short.

Worse, she felt the Ancients' disappointment about her failure. Their silence was deafening, their frustration pressing on her like a brick wall. The Skye Druids had found their earth and sky pillars once more. Edie had one more opportunity to prevent the water pillar from taking their place. She couldn't fail again. The Ancients had allowed her entry into the hidden cottage to rest and heal, but they wouldn't be so forgiving a second time.

Kerry had failed them, and she was now dead, her blood splattered on the stones of the Druid prison where Rhona had taken her. The thought of the Ancients doing the same to her left Edie cold. She would take her own life before she allowed Rhona or that Fae husband of hers to take her to the Red Hills.

The one advantage she had was that the Skye Druids didn't know who the water pillar was. That gave her time to watch and listen. Anyone she deemed might be the pillar would be removed—swiftly and effortlessly.

Edie's gaze lifted to the roof above her. The hole where Song had fallen through was gone now. The Ancients had been interested in Song joining them. It was the only reason they had stayed Edie's hand when she would've taken the Druid's life. But that had backfired, too. Song had developed feelings for Carlyle that overshadowed the dominance the Ancients had offered. Time was running out to take Druids back to a time when their magic ran free and powerful. When those without such potency had bowed to them.

She sat up on the mattress and swung her legs over the side. The first time Kerry had told her how the Ancients sought to remove Druids they deemed lacking, Edie had been horrified. Her first thought had been about her children. But that day felt like three lifetimes ago. Her eyes had been opened since, and she saw the truth of things clearly now. Druids had become meaningless, pointless. Their magic and power diminished each time they mixed with non-magicals. They stood on the brink of extinction, and no one even realized it.

The Ancients had, though. They had decided to take matters into their own hands and do what others couldn't. They had handpicked Kerry, but she had allowed the additional power granted to her to sway her from their path. And it had gotten her caught.

That's when the Ancients selected Edie as Kerry's replacement. Edie wouldn't make the same mistakes as her predecessor. A new world awaited them, and she understood the significance of her role. Already, she had surrendered any semblance of family: her mother, her siblings—Elias and Elodie—and even her children.

It hadn't been as hard to walk away as she had thought. They thought the worst of her, but she didn't care. Room had to be made for the next generation of Druids who would thrive, be bigger and brighter than even the first of their kind who had walked the Earth.

Her family was dead to her, just as her husband was. Elias and Elodie had chosen the wrong side, and they would die for that decision—her mother, no doubt, with them. As for her children, she wasn't sure where they would land. If the Ancients allowed them to live, then she would bring them back into her life. If not? Well, then that's how it had to be. She was one of the few who would survive and populate the world with more Druid babies.

The soft hush of the in-between was like a calming hand against her face. She closed her eyes and sank into the soundlessness. The cottage was special to her. Not only because the Ancients had hidden it for her, but because it had been her first home after she got married. She had loved the small cottage. That had been a time when possibilities were endless, and years of what she assumed would be happiness stretched before her.

She hated that Rhona and her group had found the cottage by accident while searching for Killian. A few had managed to find their way inside, and only then could they see the cottage. They had tainted her sacred place. It wasn't meant for any of them. Only her. And each time she entered, it became harder and harder to leave.

The world as she knew it was garish, filthy, and immoral everywhere she turned. Greed ran the world. It always had. And that would never change. The difference was the sheer number of those living on the planet. It was past time she flipped the switch on the garbage disposal and removed those not serving the greater power.

Skye had once been a Druid haven, and it would be again. It would become a place where no one but Druids dared to venture. Everything for the Druids—and the world—was just on the horizon. All Edie had to do was prevent the water pillar from being found.

That would be a lot easier if she knew who it was. But if the Ancients had that information, they weren't sharing. They hadn't known Ariah was the earth pillar, or that Sabryn was the air pillar. In all likelihood, they didn't know who the water pillar was either.

Eons ago, when the Druids on Skye had fought against some unknown beast from another dimension, they had created the pillars, each location running from north to south through the isle. Skye was nearly impenetrable when the pillars were in place.

"Edie."

The sound of the steely feminine voice rang through her head like a bell. She would never forget the first time the Ancients had spoken to her through the single voice—a sign that she had been chosen.

"There is a new Druid on the isle. We want her."

Edie frowned at the news, thinking about how badly it had gone with Song. "I can do anything you need."

"*You know better than to question us!*" the Ancients bellowed tersely.

Edie winced at the fury in each syllable. They had finally seen something in her that others had overlooked. And she wasn't ready to share that with anyone.

"*She will not replace you,*" the Ancients replied in a softer voice. "*She will merely be another of our soldiers—your soldier—to help return our kind to how we were always meant to be.*"

With a nervous lick of her lips, Edie asked, "Who is she?"

"*She's an American Druid, but do not be fooled by that. She is formidable.*"

"Just the kind of Druid we're looking for. What is her name?"

"*Rowen. She's with Rhona's contingent at the moment.*"

Edie wrinkled her nose at the news. "That will make getting to her difficult."

"*Leave that to us,*" the Ancients said with a little chuckle that made her grin.

"Is she the water pillar?"

There was a long beat of silence before the Ancients said, "*It's possible. We'll get her free of the others so you can have a little chat with her.*"

Edie ran her fingers through the short strands of her pixie cut. "And if she won't join?"

"*Let's make sure she does.*"

"I understand."

There was venom in the female voice as it said, *"We hope so. You've already failed us. There won't be a second time."*

"I'm not quite healed. I would rather not run into Rhona's crowd until I am."

"You have your orders."

Edie sighed as she pushed to her feet. She had no interest in meeting the same fate as Kerry, though Edie wasn't happy about leaving the cottage so early. She didn't have access to Healers, but she was recovering quicker in the in-between. If she left, it would slow that process and put her at a disadvantage.

She headed down the stairs. Some might think she was already at a disadvantage going up against so many Druids on her own. But she wasn't alone. Not really. She had the Ancients. They didn't just guide her, they imparted some of their magic to her. Which more than made up for the rest.

Edie paused at the back door before turning the handle and stepping out and into her time. The sun was descending into the horizon. She'd stashed her SUV two miles away. It made things difficult, but since Rhona's gang drove by the cottage often, she couldn't take the chance of it being seen parked in front of the concealed building.

It wasn't just the cottage that interested Rhona. It was the giant tear in the dimension above it. Song was the only one who could see the tear. Edie wished she could see it so she could crawl through it and discover what was on the other side. The Ancients didn't seem concerned about it when she mentioned it, so she had set aside any worry. But the tear was there for a reason. The Ancients knew everything. They knew what it was for. Whether they ever told her or not was anyone's guess.

The trek to her vehicle was over wide-open land, where the

wind howled and lashed at her. Behind her, a mountain rose in the distance as an eye-catching backdrop. She loved everything about the isle. Its bleak mountains, the spectacular waterfalls, the dazzling lochs, and the impressive ocean surrounding it. Scotland was wild and untamed, but Skye was also mystical and enchanting.

The land had called to the first Druids, summoning those with magic to its shores. It had been a safe haven, a sanctuary. Skye shone so brightly that even those without magic felt its call. They were powerless to stay away. Those early Druids should never have allowed any of them to set foot on the isle. They had contaminated the bloodlines, which had brought things to this drastic point.

Edie looked up at the deep sapphire sky as the first twinkling stars became visible. She was tainted, too. Every Druid around the world had been fouled with blood from those without magic. Her father had been a vile, disgusting man who beat her mum and Elias. He had deserved to die for his actions—just as Trevor had deserved the painful end that'd come to him for his philandering.

In order for Edie to rebuild the new world, she had to survive her next run-ins with Rhona and the others. They had been following her. She had lost them, but now that she was out in the open again, they would pick up her trail soon enough. She would have to be extra watchful. Kerry had lived in the shadows for weeks until Rhona's unit discovered that she was the one killing the Druids.

Edie hadn't had that long before they found out that she had taken Kerry's place. She would rather everyone know it was her. That way, she didn't have to pretend to be something she wasn't anymore. Yet it made moving about Skye difficult at times.

She found the car and climbed inside, just as it began to sprinkle. The engine roared to life, and she put the SUV into drive as she headed toward Carwood Manor. It was the group's favorite location because the house was sentient, making it impossible to get inside. The Ancients knew that, which meant they would get Rowen outside to her.

It was the best way for them to meet. Meeting in the village would be tough with so many others watching them. Of course, it was possible that Rowen wasn't staying at the manor. Edie would find out one way or the other soon enough. The farther away from the manor she got, the better. Edie didn't like the house—or being near it. Carwood Manor was part of the reason Kerry had gotten caught. Edie wouldn't make that same blunder.

She put her foot on the brake to slow down and make a turn. The Carwood estate was large, but she couldn't come up the drive. She would have to go the back way through the forest to watch the house. It wouldn't be her first time, and she had everything she needed to remain for several days.

The best thing was that no one ever thought to check the grounds. She grinned as she pulled off the road to a dirt section and began the bumpy ride.

CHAPTER TWENTY-THREE

SKYE DRUIDS

"You're quiet."

Mason's words jerked Rowen out of her thoughts. She glanced at him as he drove them to the cottage. "I think my brain is about to explode with everything I just learned."

"Yeah." He paused. "I had no idea that Ferne and the others had been going through all of that."

All of that had been over four hours of stories from the group, detailing their encounters with the evil and subsequent—as well as hard-earned—victories. Some had been more than too close for comfort. But a win was a win, she supposed. Not to mention, they were all still alive. That said something about their loyalty to each other and their determination to win.

She stared out at the stars, more visible on Skye than anywhere she had been before. "They walk around as if nothing is happening. I think I'd be curled up in the fetal position had I endured a single battle. How are they getting through each day?"

"I think you'd be better than you think. I've seen you in stressful situations, remember?"

"Maybe." Rowen sighed. "I know you said they were fighting evil, I guess… Well, I guess I thought you meant a person."

His voice cracked, rough with regret. "If I'd known Ferne was here, fighting, bleeding, and standing between our world and the darkness trying to rip through it, I never would've stayed away for as long as I did. If I hadn't been so obsessed with London and Thomas, we would've talked, and she would've told me everything."

"You're here now. That's what matters."

"I hope to hell you're right."

Rowen bit the side of her lip. "How do they stay in the manor after the monster in The Grey almost tore through dimensions to reach them?"

"Don't forget Finn's new tattoos, courtesy of something on the other side."

Her lips twisted. The Irishman had lifted the hems of his jeans to show his lower legs and the dark marks winding around them, that supposedly went all the way up to his hips. Something like that didn't happen by accident. She shivered, wondering what the tattoos meant.

"They stay because they believe it's safe," he added.

"The monster could get out at any time."

"The house is containing it. Plus, everyone there added wards to give the manor a boost."

"That's enough for now, but what if it stops working?"

Mason shot her a quick look. "Then the monster will be out in our world."

"That's a disturbing thought. Did you see Kirsi's face when they were talking about the beast?"

"Which one was Kirsi?"

Rowen tugged at the seat belt that ran over her shoulder to keep it away from her neck. "She was the only one who didn't speak. She's in her early twenties. Pretty. Light brown hair and striking pale green eyes."

"Ah. I think I remember her. Is she the one Callum hovered around?"

"Yep, that's her. Her face went white, especially when Callum spoke about being in The Grey. For a second there, I thought she might faint or vomit."

Mason pulled to a stop in front of the cottage and shut off the engine. "I saw that. She was terrified."

"Everyone who went into The Grey is scared. Some hid it better than others, but it was there if you looked for it. And I looked for it."

Mason turned his head to her. "You wanted to know about Skye and the Druids who call it home, but if it's too much, I can get you on a plane first thing in the morning."

She considered his offer to return home for a long minute. This was her chance to leave. She could argue that none of this was her fight, but it would be a lie. The Skye Druids were being targeted because of their strength. If they fell, everyone else would follow.

She met his gaze. "Thank you for the offer, but I'd like to stay."

"Rowen—"

"I want to help. I'm aware of the dangers. It isn't just London or the Edinburgh Druids. There's Edie, Parker, as well as the evil. For whatever reason, I was meant to be here, and that means I'm meant to contribute somehow."

He searched her face in the shadows of the car before dipping his head. "All right. If you change your mind, all you have to do is say the word."

"I will," she promised.

They opened their doors at the same time. Her gaze was pulled toward the stunning sky that was a cross between onyx and indigo, as if neither shade would allow the other to fully take control. She could stand out there and gaze at the moon and stars for hours.

"While this monster is something to be worried about, I'm more concerned about Elodie and Elias's sister, Edie," Mason said. "They know she's working with some other kind of evil. Regardless of whether it's connected to The Grey, she's a threat that's right here, and she can be stopped."

"I agree with that."

It was the jiggle of keys that shifted her attention. She walked to the cottage door just as Mason opened it.

"We should probably put up some wards ourselves," he said as he held the door for her.

Rowen nodded absently while walking past. Then she turned and faced him. It was time she got to the truth. "You've made a few proposals to pay for me to get home. Most people don't do that unless they have money. Then there was the mention of an estate, as well as your parents owning their own plane. And something about a title."

"Ah. Yes," he murmured with a slight frown before shutting and bolting the door. He faced her and shrugged. "I've not purposefully kept it from you. There just hasn't been a right time to say it."

"To say what, exactly?"

"My official title is Earl of Brannelly."

Her eyes widened as she gaped at him. "An earl? Like...a real earl?"

"I am," he replied with a slight hesitation.

"You're nobility." Even she heard the shock in her voice.

"I wasn't sure Americans knew about that."

"Oh, we know. Hard not to follow along with the royal family. Also, shows and books."

He swallowed. "My title doesn't change anything."

"I think many people would disagree with that statement."

"I'm still the man you saved."

She smiled, staring into those beautiful, stormy gray eyes. It was obvious by the way his brow had furrowed that it was important to him that she recognize the man, not the title or the wealth. So, she answered honestly, "I know."

"Good." His shoulders dropped as the tension eased from him. "Would you like some tea?"

"Some kind of herbal sounds good."

Mason chuckled as he headed toward the kitchen. "Ariah gave us a little of everything. I don't know which has magic and which doesn't, though."

"I hope they all do." Rowen followed a couple of steps behind him. She took one of the stools at the island as he filled the kettle. Her gaze lingered on the breadth and width of his shoulders—shoulders she had wiped down not that long ago. "This might be out of line, but can I ask about your tattoos? They're gorgeous."

He glanced at her as he turned off the tap, put the kettle on the warmer, and pushed a button. "I said earlier that you can ask me anything." He faced her then. "When I said I took precautions, I took every one I could. It wasn't just keeping things from others, or getting the storage units ready, it was the tattoos, as well."

The sound of the water heating in the electric kettle filled the kitchen. She leaned her forearms on the island, eager to hear more.

Mason touched his right shoulder. "The triskele represents the cycle of life, death, and rebirth and provides protection across timelines. I was being cautious," he replied at her raised brows. "The band of Celtic knotwork that unfurls from it deliberately flows and loops in on itself, and the ogham runes in the knotwork are used for misdirection. There is also the warding sigil at my elbow. Taken together, the tats mean that anyone trying to track me by magic will find themselves caught in a mental loop as if walking in endless circles." He paused and touched his left shoulder. "Here, I put the Celtic hound with its mouth closed mid-leap, representing silent guardianship and loyalty. The band of interlocking shields down to my elbow has knot-formed sigils within the spiral lines that appear like closed eyes if you look closely enough. They represent secrets kept. Lastly is the binding knot on this elbow, meant to contain energy—mine and that of others trying to touch mine. All of them mute my magical signature. No scrying spell will detect anything where I stand. As if I'm not there at all."

"That's very impressive. It also took some thought."

"Not really. Dad came up with most of it. He was considering it for himself, but he never got around to getting them done. I took what he had put together, added a few things, and had both arms done at the same time."

The water beeped that it was done. He took down several packets of tea for her to choose from.

She picked one and dished out some loose-leaf tea into a holder as he poured water into cups. "I'm glad you went to the effort, knowing what I know now about Thomas and London. Speaking of Thomas, can he take your title?"

"Fortunately, that is out of his reach. If something happens to me, it'll pass to Ferne's children. If she doesn't have any, there are cousins it will go to."

Rowen was happy to hear that, at least. "I thought that might be why he was so adamant about ending your life."

"I'm pretty sure that's because I stuck my nose where he doesn't think it belongs," Mason said with a grin.

"I think more people should do that to him," she mumbled. Rowen hadn't met Thomas, but she already abhorred the man. "There are many moving parts going on here at Skye. Where do we even begin to help?"

"I've been considering that. I thought I'd lend a hand looking for Edie. What are you thinking?"

She shrugged and watched her water darken slightly as the herbs brewed. "I don't know yet. I'd like to see more of the isle in daylight. Hearing about the Fairy Pools and the Fairy Glen made me want to visit and try to find where battles have taken place. I'd also like to see where the earth and air pillars are."

The corners of his eyes crinkled as he asked, "Are you perhaps a water dancer?"

"Sorry," she said with a twist of her lips. "My gift is the plants."

"That's too bad. It would be nice if they could find that final pillar."

"It has to be one of them, doesn't it?"

Mason shrugged and widened his stance before crossing his

arms over his chest. "You would think they would've had everyone tested after Sabryn's surprise at being the air pillar."

"What did Bronwyn call them? She used Gaelic, I believe."

Mason shook his head. "I'm not the one to ask about that. I don't know any Gaelic."

They fell into silence, each looking away at their tea. They had spent the last few days together, but she wasn't asleep now, and he wasn't fighting the pain of his injuries. They were two strangers learning about each other and their surroundings, who just so happened to be staying in the same cottage.

If she were watching a movie, she'd expect one of them to make a move on the other. Or maybe that was just her demented mind since she couldn't stop looking at Mason. The man was drop-dead gorgeous. And she was very aware that they were adults alone in a house.

Even as she contemplated the idea of a hook-up, Rowen shoved it aside. There were certain lines she wouldn't cross, despite how tempting Mason was. "How long are you staying on the isle?" she asked before she did something stupid.

He leaned back against the counter. "I won't return home until Thomas and everyone connected to him is gone."

"That could take years."

His lips thinned into a flat line. "It could. What about you? How long do you think you'll remain?"

She removed the tea strainer and set it aside before wrapping her hands around the hot mug until her skin couldn't handle the heat anymore. "That's a good question, and one Mom asked me multiple times. The answer is that I'm not sure. I've said I want to help, and it would be wrong to leave before things are solved. Unfortunately, I have no idea how long that could take. I have to factor in my lodgings and how to pay for things."

"You don't need to worry about that. You saved my life, remember?"

"That doesn't mean you have to pay my way. I'm not supposed to be in Scotland. I don't know what I'd need to do to find a job."

He shrugged one shoulder. "I have money. Please let me contribute to your expenses. I've no doubt you're resilient enough to find a way to earn money, and if you're adamant, then I'll relent. But before you make a decision, think about my offer."

Rowen did have a bit of money saved, but should she use it if Mason was offering? She didn't want to be a charity case. Then again, he wasn't treating her as one. "Let's see how things go."

"You mentioned wanting to see Skye. I'd like to look myself. Why don't I drive us around tomorrow?" he suggested. "I can ask Ferne to come so she can point out locations."

"Are you sure you wouldn't rather be alone with your sister?"

He took a sip of his tea. "I'm just happy that she's not looking at me with doubt anymore. I haven't won her over completely, and I think having you around will help."

"Okay, then," Rowen said as she slid off the stool. She put a little sugar in her tea before turning to Mason. "I think I'm going to call it a night."

"Of course. You still need to catch-up on the hours of sleep you lost. Goodnight," he said softly, his gray eyes watching her thoughtfully.

She almost stayed, but at the last minute decided to go to her room. "Goodnight."

Once the door had closed behind her, Rowen set down the mug and removed her clothes to get into the comfy sleep shirt she had found. She curled up on the bed and leaned against a stack of pillows and the headboard, then reached for her tea as she thought about the day.

She tried to remember everyone's names and put them with faces, along with their stories. Some, like Rhona, were easy to remember. Though there had been a mention of Rhona's husband, Balladyn. Rowen didn't remember meeting him, which meant he must not have been there. Rhona had glossed over her story about becoming the Druid leader, but Rowen couldn't help but think it was important, nonetheless. If she were there long enough, she might even learn what it was.

Her family would want to be caught up on everything daily. Perhaps she should've taken notes. It was doubtful she would remember all the details, but she got the gist. Rowen released a long sigh and let the soothing tea fill her body. It had been an exhaustive day, but she had met the Skye Druids.

While she couldn't say they were friends, they were friendly. Which was much more than what London had been. She hadn't met any Edinburgh Druids, but if they had aligned with London, then she could guess how they would be.

She looked at the time. Her exhausted brain took a moment to realize that it was only one in the afternoon at home. She could call and fill her family in, but that would be another long call, and she was physically and mentally drained. No doubt her aunts and a few cousins would be with her mom, and Rowen needed to be on top of her game to handle all the questions they would undoubtedly throw at her.

Her eyes grew too heavy to keep open. She set aside the rest of the tea and slid down onto her back under the covers. As she drifted to sleep, she heard Mason quietly moving about in the kitchen. A real-life earl. Should she be calling him *lord*? She'd have to remember to ask him that in the morning.

Sleep beckoned, and she eagerly went into its waiting arms. The deeper she sank into slumber, the more she melted into the cushy mattress.

"Hello, Rowen. We've been waiting for you."

CHAPTER TWENTY-FOUR

SKYE DRUIDS

Mason stood outside the cottage in the morning sunlight, staring at the mobile in his hand rather than the scenery. He had been debating calling Billings. Mason wanted to check in on him and see how the rest of the staff was doing, but the butler had no idea Mason was now in Scotland, and though he wished to talk to Billings, he didn't want to give anyone listening to the call any information. Which is why he still stared at the phone.

Billings knew the house and estate better than anyone. He would keep the staff safe while defending the manor and grounds. Mason didn't doubt the butler for a moment. It was his own worry that made him want to reach out. Thomas knew he was on Skye, but that wouldn't stop any London Druids from descending upon the estate in Mason's absence.

He blew out a breath and pocketed the mobile. He had thought he was doing the right thing by keeping everyone in the dark, but he might have only put them in more danger. If Billings had known, he could've prepared.

Mason's gaze swept over the landscape. Wildflowers were blooming, their bright colors drawing his eyes. A gust rushed past him so hard he swayed. The wind never seemed to stop. Above him, the sun did its best to penetrate the clouds that would certainly bring more rain soon.

The weather might be inhospitable, but the striking terrain more than made up for it. Skye would be special, even if there was no magic. As if the isle had been made specifically to bring wonderment and admiration from all who had the privilege to behold her magnificence. He was one of the few, and he could honestly say that he was forever changed by being here.

He wondered what his parents would think of their children breaking London's most supreme rule by being on the isle. Would they have banished him and Ferne if they were still alive? At one time, he had believed he knew the answer. Now, he wasn't so sure. His parents had had many secrets.

His dad had trained him and Carlyle for a reason, and it wasn't as a hobby or *just in case something ever happened*. It was as if his father had known he and Carlyle would need to know how to defend themselves against Thomas. Mason had asked his dad several times why they were put through such intense training, but his father had never divulged anything. The thought of his friend had Mason pulling out the mobile again.

Carlyle answered immediately. "I thought you might ring."

"Did you? Why?"

"Being here is making you think about the past," Carlyle answered. "Specifically, your dad."

Mason twisted his lips. "How did you know?"

"It's what happened to me."

"Did Dad ever tell you why he trained us?"

The sound of a door closing came through the phone before Carlyle said, "No. Did he share it with you?"

"No, and I asked many times."

"What I can tell you is that the obstacles he put us through got me through headquarters to Song. If he hadn't run us through that course as relentlessly as he did, she'd be dead. And I right along with her."

Mason squeezed his eyes closed for a heartbeat. "Why didn't he or Mum tell us more?"

"The same reason you kept what you were doing from everyone."

"I thought I was doing what was right."

Carlyle grunted. "So did your parents. It's done. All of it. There's no sense staying in the past."

"I know." It was good advice, but it might take Mason a while to actually do it. "I need to talk to Billings."

"I wouldn't do that if I were you."

Mason shook his head, his frustration festering. "London knows where I am."

"I can guarantee that they're at the estate already. They're simply waiting for you to call so they can threaten everyone there. And before you say you need to go back, let me state for the record that it would be a stupid idea."

"So, I'm just supposed to stay here protected while they suffer?" Mason bit out angrily.

Carlyle chuckled. "Of course not. There are a few ways we can get to the estate without London discovering."

"Then count me in. That is my staff and home, and I need to be there. If only to ensure no one is being harmed. Unless you still think I'm working with your father."

There was a beat of silence before Carlyle said, "Thomas might have supplied the sperm, but he isn't a father. I believe your and Rowen's stories, but I want to make it clear that if we do this, I'll be the one making the decisions. If I say we have to go, we go. No arguments."

Mason clenched his jaw. It had been a long time since anyone had ordered him about, and he chafed at the idea. Yet the opportunity to visit with Billings was too great to resist. "Then tell me who I need to speak with. Either I go with you, or I return home today by car."

"Stubborn wanker," Carlyle mumbled. "You need to talk to Rhona. Come back to the manor so we can discuss logistics. Is Rowen returning to America?"

"As of last night, she has decided to remain."

Carlyle made a noise at the back of his throat. "Really? I thought for sure she'd be on a plane home today."

"She's made of stronger stuff than that."

"As she keeps proving."

Mason recalled their plans the night before. "She and I wish to tour the isle today to get more accustomed to the important places. What time should we be at the manor for the trip to England?"

"I'll let you know soon."

The moment the line disconnected, Mason dialed Ferne. The call went to voicemail. Just when he'd convinced himself that she didn't want to talk to him, her name lit up his screen.

"I was getting out of the shower," Ferne said breathlessly when he answered. "Is everything all right? There isn't any trouble, is there?"

"We're good. Rowen and I want to take a look around Skye,

and I was hoping you'd join us to point out important locations. Plus, I'd like to spend some time with you."

There was a brief pause before she said, "That sounds doable. Let me finish getting ready."

"I don't think Rowen is up yet." He turned to look at the house over his shoulder, hoping he'd see her in the window as he had the day before. The sight of her framed in the glass, watching him, had made his blood race.

"That's fine. Let her sleep. I'll head to you once I'm dressed."

Mason smiled. "Sounds good. I'll see you soon."

He felt lighter than he had in weeks as he made his way to the cottage and entered through the back door. Instantly, his gaze landed on Rowen, who looked up as she set aside the tea kettle and offered him a smile. She had chosen a navy sweater that clung to her in all the right—infuriatingly distracting—places. But it was the way the deep color made her hair burn like fire in the light that struck him the hardest.

She moved about the kitchen without realizing how captivating she was, unaware of the way that rich blue made her skin glow, or how the curve of her neck above the collar called for him to stroke her skin. The sweater should've made her look cozy and safe. Instead, his thoughts turned dangerously carnal.

He had to turn his mind to something other than what it might be like to kiss her. Or slip his fingers beneath the hem of that maddening sweater and push it up and over her head to get a glimpse of her wondrous curves. Bugger it. He was in trouble.

"Did you sleep well?" he asked.

A small frown marred her brow. "I slept hard, but I had weird dreams."

It wasn't her words that alarmed him, but the concern that filled her eyes. "Weird how?"

She took a drink, looking at him over the rim of the cup. "I heard someone talking in my head."

"I confess that after the stories we heard last night, I had some pretty weird dreams of my own."

"That's true," she said softly, her gaze dropping to the floor.

Mason's worry grew the longer he watched her. She was leaving something out. "Whatever it is, you can tell me."

She blinked and looked up at him, waving off his words. "I'm sure it was just lack of sleep from before, coupled with the shock of learning everything."

He wasn't buying it, but he decided not to push. For the moment, at least. Trauma had thrown them together, but they didn't know each other. Not really. "I spoke with Ferne. She'll be here in a bit to take us on a tour if you're still up for it."

"You bet," Rowen replied with a smile. "I saw some of Skye when we drove in, but I'm awake now."

He grinned. "Meaning, you weren't before."

She rolled her eyes. "Ha. Ha. Very funny." Then she wrinkled her nose. "But I kinda wasn't."

"We're both in one piece. You won't hear me complaining about anything. Are you hungry?"

"I had some toast while you were outside. You seemed rather intent on your phone."

He sank onto a stool. "I was debating calling the estate."

"Did you?"

"Not yet. I called Carlyle instead."

She nodded, holding her mug close to her body. "It's good that you two are talking. At least, I assume you are."

"We are," he said with a grin. "He thinks London is already at the estate, waiting for me to call so they can threaten the staff."

"I could see that being a possibility. What are you going to do?"

"After we see Skye, I'm heading to the manor. Carlyle said they have ways to get me to the estate without London knowing."

She blinked, clearly startled by his words.

"The danger there is real, and I won't drag you into that," he said. "It's not a question of trust. I think we've established how much I trust you. It's about ensuring that London doesn't get near you again."

She drew in a deep breath and slowly released it. Her voice was soft and low when she asked, "Is going back wise?"

Mason shrugged, shaking his head. "I don't know, but it's what I have to do. It's my home, and those working for me are my responsibility. They shouldn't be harmed because of who they work for."

"Do you intend to come back here?"

"Absolutely."

She looked away, uncertainty furrowing her brow. "Good."

"I'm not in the habit of deciding things for others. You're free to do whatever you want—stay here, come to the manor, go shopping. That's your call. But I want that choice to be yours, not something tied to what I'm doing."

She bestowed a smile on him. "I appreciate that. I don't want to inject myself where I shouldn't be."

"If you're staying to help, then I think that means you can inject yourself as much as you want," he told her with a grin.

A quick rap on the front door ended their conversation. Mason opened it to find Ferne. She stepped inside and wrapped her arms around him, holding him tight without a word. He closed his eyes as he held her. For a while, he worried he might never see her again. Being with her made him thankful that fate had conspired to send him to Skye.

After a moment, she leaned back and looked him over before smoothing her hands over his shirt. Her voice was tight with emotion when she said, "I've missed you."

"I missed you, too, sis."

"Good," she said. "Now that that's out of the way, where's Rowen? It's time to go have some fun."

"I'm coming," Rowen called from the kitchen before hurrying to the front.

Mason closed the door behind them and locked it. He stood on the stoop for a moment, watching his sister and Rowen walk away together. Without a doubt, they were the two most important women in his life. One was bound to him by blood and family. The other, by blood not of kin but of sacrifice by the way she'd held his life in her hands and never once let go. They had survived together, leaning solely on each other.

"I'm driving," Ferne called as she headed toward her Mini Cooper.

Rowen opened the passenger door and glanced up at him. "I'll get in the back."

"You get in the front," he told her as he caught up with her.

She hesitated, looking up at him. He reached out without thinking and found his palm settling over hers. The world narrowed to the pale blue of her eyes. The color was clear, luminous, and utterly endless. He was drowning in something he couldn't name but craved all the same. There was no flirting, no enticing. Just her.

And that was more dangerous than anything.

Ferne's door shut, the soft thud breaking the moment. Mason forced his lungs to work as he drew in a deep breath and folded himself into the back seat as if nothing had happened. But as the car pulled away, he could still feel her warmth against his palm, and the echo of something unfinished humming beneath his skin.

His sister navigated the roads with ease, pointing out things as she drove. She told them the best restaurants to visit, pubs tourists didn't know about, and where all the best beaches were. He took it all in while casting glances toward Rowen. Once, he looked up and saw Ferne watching him in the rearview mirror. She raised a brow at having caught him staring at Rowen.

"I've been debating what to show you first ever since you rang this morning," Ferne said. "I thought I'd take you to the beautiful locations like the Fairy Pools first. It's a huge tourist spot for a reason, but then I thought it might be better to end there instead."

"Meaning you're going to show us something ugly?" Rowen asked with a grin. "I don't think there's anything like that on the isle."

Mason's gaze met his sister's in the mirror again. He had heard the change in her voice, the slight tremor that told him she didn't want to go, wherever she planned to take them, but she was doing it anyway. Which meant it must be important.

They turned off the paved road and traveled along a dirt lane that seemed to stretch on forever. Ferne's knuckles were white from gripping the steering wheel. The land was flat and open, devoid of trees or anything meaningful except for a mountain rising up like some mystical location.

"It's like we're the only ones alive," Rowen murmured.

Mason leaned to the side and looked between the seats out the windscreen to get a better view as Ferne slowed the car and drew it to a stop. She was deliberate as she put the vehicle in park, but she didn't turn off the engine. The tension that clung to her seeped into the air, thick and unrelenting, until the entire car was awash in it.

Unease filled him as he slowly looked around to see what might have caused his sister such distress. "What is this place?"

Ferne took a deep breath. "Do you remember when Ariah told you about a place where Killian had been hidden?"

"The house they couldn't see," Rowen said. "The same place Song was pulled into."

Ferne nodded. "That's it in front of you."

"Let me out. I want a closer look," Mason said.

Rowen got out to pull the seat forward so he could exit. He was surprised when Ferne met them at the front of her car. The engine was still running, as if she was afraid to turn it off and have it not start again.

"It's just a house, right?" Mason asked. "One that's hidden."

Ferne folded her arms over her chest. "It was Edie's first house with her husband."

Rowen lifted her gaze to the sky. "I can't see the house or the tear."

"From what Song says, we should be happy we can't," Ferne replied with a shiver.

Mason walked forward.

"Careful," his sister called. "You might not be able to see the cottage, but you can still get inside. And that isn't a place you want to be."

CHAPTER TWENTY-FIVE

SKYE DRUIDS

As if the weather had been waiting for them to finish their tour of the isle, the first fat raindrops didn't plunk onto the windshield until they were back in Ferne's Mini and headed to the manor. They had visited the striking rock pinnacle of Old Man of Storr, the mystical Quiraing, with its unusual hills and deep ravines, the lighthouse at Neist Point, Kilt Rock, the Fairy Glen, and ended the outing at the Fairy Pools.

Rowen was reluctant to leave the clear rock pools and numerous waterfalls. She could've remained and spent hours hiking, and she intended to do just that as soon as she could. Everywhere Ferne had taken them had been more beautiful and awe-inspiring than the last. Each time she thought she'd found a favorite place, Ferne showed her something new. But to end the day at the Fairy Pools was the cherry on top of a fantastic day.

Ferne started the engine, but she didn't back out of her spot. She stared out the window, seemingly as mesmerized as Rowen by the backdrop. Rowen glanced behind her to see Mason watching his sister in silence.

Finally, Ferne said, "This was the first place I came to when I arrived on Skye. I met Theo here that day."

Mason's lips curved into a gentle smile at her wistful tone. Rowen looked at the countryside and tried to imagine it being her first place to stop on the isle, then meeting the man that she would fall in love with. Almost as if magic had played a part in all of it.

The next time she looked back, Mason's stormy eyes met hers. She curled the hand he had touched earlier against her leg, his heat still lingering. Rowen looked away, unable to hold his stare—or experience the rising emotions.

Yet she felt his gaze linger on her.

Ferne inhaled quickly as she looked away from the scenery to her passengers as rain began to steadily pelt the vehicle. "Looks like we timed it just right. Shall we head to the manor now?" Her green gaze slid to Rowen. "Unless there's somewhere else you would like to see."

"I could spend a month here and still not see everything," Rowen said. "Thank you for showing us the important locations."

The leather in the back squeaked as Mason shifted in his seat. "Yes, thank you, sis. You can drop me at the manor. I'm not sure about Rowen."

"The manor for me, too," Rowen answered. There were still things for her to learn about the Skye Druids, and she might as well take the time to discover them.

"Sounds perfect." Ferne navigated the car park and got them onto the road.

Mason asked, "The Fairy Glen was pretty crowded when we

were there. I'd like to take a better look at where Sabryn and Kurt battled Edie. When is the best time for that?"

"Night is your best option. It'll be dark, but there won't be any tourists," Ferne explained. "It's just as popular as the Fairy Pools all year round."

Mason nodded and turned his head to look out the window. Rowen eyed the gray skies and rain that couldn't dampen the splendor of Skye. She wondered what it looked like in winter with snow. She imagined it would be just as magnificent, only in another way.

"You called the mountains near the pools the Black Cuillins. Is it just the one mountain range through Skye?" Rowen asked.

Ferne shrugged as her lips twisted. "Sort of. You'll hear locals call them the Cuillin Hills, Black Hills, and even Red Hills. The range is divided into the Black Cuillins and the Red Cuillins. The Blacks are known as the UK's most challenging mountain range. They have the high, dark, jagged peaks of gabbro rock. The Reds, on the other hand, are composed of gentler, rounded granite, which makes them popular with hillwalkers. Between the two ranges is Glen Sligachan," she said with a smile.

"What's Glen Sligachan?" Mason asked.

"It's a glacial valley that provides some truly arresting scenery. It's also good for hiking and climbing. There's an iconic bridge. When you see it, you'll recognize it. The River Sligachan runs through the valley, and there are small lochs throughout the glen. I highly recommend you take time to hike the scenic Sligachan Path."

Rowen added it to the list she had going of everything she wanted to do on Skye before she returned home. They passed people walking along the road in the rain, backpacks slung over their shoulders. "Everywhere we've gone today, people were going about their business as normal. As if the headlines about Skye and the Druids didn't happen."

"Have you seen what's going on in the world?" Mason asked. "Every day it's something catastrophic. A person can only handle so much. They pick and choose what they believe and freak out over."

Ferne nodded as she took a turn. "That's true. There's also those who don't believe in magic or Druids. They'd dismiss the story like they do anything to do with UAPs and aliens. Then there are those who *do* believe. They may or may not have magic. It's the ones who don't have other Druids to teach them that worry me. They'll likely head to Skye."

"Isn't that a good thing?" Rowen asked in confusion. "I thought the more Druids here to help, the better."

Ferne put on the blinker and slowed. "If they're on our side, yes. But if they're easily influenced, they can be drawn to the other side."

"Like Edie and Kerry," Rowen said.

Ferne's lips twisted. "I have no idea what was said to either of the women to convince them to join the other side. A part of me wishes to know while the other is glad I don't."

"You think you'd be swayed?" Mason asked.

Ferne shrugged. "No, not really. Both women were strong in their own way. Kerry was one of Rhona's deputies. She was well thought of in the community. And she turned on everyone in an instant. Edie was well known on the island as a whole. Her husband, Trevor, was a prominent attorney, and they had multiple rentals that brought in a lot of money. Now, Trevor is missing and feared dead, and Edie acts as if she doesn't have children. What could they have been told to sway them in such a way?"

"There has to be more to it that we aren't aware of," Mason said.

Ferne shot him a quick look over her shoulder. "Trevor was cheating on Edie."

"That might have played a big role in things," Rowen guessed. "Anything like that with Kerry?"

"Not that I'm aware," Ferne replied with a shake of her head.

They rode in silence the rest of the way to the manor, each lost in thought. It was easy to get caught up in the beauty of Skye and forget what was really going on. Though she could only take everyone's word for it since she hadn't seen anything for herself.

Once Rowen was inside the grand house again, she paused in the entryway and took a deep breath. It was like the walls were armor surrounding them. She felt safe within the long-standing building. Her gaze lifted to the second floor, where the monster had tried to break through, and Finn had gotten the tattoos. Perhaps she wasn't completely safe, but it was safer than being outside. It was a weird feeling she didn't quite understand.

"You feel it, don't you?" Bronwyn asked as she walked out of the library.

Rowen turned her head to her and raised a brow. "Feel what?"

"The house," Bronwyn clarified.

Rowen studied the walls and ceiling around her. "It does feel different."

"Because it is," Ferne replied with a smile.

Mason looked between the women. "What are you talking about?"

"You didn't tell them?" Bronwyn asked Ferne with a secretive grin.

Ferne shook her head. "I haven't had a chance. I was taking them to see the places we've had…encounters."

Bronwyn walked to a wall and placed her hand on it. "One of those battles was right outside."

Rowen watched the way Bronwyn seemed to pet the wall. She frowned at Mason, who shrugged, his eyes filled with confusion.

"This house was built on land filled with magic, by Druids who infused every piece of wood, and every nail, screw, and brick with their power, wards, and sigils." Bronwyn dropped her hand to her side as she looked at them. "The house sees and hears everything."

Mason's brow furrowed into deep grooves. "Are you saying the manor is…?"

"Is what?" Rowen asked as she struggled to fill in the blank.

Bronwyn grinned. "Aye, Mason, the manor is sentient."

Rowen looked around her again, this time with a new perspective. "How do you know?"

"It kept the monster from getting out," Ferne said. "It has also kept enemies from entering."

Bronwyn patted the wall once again. "It's done many other things to protect me." She faced them with a cheery smile. "Well, if you're wanting to see all the places we've battled, then you need to see the room on the second floor. I can show you before I take you up to our command room."

"Command room?" Rowen asked as she followed Bronwyn to the stairs.

Ferne moved beside her. "It's where we hold a lot of our meetings. There are whiteboards, tables, chairs, screens, etcetera…"

"Impressive," Mason mumbled as he brought up the rear.

Rowen looked over her shoulder at him, their gazes meeting. Her hand skimmed the railing as they climbed to the second floor. Prickles of awareness skimmed over her skin, making the hairs on her body rise. She didn't know if it was something in the house, or if it was just her imagination.

They came to the landing. Bronwyn was talking about the rooms and those available if she and Mason wanted to stay at Carwood, but Rowen barely heard her. She looked down one long corridor, and then the other, peering at door after door. She didn't realize she had halted until Mason came up beside her, his hand gently touching her back—not to push, but to offer support.

"You don't have to see the room," he whispered.

Rowen swallowed. "I know. But I need to."

"Nothing will harm you," Bronwyn said, overhearing them. "The monster tried to break through, but it didn't."

"It couldn't," Ferne stated.

Rowen noticed how Bronwyn gave her a quick look. Did that mean the monster—or whatever kind of fiend it was—*could* get through? That it just didn't happen the last time?

"Something got through if it attacked Finn," Mason pointed out.

Neither of the women replied to that as they walked to the left. Rowen's heart began to beat rapidly, her breath quickening. She stared at every door as they neared it and sighed once Bronwyn walked past. When they got to the second-to-last door on the right, Bronwyn finally halted. Nothing about the closed door announced that it led to anything but a room. And that's what made it so scary.

Rowen moved to stop Bronwyn as her hand closed around the

door handle, but the door swung open before she could. Rowen's breath caught in her chest the moment her gaze landed on the empty room. Bronwyn walked inside, followed by Ferne. Mason trailed them a few seconds later. Rowen hung back as she continued to inspect the room that was devoid of furniture. She had to physically lift her foot and place it across the threshold.

She stilled once she was in the room, waiting to see if something would suddenly come for them. But nothing happened. She turned in a slow circle, looking more closely at everything. It all looked untouched until she turned and found herself facing the opposite wall. A jagged crack split the surface, drawing the others' silent attention. Mason stepped forward, running his hand along the fissure before turning to his sister.

"Yes, that's exactly where Theo and the others brought me back through from The Grey," Ferne explained.

Rowen shivered at the thought of being taken by something unseen and dropped into another dimension, stranded and exposed. Ferne's story had left her shaken yesterday. Rowen hadn't had time to freak out about any of it before the others had moved on to the next encounter. "How are you still standing after all of that?" she asked.

Ferne smiled softly. "Theo." She then looked at Bronwyn. "And the rest of the Druids here. We're a family."

"We look out for each other," Bronwyn confirmed with a soft smile.

Mason took a step away from the wall. "You were taken once. Can it get to you again?"

"I believe it's moved past me," Ferne replied, her face lined with trepidation.

Bronwyn wrinkled her nose and sighed. "With every defeat

we've given the evil, they ramp things up. It could try to take anyone at any time."

"Its focus is on Kirsi, at the moment," Ferne said.

Rowen thought of the younger woman. "Kirsi is who brought you to Skye to begin with?"

Ferne nodded. "Because she will be the one who fights it in the end."

"Why her?" Mason asked. "Why not someone else?"

Bronwyn walked toward the door. "She was chosen. By what or who, I can't say. We all have parts to play." She turned to face them. "I was the one who first opened the portal between the dimensions and hid my unsuspecting, unconscious cousin, Beth, there. I believe that putting her there weakened this particular section between our worlds."

"You can't know that," Ferne argued.

Bronwyn's smile was fleeting. "My part also brought the Knights to Skye, giving us more allies. I wouldn't be here now if it weren't for Elias and the others."

"Don't forget the manor," Ferne pointed out.

Bronwyn touched the wall reverently. "That's right. This house has also played an important role." Her hazel eyes landed on Mason and then Rowen. "You were brought here, which means you're both a part of the story now. I can't wait to see what parts you will play."

"I think I've done my bit by saving Mason," Rowen said.

Ferne laughed softly. "While that was an important part, for which I'll never be able to properly repay you, I think there's more in store. You've decided to stay, remember?"

They quietly filed out of the room. Rowen shot Mason a quick look, but he was deep in thought. Ferne led them down the corridor to another room. Even before they approached, she heard voices from within, as multiple conversations were happening at once.

At the doorway, Rowen saw tables set up in a U pattern with chairs lining the outsides. There were several whiteboards situated around the room, a corkboard with a map of Skye and pins stuck in areas, and a large screen hanging on one wall. Everyone was already seated and waiting. Upon closer inspection, she realized that Kirsi, Theo, and Ariah were missing. Rowen took one of the empty chairs beside Mason and settled into it, unsure what was about to happen.

"Good, you're here," Rhona said when she noticed them. "Let's get right to the matter at hand. Mason is concerned about his staff at Crawford Estate and any leverage London might attempt to take. I've spoken at length with Carlyle about this. I don't take Mason's request to return there lightly. However, I won't be the one getting us there, so I thought it only fair that the one risking the most gets the final vote. Balladyn?"

Rowen looked around at the faces, but she recognized all of them. Suddenly, a man materialized beside Rhona. He stood tall and imposing, his black and silver hair falling well past his shoulders in a thick curtain. It was his silver eyes ringed in crimson that caught her attention.

That, and the fact that he was staring directly at her.

CHAPTER TWENTY-SIX

Mason had heard stories about the Fae, but he'd never imagined he would come face-to-face with one. Nothing about Balladyn would make anyone think him a mortal man. It wasn't just his unusual coloring or the commanding way his very presence filled the room. It was what Mason saw in the Fae's eyes: war, death, betrayal, love, and everything in between.

Balladyn had lived through it all and stood before them now, taciturn and vigilant. It was obvious as the Fae looked first at Rowen before his eerie gaze landed on Mason, that Balladyn was seeing if they were worthy of his help.

Mason slowly got to his feet. "I realize I ask a great deal by requesting to check on my home. While the house and lands hold sentimental value because it's where Ferne and I grew up," he said, motioning to his sister, "my main concern is the staff. The majority have been with us for over a decade."

"Billings is like a second father," Ferne chimed in.

Mason didn't look away from Balladyn. He knew the Fae were split into Light and Dark, but that was the extent of it—vague rumors, whispered warnings, and half-remembered stories from his youth. Balladyn was obviously trusted by those in the room. "I don't expect you to put your life on the line alone. I will share that burden. If I could get there on my own without notice, I wouldn't ask for help."

"What do you hope to gain by returning?" Balladyn asked. "Is it just to see that they're alive?"

The Irish accent took Mason aback. He had half-expected the Fae to sound Scottish. "I'd like that confirmation, yes, but if I had the means, then I would secure them somehow so that no harm could come to them."

That was an impossible task. The only way Mason could do that is if he took all the staff members out of England. And most had families they wouldn't leave.

"Do you think any of them is working for London?" Elias questioned.

Mason ran a hand down his face. "I don't think so, but anything is possible. The only one I'm sure of is Billings."

"He's alive," Balladyn stated. "They all are."

The proclamation came out of nowhere. Mason blinked as his gaze swung back to the Fae. "When did you go?"

"A few moments ago."

Rowen held up a hand, a look of confusion creasing her face. "I, ah, hate to interrupt, but can someone please tell me how he was able to go to England a few minutes ago when it took me twelve hours to drive?"

"Have you never heard of the Fae?" Balladyn asked.

She shrugged and cut a glance to Mason. "Sure. They're in

many Druid stories handed down through my people. But they're gone."

"They're far from gone," Rhona replied and cut a look at Balladyn.

The Fae widened his stance, his body relaxing slightly. "The Fae are everywhere. You've probably passed us on the street and never knew. We can use glamour to change our appearance."

"You're Fae?" Rowen asked, shock causing her voice to dip into barely a whisper.

Balladyn dipped his chin. "Aye. We've been here a very long time. The Fae chose Ireland as our home long ago when our world was destroyed during a civil war. The Light took the top half of the island, and the Dark the bottom."

"Which are you?" Mason asked.

At this, the Fae's lips curled slightly. "Both. And neither."

Rhona touched Balladyn's arm. "He was a general in the Light army before being betrayed. Then he became King of the Dark."

"Before being betrayed by the same bitch a second time." Balladyn's voice was even, but there was a depth of emotion in every syllable. "I'm now a Reaper, working for Death. She is the judge and jury, we're the executioners. Neither Dark nor Light. Something in between—and much more powerful."

Bloody hell. Mason stood in awe of the Fae, er, Reaper before him. He had known Balladyn had seen a lot, but he couldn't have imagined to what extent.

"Wow. Okay, then." Rowen drew in a shaky breath.

Balladyn's intense gaze slid to Rhona. Something silent passed between them before she gave a barely perceptible nod. The Fae turned back to Mason. "I'll take you, if you still wish to go."

"I'll tag along," Kurt said. "I have some cameras we can put up so Mason and Ferne can check in at any time. They're small. No one will notice them. I also have something for the phone lines."

Carlyle caught Mason's eye. "Count me in."

"The four of you, then," Rhona said as both Elias and Finn started to speak up. "We don't all need to go."

Finn let out a loud snort. "Maybe we should if London's there. They've been wanting a fight."

"That'll come soon enough," Sabryn said.

Finn nodded and slid down in his chair.

"I can keep us veiled, but we must remain silent. People won't be able to see us, but they will be able to hear," Balladyn informed.

Mason nodded once in understanding. "I'd like to talk to Billings, but I'd rather the rest of the staff not know we're there."

"Is there anything we can do to keep London off the estate and out of the house for good?" Ferne asked.

Rhona shook her head. "Nothing that won't draw attention. The best thing we can do now is have eyes and ears to keep watch on what they're doing."

"Are you ready now?" Balladyn asked.

Mason found himself looking down at Rowen. Apprehension lined her face. "I won't be long," he told her.

"They could be waiting for you," she said.

Ferne shook her head. "Balladyn will get them there and back safely."

Still, Mason hesitated as Rowen stood up. "Will you be all right?"

"Don't worry about me. I'll be fine," she said.

"She'll be with us," Ferne told him.

Mason glanced over when Carlyle called his name. He knew

Rowen could handle herself, and she would be with Ferne and the others, yet he found he didn't want to leave her.

"Go," Rowen urged. "And be careful."

He lingered for a moment longer before crossing to Carlyle and Balladyn. Kurt hurried over, a rucksack slung over one shoulder. With a nod from Balladyn, Carlyle and Kurt each placed a hand on Mason. Balladyn reached out and touched them both. Mason barely had time to register what was happening before the world blinked. His knees went weak when he found himself standing in his room. A rush of dizziness hit him hard, the floor seeming to sway beneath his feet as his mind tried to catch up to his body.

"It'll pass," Carlyle whispered beside him.

As the spinning slowed and the room settled around him, Mason realized they were alone.

Balladyn released them. "I'm going to have a look around. Don't leave this room."

Carlyle lifted a hand in acknowledgment while Kurt strode to the phone line and pulled out a laptop. Mason looked around the bedroom, exactly as he had left it. The space hadn't changed. Same walls, same furniture, same muted colors. But the shadows seemed longer, the space somehow smaller.

No, the room hadn't changed. *He* was the one who had transformed.

"Do you want to grab some clothes? I can help you pack," Carlyle offered.

Mason walked to his closet and opened it. "Good idea."

Within moments, two suitcases sat next to the bed. He eyed the door and fought the urge to go out and shout for Billings. It was wrong to hide in his own bloody house.

"Damn," Kurt mumbled.

Carlyle walked to him. "What is it?"

"Someone is already listening in."

Mason crossed his arms over his chest. "I told you they were."

"Can you remove it?" Carlyle asked.

Kurt threw him a flat look. "Of course, but I don't want to. It would alert them that I was here." His fingers flew over the keyboard. "Just give me a moment. I'm going to piggyback on them."

Mason paced the room as the seconds ticked endlessly by, and the quiet became as heavy as death. Finally, Balladyn returned.

"What did you find?" Carlyle asked before Mason could.

The Fae's lips were pinched. "I think someone from London has been here. They may still be here. I've not looked in every room."

"Can you get me to Billings? He'll know," Mason said.

Balladyn walked to the door and leaned against the wall. "I slipped a note into his pocket. He should be on his way up soon."

"Done," Kurt said. He smiled as he turned to them. "I need to set up the cameras now."

Mason glanced at the door, hoping Billings would walk in. "Where are you thinking?"

"I brought a dozen. If we can put them all up, that would be great. I don't know if we'll have time, so I'd like to start with the important areas. The doorways and anyplace you think London would be interested in."

Carlyle sank onto the corner of the mattress. "Better put one in Mason's office."

"Because Thomas sent Song to search it?" Mason asked.

Carlyle's lips twisted. "Exactly."

"There's nothing there. I made a great show of putting papers inside, but they're either blank or have nothing to do with my investigation. I did it in case someone was watching."

"Someone was," Balladyn said.

Mason's smile vanished. "So, they were."

"Are you sure you can trust Billings?" Kurt asked.

"Yes," Mason and Carlyle replied in unison.

Kurt tossed something to Mason. "Then this is for him."

Mason looked down at the mobile phone and nodded a thanks to Kurt. Balladyn held up a hand as he turned his ear toward the door. The next second, he strode to them and motioned them together. Once they each had a hand on the other, Balladyn touched them. Mason didn't feel any different. He wasn't sure what the Fae had done, but he got his answer when the door opened, and Billings slipped inside, shutting the door behind him. A frown marred the butler's face as he scanned the room.

Mason dropped his hand from Carlyle's shoulder. Billings' eyes went wide when he saw him. The happiness in the older man's dark features brought tears to Mason's.

"My lord," Billings said, his smile bright. "It's good to see you."

Mason walked to his butler and shook his hand, clapping him on the shoulder with the other. "It's good to see you, too."

The butler's expression turned worried as he looked back at the door. "You shouldn't be here. It's too dangerous."

"I had to know you were all right."

"Don't worry about me. I'm keeping things in order."

Mason looked toward the others, but he didn't see them. He cleared his throat. "I think someone on the staff is working for London."

"I've come to that same conclusion myself, my lord. Unfortunately, I don't have any names to give you."

"Names?" Mason asked. "You think there's more than one?"

Billings' thin lips flattened. "I'm afraid so."

"Has anyone been here?"

"A few visitors stopped by, wanting to see you, but none left their names. One dared to shoulder his way in."

Fury filled Mason. "Were you or anyone else hurt?"

"I handled him. And no, sir, no one was harmed."

Mason rubbed the back of his neck. "There may be more of them, Billings."

"Then it's as I suspected. You found something out about your parents' deaths."

It was on the tip of Mason's tongue to tell him everything. He had often shared things with Billings that he hadn't told his father. Yet the less Billings knew, the better. For the time being, at least. "Let's just say that London would prefer I wasn't breathing."

The butler's nostrils flared as he straightened his spine another degree. "Not if I have anything to say about it. No one will know you're here."

"I can't stay. I just needed to know you were okay, and to tell you to be careful."

"I have things firmly in hand, my lord. Don't worry about us," Billings stated confidently.

Mason gave him the mobile. "This is secure. Call me on this."

"Splendid. I'll make sure no one finds it." Then he looked Mason over with an approving nod. "Until next time, Lord Brannelly."

Mason's throat clogged with emotion as Billings left the room. He hoped it wasn't the last time he saw his friend.

CHAPTER TWENTY-SEVEN

SKYE DRUIDS

Rowen found her gaze drawn to a beam of sunlight that broke through the clouds, illuminating a section of the woods at the back of the manor. She walked closer to the window, drawn to the sunbeam like a spark chasing dry grass.

She had never been one of those girls attached at the hip to a guy, but she couldn't dismiss the fact that she felt…well, the only way to put it was adrift once Mason left. Actually, he had vanished. One moment, he was there. The next, gone. Rhona had attempted to explain how the Fae could teleport, but Rowen hadn't been paying attention. Her thoughts had been on Mason heading straight into danger.

She was no one from a small island in the Pacific Northwest. And he was a man she barely knew, who was embroiled in a tangle of malevolence that made her head throb anytime she thought about it too hard. She might be a Druid, but she didn't have the kind of magic the Skye Druids possessed. It was her curiosity that kept her on the isle, not because she actually believed she could make a difference in this war they were in.

"Want to talk about it?"

The deep, Irish accent jerked her out of her thoughts. She turned and found Finn, his fingers stuffed into the front pockets of his jeans, his head of dark waves tilted to the side as he regarded her with his deep brown eyes.

"Talk about what?" she asked.

He shrugged, his lips twisting. "You tell me. You've been thrown into the deep end of the ocean here. Most would have been sucked under by now, but you're staying afloat. Rather well, I might add."

"I'm not so sure about that."

He chuckled and glanced at the floor as he shifted his weight to one foot. "Trust me. You're doing better than most."

"How do you handle it?"

"Hmm," he replied, his brows raising as his gaze went distant for a heartbeat. "Good question. I think we're all doing the best we can. Some days are good. Some…aren't."

She rubbed a hand up and down one arm, unable to chase away the chill. "Yet you're still here."

"So are you," he said with a grin.

"I thought I could help."

He nodded slowly. "Then that means you can."

"I'm not a Skye Druid."

"Neither am I. Neither are several others here. But that doesn't matter. According to Rhona, every Druid in the world can trace their roots to the isle. This was the Druids' home once."

She pressed her lips together and debated whether to talk to him about her concerns.

"I can see you have questions. I can't promise I'll know the answers, but someone here certainly will."

She hadn't been able to talk to Mason. Maybe it would be better if she spoke to someone else about what was weighing on her. "Have you ever heard the Ancients?"

He shook his head, smiling sadly. "I wish I could say I had. Have you?"

"I've not been that lucky."

"But you know of them? You were taught about them?"

"Oh, yes. The leader of the Salish Druids in the forties heard them. I can't imagine anyone who knows they are a Druid who hasn't sought out the Ancients' guidance and wisdom."

Finn's dark eyes were sharp and penetrating as he stared. "You remember Ferne's story from the other night, right? Where the Ancients managed to speak through her and let us know their voices were being suppressed."

"Yes," she replied warily.

His brow furrowed for a heartbeat. "Have you heard something claiming to be them?"

"No." But it didn't come out as firm as she had hoped.

"Rowen, this is serious," Finn said as he took a step toward her. "Have you heard what you thought was the Ancients?"

She fought not to back up. "Of course not."

"Are you sure? Because your face says otherwise."

Rowen turned her head to the side. It had been a mistake to talk to Finn. She should've kept this to herself, or, at the very least, spoken to Mason. "It was a dream. That's all."

"What was?"

"It was nothing, okay?" she stated, her tone defensive as a

thread of anger wove through it. She didn't like the way he was staring at her as if she were a potential enemy. "Just a dream."

Finn held up his hands in a gesture of surrender, his lips twisting. "All right. If you say so. Just be sure. Because what may seem like nothing could be something. Especially here on Skye."

Rowen nodded, knowing he was right.

"Something made you ask about the Ancients. That means something about the dream didn't sit right."

She sighed, unsure what to do. Did she voice the fear that had been with her all day, feasibly giving everyone a reason to question her again? Did she stay silent and possibly give evil a foothold? Rowen studied Finn for a long minute before wrinkling her nose and shrugging. "It was when Mason and I got back to the cottage last night. I was out as soon as my head hit the pillow."

"And? What happened?" Finn pressed when she paused.

She bit her lip, teetering on whether to continue. But she had started, so she might as well tell him the last part. "I heard someone say my name, and then they said they had been waiting for me."

"Did you see anything in the dream?"

"Nothing. I just heard the voice."

"Do you dream often?"

She tucked her hair behind her ear and began to pace nervously. "I have a couple a month that I might recall parts of when I wake."

"How clear were the words?"

Very. "Clear enough."

Finn considered her for a moment. "How many voices did you hear?"

"Just one." Rowen halted and faced him. "It was a female

voice. Maybe I was just thinking about being here, and I dreamed of an ancestor."

"Could be."

But he didn't sound convinced. She struggled to remain still and not fidget. "You don't think so."

"I've learned to keep my mind open to all possibilities. Nothing is what it first appears on Skye."

"Does that include you and the others?"

The corners of his eyes crinkled as he grinned. "I like your grit. You're going to need it."

"You didn't answer my question."

"Everyone here has had to choose a side. You will, too."

She shot him a look. "I already have."

"You might think so, and I hope it never comes to it, but you just might be faced with that choice."

"It was only a dream," she stated again.

Finn's smile was quick and fleeting. "I hope so, for your sake. Just know that the Ancients have been stifled. If something comes to you claiming to be them, it's a lie."

"How do you know that what spoke through Ferne wasn't the lie? How are you all so sure that you haven't been deceived on a grand scale to fight *with* this evil against the Ancients?"

"We've all come face-to-face with Kerry and Edie and whatever turned both of them. There's no denying the malice in their deeds and words. There's nothing any of us can say or do to persuade you if our stories haven't convinced you. What I can promise you is that if I think for even a second that you're working with the evil, you'll never see me coming."

Rowen stood shaken as he walked away, whistling. He had

allowed her to glimpse the fury in his eyes, and she knew he would carry through with the threat.

Sabryn leisurely rounded the doorframe. One side of her jaw-length black hair was tucked behind an ear, showing studs running from her lobe all the way up the cartilage. She glanced at Finn's retreating back before swiveling her head to Rowen. "We're the only family he has, and he's very protective of us. Then again, we're pretty damn protective of each other."

"I take that to mean you heard our conversation." Great. Just what she wanted.

"Not intentionally. I was getting coffee. And you weren't exactly whispering."

Rowen propped herself against the windowsill. "It was just a dream."

"You keep saying that. I'm wondering if you're trying to convince us or yourself." Sabryn shrugged as she crossed her arms over her chest. "Do you mind if I ask you a question?"

"Sure. Go ahead." What could possibly make any of this worse?

"What did the words in your dream make you feel?"

A dark knot formed in Rowen's chest, and it felt like icy fingers were tracing slowly, menacingly down her spine.

"Wow," Sabryn said. "That bad, huh?"

"I didn't say anything."

"You didn't have to." Sabryn pushed away from the doorjamb. "It was all over your face. Have you heard anything since?"

Rowen shook her head. "Nothing. I was still exhausted, and I had heard stories about the horrors you all have faced. I chalked it up to that."

"Not sure if it's nothing if it bothered you enough to talk to Finn about it."

Was she right? Was there more? Rowen was out of answers—and that scared her. "I stayed because I want to help. I've chosen my side. I stand with all of you."

Sabryn glanced behind her when voices drew near. "I believe you. We're all here for you. Don't forget that." She motioned behind her. "There's food in the kitchen if you get hungry. Help yourself."

Rowen watched one more person walk away. It was just a dream. She wanted it to be nothing more than her subconscious working through everything she had absorbed since landing in London, but she was no longer sure that it wasn't something more.

Filip poked his head into the room. "There you are. I'm heading to the co-op. Do you need anything?"

"Thank you, but I'm good."

"I've got my mobile if you change your mind." He paused. "Are you okay?"

Rowen forced a smile she didn't really feel. "Just still taking it all in."

"Doona worry. Balladyn will get everyone back safely."

"Thanks."

She waited until he had left before finding the back door to the manor and heading out. It rained more on Skye than it did back home. Orcas Island had sunnier, drier summers, and from what she had learned, Skye seemed perpetually cool, wet, and cloudy. Yet that didn't keep her from walking outside. She didn't care if the sky opened up again and drenched her. She needed to clear her head, and she could only do that by being among nature.

Rowen crossed the lawn where patches of wildflowers sprouted.

She reached for her gift and heard their song, soft to her ears. The clouds had swallowed the sunbeam from earlier, casting everything in a dull, damp cloud, but she found it appealing all the same. There wasn't a glimpse of blue through the thick cloud cover that hid even the sun.

A cool gust of wind whipped around her, tangling her hair in her face so that strands caught in her lashes. She shoved it away and lengthened her strides to get to the trees. Their song rang the loudest. The forests always did.

She burst into the tree line and put her back to a trunk as she closed her eyes. The deep, resonant melody vibrated through the earth and up into her body, the trees' tranquil strength quieting her racing heart. A softer melody, gentle and calming, filled the notes between the trees, proclaiming its name. She opened her eyes and searched for the flower responsible, finding the plant low to the ground, its pale yellow color bright against the green.

"Primrose," she murmured as she squatted and ran her fingers along the petals.

Its song rose louder at her attention.

"Spring's first promise."

Other tunes reached her then. The deep timbre of different trees, along with some quieter and sharper notes of other plants. She heard each of them singing their names for her, and with each passing moment, the knot that had tightened in her abdomen loosened.

The voice had been nothing but a dream.

CHAPTER TWENTY-EIGHT

SKYE DRUIDS

Edie crept through the trees to get closer to her quarry. She had seen Rowen leave the house and smiled in anticipation. The Ancients were right once more. Then again, they always were.

She still didn't much like that they wanted this American, but she would make sure Rowen joined them. Edie grunted when she saw Rowen press her back against the tree and smile. Perhaps she should've asked the Ancients what kind of power this Druid had. Though she'd find out soon enough.

Edie crept forward silently, careful where she placed her feet. The next time she looked up, there was no sign of Rowen. Panic sent her heart knocking against her ribs. She couldn't be this close and have lost her. Edie quickened her pace as much as she dared. She didn't want to alert Rowen to her presence until she was closer, in case the woman bolted. She wanted it to appear as if she'd just happened upon Rowen.

A branch suddenly broke beneath Edie's foot, making her scowl. She froze and peered around a tree in Rowen's direction, but she couldn't see the woman. Edie glanced toward the house. There was no sign of Rowen making her way to the manor. That meant she was still in the woods.

Edie gripped the trunk of the oak in front of her and shifted to look around the other side. That's when she spotted Rowen peering through the branches of a fern in Edie's direction. Now was the perfect time to stumble out and act as if she had caught her toe on a root. All Edie needed was a few minutes with Rowen. The Ancients would do the rest. Just as Edie was stepping from behind the tree, someone called Rowen's name. They both looked toward the manor, where they saw a man.

"I'm here!" Rowen called and jogged toward him.

There was something in the man's smile that brought back a memory of Edie's first date with Trevor. When her husband was in love with her.

"You got away this time, but you won't the next," Edie murmured, watching the couple.

CHAPTER TWENTY-NINE

SKYE DRUIDS

"Well?" Rowen asked as she reached him, her blue eyes searching his face. "How did it go?"

He took the time to look her over quickly, as well. Her bright smile as she rushed to him had made his heart clench excitedly. "It went as well as it could have."

"Billings is okay, then?"

Mason nodded and turned toward the house. They fell into step, walking slowly. "I feel a huge relief in knowing he is unharmed. I was able to speak to him privately."

"You appear as if a large weight has been taken off you."

"It feels as though it has."

She briefly looked away toward the house. "I'm glad to hear it. Does that mean London wasn't there?"

"Oh, they're there. As a matter of fact, Billings suspects at least one of the staff members is working for London."

"I hope he's going to ferret out who it is."

Mason chuckled and clasped his hands behind his back. "He

will. I have no doubt. Billings will be careful. He knows the stakes."

"What about Kurt and his cameras?"

"Balladyn took him around, and they got them placed all over the house. Kurt even figured out a way to tap into London's surveillance, so we're listening to them listen to calls made to the estate."

"That's all great news. Tell me, how was teleporting?" she asked, cutting her eyes to him as she smiled.

He grimaced. "I confess, it took me by surprise. I should've asked how we were getting to London. I had a moment of concern when we stood in that circle, but there was no time to comment on it. One moment, I was on Skye, and the next, in my bedroom in England. The second time was much easier."

She laughed, the sound light and full of life. "It was a shock to see you all vanish."

They strolled for a few steps in companionable silence. The air was thick with the promise of rain, saturated with the earthy tang of damp soil. Layers of clouds covered each other, some moving fast, others taking their time to gradually skate across the sky. He had taken many strolls before, but this one hit differently. And he knew why.

Mason looked at Rowen. He had been about to ask what she had been doing when he saw her puckered forehead. Immediately, he wondered if someone had been unkind. "Was everything good here?"

"Of course," she replied, smiling as she met his gaze. "You weren't gone that long."

They reached the back door. He held it open for her and then followed her inside. There was more he wanted to say since he wasn't completely convinced, but he decided to wait until they were at the cottage. He couldn't imagine anyone being rude to her, but he also couldn't shake the notion that something had happened.

Just as they rounded the corner, he caught sight of Sabryn—or rather the concern lining Sabryn's face as she watched Rowen. It confirmed his suspicions.

"Everyone is in the library," Sabryn told them as she headed in that direction.

Mason caught up with Rowen. She glanced at him, and to his relief, he saw no sadness, fear, or anger. Maybe he had misinterpreted things. With all that was happening, he might be looking for things that weren't there.

Elias straightened from stirring the fire in the hearth. Balladyn was with Rhona, the two sharing a quiet word together near the window. The sofa was taken, as were both chairs. The rest of their group stood so everyone could see everyone else. It was apparent that they had gathered in here before, given the way everyone had their positions.

There was something comforting about the floor-to-ceiling bookshelves, the tall windows, and the fire's glow. Mason's parents had passed on their love of books to both him and Ferne. Anytime he needed to look for Ferne, he always searched their library first. He had sent the crates of books to her in an attempt to mollify her anger when he pushed her away. He knew it for the poor attempt it was. He had only just learned that Ferne intended to open a bookstore on the isle, and he couldn't wait to see it.

Rhona stepped forward, getting everyone's attention and ending the conversations. "I know we're missing some of our group, but I don't expect Kirsi for a while. Speaking of her, the funeral is tomorrow. We need to be vigilant. I don't think anything will happen, but I also don't want to let our guard down."

Balladyn stood behind Rhona, his voice calm and resolute. "I'll be there veiled. If someone means to start trouble, I aim to catch it before it escalates."

"Doona forget about the news article. The stranger draws in the stranger," Elias stated.

Theo's expression hardened. "I've already spoken with Chief Superintendent Boyd. She granted my request to have plainclothes officers at the funeral. Just in case."

"You think the press will actually show up?" Willa asked dubiously.

Scott let out a dry snort. "I wouldna put it past them."

"There has been some chatter about the funeral," Kurt pointed out as he propped his hip on the arm of the sofa and pulled his laptop out of his bag. He clicked a few keys. "A few more articles have come out. Some claiming they know Druids. Others debating our existence." He looked up from the screen. "I agree with Theo. We need to be prepared, just in case. We wouldn't want the funeral to become a spectacle."

Sabryn nodded. "Don't forget that Parker is still out there. It would be just like him to show up with more Edinburgh Druids."

"I was unaware that someone had passed. Whose funeral is it?" Rowen asked, her voice soft with respect.

Killian spoke up. "Nora, Kirsi's mother."

"Was she attacked?" Mason asked.

Ferne shook her head. "She was ill. I should've told you today. It slipped my mind. Sorry."

Mason waved away her words. He hadn't thought to pack a suit. Hopefully, he would be able to borrow something from one of the other guys. He glanced at Rowen to see her furrowed brow as she sidled closer to him, and the conversation turned to the trip. Kurt explained where he'd set up the cameras at Mason's house.

She leaned toward him and whispered, "I don't have anything to wear."

"Me, neither. We'll sort it out," he said in a low voice.

Ferne tilted forward on the chair to catch Mason's gaze when Kurt finished. "Did you talk to Billings?"

"Indeed," Mason answered. "Billings, being Billings, he had planned for such an event and kept things running. He confirmed that at least one among the staff is a spy."

Ferne's lips flattened. "I expected that, but I still don't like it. He knows to be discreet about discovering who it is, yes?"

Mason dipped his head. "Billings can't be anything but discreet."

His sister grinned and eased back in the chair.

"Um…" Kurt murmured, his brow wrinkling as he scanned his laptop screen. He looked up, disbelief and alarm etched in his features. "I tagged a few names to send an alert if there was any mention of them in the press, from the police, etcetera." He nodded toward Carlyle. "Thomas is one. Parker is another. I also did one for George."

Rhona stiffened slightly. "Let me guess. She gave an interview on the article about us."

Kurt ran a hand over his mouth and jaw. "Actually, she's dead."

The room went silent as everyone digested the information.

"George?" Rowen mouthed as she looked at him in confusion.

Mason put his mouth next to Rowen's ear and said, "Georgina Miller, who goes by George."

"Oh, right. She was in charge of the Edinburgh Druids," Rowen said.

Filip was the one who finally asked, "How did she die?"

"Does it matter?" Scott asked, his voice angry and hard.

Jasper dipped his chin to Scott. "I agree. I really doona care after what she's done to us."

"I want to know," Elias said. "After all, she made it her mission to kill me."

Kurt balanced the laptop on one hand and used his other to scroll to a page. Then he began to read. "Police have launched a murder investigation after the body of a woman was found in a commercial warehouse in the Leith area early Tuesday morning. The deceased has been identified as Georgina Miller, whose body was discovered on the premises. Emergency services responded to the call shortly after one a.m. Ms. Miller was pronounced dead at the scene. According to authorities, she suffered a fatal wound to the throat. No suspects have been identified, and no arrests have been made. A spokesperson for Police Scotland said they are treating the death as suspicious. They urge anyone who may have seen or heard anything in the area to contact them."

"She had her throat sliced?" Ferne asked in astonishment.

Rhona looked stunned at the information. "It appears so."

"She pissed off a lot of people. If she was attempting to work with Beth to get the book, then…" Bronwyn's voice trailed off as she shrugged.

Kurt closed the computer and set it aside. "It wouldn't surprise me to learn that Parker was involved somehow. I'm running facial recognition around the area, starting an hour before and leading up to George's murder, to see what I find."

"And if you find something?" Elodie asked. "Will you send it to the police?"

All eyes were on Kurt as he considered the question. "I will."

"Keep us updated," Rhona urged. Then she sighed as she looked around the room. "I know we all wish for a break where we can forget about London, Edinburgh, and the ever-present darkness that's steadily growing over the isle, but we can't. Not when we're at home settling in for the night, not at the funeral. Not anytime. The moment we let our guards down is when one of our enemies will strike."

Balladyn put a hand on her shoulder as he moved closer to her. "We've been successful against our enemies despite always being one step behind. Being on the defensive is not where I like to be, but we've not been able to play it any other way. Yet."

Rhona briefly met his gaze before covering his hand with hers. "Each time we face one of our foes, the stakes get higher. We have two of the three pillars. Things will only get more intense."

"Kirsi isna up to fighting the evil," Callum stated from his spot against the far wall. He had his arms crossed over his chest, his shoulder-length caramel locks pulled back in a queue at the base of his neck. "She wasna before, and she certainly willna be now that her mum's gone."

Ariah shot him a look filled with sadness. "None of us is ever ready for such things, but we have to do what we have to do."

Callum shook his head. "You doona understand."

"We'll talk to her," Willa promised. "She's going to need all of us more than ever."

Elodie nodded. "And we'll all keep an eye on her."

Mason noted that Callum didn't look convinced. Killian

seemed to realize that, too. "What if Kirsi doesn't fight the evil?" Mason asked.

Ferne made a sound at the back of her throat. "Then everything we've done has been for nothing."

"How is that possible?" Rowen asked. "If you find all the pillars, doesn't that count for something? What about Balladyn since he's the Warden of Skye? What about the rest of the Druids on Skye? It can't all be up to Kirsi."

Rhona pulled a face. "I'm afraid it is. What's happening now is a cycle that dates back as far as Druids have recorded history. There's no rhyme or reason for when things begin to occur, but there is always something from another dimension that wants to break through to ours. There have always been three pillars who help safeguard Skye, but there is one Druid who must face the evil head-on."

"That's messed up," Rowen mumbled.

Mason nodded in agreement. "It's too much for any one person to shoulder."

"They've done it in the past," Filip replied.

Jasper said, "That doesna mean it will happen every time. Hence why this battle plays out again and again over the millennia."

"We can no' force Kirsi to do anything," Killian said.

Ferne's face twisted with regret. "Maybe I shouldn't have told her that it was her I saw."

"It was better for us to know who it was so they could prepare." Rhona scratched her jaw. "But I, too, am worried about Kirsi. She's becoming more and more withdrawn the closer it gets to the final battle."

Mason was playing catch-up with all of this, so he might have missed something. "Is there a set date for when this battle takes place? How do we know it won't continue for months or years?"

"There isn't a date," Rhona answered. "I have no idea when any of it will happen. It's just a feeling."

Bronwyn nodded solemnly. "It grows each time we triumph over an enemy."

"As if they're becoming desperate and angrier," Finn murmured.

Mason exchanged a worried look with Rowen before asking, "Can the big battle take place before the third pillar is found?"

"I don't remember anything about that," Bronwyn said as she looked at Elodie and Rhona.

Rhona shook her head. "Me, neither."

"I have a vague recollection about the pillars coming first, but that could be wishful thinking," Elodie said

Callum shook his head in exasperation. "Fuck me. Are you saying there's a chance this battle could happen right after the funeral?"

"Or during," Balladyn added.

Callum ran a hand down his weary face and shook his head again.

"Sounds like we need to focus on the third pillar. How do we find this person?" Rowen asked. "Surely, there have to be water dancers on Skye. Can't you test them?"

Rhona flashed a tired smile. "My deputies have already put out a call for water dancers. If we're lucky, the pillar will be a Skye Druid."

"Ariah was, but I wasn't," Sabryn pointed out.

Mason wasn't surprised when Ferne suddenly jerked her head to him, her eyes wide with excitement. He knew what she was thinking, but he shook his head. It wasn't him. Whatever abilities he'd had with water ended when he was just a boy. And they hadn't returned.

CHAPTER THIRTY

London Druid Headquarters

Thomas slammed his hand down on the desk, glaring at the Druids around him who had failed him. "Give me something!" he bellowed.

David Smythe stepped forward, his dark head bowed. "Sir, we've looked everywhere for both Lord Brannelly and Ms. Thornevale."

"Everywhere?" Thomas asked in a deceptively calm voice. He caressed the top of his fifteenth-century mahogany desk as he leisurely walked around from behind it to stand before David. The man had never disappointed him before, and Thomas wasn't taking this setback well. "Is that true? You've looked *everywhere*?"

David kept his gaze on the floor, refusing to look up.

Thomas turned his attention to the others in the room. The only one who dared to meet his gaze was Ella. She had ambition for power and influence that nearly matched his. And she was willing to do *whatever* it took to get to the top. That alone brought her into his close circle of those he could count on.

Yet tonight, even she had failed him. That simply wouldn't do.

"And what do you have to say for yourself?" he asked Ella. "All you had to do was stay with Rowen, and you couldn't even manage that simple feat."

Ella lifted her chin a notch. "I couldn't exactly follow her to the toilet."

"You should've waited right outside the door. Instead, she managed to not only slip past you but leave through the front door. And head right to Mason. If I didn't know better, I'd say it had been planned."

Defiance glittered in Ella's brown eyes. "Rowen was hesitant about us from the moment she walked in. It was too much for her. We should've started with a more intimate meeting as I suggested."

"Are you telling me how to do my job?" Thomas demanded, letting anger tinge his words—the threat clear. Her lips parted as she prepared to answer, but he spoke over her. "If not for Rowen, Mason would be dead now. An impressive display of incompetence, Ella. You've all but managed to orchestrate a calamity I'd previously thought impossible."

"We located the Aston Martin at the storage units. I'll track them down," she said.

The four men knew their place, but Ella had no idea when to shut her mouth. Usually, her impudent behavior amused him.

But not tonight.

Thomas curled his hands into fists as he turned away, his fury rising at the thought of Mason on Skye. "Oh, we're past that, my dear. I'd wager that both are in the very place I was trying to keep them from."

"But..." Ella began.

The last thread of his restraint snapped. In the space of a heartbeat, seething rage ignited in his veins. He spun with a roar, magic bursting from his hands.

Ella didn't even scream. Her gasp caught in her throat as his strike hit her chest, caving it in. She stared at him with stunned, wide eyes as she raised a shaky hand. Then she crumpled, dead before she hit the floor.

Magic crackled around his fingers, alive and hungry, the air scorched with its residue. His own chest heaved from the sheer force of his fury. He didn't pull back his magic. Instead, he let it swirl in his palms, its thick essence sliding beneath his skin like a predator straining at its leash.

He stood over Ella's body and looked at the others, daring them to try their luck. "Anyone else want to speak?"

He wanted—no, he *needed*—to take another life, to expel some of the indignation roiling through him. But he had to be careful. Everyone had limits. Even him. He had let his anger get the best of him twice, and both times he had nearly lost control of London—of everything. It was a mistake he couldn't repeat. Everything was finally falling into place. All he had to do was keep it together.

But if one of the bloody fools provoked him, no one would blame him for reacting.

It seemed they were far more intelligent than the pretty Ella. He had enjoyed having her on her knees with his cock in her mouth, but there were plenty of others ready and willing to take her place. Had she not blundered so badly, he wouldn't be trying to sort through this debacle.

Bloody hell. He had been so close to being rid of Mason once and for all. The bastard had dared to dig into his parents' deaths. Thomas had thought he'd put enough things in place to prevent Mason from linking him to the accident, but he'd been wrong. So fucking wrong.

Mason had been good at hiding what he was about, but Thomas was too clever for that. He had unlimited money and people at his disposal, and he had used every one of them to get the information he needed. Now, the only thing standing between his total domination of the Druids and losing it all was Mason and the information he had obtained.

Dozens of individuals were scouring the entirety of London for the documents, as well as a couple at the Crawford Estate. Every electronic device Mason owned had been searched. Thomas even had everyone Mason had the slightest connection to investigated and their homes and offices searched, all to no avail.

And time was running out.

Thomas rolled his shoulders to relax, gradually pulling back his magic until it was contained—until he was in control again. Then, he tugged at the cuffs of his starched dress shirt and walked behind his desk. He lowered himself into the chair and rested his arms atop the wood as he regarded the men. "Options?"

"We go to Skye," David suggested.

Thomas pondered that. "Whoever goes will be banished."

"It would be worth it if we could get to him."

"That's just it. You'll never get to him." Thomas shook his head. "That option is off the table. I'm not risking one of you to go up against anyone on Skye. Yet," he added.

Jimmy, the youngest of the group at only twenty, said, "Then we take Crawford Estate."

Thomas chuckled. "Mason is very much alive, and even if he

weren't, the estate would go to Ferne. I don't care about his title, lands, or homes."

"We could hurt him that way, though," Jimmy argued.

David cut the younger man a dark look, telling him to shut his mouth. Then he glanced up at Thomas. "If Mason had the information, he would've released it by now. Especially after we tried to kill him."

"Maybe." Thomas drummed his fingers on the desk. "And maybe not. Mason is his mother's child. Alicia Crawford was too smart for her own good. She and Shane fooled me, and I wasn't about to fall for the same thing with their son."

The shrill ring of a mobile broke the heavy silence. Irritated, Thomas motioned for David to answer when the man hesitated. David pulled the phone from the inside pocket of his suit jacket and answered. A beat later, David's eyes jerked to Thomas. Another few moments passed before David pressed the mobile to his chest and said, "It's Parker Barclay. He's demanding to speak to you. He claims he has news you're going to want."

"Does he now?" Thomas debated whether to take the call. He didn't care for Parker much, even though the lad always did as ordered. There was just something about him that rubbed Thomas the wrong way. Yet the fact that he had called instead of his mother, Diana, intrigued him. Thomas motioned for David to bring the mobile. "What is it, Parker?"

"Right down to business. All right, then. How do you think the relationship is going between London and the Edinburgh Druids?" Parker asked, his enjoyment clear.

Thomas narrowed his eyes as he leaned back in his chair. What did the boy know that he didn't? Diana was there, keeping George and her Druids in line. Or she should be. He wrote a quick note on a piece of paper for David to check on Diana and handed it to him before he said, "I think George is taking far longer to get us results than I had hoped. Are you suggesting that you have a way of moving things along faster than your mother?"

Parker laughed, the squeak of a chair coming through the line. "You could say that."

There was something different in the way Parker spoke. Almost as if he believed himself in charge. Thomas watched David across the room, trying to reach Diana. He saw Thomas looking and shook his head, letting Thomas know she wasn't picking up.

"You see," Parker continued, "George is no longer running Edinburgh. I am."

Thomas let that sink in. His anger had been growing rapidly up until that point. At first, he'd believed that Parker would ruin things just as Mason had tried, but now he was second-guessing that. "What a nice surprise."

"It was certainly a surprise for George."

"How did such an…event come to pass?" Thomas inquired.

Parker chuckled, the sound dry and edged with confidence. "Fairly easily, actually. She never saw it coming."

"I didn't think you had it in you. What is it you want, Parker? You wouldn't be ringing if you didn't want something."

There was a pause before Parker said, "My due."

"Ah. I take that to mean you've outgrown your family."

"Diana is dead."

Thomas sat up in disbelief, his mind racing. No one harmed one of his Druids without repercussions. Was it one of the Edinburgh Druids? Or was it someone from Skye? "How? When? I need to know who did it."

"A few hours before George. And as for the how, it was with a knife. She, too, never saw it coming. I was honestly surprised she didn't fight back. I always expected her to fight me."

Shock shuddered through Thomas as he slowly rose to his feet, his heart pounding in his chest. "You killed her."

Parker's laugh floated through the line, the sound grating. "Believe me, it was a long time coming."

This was an unexpected and unwelcome outcome, but there was time to ponder Parker and his motives later. Right now, he needed to keep the youngest Barclay on his side. "Well, you've certainly become someone I didn't expect. What can you do outside your family's shadow?"

"For that, you'll have to wait to find out."

Thomas lowered himself into his chair once more. Parker had surprised him, but now it was time to do what he did best—take power. "Now that we have control of Edinburgh, there are a few things I need from you."

"You aren't in control of anything. *I* am."

Fury sizzled through Thomas's body, sharp as lightning. It was never good to get him angry, and Parker was teetering on a precipice as it was. Diana had known her place and had gotten things done. She had been useful. Finding her replacement wouldn't be easy. That, on top of the Mason and Rowen fiasco, only created more turmoil when there should have been none.

"Careful, son," Thomas replied coolly, violence hanging on the syllables. "You have no idea how long my reach is."

"And you have no idea what I'm capable of. Try to take Edinburgh from me, and you'll find out," Parker snapped.

Thomas clenched his jaw. He could've taken the Druids from George at any time, but he hadn't wanted to. His focus had been Skye. If Parker pushed him, he would rain hell upon the city the likes of which none had ever seen. He had been saving that for Skye, but he wasn't averse to using Edinburgh as a test site. "Did you call to gloat about your kills, or was there something more you wanted?"

"You needed to be made aware of my claim over Edinburgh. However, if you're amenable, we can come to an understanding."

Thomas seethed with outrage. Who did this bastard think he was? "What kind of *understanding*?"

There was a smile in Parker's voice when he replied, "An agreement similar to what you had with George. I need to think about my future, you understand."

Thomas looked down at his hand as he turned it over and let magic flood into his palm. Maybe Parker wasn't as shrewd as he had first thought. "And no doubt you've been cut off from your family's funds."

"Unfortunately. I do have a little put away, but I require a certain type of lifestyle. Besides, you don't want to waste any of your precious Druids going to Skye. That's what those in Edinburgh are for."

A slow smile spread over Thomas's face. "Do you have Druids on the isle now?"

"Of course. Who are you looking for?"

"I'm after an American woman and Mason Crawford."

Parker chuckled softly. "I can guarantee that Mason will be with his sister. He'll be easy to locate. Not sure about the American. Do you have a photo?"

"You'll likely find Rowen with Mason."

"Do you want me to find them or kill them?"

"Find them," Thomas answered. "Contact me the moment you do, and we'll discuss your…requirements."

Parker lowered the mobile to the table and looked across the room to the Scottish beauty lying against the headboard, tangled in the sheets, one shapely leg exposed.

"You're smiling. That's good," Mara said.

He shifted lower in the chair and placed his feet on the seat of the one opposite him. "It went fabulously. I wish I could've seen his face when I told him about Diana."

"Which part?"

"Both."

Mara's smile grew, crinkling the corners of her hazel eyes. "It's going just as you want, baby."

It was going better than that. His plan was falling into place easily. He should've done this years ago instead of remaining in Kurt's shadow.

"Do you think Thomas will give you any money?" Mara asked.

Parker shrugged. "I don't care if he does. It was just a ploy to get him to think I need it. He'll attempt to use it as leverage. He thinks he's smarter than everyone else, but he'll learn soon enough."

"Oh, I do love it when you talk like that." She threw off the covers and rose from the bed to walk naked to him. She straddled him, sliding her fingers into his hair.

He didn't move as she lowered her mouth to his, sliding her tongue along his lips before kissing him. He had always had a weakness for breasts, and Mara's were fabulous. And she knew just how to use them. He groaned as she pressed the large globes into his bare chest and began to kiss down his neck. He grasped her firm arse and pulled her tighter against him.

Suddenly, she sat up, a frown marring her pretty face. "Still nothing from your dad?"

"Not a peep." He tried to retake her lips.

Mara pulled away. "Surely, he's been told about Diana by now. And for that matter, Kurt. He should've contacted you about the funerals."

"I don't care. There's nothing he can do."

"What if he knows you're responsible for their deaths?"

Parker shrugged and wound his hand in her long, brunette locks to force her back to him. "I don't care if he does. I'm his only child now, which means I inherit *everything*."

Her eyes sparkled. "Maybe sooner rather than later."

"We have enough to handle here at the moment."

"It would only be a wee trip," she said and nipped at his lip. "There and back before anyone misses us."

Parker got to his feet and carried her to the bed. "No more talking," he said before claiming her lips.

CHAPTER THIRTY-ONE

SKYE DRUIDS

Mason was glad Rowen wanted to drive back to the cottage since his mind was too preoccupied to be behind the wheel. His thoughts moved from Billings to the estate, London, the water pillar, and everything else like a bird flitting from one tree to the next. When he blinked again, they were already parked at the rental, and Rowen was out of the car. He climbed out and trailed her to the porch.

"We need to ward the cottage," she said as she unlocked the door.

He waited for her to enter before stepping inside and closing the door. "I did that the first night while you slept. Balladyn told me that he had also added his magic."

"Really?" she asked in surprise and headed into the kitchen.

"I was surprised, as well, but Ferne said he's done that for everyone in the group, and lots of other Druids who have no idea."

"A real-life Fae," she murmured, shaking her head. Suddenly, she stopped and faced him. "Are you good? You seem kinda out of it."

"I'm fine." Mason rubbed his head, not wanting to get into it. "I know I already asked, but what about you? Are you sure nothing happened?"

Her expression fell.

He walked to the counter and grabbed a bottle of wine. "You don't have to tell me. I just want to make sure you're okay."

"I should tell you. I'd rather you hear it from me than from your sister. Besides, I get the idea that there aren't secrets in this group, which is a good thing."

Mason quietly studied her as he opened the wine and got out a glass. He raised his brow, and at her nod, he pulled a second one down, filling it before handing it to her. "Everyone has secrets. There's no getting around that, but in this situation, where so many are relying on others to watch their backs, I can understand where they don't leave room for them. If this is personal, however, then it should remain that way. I'll tell them to back off."

"Thanks, but I can do that myself." She sipped the wine. "The thing is, while it is sort of personal, it also involves this," she said, swirling her hand. "I think I need to sit."

He shadowed her to the living area. Rowen took the sofa, and he claimed one of the chairs. Her face was pinched, and she kept worrying her bottom lip with her teeth. "We don't have to do this n—"

"I thought I heard something," she blurted out.

Mason took a deep breath. "Okay. When?"

Her face creased as she briefly squeezed her eyes shut. "Last night. I asked Finn if he had ever heard the Ancients. I hadn't, you see, and I was curious if he had. I wanted to know what they sounded like."

"Had he?"

"No." She sighed and took another drink, her gaze on the floor. "When we got back last night, I went to bed because I was still so tired. I heard someone. A voice, really. I thought it was a dream. I *still* think it's a dream," she hurried to add as her eyes met his.

Mason's alarm grew as she spoke. She was desperate to make it seem like it was nothing, but it evidently was something. To what extent, though, remained to be seen. He hoped Finn hadn't scared or upset her. At least not until there was something to worry about. "What did the voice say?"

"'Rowen, we're so glad you're finally here.'"

"That's not creepy at all."

She let out a burst of laughter, some of the stiffness leaving her body. "Right? I thought so, too."

"Are you sure it was a dream?"

"I was falling asleep. You know that place where you're asleep but also kind of awake? If I had heard a voice, I think I would've woken up, but I can't be certain. It's all so hazy." She shrugged. "I made the mistake of telling Finn, and he immediately got all weird, saying that it might be the evil that had converted Kerry and Edie. He told me that if he thought I was a threat, I'd never see him coming."

Mason was instantly defensive of her. How dare Finn threaten her? Though he also understood why Finn had gone to such lengths. Everyone had been living with constant danger for weeks now. He and Rowen had not.

They were the newcomers, the ones who had yet to prove

themselves or their loyalty. If he were in Finn's shoes, he'd likely wonder if Rowen's voice had been a dream.

Rowen nervously tapped the wineglass. "Sabryn came in after Finn walked away. She had overheard, and she didn't seem to think it was a dream either. Now, I think I'm back to being someone they don't trust. Or maybe they never did." She brought the wine to her lips and drank.

He watched her mouth, his gaze moving to her throat as she swallowed. He was torn between sitting next to her, wrapping his arm around her, and telling her everything would be fine, and driving back to the manor and having a word with Finn and Sabryn. The only other person he'd ever felt so protective of was Ferne. At first, Mason thought his feelings had developed to that degree because Rowen had saved his life, but he wasn't so sure anymore.

"Say something. Please," she begged, her pale blue eyes pleading. "I promised them I had already chosen a side, but neither seemed to believe me. Do you?"

Mason remembered seeing her come out of the darkness behind the building and help him to his feet. He recalled her soothing touch as she wiped his fevered skin after sewing his wounds closed. And he would never forget watching her walk out of the trees with a bundle of flowers clutched in her hand.

He didn't know her favorite food, the names of her family members, if she had a boyfriend, or what her occupation was, but that didn't mean he didn't know her. Their dangerous journey had put them in situations where they saw each other's true depths. It was rare to get a glimpse into someone like that, and he didn't take it lightly.

"I believe you," he replied.

Her shoulders drooped as she sighed, her brow furrowing as she held back tears. "Thank you."

"I hope it was nothing more than a dream. Had you heard anything like that before?"

"No. Never."

That was a relief. "Then it could've been a dream. However, maybe consider what you will do or say if it wasn't."

Rowen dropped her head back against the sofa cushion and stared at the ceiling. "I knew you were going to say that. It's the right thing to do, but I just want to forget it."

"I'm afraid we can't do that."

"Yeah, I know. I'm just not happy about it," she grumbled. "I want it to be nothing."

Mason smiled at her reply. She didn't hold back, at least not with him. "I know."

"Maybe I'll just tell it to fuck off."

He chuckled, not realizing until that instant how much he had needed to laugh. "That might work."

Her grin faded. "But if it doesn't, I'll need something more."

"You aren't in this alone. I'll be right there with you every step of the way."

"Thanks." She took another drink. "I won't be keeping anything from you. I need you to know that. If it happens again, I'll tell you."

"Good."

She ran her fingers through her hair as she shoved it back. "What did Kerry and Edie do?"

"I'm not sure anyone ever asked them. They might have joined immediately. I mean, you heard the voice and thought it was the Ancients."

Rowen grimaced. "It was the first thing I thought of."

"What if this evil is claiming to be the Ancients? Would you, a Druid who has waited her entire life to hear them, turn away?"

Rowen's face paled as her mouth went slack. "Oh, my god. No, I wouldn't. Do you think that's what's happening?"

"It's a theory. Not sure if it's accurate or not."

"It's a terrifying thought, though."

Mason nodded solemnly. "That it is."

"But I know the Ancients are being silenced now, and I've passed that on to my mom, who is telling others. Surely, this evil—whatever it is—will know that word is getting out. It wouldn't be that stupid to approach me, claiming to be them."

"Who knows what it's thinking? If you hear them, I don't care what time it is or where you are, come find me. I'll help."

Her eyes softened as she stared at him for a long moment. "I'll do that." She cleared her throat and sipped the wine. "Now. Enough about my issue. What about yours?"

"It's nothing."

"Neither was mine," she pointed out.

Mason laughed softly. She had opened up to him. It was only fair that he do the same. Besides, this wasn't the time for secrets. "Do you remember in the library when we were talking about finding the next water dancer?"

"Hard to forget that. I also saw Ferne give you a look."

"That's because I was able to move water when I was young."

Rowen lowered her wineglass to her lap, her eyebrows shooting up on her forehead. "Are you telling me you're a water dancer? Why didn't you say anything?"

"Because I'm not. It was a fleeting ability that stopped the summer of my tenth year."

"I don't understand," she said, frowning.

He downed the last of his wine and set the glass aside. "There's nothing to understand. It wasn't as if I had any major control over water. I was able to do a few small tricks. My parents thought I might have that gift, but it turned out I didn't."

"Have you tried it since?"

"I have, and there's still nothing there."

She tucked her legs up against her as she shifted onto one hip. "That's weird, though, right? To have that ability and have it just stop?"

"My parents thought so, yes. They took me to see some Druids, who did tests. One was a water dancer, and each of them proclaimed that I was not one." He shrugged. "Ferne and the others are looking for a miracle, but it isn't me."

"It got you thinking, though," she said softly.

Mason flashed a smile. "It did. Who wouldn't want to be one of the pillars?"

"Me." Rowen chuckled. "Think of the responsibility. Not to mention, both Ariah and Sabryn had to fight to claim their pillars."

He looked toward the window, unable to stop himself from wondering if he would be able to defeat whatever came at him if he were the water pillar. His father had prepared him for battle. Mason had always thought it was for something grand, but it looked as if it had been to go up against London. He couldn't be upset about that. Both he and Carlyle had benefited from the effort his father had put into them. And Mason intended to carry it forward. When he slid his gaze back to Rowen, it was to find her watching him.

"Thinking about being in one of those battles we heard about?" she asked with a small grin.

"Hard not to."

"Tell me about it. Everyone there is a complete badass."

He laughed and pushed to his feet. "I think I'm going for a walk. I want to get better acquainted with the land surrounding us."

"Mind if I tag along?"

"Not at all."

Within minutes, they walked out the back door and headed along one of the trails he had seen. They fell into the easy silence of the evening. It was about an hour before sunset, so there was still enough light to see the wonders around them.

"Finally, blue sky," Rowen said, pointing upward.

Mason followed her finger to see a patch of cerulean through the clouds. "We shouldn't go far in case it rains."

"Getting caught in the rain is half the fun."

The smile in her voice caught him off guard. He came from a world where women did whatever they could to avoid getting caught out in any weather for fear it would mess up their hair, makeup, or clothes. Rowen was the opposite in every way. She embraced the messy and welcomed the complicated.

"This place," she murmured. Almost immediately, it was followed by a delighted gasp. "Look at the waterfall."

It was a small one that tumbled from the rocks and meandered its way to a stream down below. A herd of sheep grazed in a pasture farther afield, looking like fluffy white dots against the deep green of the grass, while a stone fence separated the land into sections. What a wild, picturesque land. He wondered what Skye had looked like for the first Druids who found the isle and walked the very steps he was taking. Had it been just as untamed? Or had it been wilder?

"Mason."

He swung his head at the sound of his name to see Rowen at the waterfall. She plopped down on a large stone and patted the seat beside her. There was no way he would pass up the opportunity to be next to her. He still missed having her beside him, his arms around her shoulders, but at the same time, he was glad to be healed.

Her grin was wide as he sat beside her, their shoulders brushing. Then she motioned with her hand.

His breath locked in his chest when he beheld the dazzling splendor before him.

"I know," Rowen said softly. "It takes my breath away, too."

CHAPTER THIRTY-TWO

SKYE DRUIDS

In that instant, that very moment, Rowen felt more connected to the earth than ever before. There was a deep, multifaceted bond with the man sitting beside her, as well. She watched him out of the corner of her eye, a look of wonder and admiration on his face. The overwhelming urge to reach for him, to place her palm against his, engulfed her. Instead, she wrapped her arms around her middle and drank in the grandeur surrounding her.

One day, she would think back to this moment, and she wanted to be able to call up every detail. The soft focus of the sun playing hide-and-seek behind the clouds. The green of the grass and the gray of the stones protruding from the ground. The earth, darkened by rainfall. The soft murmur of the wind.

And the warmth of the man beside her.

She opened her ears and heard the melodies of the plants, adding to the impressive backdrop. It was a rare moment, when she was able to glimpse the world in all its magical delight. She held her breath, wanting it to last, but understanding—and accepting—how fleeting it all was. The rain began as a sprinkle, but within moments, it was a light, steady rainfall.

Mason grumbled something about raincoats, but she wasn't listening. She jumped up and spread out her arms as she twirled in a circle, her face tilted to the sky so the drops could pelt her skin. She stopped and looked at Mason, blinking through the rain as she lowered her arms. His smile was wistful and sexy. And his gaze was locked on her.

There was no denying the pull she felt to him. The attraction was strong and only growing stronger. If she were anyone else, she wouldn't hesitate to find out what it would be like to be his lover. But now, after sharing her fears, she felt vulnerable. Needy.

She shook herself before she did something stupid. "Race you back to the house," she called before turning and running.

Rowen heard his footfalls behind her as he swiftly closed the distance between them. She had difficulty keeping her footing on the slippery grass and undulating ground. Each time she slipped, she laughed, and to her delight, she heard him laughing with her. Her gaze stayed on the ground as she navigated the stones she saw, as well as the ones she couldn't.

She felt Mason behind her and ran faster. His answering chuckle only made her smile grow. Strands of hair stuck to her face as rain slid between her collar and rolled down her back. One moment, she was upright. The next, she saw the ground coming at her, fast.

A strong, steady arm locked around her from behind and set her back on her feet, without Mason missing a stride. Somehow, his hand found its way to hers as they ran the last few feet to the front door.

Their laughter tangled with the soft rhythm of the rain as they burst inside, dripping water on the floor. Breathless and flushed, she became aware of their linked hands. Rowen turned to face him. Their gazes caught, held. And something shifted.

The laughter faded. The smiles melted. Silence stretched, thick with unspoken things. The warmth of his palm against hers burned hotter as awareness prickled across her skin. Only a couple of inches separated them. Her breath caught when his eyes darkened into a stormy mix of emotions that she was too afraid to contemplate.

Or name.

The look made her stomach feel as if a thousand butterflies had taken flight. She wanted to lean against him, to take his face in her hands. She craved to know the feel of his lips against hers, the taste of his tongue.

The strength of his arms as he held her against him.

The rain droned louder as it pounded angrily against the stone path that led to the back door and pinged against the windows. His mobile rang, the piercing tone severing whatever had held them in thrall. They released each other simultaneously. Rowen walked away, shaken by what had just happened.

With every step, she was sure her legs would give out on her. She had nearly made a fool of herself. She left a trail of water in her wake as she hurried to her room. Once inside, she leaned against her shut door and shook her head at herself. It had been a long time since she had felt so out of control around a guy.

She pushed away from the door and stripped out of her soaked clothing. Each item removed sent a chill through her, and she hurriedly reached for some sweats. As she turned away, she caught her reflection in the bathroom mirror and stared at the disheveled mess that looked back at her.

That image faded, and she was back in the doorway, her hand linked with Mason's as they stared at each other. She blinked the memory away and combed the tangles from her hair. Through the door, she heard Mason's deep voice talking, though she couldn't make out the words. Her gaze slid to her cell sitting on the table. She missed the sound of her mom's voice. It would be a good time to call and fill them in about everything, and maybe let them know she was coming home.

While she wanted to stay, she didn't like being looked at as untrustworthy, and her confession to Finn had only made things worse. Without a doubt, she knew where she stood. Did that mean she wanted to go up against whatever this thing was that the Skye Druids were battling? Absolutely not.

She wasn't a coward, but she didn't go seeking problems either. Maybe the voice had been nothing but a dream. But if it had been this evil? Well, why stick around to see if it tried to turn her against those she cared about? Because she did care about them, damn it. Watching someone nearly die had a way of doing that. Then meeting Mason's sister and seeing their bond made her care deeply about Ferne.

And the rest by extension.

Her head swiveled toward the door as her thoughts turned to Mason. She wasn't ready to leave him, which was a dangerous thing to admit. He was a noble. A man with a fucking title. She was no one from a small island in America. Even if he was attracted to her, it wouldn't work. She would leave. She *always* left. It was the one thing she'd gotten from her father.

Yet none of it mattered, because they were in the middle of a war. It might not be plastered in the headlines, but it was happening. There was no time for romance.

She set the comb down and considered returning home. There was a great deal she could teach the others about what she had witnessed and learned. No one would stop her from leaving this time.

There was a soft rap on her door. Then Mason's deep voice. "Rowen?"

"Yeah?" she asked, her head swinging toward him.

"That was Ferne. She found clothes for us to wear to the funeral. If you want to go, that is."

"I'll go." She almost added *If I'm still here*, but the words got stuck in her throat.

"Okay. Good."

It felt as if he were hesitating at the door, like he might want to say more. She could go to it. Maybe open it. But what if he was there? Would she reach for him? Kiss him? Ask him to hold her?

"Would you like some tea?" he asked.

She needed to act normal, as if she weren't in the middle of a crisis, because she didn't want him to begin asking questions that didn't have answers. "That sounds nice."

Her ears strained to hear him walking away. Several seconds ticked past before she finally heard his footsteps fade. She curled her cold toes in the rug and sighed. She was making things weird without even trying. It was a gift that seemed to come out of nowhere. The awkwardness would be next, and on the heels of that, questions. Lots of them. She hated it when that happened. If only she could pretend the moment by the door hadn't occurred.

If only she could ignore the ever-present desire.

Rowen found some socks to cover her icy feet and then made her way to the kitchen. Mason had his back to her, searching through the myriad teas. He was now in dry clothes, the long-sleeved maroon tee hugging his broad shoulders and showing off his muscular arms. He had a bag of tea in each hand as he turned around. The moment he looked up and saw her, he halted, a smile pulling at the corners of his lips.

His happiness at the sight of her made her knees go weak. She wanted to be the kind of woman who had relationships. The kind who knew how to be a long-term girlfriend.

The kind who stuck around.

"I was about to ask you which one you wanted." He held up his left hand. "Herbal meant to warm and calm? Or this white tea blend for mental clarity?" he asked with a grin. Then looked behind him to the counter. "Or one of the dozen others."

Why did he have to be so damn handsome? And kind. And generous. Men like him weren't supposed to be real.

"The white sounds nice," she replied.

He studied her for a moment, the barest frown puckering his brow, as if he'd noticed something different about her. Thankfully, he nodded and punched the button on the kettle instead of asking. She smoothed out her expression to make sure there was nothing there that would make him question her.

Mason rubbed the back of his neck. "Ferne is going to drop the clothes by in a bit. Theo is lending me one of his suits, but Ferne needs to check to see which one he's wearing first."

"Everyone has been so generous." Ugh. Things were getting awkward. Why did she always do this?

He glanced at her, nodding. "I'm not sure the same would've happened with the London Druids. They've all become close here. A family."

She heard the catch in his voice. "Ferne is your sister. Nothing will ever change that."

"I know. But I feel like an outsider. It's strange."

"That'll change the longer you stay."

The kettle beeped, and he poured water into two cups before sliding one across the island to her. "Perhaps."

"You have nothing to worry about."

"Except being able to go home, finding the spies among my staff, and bringing Thomas and the others responsible for murdering my parents to justice."

Her face creased as she grimaced. "Yeah. There's that."

"I, ah," he hedged, slowly walking around the island until they were a foot apart. A small frown furrowed his brow as he glanced away. "Perhaps I'm wide of the mark, but I thought we had a moment earlier."

She blinked, not entirely sure her mind hadn't interjected the words she longed—and dreaded—to hear. The longer she stared into his eyes, the more she realized that he had, indeed, said them. She knew how she wanted to respond, but she also knew it was the wrong thing to do.

He forced a tight grin and looked away. "Okay. No problem."

The sight of his dejection gutted her. Not because he looked hurt—though, he did—but because she knew why. He thought she didn't want him. It was in the stiff line of his shoulders, and the flicker of something lost in his eyes before he turned away. He tried to mask it, but she saw the ache.

The regret.

And it splintered something inside her.

"We had a moment." The words were out before she had time to think about them.

He froze, and his gaze swung to her. Hope flooded his eyes, shifting the turbulent gray to a softer, gentler hue. It was the absolute worst thing that could've happened, because now she couldn't turn away. She should've kept her mouth shut. She should've lied. She should've done anything but speak the truth.

But what was done was done.

There was no turning back now, no ignoring it.

No forgetting.

She closed the distance between them and brought his head down to her mouth. For a heartbeat, he didn't move, then his arms snapped around her, crushing her against him as a low, guttural groan escaped him. His mouth found hers, rough and hungry, and when his tongue swept past her lips, it wasn't a kiss.

It was a claiming.

CHAPTER THIRTY-THREE

SKYE DRUIDS

Every fantasy that had drifted through Mason's mind about Rowen had begun and ended with this moment. He had dreamed of what she would taste like, but he wasn't prepared for the light, the heat, and everything he never knew he craved. None of his dreams had ever touched the wild sweetness or the fierce passion of her lips.

He deepened the kiss, ravenous for more. Her arms held him tightly while her fingers slid into his hair. Her soft curves molded against his aching body, causing his blood to singe his veins. His smoldering desire erupted into something primal and reckless—and past the point of no return.

Mason turned them so she was pressed between him and the fridge. He slipped a hand beneath the hem of the sweatshirt and touched warm, silken skin. Every fiber of his being yearned to bare her body and lay claim to it. It was a battle of control and craving. And he was losing.

Their tongues tangled in a kiss that burned with raw hunger and unspoken need, one that left no room for breath or doubt. It was a searing, soul-deep storm of passion that would forever ruin him for another.

To his surprise, his hand trembled as he caressed her side. He had never wanted everything to go so perfectly as he did in that moment. Her skin was satin beneath his touch, tender as temptation itself. She carried the wild scent of pine and stone upon her rain-kissed skin and wind-washed hair. He dragged in a deep breath, letting the aromas seep into his very soul.

His fingers grazed the outside of her bra as need thrummed fiercely, fervently through him. Their tongues danced, the kiss frantic and blistering. His heart thumped so loudly he could hear it. Her fingers dug into his shoulders, holding him closer. His heart hammered even louder, but he didn't care. Rowen was finally in his arms, and nothing was going to yank her away.

Gradually, he realized the pounding he heard wasn't his heart at all. Mason bit back a howl of anger when he realized the sound was someone knocking. And they weren't going away. He grudgingly ended the kiss and stared down at Rowen in wonder.

The sight of her kiss-swollen lips made him want to lay her across the table and sink into her wet heat, locking their bodies together forever. She opened her eyes. Need, hypnotic and dark, filled the pale blue depths. He gently touched her face, unable to believe what they had just shared.

But that wild passion started to dim in her eyes. He watched in horror as it turned to dismay, then to regret. She purposefully removed her hands from his body. He took a step back, the pain cutting into his heart as sharp as a blade. He wanted to know what had made her pull away. He wanted to kiss her again, to take them back to that incredible place.

More knocking, even louder this time.

Mason intended to ignore them. He knew if Rowen walked away, he might never hold her in his arms again. Her mobile rang from her room before he had a chance to form words. She said nothing as she slipped away to answer it. He clenched his jaw as the pounding at the door continued. He stalked to the front and wrenched it open, ready to tear someone's head off, but he found his sister standing beneath the awning, holding two garment bags.

Ferne's smile died as she stared. "I interrupted something."

He didn't answer. He couldn't. He was too upset—at fate for giving him what he desired most and then taking it away, at Rowen for kissing him to begin with, and at himself for wanting her so desperately.

Mason pushed open the door and moved aside for Ferne to enter. She gave him a hesitant look before walking past. He shut the door and followed her into the kitchen. His gaze turned down the hall, where he heard Rowen on the phone.

"I'm sorry," Ferne whispered.

Mason blew out a breath and shook his head as he swung his gaze to her. "Forget it."

"Hard to do when you looked ready to filet me a second ago."

He grabbed the back of the chair and squeezed it, his thoughts on the unbelievable kiss followed by Rowen's regret. She had been as involved in the kiss as he had. There was no mistaking her need or the fact that she had kissed him. So, what had changed?

Mason looked down to find his sister's hand on his arm. He raised his head to stare into her worry-filled eyes, matching the frown that creased her forehead. "I'll be fine," he said.

"Bollocks. You forget how well I know you."

"I don't want to discuss it."

She nodded and held out the two garment bags. "I brought

clothes. Rowen has a couple of options. I didn't know if she would prefer a dress or pants, so she has both. You have two ties to choose from."

"Thanks," he said and accepted the bags. "I'll find a way to repay everyone."

"There's no need for that. We're going to the wake tonight. I wasn't sure if you and Rowen wished to come. It would be a good way to meet some of the locals. I don't know how long you plan to stay—"

He shrugged. "I don't know myself."

"The Druid community here is close-knit."

"Which means, getting to know them is in my best interests."

She grinned. "For both you and Rowen."

He could still hear her on the phone. "I'll see what she wants to do."

"Okay," Ferne said as she set her keys on the table.

Mason held the bag with Rowen's clothes in his right hand as he walked to her room. The door was pushed to the jamb but not closed. It opened wider as he rapped softly, and he poked his head in. She held up a finger when she saw him.

"Hang on, Mom." Then she turned the mobile away from her face and looked at him, not quite meeting his gaze.

"Ferne brought some clothes for tomorrow. The wake is tonight. I'm going to go meet some of the other local Druids. Would you like to come?" He knew the answer before the words left his mouth.

She wrinkled her nose. "I think I'm going to catch up with my mom and aunts. There's a lot to pass on. Besides, I'm still chilled from getting caught in the rain."

"Okay. I'll see you later."

Mason closed the door and remained for a heartbeat before heading to his room. After he'd hung up the suit, he quickly changed and returned to the kitchen, where Ferne waited.

"I heard," she said before he could tell her about Rowen staying.

They said nothing as they headed outside. Mason locked the door behind him and started toward his car.

"I'll take you," Ferne offered.

Mason altered his steps and climbed into the passenger side of her Mini.

"That was quite a storm we had a little while ago," Ferne said to break the silence as she drove. "We get a lot of those. It rains often, but not usually for long periods of time."

"We got caught in it." Mason had no idea why he'd told his sister that. He kept his gaze out the window, watching the passing scenery while imagining Rowen twirling in the rain.

Ferne turned down the radio until the music was barely audible. "It's okay for you to find someone to be with, you know. When was your last real relationship since Madeline?"

"Madeline and I only dated for three weeks when Mum and Dad died. I wouldn't call that a relationship."

"She did. She was devastated when you called it off."

He shrugged, uncaring. "She was a nice girl, but if I had felt something for her, I wouldn't have ended it."

"And since?"

"You make it sound as if I've been alone. I haven't. I've gone on dates."

Ferne snorted a laugh. "You've never had a problem finding women, Mas. They fall all over you."

"Because of the title. They never see *me*."

There was a long pause before Ferne said, "You never let anyone close enough to find out who you really are."

He swiveled his head to her. "The moment I suspected our parents were murdered, I knew I couldn't bring anyone else into the family until things were straightened out."

"That's an excuse, and you know it," she stated angrily, not backing down.

Mason ran a hand over his face and focused his gaze out the windscreen. "We kissed."

"Who?" Ferne asked as she glanced over at him. "You mean you and Rowen? That's good, isn't it?"

Was it good? He had thought so at first, but now he couldn't unsee the remorse. "She knew me, not the titled, wealthy lord. She had no idea who I was when she helped me."

"I knew there was something between you," Ferne said excitedly. "We've all seen it."

There was a smile in her voice, a thread of eagerness that made the pain of Rowen's guilt even worse.

"I interrupted the kiss, didn't I?" Ferne's voice was soft, apologetic.

Mason nodded as Ferne slowed and turned onto a street.

"That explains your irritation, but not the sadness."

He blew out a breath and wished he hadn't said anything to her. "Forget it."

She pulled alongside the curb and turned off the ignition before looking at him. "Can't do that. Tell me what happened."

"She regretted it."

"I don't believe that. I've seen the way she looks at you."

Mason threw open the door and got out. "Trust me. I know what I saw. Hard to mistake such a look."

"I'm so sorry, Mas," she said as she exited and faced him.

"Don't," he told her. "Just drop it. I don't want to talk about it anymore. With you or anyone else, so don't speak of it again."

Ferne's green eyes held his for a long minute. "Okay."

"Good. Now, which one is Kirsi's house?"

Ferne directed him to the home of Matt and Nora Brown. It was nestled along a narrow, winding lane just off the village green. Constructed from stone and whitewashed harling, the exterior was simple but solid. It had been weathered by years of salt air and rain. The slate roof was dark and uneven in a few places, with a thin chimney protruding. He noted the deep-set, small-paned windows that graced the older homes on Skye. He had learned they had been designed to retain heat and keep the wind out.

A wooden front door painted a muted green stood open as people came and went. The narrow entryway had worn wooden floors. The low-beamed ceiling forced him to duck so as not to bonk his head. The house was packed with people. Ferne meandered into the compact kitchen with open shelves and original, meticulously cared-for cabinetry.

Mason recognized a few faces and nodded in greeting. He found Matt Brown at a table with Kirsi standing behind him, both looking lost and grief-stricken. He and Ferne had been there once. It had been hell to climb out of. He empathized with the road they had before them, but they wouldn't be alone.

Ferne touched his arm to get his attention and began more introductions. After about ten minutes, he noticed Callum standing in a corner, his gaze never leaving Kirsi. Callum kept emotion from his face, but that didn't stop Mason from seeing the truth. A man didn't look at a woman like that if he wasn't in love with her.

Mason glanced to the side, expecting to find Rowen. He remembered then that she had remained at the cottage. It felt wrong to be there without her. As if, somehow, in the days they had been thrown together, their fates had become forever entwined.

He rubbed his thumb over the pads of his fingers, recalling the feel of her skin.

And craving more.

CHAPTER THIRTY-FOUR

SKYE DRUIDS

"Ro, honey? Did you hear me?"

Rowen peeked through the blinds and watched Mason and Ferne drive away. "I'm listening."

"You don't sound like it. What's going on?"

Too much, but she didn't want to get into it with her mom. At least, not yet. She needed to sit with it more before she discussed it with anyone.

"Ro, you're scaring me."

She grimaced at the rising tone of her mom's voice. "Nothing bad has happened, Mom. Promise. I'm still getting used to things here. There's a lot to absorb. There is so much about the Druids here that is similar to us, but twice as many things that are different. The Skye Druids retained and maintained traditions we lost."

"And a handsome guy is staying in the cottage with you," her mom pointed out.

Rowen fell back onto the bed and closed her eyes. "I never should've told you that part."

"Which? That he's handsome, or that you're living together?"

"We're not living-living together. It's a temporary arrangement. We're just roommates."

"Mm-hmm. Sure," her mother teased. "By the way, I did a little search on Mason."

Mortification burned through Rowen. "Oh, god. No. Please, don't. I can't handle your description of him." Her voice cracked with desperate hope that her mother hadn't pieced together that Mason was an actual earl.

A pause hung in the air, quiet and telling. The next time Maris spoke, her words were soft, but serious. "It's okay to let yourself love, sweetheart. Not every relationship will work out. They aren't supposed to. They're meant to teach you what you like and don't like. What you need and don't need. So that when you do meet *The One*, you'll know."

They'd had this conversation since Rowen was fourteen. She had thought things might change by now, but they hadn't. And they never would. "I know."

"Do you? Because I'm not sure you do."

"I promise, I do." It was just that she couldn't allow herself to love anyone. She had tried too many times, and the outcome was always the same. She couldn't stand seeing another angry or miserable expression on a man's face.

Even though she had seen it on Mason's face a short time ago. She shouldn't have kissed him. What had she been thinking? Now, everything between them would be strained and uncomfortable. All because she'd had to know what his kiss was like.

A loud sigh came through the line. "Not every man is going to be like your father. There are assholes, sure, and there's no getting around that, but there are good men, too."

Rowen couldn't take another, *You'll find the right guy when it's time* talk, especially not now. "I'm really tired, Mom. I'll check in tomorrow. Okay?"

"All right, honey. I love you."

"Love you, too, Mom."

Rowen ended the call and let her arm fall to the side. The phone tumbled from her hand, and for a long time, she simply lay there, staring at the ceiling as her thoughts returned again and again to the kiss. That unforgettable, soul-stirring, toe-curling, go-weak-in-the-knees kiss.

Tentatively, she touched her lips, remembering the way his tongue had teased them apart before mapping the contours of her mouth as if he were memorizing it. She had been lost at the first meeting of their lips.

And every lingering press of his mouth had unraveled her further, deliberate and devastating in its tenderness.

She had felt his longing. It was the same need that burned through her. It had been in his gaze even before their lips touched. Then in his kiss, and his touch afterward. The world had melted away, leaving just the two of them—and a passion so intense that it had scorched everything around them.

Her body ached to be cradled in his arms once more, to feel the hard length of his body pressed against hers, his thick arousal between them. To lose herself in the heat of his kiss, the sweep of his hands. She groaned, recalling how he'd touched her as if she were both precious and necessary. Like the world itself might stop spinning if he let go.

Maybe she had always known he would affect her so, but she

hadn't been strong enough to withstand the pull. That kiss lived in her psyche now—too deep to dislodge, and too sweet to deny.

Too intoxicating to escape.

After him, every other kiss would taste like ash. Would be lacking and uninspiring. She had been ready to give him her body, to lay herself bare and allow him to have his way with her for however long he wished.

If only she could've stayed in that sweet bliss.

If only Ferne hadn't interrupted them.

If only she could forget the past.

If only she were different.

If only…

Rowen sat up and found her shoes. She needed a good walk to clear her head. The longer she let herself dwell on the kiss and her actions afterward, the harder it would be to stay in the cottage with him. And she wanted to stay. She wasn't ready to say goodbye to Skye. Or Mason.

She walked through the kitchen, her gaze immediately going to the fridge, where she had been sandwiched between his body. She hastily looked away and hurried out the back door, no destination in mind. Twilight was coming fast. Perhaps that's why she fell back onto the trail they had walked earlier. She didn't go to the rock like before, though. Instead, she headed toward the fence, since the sheep were grazing nearby. The animals barely paid her any mind. She whistled and clicked to them, but they continued munching on the grass, ignoring her.

Her lips parted, ready to ask Mason if he had sheep, when she remembered that he wasn't there. They had spent so much time in each other's company that she automatically assumed he was with her. He had wanted her to go with him and Ferne to the wake.

He'd tried to hide his disappointment when she said no, but she had seen it anyway.

It hadn't been as bad as watching his joy melt into a carefully placed mask of indifference, though. All because she had been appalled that she had given in to the temptation to know his kiss. Because she didn't want to hurt him. She liked him. Too much, it seemed.

Maybe she should've sucked it up and gone with him. She bit her lip, wondering if she should get directions and meet him there.

"Hello?"

Rowen startled at the sound of the voice and turned to see a woman making her way over from the other side of the fence. Rowen lifted her hand in greeting. "Hi."

"Are you lost?" the woman asked, concern coloring her blue eyes.

"No, no. Just taking a bit of a walk."

The woman stopped a few feet away and leaned against some rocks. "American, huh? Where from?"

"The Pacific Northwest. Near Washington."

"Skye gets visitors from all over the world. I'm always curious where people hail from."

Rowen glanced around. "With a place like this, it's no wonder. Do you live here?"

"Born and raised."

"You're very lucky. I've only been here a few days, and I have to admit, it's going to be tough to leave."

The woman laughed as the wind ruffled her short, blond hair. "Every place has its pros and cons. Skye is no different."

The more Rowen stared at her, the more she looked familiar. If they had met, surely the woman would've reminded her of that. A niggle of worry began in the back of her mind. She held out her hand. "I'm Rowen, by the way."

The stranger smiled, her gaze never wavering as she grasped Rowen's hand and said, "It's nice to meet you. I'm Edie."

The instant the name hit her ears, Rowen's chest tightened, and fear surged. Icy dread pooled in her gut. Her movements were jerky as she dropped her hand to her side. No wonder the woman had looked familiar. She could see the family resemblance between Elias, Elodie, and her. "That's an unusual name."

"Let's dispense with this, shall we?" Edie suggested with an easy smile. "You know who I am."

Rowen nodded warily. "I do. Why are you here?" Edie hadn't come upon her by accident. Now, more than ever, Rowen wished she had gone with Mason.

"To talk to you. You've not been alone. It has made it difficult for us to have a wee chat."

"We're nice people. You could've come to the door."

Edie chuckled wryly and propped a hip against the rocks. "We both know how that would've gone. Mason isn't going to allow anyone near you that he doesn't deem…oh, what's the word?" she mumbled to herself. Then she smiled like a cat toying with its prey. "Appropriate."

"First, I can take care of myself. Second, do you believe yourself *appropriate*?"

"I imagine if you ask any general in any army, they would tell you they were in the right, and those they fought against were on the wrong side."

Rowen's brows rose. "Comparing yourself to a general? Thinking mighty high of yourself, aren't you?"

Edie's smile was slow, dangerous. Predatory. "You were brought to Skye for a purpose, Rowen."

That was the second time she'd heard that, but coming from Edie, it felt tainted, oily. Like something rotten slithering over her skin. "I wasn't brought here."

"Sure you were. But if it helps you to reconcile what's going to happen, then believe what you want."

Rowen bristled, her nerves frayed to the point of anger. She swallowed her response at the last second. It was better to learn what Edie wanted.

"The one thing we can agree on is that a war is happening on this isle. You've been chosen by the Ancients to join us," Edie said, her voice serene, as if they were talking about the weather.

"The Ancients have been silenced."

Edie laughed softly as she glanced at the ground. Then she took a deep breath, smiling as she shook her head. "They've not been silenced, dear Rowen. They are the ones leading this movement. They can no longer stand by and watch the power and might of the Druids fall away. Something must be done, and they're guaranteeing that a change happens."

Dread spread into Rowen's body. Edie sounded so certain, as if the fall of Skye was inevitable. "How are these supposed Ancients going to do that?"

"Druids are losing their magic. The more we mate with those who don't have any, the more our blood gets diluted. Soon, there won't be any of us left. The Ancients are weeding out the weak and selecting those they deem worthy to lead the next generation into a new day. *You* are one of those chosen."

Rowen was going to be sick. Her hands were clammy, her mouth was dry, and her heart was beating so hard and fast that she wondered if it might burst from her chest at any second. She desperately wanted to take a step back and put some distance between them, but she refused to show any weakness. "Chosen, huh?"

"Don't be so dismissive. It's a great honor."

"The same kind given to Kerry? I heard how she was killed. Or should I say obliterated?"

Edie shrugged a slim shoulder. "No one wants their secrets leaked to the enemy. Think about what I've told you. The Ancients are willing to give you a little time to consider their offer, but don't take too long."

"And if I refuse their proposition?"

Edie twisted her lips as she turned to walk away. "The Ancients have already spoken to you once. Listen for them. They speak to their chosen ones in a single voice."

Rowen stood, her knees weak, eyes fixed on Edie's retreating form until she disappeared over a hill. Only then did she release the breath she had been holding. She placed a trembling hand on her stomach and whirled around to hurry back to the cottage, looking over her shoulder every few steps to make sure Edie didn't return or follow. The minute she was inside, she bolted the door and warded it.

Her hands were still shaking when she pulled out her phone to call Mason. Her finger hovered over his name in her contacts. Just before she pressed *call*, she lowered the phone. Edie had been watching her. She could've come into the house, but she had waited to approach until Rowen was outside. Edie could've tried to take her, but again, she hadn't. She had simply talked. This time.

Rhona's group believed someone was silencing the Ancients. Ferne had been adamant that it had been the Ancients who'd spoken through her. In what little Rowen knew about the Ancients, she'd heard they all spoke at once, so it sounded like thousands of voices. Edie was just as positive that it was the Ancients going through her, and that they had coalesced into one voice.

Rowen had believed the stories she'd heard from Ferne and the others because they had all experienced them. But she had to admit that Edie's version had credibility, too. Rowen knew for a fact that Druids were losing their powers since it was happening on Orcas.

Could the great evil that Mason was willing to fight actually be the Ancients? Could that be what was trying to get through the dimensions? Had the Ancients reached out for Finn and branded him? More importantly, could they really have chosen *her*?

Knowing who to believe had been simple until she'd talked to Edie.

She didn't know how long the Ancients would give her before they demanded an answer, but if she was to survive, she needed a plan.

CHAPTER THIRTY-FIVE

SKYE DRUIDS

Edie concealed her vehicle once more and started the long walk to the cottage. She lifted her face to the cool, damp wind, quickening her steps as she hurried across the open land, ready to be within the concealed building once more.

It wasn't that long ago that she had been consumed with the knowledge of her husband's affair. Her rage had been indescribable, her suffering unbearable. His betrayal had left a wound no blade ever could. It had hollowed her out in ways she hadn't known were possible.

And just when she thought she might crack under the weight of his disloyalty, the Ancients had thrown her a lifeline. It had come by way of Kerry, and Edie hadn't been sure about any of it at first. But she had learned quickly enough. Once she let go of all the pain and heartache, all the insults and despair, she turned her fury into something terrifying and powerful. She had a purpose now, a drive she'd never had before. All because the Ancients had seen something in her.

Edie stepped into the cottage and closed the door as the magic hiding the structure closed around her. A sigh escaped her as she leaned back against the wood. Gingerly, she touched the wound on her left side.

Sabryn had gotten off a lucky strike. A little more to the right, and Edie wouldn't be standing here now. The injury was nearly healed. Just a little longer inside the cottage, and she would be fully back to normal. She pushed away from the door and started up the stairs.

"Edie."

She paused at the sound of her name in her head. No matter how many times the Ancients spoke with her, it always gave her chills of excitement. "Aye?"

"You did well with Rowen."

"She didn't seem interested. Granted, she didn't run away or attack, but I need another go to convince her."

"Leave her to us."

Edie slowly began climbing the steps again. "She has a strong connection to Mason. I saw it myself."

"We're aware."

"There are also Edinburgh Druids on the isle."

"Do not concern yourself with them. They're serving another purpose. You have the names of those who need to be dispatched."

Edie wished she had more details about the plan at times, but she knew why the Ancients kept them from her. They had told Kerry many things before she was captured. "I won't let you down. Nor will I betray you. I believe in this cause."

"We saw the fire within you long before you felt it. The inferno rages within you now. Druids have forgotten what that was like."

"Not for much longer. I'm ready to restore our kind to the

power we once commanded." She headed toward her room and sank onto the mattress.

"Soon. Very soon. You need to let the cottage finish your healing. We need you at your best the next time you face them."

Edie rolled over and stared up at the ceiling. "Sabryn got lucky. That won't happen again."

"It'd better not. And we don't need to warn you about what will happen if you're captured."

She might not have seen what the Ancients did to Kerry, but she had heard about it. "I'll kill myself before they have a chance to take me."

Edinburgh

"I don't like this," Madeline grumbled for the second time as they walked toward the warehouse beneath gloomy skies. "The wanker should be coming to you, bowing at your feet and swearing his loyalty, not sending for you."

Beth grinned at her bodyguard's back. She didn't really need anyone protecting her, but Madeline refused to listen. "Look around, my friend. We're not in medieval Scotland, I'm not a queen, and I don't have a throne."

"Not yet." Madeline glanced back and winked.

Beth adjusted the strap of the tote on her shoulder as they crossed the street. Her arm lay atop the open purse, one finger dipped inside to rest against the worn leather of the thick, ancient book within. It was the price the tome demanded.

Well, one of them, anyway.

Madeline halted at the door of the warehouse and turned to Beth. "He sliced George's throat."

"I read the article, too, remember? George wouldn't have lasted much longer in this war. You know that."

"I do, but a blade? We're Druids."

"If George wasn't prepared for an attack, then she deserved what she got. Besides, Parker did us a favor."

Madeline's lips twisted. "He may not be as easy to control as George."

"Oh, I doubt he will." Beth felt the book pulse beneath her finger. It desired to be opened, so that the words within could be consumed. The book never stopped tempting her to crack open its cover and read. She used to yield to its call, but she had begun to ignore its enticement for as long as possible. "Parker should've masked how he executed George to make it look like magic was used. Instead, he's allowed us to know his secret. Which means, we'll be prepared for such an attack."

"I almost hope he's stupid enough to try something today," Madeline murmured angrily and opened the door. She stepped in first and looked around before moving aside.

Beth crossed the threshold and was enveloped by the shadowy light of the warehouse as the door closed behind her. No sound came from Madeline's black combat boots while the metallic tick of Beth's heels reverberated against the concrete, each footfall announcing her presence with ruthless certainty.

Much like the book.

While Madeline blended into the shadows in her solid black attire, Beth stood out in her cream blouse and matching trousers. She wanted all eyes on her. Gone were the days of jeans, tees, and trainers. That time seemed a lifetime ago instead of mere months. She was even growing out her short hair. The ends now reached her chin. And the face she saw in the mirror no longer looked like her.

She was different, *had been* different from the instant she opened the book. Even before she'd read the first line. Everyone felt the tome's power, but no one ever spoke about the consequences. And there was a reason for that. Because no one lived long enough. It was something she'd discovered shortly after using the book.

Some part of her blamed her cousin for all of this. After all, it had been Bronwyn who'd started her on this journey. Soon enough, Beth would face her again.

"Eleven o'clock," Madeline whispered. "Three o'clock."

Beth cut her eyes in both directions and spotted the Druids watching them. There were others, too, all peering out for a glimpse of the visitors. It was unclear yet how they felt about a Brit taking over their faction. Though she was quite certain she'd discover the answer soon enough.

Light from the offices looming before them was blinding against the murky depths of the empty warehouse. A man rose from a chair and leaned against the doorway, his hands in the pockets of his custom-made suit pants. Beth felt Parker's gaze sizing her up, much as she did to him.

If she didn't know who he was, she'd think him attractive with his athletic, six-foot frame, thick, perfectly combed, caramel-colored hair, bright blue eyes, and charming smile. She might even be lured by his posh playboy attitude, but not for long. She preferred her men darker, edgier.

Rougher.

Beth halted before him, unfazed by his looks or the affluence he wore like someone who had been born into it.

"Delighted you could make it," Parker said, each word dripping in refined British charm.

"That was a bold move."

His grin widened as he gave her an appreciative look up and down. "Fortune favors the bold, does it not?"

Madeline stiffened beside her the same instant Beth saw a figure out of the corner of her eye. The buxom brunette's hazel eyes glittered with rancor as she glowered at Beth.

"Please," Parker said as he turned to the side and held out his arm to them. "Come inside and have a seat. I'm eager for us to become friends."

Beth had never cared for George. They'd had an uneasy alliance that threatened to be dissolved often. George had coveted power, demanded it. It had gotten her far, but it never would have taken her as far as she had dreamed. George was always going to die, but Beth had thought she would be the one to snuff out her life. Still, it was strange to see George's uncluttered, austere industrial office transformed into something that could almost be deemed warm and inviting.

The concrete was now obscured by an enormous, red Oriental rug. Sitting atop it against the wall to the left was a tufted leather sofa with rolled arms. Two matching tufted chairs sat on either end, facing each other, while a five-foot-square chest stood in the middle, acting as a coffee table. To the right, where George's beat-up, hundred-year-old metal desk had once rested, was a desk with modern legs that held up a top plucked from another century.

Behind the desk were bookshelves filled with art and various pictures of Parker with famous and influential individuals.

"Would you care for something to drink?" Parker asked. "Tea? Or perhaps something stronger?"

Beth bestowed a smile on him as she headed to the sofa. "Whatever you would like is fine."

She sank onto a cushion and watched him pour two glasses of whisky from a nearby bar cart. Madeline remained near the door while the brunette crept closer to Parker, but the two women continued staring at each other. Beth dimly heard Parker talking about converting the office to his liking, but she wasn't listening. She was studying the brunette. Perhaps it hadn't been Parker who'd killed George, but this woman.

"Here you go," Parker said and set her glass on the coffee table.

She blinked and slid her gaze to him as he took the other end of the couch and sat sideways, one arm thrown over the back of the sofa and his ankle crossed over his knee. He was a man who had been given everything from the day he was born, someone used to getting whatever he wanted. There were so many like him wandering the world. If she asked the book, it would tell her exactly how to kill Parker to deliver the most pain.

The tome pulsed once more, eager to give her what she wanted. How many more times could she open it before it consumed every ounce of her soul? Ten? Five? One? It was hard to say. Plying that kind of command created such a buzz. But it was an addictive kind of high. Too much power was within the pages, too many spells. Too many souls had been claimed by it.

The history of the Druids was all there, written over the generations. There were secrets long forgotten, and abilities waiting to be seized.

"Do you like what I've done with the place?" Parker asked, his blue eyes briefly slanting toward the tote resting on the cushion beside her, the straps still on her shoulder.

"You seem to have moved in quickly."

"There was a bit of cleanup once the authorities cleared out." He flashed a grin. "It's all about who you know."

"Is this when you tell me exactly who it is you know?" she asked coolly.

He chuckled and took a sip of the liquor. "You seem like a smart woman, Ms. Stewart. I believe you can figure that out for yourself."

"Why did you ask me here then?"

He studied her for a long, quiet moment before inhaling quickly and sitting up, leaning his forearms on his knees. "I want to buy the book. Now, don't attempt to tell me that you don't know what I'm talking about, or that you don't have it. Every Edinburgh Druid I've spoken with has told me they've seen you with it."

"I'm not denying anything."

"Good." He smiled, self-assured and expecting to get what he wanted. "I would really hate for our relationship to start off… difficult."

The book sent out an intense pulse that vibrated through her finger and into her hand, running up her arm to mix with her outrage and need for violence. It was a heady, dangerous combination. Her fingers curled around the spine as she struggled against the desire to whip out the tome and show Parker just how *difficult* things could be. She could picture him writhing on the floor, his screams echoing around him. It would feel so good to put him in his place.

Slowly, she loosened her fingers and drew in a breath. It would likely end exactly as she'd pictured, but she would control that urge.

For now.

Madeline moved closer, taking Parker's words as well as the book had. He glanced at Madeline with cold eyes and smiled as if daring her to try something. He honestly believed he had them cornered and at a disadvantage. It was almost comical. Few had witnessed what the book could do. Beth had never used it in front of George, so none of the Druids would know the extent of its dominance or authority. She doubted Parker even knew what it could do. He had likely heard about the book from the brunette and decided he needed it.

"How much do you want for it? A hundred thousand? Two hundred?" he offered.

Beth reached for the drink and tossed it back, letting the warmth of the whisky burn down her throat to her stomach. She set the tumbler down and slid her gaze to him. "It isn't for sale."

"Everyone has their price. Five hundred thousand pounds."

Beth rose to her feet. "I've given you my answer. We're finished here."

She turned to leave and felt something pull at her tote. There was a commotion behind her, and she shifted to see Parker flat on his back with his suit scrunched up and eyes wide with disbelief. The brunette was crouched beside him as she stared up at Madeline, half in fear, and half to keep him down.

"How the fuck did you just do that?" Parker demanded.

Beth raised a brow as she looked at Madeline.

Her bodyguard shook her head. "It wasn't me. He tried to take your bag."

Beth looked down at the tote to the book inside. It had been stolen many times. She had been the one to steal it last, but it had never fought back as it had just now. She stroked the leather with her finger, feeling the connection between them. It seemed it now claimed her just as she had once claimed it.

She shot Parker one last look before walking away.

CHAPTER THIRTY-SIX

SKYE DRUIDS

Rowen stretched with a silent groan, absently scratching the side of her nose. She shifted to roll over, only to be met with the firm cushions of the sofa—and the unwelcome reminder that she wasn't in bed. Because she had been waiting for Mason to get back.

She cracked open her eyes and frowned, bleary-eyed, at the blanket, then at the dark room. Mason must have covered her and turned out the lights. The gesture was sweet, but she wished he had woken her.

The house was still, the hush of silence like that of someone holding their breath. Her entire evening had been spent in a cycle of worry, planning, and thinking. She checked her phone for the time and saw that it was after two. Only a few more hours until morning. She had waited this long. Another little bit wouldn't hurt.

She rose to her feet, the familiar weight of dread settling on her like lead. She'd spent the night checking the time every few minutes, anxious for Mason to return so she could tell him everything. When she found the keys to his car, she had gotten inside it twice to go find him, only to change her mind at the last minute. She wanted to talk to him first, and if she arrived at the wake looking frazzled and scared, everyone would know.

Rowen headed to the kitchen for some water, but she found herself walking down the hall instead. No light shone under his door, and no sounds came from within. Yet she remained in the corridor, unable to move as the memory of their sensual, carnal kiss returned, slamming into her with the force of a hurricane.

She had been anticipating his return all night, eager to see him and share what Edie had said. It was only in that instant that she understood she'd waited for him for something else entirely. Rowen put her palm on the wall as desire, slick and scorching, swelled and spread. She pressed her other hand to her stomach in an effort to stanch the throbbing of her center, but there was no stopping what Mason had ignited.

There was no way they could remain in the same house together now. She would have to leave. Bronwyn would let her stay at the manor. Or maybe it was time for her to return home and put everything out of her mind: Mason, London, Skye, and that earth-shattering kiss.

That was the problem, though. She would never be able to forget it. How could she erase such a kiss? Even now, the memory of his lips against hers haunted her. Tender, consuming. Like she was something to be cherished, then devoured.

Claimed.

She could still taste him—warm, heady, and addictive. It was a kiss that had undone her from the inside out. Her eyes closed as she swayed, wishing his deliciously hard body was there to hold on to, that she could sink her fingers into his hair.

The worst thing she could have done was kiss him. But there was no turning back the clock now. She would have to live with the heat, the ache. The longing.

Her eyes opened, and before she knew it, she stood at his door. Her hand was on the handle as she pressed her ear against the door to listen. Her blood roared, making it impossible for her to hear anything. She shouldn't even be contemplating going inside. She was playing with fire. But despite knowing she would get burned, she couldn't turn away.

As if someone had taken control of her body, her hand twisted, opening the door. It swung open soundlessly, and she stepped inside, only to halt when she found him lying on his back, his head turned away from her, and the covers bunched at his hips, revealing his spectacular, bare chest. One arm was bent, his hand near his face, while the other lay on his stomach. Even asleep, the man stole her breath.

A million wants roared through her in that instant, and none of them were within reach. Not really. Not if she wanted to be able to look at herself in the mirror again. Mason was a temptation the likes of which she had never encountered before. Their attraction was white-hot, which only meant it would fizzle out quicker. It was better to save them both a lot of misery and stop things before they went any further. It was the smart thing to do.

Her gaze lingered on him for a moment longer, imagining all that could be if she were a different person. The nights of passion, the joy of being with him, of starting a life…of growing old together.

The longer she looked and fantasized, the harder it was to bear. For the first time, she saw all the things she had always wanted within reach, yet still miles away. She turned around and drew the door closed behind her.

"Rowen."

The sound of her name on his lips, low and raspy with sleep, undid her. She should keep going, but she couldn't shake the deep timbre of his voice. Slowly, she turned to face him and saw that he had risen up on an elbow, his brow furrowed in worry.

"What is it?"

She shook her head. "Nothing. Go back to sleep."

"It's something. I can tell."

Oh, it was something all right. An unwavering, unquenchable firestorm of yearning. For him. *All* for him. It felt as if she might go up in flames at any second if he didn't touch her, if she didn't bridge the space between them and mold her body to his. It felt as if their souls belonged together. As if he were someone she had been searching for from the moment she came into this world.

"Stay," he urged.

She might not be able to see his eyes, but she felt the intensity of his gaze. Heard his need-roughened voice. The slim thread of control she had grasped so tightly slipped through her fingers. She wasn't leaving. Maybe she had known that before she even entered his bedroom.

Admitting it, however, was impossible.

"All I can offer is one night," she told him. "Don't ask for more. I won't be able to give it. I don't do relationships. I hurt everyone I get close to because I don't stick around. Ever."

If she thought her statement would change his mind, she was wrong. He lifted the edge of the covers and simply waited. It was all the encouragement she needed. She tugged the sweatshirt over her head and let it fall from her fingers. The sweats and socks followed as she walked toward him, unhooking her bra. The straps loosened on her shoulders and fell down her arms. She tossed the garment aside as she reached the bed. There, she stopped and removed her panties, his gaze following her movements. Her breath was coming fast, her blood hot, her body ready. Before she slipped between the sheets, their eyes met.

There were no words as he pulled her against him, flesh against flesh, heat against heat. Her breath came quicker when she realized he was already naked. His cock throbbed hot and hard between them as he rolled on top of her.

The passion was palpable, tangible, so fiery it sparked around them as he lowered his mouth to hers. The kiss was slow, erotic. Utterly carnal. A decadent claiming that spoke of a need long restrained. His lips moved over hers with purpose and hunger, as if he had forever to explore and savor her.

Every brush of his lips ignited something primal. Every tilt of his head was a silent vow that this would never be enough. Their breaths mingled as the heat between them soared with each deliberate pass of his tongue, until the world fell away, leaving only sensation and the helpless, spiraling crash into each other.

She caressed his back, exploring his shifting muscles as he moved. Then her fingers found his face. He tore his lips from her mouth and turned his face into her palm, planting a hot kiss there. She forgot to breathe as she traced his full lips with her thumb. His gaze met hers. A storm churned in the gray depths, one of yearning, of longing.

Of an ache only she could satisfy.

He rocked against her, dragging his arousal against her throbbing center. She sucked in a quick breath as pleasure shot through her like lightning, raw and uncontrollable. Her legs wrapped around his hips. Desire blazed in his eyes as he reached down and brought his cock to her entrance.

She bit her lip, moaning as he rubbed the blunt head against her sensitive flesh in the same slow and deliberate way he had kissed her. She might have said there would only be one night, but he was making sure to imprint their time onto her soul so she never forgot a second of it.

Her fingers dug into his back as he gradually slid inside her. She pulled him close, needing him deep, but he clearly had no intention of rushing anything given his measured movements. Her craving for him only grew as her body stretched the deeper he went. Just when he was fully within her, he pulled out until only the tip of him remained.

She forced her eyes open and found him gazing down at her. Tremors coursed through his arms, telling her he was driving himself as mad as he was her. Mason was nothing like other men. Everything about him was meaningful and substantial. She should've known sex with him would be just as evocative and earth-shattering.

He gave a small thrust of his hips and slid deep inside her, burying himself completely. At last, their bodies were finally, irrevocably joined. It felt as if the Universe let out a sigh. Then he was moving, driving in and out of her body in a rhythm that sent pleasure spreading through her like wildfire, fierce and unrelenting.

She shoved away the covers as their bodies rocked against each other. Their lips tangled in a fierce, hungry kiss. Then he rolled onto his back, taking her with him. His hands stroked down her back to cup her ass and grind into her. She groaned, lost in ecstasy. Had she really only said one night?

Rowen sat up, slowly running her fingers over his chest. She had bathed blood from those hard muscles, wiped it from his wide shoulders while trying not to notice him. Now, she was able to touch him as she had wanted to that first night. Learning his body, absorbing his warmth.

Feeling his passion.

He flattened one of his large hands over her stomach and caressed upward. She held his gaze as his hand slid into the valley between her breasts. Her nipples puckered, eager for his touch. He cupped one and rubbed his thumb over the turgid peak. Her head dropped back as she sighed, arching her back to press her breast into his palm while moving her hips in slow circles.

A deep, guttural groan filled the room. In the next instant, he sat up and closed his lips around a nipple, pulling softly. She grasped his shoulders and lifted her head as their bodies continued to move.

His tongue licked, laved, and suckled first one breast and then the other until she was quivering in his arms. Pleasure coiled low in her belly, growing heavier and tighter with every second.

She found herself on her back once more, Mason over her as he thrust hard and deep in a steady, driving rhythm. The climax built quickly and crashed through her swiftly. The breath locked in her lungs as pleasure surged fast and sharp, stealing control and unraveling her. Even as she rode the delicious waves, she knew she would never be the same. Mason's touch had changed her, altered her to her very core.

Rowen screamed his name as a second orgasm rocked her. She had been unprepared for another and could only hold on to the man who shattered every one of her defenses.

CHAPTER THIRTY-SEVEN

SKYE DRUIDS

Mason's release came in a powerful wave he couldn't outrun. He gave in to the fire, the devastating need to be hers with one final thrust. Then he broke apart with a raw shout, helpless against the way her body pulled him in—tight, relentless, and achingly intimate.

When he finally came back into his body, he looked down at Rowen. Her strawberry blond tresses were spread out around her, stark against the navy sheets. Her eyes fluttered open, and he stared into her pale blue depths. It had been risky giving her just this one night, because he had known for some time that he wanted more. But he would rather have one night than never know what it was to claim her body.

He lowered his head and brushed his lips over hers. Her body clenched around him once more, causing him to groan and rock his hips. She answered with a moan of her own. He would give up every ounce of his magic if he could stop time and hold on to what was left of the night to have more time with her.

Her lips curved into a sexy smile as she tenderly touched his face. "Wow," she whispered.

He knew exactly how she felt. What'd happened between them was...he didn't have words for the visceral, intimate, and utterly carnal meeting of their bodies. All he knew was that it was rare and extraordinary, something that few ever experienced. He couldn't understand how she could walk away from something like that. Because he certainly couldn't.

Mason took her hand and kissed her inner wrist before softly pressing his mouth to her forehead, nose, and lastly, her lips. "I'm glad you came into my room."

"Me, too."

Their bodies were still joined. He was loath to break the connection, but he was cognizant of his weight on her. Reluctantly, he pulled out and rolled onto his back. As he did, she moved onto her side and propped her head up with her hand. He met her gaze and touched a lock of hair that a moonbeam caught through the edge of the blinds.

He could tell her about the wake or ask her about her evening, but he didn't want to talk. Not yet. Not after such an earth-shattering moment. He pulled her against his chest, and they lay in comfortable silence until Rowen's stomach grumbled with hunger. Her nose wrinkled as she dropped onto her back.

"Did you not eat?" he asked.

"I couldn't."

A note of disquiet in her voice had caught his attention. Something had happened while he was out. She would've called him had it been serious. Or would she have?

Mason propped himself up with a hand and looked down at her, wondering if he should push her to tell him. "Let's get you something to eat. You need your energy, because the night isn't over, and I'm not done with you yet."

He sat up and held out his hand to her. A heartbeat later, she took it. He pulled her up. His gaze lingered on her stunning body—perfect breasts, the indent of her waist, and the sensual swell of her hips—as she headed to the door. He followed her, torn between wanting her again and wanting to know what bothered her.

They moved about the kitchen, the darkness broken only by the bright light of the fridge when the door opened. She munched on some soft cheese spread over a fresh piece of bread. When she offered him a slice, he accepted.

"I had a visitor," she calmly said after a few minutes.

Mason stilled, the bread halfway to his mouth. He watched her across the island, looking for minute emotions, but she gave nothing away. "And whom might that have been?"

"Edie."

Surprise jolted through him as he lowered the hand holding the snack to the island. "She came to the cottage?"

"Sort of. I went out for a walk, and she found me out there."

"Why didn't you call me?" he demanded, angry and upset that she had been here alone. "Or someone? Did she hurt or threaten you? What did she want?"

Rowen put her hand atop his arm and looked into his eyes. "I'm fine. She didn't threaten me, and I didn't call because I needed time to sort through what she said."

"And what was that?"

Rowen took a long drink of water before she answered. "She's convinced she's working with the Ancients to make a new world order of Druids. She said they have chosen me to join them."

"Bloody hell," he murmured and sat on the barstool next to her. His mind was in turmoil, thinking of all the things that could've gone wrong. The thought of losing Rowen was incomprehensible. Finally, he looked into her eyes. "What did you tell her?"

"Nothing. She told me to think about it, and that the Ancients would contact me."

He ran a hand down his face. "Fuck. They're going to contact you. So, you did hear a voice?"

"Seems so," she murmured. "I have a feeling I don't have long to make a decision."

"What happens if you refuse their offer?"

She shrugged and looked at the half-eaten slice of bread. "I'm not sure."

Mason tucked a strand of hair behind her ear so he could better see her face. He knew exactly how these supposed *ancients* would react, and it wouldn't be pretty. "This decision is solely yours. Just because you brought me to the isle and are staying here doesn't mean you've chosen a side."

Her eyes lifted to his. "You believe Edie is working with the Ancients?"

"I don't know who or what Edie is working with, but it isn't the Ancients. I have the privilege of knowing Ferne and Carlyle, which means I trust what they've been through. Saying that, I'd be cautious of taking everyone at their word without seeing things myself if I didn't know them."

Rowen turned in the seat to face him. "I don't have a decision to make, because I already chose a side. I stand with you and the others."

Relief poured through Mason. He hadn't realized until she said the words how worried he had been about her choice. He cupped her face and kissed her. Now, he had a new fear. Edie wasn't done with Rowen, and neither were the false Ancients.

Those thoughts scattered like the wind when Rowen's hand wrapped around his shaft and began to stroke it. Heat surged straight to his cock. His body responded instantly, thickening with need. He slid his fingers around the back of her neck as the kiss turned urgent, fiery. Her hand worked him into a frenzy of need within moments. He stood, dragging her with him. She dropped to her knees and looked up at him before her lips enveloped him.

She took him in with a confidence that stole his breath. The first glide of her mouth on him sent a jolt of white-hot pleasure straight to his core. His hands fisted in her hair as every muscle drew taut, and liquid heat ran down his spine. Her mouth was warm and wet—and maddeningly slow. Every lick undid him.

He tried to savor each languid pull, but his hips betrayed him. A low groan slipped past his lips as she hollowed her cheeks. The physical pleasure reached heights he had never touched before, but it was more than that. It was Rowen. The way she watched him, the hunger in her gaze, as if he were hers to unravel. The fire that burned inside her.

The way she drew her tongue along his length as if she knew exactly how close he was to breaking.

His heart thundered in his chest. Desire coiled so tightly it bordered on pain, but still, she took her time, driving him closer to the edge with each torturous stroke of her velvety tongue.

Her hand reached his base as her mouth worked him deeper. The sight of her lips wrapped around him was a fantasy come to life. His control hung by a thread that was quickly unraveling.

"Rowen," he called, shocked by the rough sound of his voice. "I'm too close," he warned.

She kept at it, sucking, licking, touching. He tightened his fingers in her hair, but he couldn't make himself pull her away. It felt too good.

Then she moaned—*moaned*—around him. The release ripped through him like a detonation, pleasure crashing in waves so intense his legs nearly buckled.

He gripped the island to stay upright as she licked him clean. Still panting from such a wild orgasm, he pulled her to her feet and seized her mouth for a passionate kiss full of emotion he couldn't put into words.

Mason set her on the island and stood between her legs. He didn't dare look at the clock because that would give time power over him, and right now was *their* time. If it was all he had with her, then he would grasp every minute.

"I wasn't finished with you," she said as he kissed down her neck.

He lifted his head to look at her. "It's my turn now."

Her mouth parted as her eyes flared with need. He shoved everything off the island and lay her back. Her chest rose and fell rapidly, drawing his gaze. He ran a finger around first one nipple and then the other, watching them pebble, before rolling one peak between his fingers.

The sound of her breath hitching was music to his ears. Mason bent and placed a kiss on her stomach. Her legs widened farther as she arched her back. He grinned, kissing her hipbone as he stroked down the tops of her thighs.

He looked up in time to see her back arch, her hands reaching for him. The instant she found his arm, those fingers dug into his flesh, her grip conveying her need and the unmistakable demand for more—more of his mouth, his fingers. Him.

And he would give her every last drop of his soul.

His mouth hovered over her sex. She lifted her hips, urgent and seeking. He leaned just far enough away so he didn't touch her. She whimpered and dug her nails deeper, but he wouldn't relent. If he only got one night, he was going to take full advantage of it.

He lightly ran his fingers along her sex that glistened with her desire, pausing at the top. His finger circled the hood covering her swollen clit. Slowly, deliberately, he pulled it away to reveal the tiny nub. Then he lowered his mouth to it, letting his tongue flick back and forth.

Rowen groaned and rocked her hips against his face. It wasn't long before she was panting, her chest heaving as he teased and tormented her body until she was a quivering, writhing mass of nerves perched on the precipice of ecstasy. He refused to allow her to fall. Each time he felt her body tensing, he eased back on his ministrations, but he never relented.

He wanted—no, he *needed*—her screaming from the exquisite pleasure only he could give. To drive her past the edge and watch every tremor, hear every cry that ripped free of her. He craved her surrender as proof that she, too, felt the desperation, the need, the wildfire that roared, unstoppable, between them.

Mason feasted upon her sex and slid first one finger and then two inside her, pumping his hand in and out of her. This time, when he brought her to the edge, he sent her plummeting hard and fast. Her body stiffened as pleasure rolled through her, her inner walls spasming around his fingers.

The sight of the ecstasy claiming her was the most beautiful kind of torment. He drank in every shudder, every moan, drawing out her climax until she lay limp, his name caught on her breath. And he fell—utterly, irrevocably. Hers.

He pressed a kiss to the inside of one thigh and then the other while slowly withdrawing his fingers. Her eyes were closed, her chest heaving. Her pleasure coated his fingers and lingered on his tongue, and he knew in that moment that there would never be another woman for him. He loved Rowen.

It was a quiet love, a calm love. Yet it was fierce. Violent.

Savage.

And he would tear anyone apart who contemplated harming a single hair on her head.

He wanted to tell her and swear to always stand by her side, but he held the words in. Maybe one day he would tell her. For now, he remained silent and buried his love. There were still a few hours yet of their night. There was no need to disrupt their enjoyment with anything but more pleasure.

The dawn would bring enough of that.

CHAPTER THIRTY-EIGHT

SKYE DRUIDS

Rowen was so sated and content she couldn't even lift her eyelids. She drifted on water, or maybe it was clouds. Not that it mattered. She was too lost in the utter satisfaction of her body. No one had ever come close to giving her this. *She* hadn't even been able to reach this level of gratification herself.

No, it had come from only one person: Mason.

Had she subconsciously known the sex would be that mind-blowing, that his kiss would be so intoxicating, that his touch would stir her to such depths? If there was ever someone who made her wish she were the kind of person who could be in a relationship, it was him.

Strong arms lifted her from the island, cradling her against his chest. She leaned her head on his shoulder, comforted by the steady beat of his heart. Rowen thought he was taking them to bed, but she soon found herself situated before a hearth and a roaring fire.

"You were chilled," Mason said as he settled her between his legs, her back to his chest.

They sat on several thick blankets with pillows scattered around them. There was a myriad of food close at hand, as well as drinks. While she had been gliding upon waves of bliss, he had been busy. Rowen had thought men like him only existed in fiction, but he was proving her wrong one day at a time.

She turned her head up and back to look at him and smiled. "This is incredible."

His lips curved into a grin. "I'm glad you think so. We can stay for as long as you want. Let me know when you get tired."

That was the thing. She didn't want the night to end. Ever. She might like romance and the idea of commitment, but they were anti-Rowen to the extreme. Love always took one look at her and ran the other way. She had tried to catch it a few times, but it had only ever ended in disaster. It had shown her where she fit in the world, and she had accepted that.

She returned her gaze to the fire and rested her arms over Mason's, which were wrapped around her. "To think that just a few days ago I was angry at being sent to London…"

"And I was bleeding out in the street," he replied. "Do you know what I noticed first about you that night?"

"My hair?" she guessed.

"Your eyes."

She scrunched up her face and snorted. "You're kidding."

"Not in the least. They were bright and clear. Such a beautiful blue that I couldn't look away. Then you got me on my feet, and I didn't think a little thing like you could keep me up. You're stronger than you look."

Rowen chuckled. "I nearly didn't stay on my feet. You have no idea how many times we both almost crashed to the ground. We can smile about it now, but I was terrified at the time."

"Me, too," he replied somberly. He pressed a kiss to the top of her head as the fire crackled.

It was, hands down, the most romantic event of her entire life. Not only had he given her mind-blowing sex, but he was a true gentleman. Maybe that had to do with him growing up as a noble, but she rather thought it was just who Mason was as a human.

"How was the wake?" she asked.

He made a sound in the back of his throat. "As horrible as any wakes are. Matt, Kirsi's father, was a mess. The man never stopped crying. He looked downright lost. As if he didn't know what to do with himself now that his wife was gone."

"That sounds horrible." She couldn't imagine loving someone that deeply. She supposed it existed. Ferne and Theo might have that kind of relationship, so she figured it was in the realm of possibility. "How was Kirsi?"

"More withdrawn and pale, if you can believe it."

"Poor thing," Rowen murmured.

"Ferne told me that Kirsi was very close to her parents. I'm happy Matt is still here for her. I don't want anyone to know the pain of losing both parents at once."

She squeezed his arms. "I can't even imagine. I'm so sorry."

"I'll avenge them."

"I have no doubt."

He pressed the side of his head to hers. "There was something else I noticed."

"What's that?"

"I think Callum is in love with Kirsi. He was never far from her, but he also never got too close. Yet he rarely took his gaze off her."

Rowen shifted to get more comfortable in his arms. "That's interesting. I thought I saw something between them, too. Did you ask Ferne?"

"I didn't get a chance. Too many people were around, and I didn't want them to overhear. I wasn't the only one who noticed, though. I saw several of our group taking note of the pair. Killian and Callum, it seems, have a close friendship. That was nice to see, since some outright ignored Callum."

"Why? What has he done?" she asked, offended for him.

Mason blew out a breath. "I did manage to get that from Ferne when she brought me home. It seems Callum's family is not well thought of. Every generation, the men become drunks and abuse their wives and children."

Rowen sat up and turned to look at him, aghast. "You mean that everyone knows Callum and his mother are being abused and no one steps in to stop it?"

"Callum won't talk about it, and he has asked Killian and Ariah to stay out of it."

"If they were his friends, they wouldn't."

Mason's lips twisted as he nodded. "I feel the same. Ferne said everyone calls it the Kilmuir Curse."

"Hasn't Callum's mother asked for help? Surely, the Druids would do something."

"She's gone. Left Skye with Callum's younger brother years ago."

Rowen's heart broke. "So, Callum experiences the full brunt of his father's rage. That's horrible. I'm not sure I could remain silent and do nothing."

"Perhaps I'll speak with Killian. We're outsiders. Maybe we don't know the full story."

"I'm not sure that matters." She settled back against his chest. "Now I want him and Kirsi together even more."

Mason grunted. "I don't think that's going to happen."

"You have to be wrong. I need some good news right now, and those two could be it."

He shifted his leg closer to hers. "It's a secret. Ferne isn't even supposed to know, so you can't say anything."

"My lips are sealed. Now, spill the tea," she urged him, grinning. There was something exciting about learning a secret that no one was supposed to know.

"Callum has sworn to break the family curse."

She frowned, letting that sink in. "The only way that will happen is if he doesn't have a rela—oh, my fucking god. He's not going to be with Kirsi, is he?"

"No, he is not."

"He would rather be alone and lonely than be with someone he obviously cares about?" As soon as Rowen said the words, she hoped Mason didn't compare their scenario to the couple in question. Because it wasn't the same.

Or was it?

No, it wasn't. She was sure of that.

Mason's chest expanded as he drew in a deep breath before slowly releasing it. "Apparently, most of the men in his family swore they wouldn't turn into their fathers, and inevitably, they did. Callum wants to make sure he doesn't continue the generational abuse in any of its many forms."

"Damn. I'm sad for him. And for Kirsi, for that matter. Yet I also applaud him for taking a stand."

"If he can go through with it."

She glanced back at him. "Meaning?"

"What if Kirsi asks him out? What if she initiates sex? Can he remain strong and refuse her?"

"Maybe it's as simple as Callum not becoming a father. Kirsi could ensure that she never has children."

Mason slid his fingers between hers and curled his hand inward. "Maybe."

"We have to be able to help."

"And what if we aren't supposed to?"

She lightly elbowed him. "Don't ruin my moment of planning with common sense."

"Why do you want them together?"

She was about to give a flippant answer when she paused and reconsidered. "I think it's because I saw how he watched her. Even as he kept all his emotions hidden, there was something in his eyes."

"Yearning."

"Yes. He tries to hide it, but there's no concealing that kind of sentiment. Then there's Kirsi."

Mason softly rubbed his cheek against hers. "Ah. You mean the way she desperately tries not to look at Callum, only to throw a surreptitious glance his way. She doesn't mask her longing. She puts it out there for the world to see, hoping and praying that he not only sees it, but responds."

Rowen swallowed hard. "Yep. That, exactly."

"She's young to be the one who has to face the evil when the time comes."

"I don't think it's happenstance that everyone in this fight is in their twenties and thirties. This battle was meant to pit the young against the ancient. They expect us to fall."

"Us?" Mason repeated softly.

She leaned her head back and pressed her lips to his. "I told you I chose a side already. I'm not changing my mind."

"I don't think Edie or whatever it is she's following will give up so easily."

"Probably not, but I don't care. I'll deal with it."

He cupped her face, his gray eyes darkening. "Not alone. I'll be there in whatever capacity you need."

"That's good to know."

He rubbed his thumb over her lower lip. "I shouldn't have left you alone last evening."

"You can't be with me every second of the day."

Those wonderful fingers of his lightly trailed down her neck. "If I thought sending you away would keep you safe, I'd do it in an instant."

"Safety is an illusion. Nowhere is truly safe." Though right then, she'd never felt more secure and protected than she did while cradled in his arms. "If they want to get to me, they'll find a way."

His head lowered as he placed a delicate kiss on her jaw. "Do you think Edie will visit you again?"

Rowen was having difficulty thinking as his warm lips left a hot trail of kisses down her jaw and then behind her ear. "I-I... don't know. Maybe."

"They've not approached any of the group before."

"That we know of." She was breathing harder the closer his hands moved to her breasts.

She was suddenly lying across his arm, and she couldn't remember getting into that position. He trailed a finger from the hollow of her throat down between her breasts and then lower to circle her navel. Her sex clenched greedily, impatient to have his long, thick length inside her once again. His fingers and mouth had been sublime, but nothing could replace his cock.

Her breath caught as his exploring fingers drew close to the triangle of curls between her thighs. She widened her legs and waited for him to slip his fingers lower. Instead, he caressed back up to her throat.

"Hmm. That is something to think about," he murmured near her ear, his warm breath brushing across her skin.

What was he talking about? Oh, yes. That's right. She had said something about…her thoughts scattered as he lightly rubbed his knuckles over a nipple.

"Please," she begged.

"You never have to beg me," he said before taking her mouth in a desperate, frantic kiss that held all the fire and need that consumed her.

CHAPTER THIRTY-NINE

SKYE DRUIDS

The sky was still gray when Mason grudgingly extracted his body from Rowen's. They had spent hours exploring each other, and she had finally fallen asleep a few minutes ago. He considered remaining next to her and finding sleep himself, but he couldn't. There was a big difference between having sex with someone and sleeping with them. It was a level of intimacy he greatly wished for, but one that would be harder to get over.

Not that he would ever be able to forget the feel of having her in his arms, their skin slick with sweat, gliding against each other, or the sounds of their bodies slapping together as they each feverishly reached for release. Those memories would be difficult to bear, but he wouldn't survive knowing what it was like to fall asleep with her warm softness against his and know he'd never have it again.

It was a small way of protecting a corner of his heart. He had known Rowen was different, and that she would leave a lasting mark on him. Though he hadn't expected just how deep that mark would be.

Even if he had, he wouldn't have changed anything.

He gently covered her with a blanket and quietly picked up the remnants of their food. Their sessions were as wild and carnal as they were long, and they had both needed to refuel often. He smiled down at her. The image of her body flushed with pleasure would be forever stamped in his mind.

Mason entered the kitchen and paused beside the sink to set the dishes aside. He looked out the window to the area where Edie had approached Rowen. He was deeply troubled about Edie's visit as well as the conversation between the women. No one knew if whoever Kerry and Edie worked for was the same evil that hovered over the isle, though everyone suspected it was. The real question was, was it the same as The Grey and the monster within?

He braced his hands on the edge of the sink. The evil had created a killing mist and had given Kerry control over it. That same malevolence had gotten through Rhona's *and* Balladyn's magic in the Druid prison to obliterate Kerry. What could anyone on Skye have that would keep it away from Rowen?

Not a bloody thing.

There wasn't much time to come up with a plan, either. His gaze dropped to the faucet, thinking about the way he had once been able to move water. He turned on the tap and watched the water pour out as he extended his hand. If he were a water dancer, he would hear it, and he had never heard it.

Skye needed its water pillar, and he would be happy to fill that role. Then all three pillars would be in place, and it would give the isle an extra layer of protection. Plus, if he were the third pillar, maybe it would unlock something that gave him what he needed to keep Edie and the evil away from Rowen. All he had to do was find the ability that had been lost to him.

Mason let his magic pool in his palm and attempted to use it to move the water. There was a chance he had been too young to understand what was happening, but he didn't buy that either. Yet no matter how long he sat there trying to link with it, nothing happened.

Maybe he couldn't hear the water, but it understood *him*. After all, he hadn't been the only one to see that he could move it. His parents had witnessed it several times. It hadn't been some wild dream or delusion that he had made up. He had actually done it. And right now, he needed to do it again.

He reached out with his mind then, picturing the water turning at a ninety-degree angle. For a moment, nothing happened. Then, the water shifted slightly. A bright smile spread over his lips. Mason adjusted his footing and focused again. Skye needed him. The Druids needed him. Rowen needed protection. He could do this.

He *would* do it.

Mason kept the same picture in his head and poured his magic through his fingers. He strained, calling to his magic as he stared at the water, waiting for it to move again. When nothing happened, he changed the image in his mind and tried again. And again. And again. To no avail.

He braced his hands on the sink and hung his head. Skye could have its third pillar if he could just break through whatever kept him from reaching the water. He'd failed his parents, neglected to keep his staff safe, and he feared he wouldn't be able to protect Rowen.

"What are you doing?"

His head jerked up at the sound of her voice. He turned to find her standing behind him, the blanket wrapped around her, and a frown furrowing her brow. "Seeing if I can command water like I did as a boy. I was hoping maybe I *was* the water pillar." He shrugged away his words. "Turns out, I'm not."

"They'll find the last pillar. They've done it every time they've faced the evil before. They'll do it again."

"I hope so," he said as he shut off the tap. Then he faced her. "Did I wake you?"

She hesitated for a moment and then briefly shook her head. "I heard the voice again."

Fear cut through him, sharp and deep. "What did it say?"

"I couldn't make it out, but it was there."

And he hadn't been. Bloody fucking hell. Could he do anything right? "It's early, but I think we need to get to the manor."

"I agree. I'll grab a shower."

"I'll ring Ferne to alert her."

He followed Rowen down the hall until she peeled off to her room. His footsteps ate up the distance to his bedroom, where his phone lay charging. He sank onto the bed and dialed his sister.

"Are you okay?" she asked groggily, panic edging her voice.

"We're not in immediate danger, but we're heading to the manor shortly. Edie paid Rowen a visit yesterday."

"What?" Ferne shouted. "What happened?"

"What's going on?" Theo asked in the background.

"It's Mason. We need to get to the manor," she told him. Then her voice became stronger as she repeated, "Mas, what happened?"

He squeezed his nose with his thumb and forefinger. "It's

better if Rowen explains. It's why we're going to the manor, so she only has to do it once."

"Why didn't you call earlier?"

He heard the shifting of covers as Ferne got out of bed. That was a question the others would ask, too. And a valid one. But not one they would get the complete truth of either. "We've been discussing it."

"You've not slept at all?"

"Rowen got about thirty minutes."

Ferne dropped the mobile and quickly picked it back up. "We're getting ready now. We'll meet you over there. Should we come get you?"

"I don't think it's going to matter."

"You're not making me feel better about this."

He winced at the fear in his sister's voice. "We'll be there as quickly as we can."

Mason hung up and jumped in the shower. Within minutes, he was out and pulling on clothes. He ran a hand through his wet hair as he walked out of his room, only to jerk back when he saw Balladyn waiting in the hallway.

"Ferne called," the Reaper said. "I've added another layer of protection to the cottage."

Mason would need to thank Ferne later. "Will it be enough?"

Balladyn's red-ringed silver eyes held his for a long moment. "I have no idea."

Suddenly, Rowen's door opened, and she looked out to see them. She was dressed, shoes in hand, and her hair was wrapped in a towel. "I thought I heard voices."

"I'm here to take you to the manor," Balladyn said.

Rowen glanced between them. "You really think something could happen as we drove?"

"I'm not taking any chances," the Reaper answered.

Mason moved to stand beside her. "It's not a chance we want to take either."

"That doesn't make me feel any better," she murmured. Then she pulled off the towel and ran back to put it in the bathroom.

The moment she walked out, Balladyn touched both of them, teleporting them to Carwood Manor. Despite it being a little after dawn, the house was abuzz with conversation and movement. Delicious smells wafted from the kitchen. A flash of beige fur, then gray, rushed past him as two felines slipped through the swinging kitchen door when someone opened it. Mason caught a glimpse of Carlyle at the stove.

"Come," Balladyn urged.

Mason and Rowen followed him into the kitchen. She still carried her shoes and dropped them next to the wall. The kitchen was enormous, and the table was already crammed with people while Carlyle moved about happily, tending to multiple pans.

Ferne and Theo walked into the kitchen a few seconds later. Ferne wrapped her arms around Mason for a quick, tight hug before moving to Rowen. It seemed just about everyone who didn't reside at the manor had beaten them there. Even Kirsi was in attendance this time.

Mason motioned for Rowen to take one of the last chairs while he remained standing. The noise of conversation and cooking was so loud that his ears rang with it, yet he loved being amid such a group. They bickered, joked, and loved like siblings. It was a level of camaraderie he hadn't experienced before. He'd had something close at university, but it was a pale comparison to what surrounded him now.

Carlyle jabbed his arm with his elbow. "You good?"

"Right this moment, I am."

His friend grinned. "I know that feeling. This is something unique and extraordinary. I'm glad your first thought was to get Rowen here."

It was far from Mason's first thought. He prayed that taking their night together hadn't put her life in more danger than if he had brought her straight here the moment she'd told him.

"We'll get it sorted," Carlyle vowed. "You'll see."

He handed Mason the plate he had been holding. Mason's stomach growled at the array of food: scrambled eggs, sausage, crumpets, and mushrooms roasted with butter and thyme.

"I hear you're a pretty good cook," Mason said.

Carlyle chuckled. "Give it a try and let me know."

For the next fifteen minutes, the kitchen quieted as plates were passed around and everyone dug into the tasty spread Carlyle had provided. Mason devoured his quickly, somehow not surprised that Carlyle had found his way to such an interest.

All too soon, their meal was finished and the plates stacked next to the sink. Once everyone had tea or coffee, the attention shifted to Rowen. She looked his way, and he gave her a nod of encouragement. Not that she needed it. She had an inner strength unlike anyone he had met before. If anyone could stand against Edie and the evil, it was Rowen. He just wished she didn't have to.

"I could say this has been blown out of proportion, but that would be a lie." Rowen leaned her forearms on the table and lowered her gaze to her mug of tea. "I…well, there's no easy way to say this, so I'll just say it. I went for a walk around the cottage yesterday evening. It was still light out, and I stayed within sight of the house at all times."

Mason decided to speak up then. "She didn't cross any of the fences."

No one said a word as they waited for Rowen to speak. Finally, she took a deep breath and lifted her head. "That's when Edie approached me."

CHAPTER FORTY

SKYE DRUIDS

It hadn't been difficult to tell Mason what had transpired, but that wasn't the case now, sitting in the manor's kitchen. Rowen was extremely aware that Edie's siblings were listening to every word. Elodie's shoulders were hunched, and her face had drained of all color. Elias's hands were clenched so tightly his knuckles had turned white, and his lips were compressed into a tight line as fury emanated from him.

The rest of the room showed various reactions, ranging from shock to anger. The only one who didn't seem surprised was Balladyn. The Reaper withheld all emotion. As someone who was several thousand years old, Rowen could only imagine the things he had witnessed from the Fae as well as humans. Perhaps nothing astonished him anymore.

"She waited until Rowen was alone," Theo said, breaking the silence that had fallen with Rowen's last word.

Mason nodded slowly. "That was the first thing I said, too. She's been watching Rowen."

"To know exactly when she would be alone," Ariah said.

Callum leaned back in his chair. "How many others are watching the rest of us?"

"It doesn't matter. It changes nothing," Rhona stated.

Rowen had been thinking a lot about her encounter with Edie and what the next steps could be. She had no intention of joining the woman, but that didn't mean she couldn't use the evil's intent in her favor. "Why don't we use Edie's interest in me to draw her out?"

All eyes swung to her, but it was Mason's gray gaze she met. She saw the trepidation there, the fear.

"You want to use yourself as bait?" Balladyn asked.

Rowen looked at the Reaper and found approval in his eyes. "You've been after her for some time now. Sabryn nearly got her, but I can draw her in, let us get closer."

"She'll be expecting something," Elias cautioned. "She might be off her fucking head, but she has added power, just as Kerry did. I also need to point out that while Kerry was addicted to the authority she commanded, Edie isna. She's bought into this shite from the false Ancients completely."

Killian sighed. "Can we save her? Perhaps prove that she's been deceived?"

"Nay," Elodie and Elias replied in unison.

Elodie licked her lips, swallowing hard. "The Edie walking around now isn't my sister. Edie loved her children more than anything. She never would have left them. Never."

"What about Trevor?" Kirsi asked.

Elias and Elodie exchanged glances before Elias said, "That cheating son of a bitch deserved for Edie to take him for all he was worth in a divorce, but the fact that he's missing is concerning. If you had asked me two months ago if Edie would ever harm anyone, I would've emphatically said nay. I believe this new Edie is more than capable of taking another's life. We all saw her fighting Sabryn and Kurt."

"We doona know if she has help either," Scott pointed out.

Finn snorted and hooked one arm around the back of his chair. "Setting a trap could backfire on us."

"It's worth it, though," Willa said. "It put a cramp on things when Kerry was captured. We can do the same with Edie."

Filip made a derisive sound. "Really? Look how that turned out with Kerry."

"Then we do things differently this go-round," Kurt replied.

Sabryn shook her head. "Kerry was exactly where she needed to be. That's the only place Edie can go. We can't do anything differently."

"I think everyone is forgetting one thing," Song said.

Carlyle's brow was furrowed as he turned to her. "What's that?"

"There is only one person who gets to decide if this moves forward." Song swiveled her head to Rowen. "The one standing as bait."

Rhona blew out a breath. "Song's right. You suggested this, Rowen. We'll figure out a way to make it work if this is truly something you want to do, but I want to point out that I'm unsure about going through with it."

"Even if we do, I think Rowen should be able to back out at any time," Mason added.

Rhona nodded in agreement. "Of course. If she feels something is off or changes her mind, then all she has to do is say the word."

Rowen had the insane urge to reach for Mason, just to feel his sturdiness, his strength. She had never been the kind of person who needed others' strength, but this wasn't any ordinary situation or decision. A myriad of things could go wrong, ending in her getting hurt or worse—dying.

"You don't have to do this," Sabryn said.

Rowen's stomach roiled viciously, making her wish she hadn't eaten so much. Or drank that last cup of tea. "While I've never believed things are predetermined before we are born, I do think I was brought to London to meet Mason in order for me to be here, right now. I tend to avoid confrontation. I can—and do—stand up for myself, but what I'm trying to say is that I know nothing about battle or using magic *in* battle. I chose to stand with all of you, and I will fight these false Ancients. But this is a prime opportunity. For some reason, they want me. And if I can use that to give us an advantage, then I'm going to do it."

"Only a warrior would say such words," Balladyn replied.

Rowen was pretty sure he'd said that just to make her feel better. "I'm not a warrior."

"Don't sell yourself short," Finn said. "It takes some serious stones to do what you're offering."

Elias flexed his hands and gave a slight shake of his head. "Edie has to be stopped. I know we said we'd let her be since we knew she was working with the evil, but now I think that wasna a wise choice."

"It was the best decision at the time," Rhona said. "Things have changed, which means we alter our plans to compensate for that. The oppressive evil over Skye is steadily growing. I don't know how much time we have before the ultimate showdown arrives. We've had some success, but I'd like to give us a leg up on our enemy."

"Enemies," Mason corrected. "Don't ever forget about London."

"Or Edinburgh," Scott added.

The sheer amount of stress on Rhona's shoulders made Rowen doubly glad she wasn't in her position. How were they supposed to triumph over so many enemies? Could they even do it?

And at what cost?

Carlyle put his elbows on the table. "Thomas worked hard to get someone from Rowen's group to London. He's likely doing it with others to build up the London Druids. Not only did Rowen get away, but she also helped Mason. Thomas won't let that slide. He's methodical. He might not hit now, but he will very soon."

"Not with his own Druids. He'll outsource it, and I've a feeling Parker is helping with that now that he leads Edinburgh," Kurt said.

Mason set aside his empty cup. "Then use me as bait for Thomas."

"One trap at a time, please," Rhona said as she held up her hands when the room erupted in response.

Rowen was aghast that Mason would want to do such a thing. Dozens of words came to mind to convince him to change his mind. Then she considered what she wanted to do. How could she ask him not to put his life in danger when she was intending to do the same?

"Parker will return to Skye," Sabryn stated. "It's just a matter of time. As far as we know, he still thinks Kurt is dead."

"That won't last long. Especially if Parker has indeed taken over Edinburgh as we suspect," Kurt replied.

Finn twisted his lips. "We need to get ahead of at least one of our foes. Defending against all of them will only bring us down. We're spread too thin."

"We could ask the MacLeod Druids," Bronwyn offered.

Rowen perked up at the mention of more Druids. She was hoping to learn more about them, but that was quickly squelched.

"This isn't their fight," Rhona said.

Balladyn shrugged from behind her. "Maybe it should be. They have strong roots here. So do the Druids at Dreagan."

Rowen tried to keep up with it all. There were obviously groups she didn't know about, and by the confusion on Mason's face, he didn't either.

Rhona turned in her chair to look at Balladyn. "You're serious."

"This is an attack on Skye, sure, but it's also an attack on the Skye Druids. You welcomed Mason, Rowen, and others to join the fight. Why not them?"

"Because we would be asking them."

Balladyn took her hand in his and squatted down beside her. "They can refuse."

"They won't."

"Nay, they won't. Because they understand the significance."

Rhona went silent for a long moment.

"I'd also like to remind you that another Reaper is mated to a Skye Druid," Balladyn added.

Rhona's frown deepened. "Do you think Erith would allow Sorcha to return?"

Balladyn shrugged. "There's only one way to find out."

Rowen swung her head to Mason and lifted her brows, hoping he knew who Erith was. He gave a small shrug and shook his head.

"The MacLeod Druids are allies," Ferne explained to Rowen and Mason. "They, along with their immortal mates, live in an area of the Highlands hidden from outsiders. Some of the Druids there are hundreds of years old and very powerful."

Mason grunted. "And Dreagan? You aren't talking about Dreagan whisky, are you?"

"The verra same," Scott replied with a grin. "Dreagan is Gaelic for dragon."

Rowen looked at Scott. "What does that mean?"

"It means it's home to the Dragon Kings," Elodie told them.

Mason jerked back at the news as if slapped. "You're serious."

"Dragons?" Rowen murmured, afraid she hadn't heard correctly.

Theo tapped a finger on the table as he glanced at Rhona. "The dragons once ruled this world. It's a verra long story, and we'll share it."

Rhona and Balladyn stared at each other during the exchange. Finally, she released a long sigh and looked at everyone in the room. "Some of us were born here and grew up learning the past and about the great battle that returns again and again. We never expected it would fall to us, but I doubt any of the others who fought in the past thought differently. Each of you is here because you want to be. No one coerced or forced you. You're here because of family or love or friendship, and you've stayed, fighting with everything you have."

She paused and swallowed. "There have been injuries. A couple of attacks that nearly took one of us off the playing field. It's been our unity and devotion, not just to each other but to vanquishing that which wants to end us, that has kept us moving forward and overcoming every obstacle placed before us. We were taught that the Skye Druids won in the past. And it was made to seem as if they did it on their own. But we can't know for sure. It never felt right asking others to join our fight. But," she said, drawing out the word as she glanced at Balladyn, "this isn't just a fight for the Skye Druids. It's a fight for Druids everywhere. And we won't win if we don't know when to ask for help."

Balladyn smiled and kissed Rhona before straightening. "I'll speak to the others."

"The sooner, the better." Rhona looked at the rest of them. "We need to formulate a plan for Edie's capture."

The energy in the room was electric as the others smiled, eager for this next step in the war. Rowen's heart clutched painfully. It didn't matter if the evil talking to Edie wasn't the Ancients. It was still formidable. And none of them could forget that.

Sabryn called to Rowen. "The one thing I know about Edie is that she'll come at you in ways you least expect."

Kurt nodded. "Her magic is potent. Don't fight her alone."

"Rowen won't be alone," Mason stated.

CHAPTER FORTY-ONE

SKYE DRUIDS

The wind whipped viciously at the gravesite later that morning as Nora Brown was laid to rest. Matt's shoulders were hunched as he sobbed while the minister spoke. Kirsi stood as still as a standing stone, tears rolling down her cheeks.

Mason opted to stay at the back, giving those who knew the family an opportunity to get closer. Rowen remained with him, along with Sabryn, Kurt, Finn, Carlyle, and Song. Mason scanned the crowd discreetly. Midway through the funeral, Rowen nudged him on his left side. He looked her way to see her watching something behind him. Mason followed her gaze to find Callum standing fifty yards back next to a tombstone, watching the funeral.

When the service finished, Callum was nowhere to be found. No one mentioned noticing him, nor did it seem as if they were looking for him either. Mason looked toward the gravesite where Kirsi held her father up as they lingered.

"They'll be fine," Carlyle said.

Mason briefly met his gaze as they began walking toward their vehicles. "How do you know?"

"Callum is near."

So, they *had* seen him. Or maybe everyone realized the lengths Callum would go to for Kirsi and her family.

Sabryn added, "Rhona and Balladyn will check on them, too."

Rowen put her hand on his arm and slowed. He halted beside her as she waited until the others were out of earshot.

"Do you mind if we linger for a moment?" she asked.

"Not at all. Is something wrong?"

"No, I just want a moment."

"Would you rather be alone?"

She shook her head as the wind whipped her hair around her. "No." She faced him, her eyes closed. "I wish you could hear the flowers."

Mason saw wildflowers here and there, but there was a rather varied array of cut flowers near the gravesite. "What do they sound like?"

"Each has a melody."

"Like a song?" He hadn't expected that. He'd always assumed they communicated with words.

Her lips curved softly for a heartbeat. "Exactly that. The smaller the flower, the higher the note. Trees are the deepest. Today, though, they sing a sad song."

"For Nora?"

"Everything is connected on this isle. The magic is within the ground and flows with the water. It swirls in the air and moves with the clouds. It's in the Druids who call it home." Her lids lifted, and she speared him with her pale blue eyes. "They know each Druid. And they mourn those who have moved on to the next stage."

He brushed away the single tear that fell onto her cheek. "They liked Nora."

"Very much. They like you, too."

Mason felt himself grinning. "That's nice to hear."

Suddenly, she winced, her entire body shuddering.

"What is it?" he asked worriedly.

She put her fingers to her temple. "Someone was trying to get in my head."

"The evil?"

"Maybe. It's hard to tell. I felt them there, but I didn't hear anything."

He glanced around to see that nearly everyone had left the cemetery. "Perhaps it wasn't trying to say something."

"It was. I could tell."

"Are you purposefully keeping it out?"

She pulled some hair out of her eyes and turned to face the wind. "Not that I'm aware of. I think our time is up, though."

He wasn't ready. Even with all the planning and discussion, Mason still wasn't convinced that Rowen using herself as bait was the right thing to do. If there *was* a right thing to do. They were all in danger just standing there, but he couldn't shake the feeling that something could go horribly wrong and he might lose Rowen forever. Not that she was his in any sense of the word.

Before he knew it, they were in the vehicle, driving to the cottage. Rowen sent out a message to everyone that it was time to put the trap in place for Edie. Everyone knew their roles.

"It's going to be all right," Rowen said.

There was a pit in his stomach that said otherwise. Mason

couldn't believe she was reassuring him when she would be the one coming face-to-face with a foe. He tried to come up with reasons that might change her mind, but each one sounded more absurd than the one before. All too soon, they pulled up to the cottage.

"I should've driven slower," he said as he put the vehicle in park.

"There's no stopping what has to happen."

"We don't know if everyone is in place yet."

She turned her head to him. "They will be."

"Take your time changing."

Rowen flashed him a quick smile before grabbing her bag from the back seat. He had wanted things to go down at the manor, where they had transferred their belongings, but Rowen had been adamantly against it. Everyone assured him they would keep Rowen safe. That should make him feel better, but it didn't.

Mason was two steps behind Rowen through the front door. She immediately went to her room to change. He tugged off his tie and tossed it onto the kitchen table before shrugging out of the suit jacket and laying it over the back of a chair. As he unbuttoned the neck of his dress shirt, he looked out the kitchen window. All he could see was sheep and a cottage in the distance.

It was barely after noon, but he poured himself a glass of whisky and tossed it back. Rowen wasn't going to fight Edie alone. He and the others were there to step in when the time came. They knew how Edie fought, and he would take his cues from them. Sabryn and Song had shown Rowen a few moves that she, thankfully, picked up quickly. She wasn't defenseless, but she wasn't battle-ready either. Even with all his experience, Mason didn't consider himself prepared.

He turned when he heard a noise and found Rowen standing

behind him, dressed in jeans and a white sweater. Her hair was pulled into a high ponytail to keep it out of her face. He walked to her, stopping short of taking her in his arms, even though he craved the feel of her. It would wound him too deeply if he tried to embrace her and she pushed him away.

So, he kept his hands to himself, though it was nearly unbearable. He knew how easily she fit against him, how good she felt in his arms. He had witnessed her pleasure as she writhed and shivered as she climaxed. He had kissed every inch of skin, learned every valley, tasted every peak.

She had given him a single night.

And he would relive it every night hereafter, suspended in a kind of purgatory.

"I'm going to be fine," Rowen assured him.

Her voice was steady, her words firm. Yet her mouth was pinched, and her face was pale. She was scared—as anyone in their right mind would be. If she were to come out of this alive and unharmed, he needed to be her confidant, give her the words she needed to hear. Even if he didn't quite believe them.

"That you will," Mason replied with a nod. "The plan is solid. The others have been through this several times already. You and I may be new to this conflict, but you have seasoned warriors watching over you. And me," he added, grinning.

Her mouth eased into a smile. "I'm pretty sure you can hold your own."

"Just remember, while it may seem like you're alone, we're here. I'm the closest, and I'll get to you, no matter what. You understand that, right? I *will* get to you."

She nodded, her gaze locked with his. "I know you will."

"You're strong. Trust yourself and your magic, and all will be well."

"Do you really believe that?"

Unable to help himself, he grasped her shoulders and ran his palms down her arms until he held her hands in his. "Without a doubt."

She didn't push him away. Instead, she gripped him tightly. "I'm glad you're here."

"There's nowhere else I'd be," he told her.

She inhaled before releasing him and turning toward the back door. He followed, fighting the urge to keep her inside. At the door, she turned and threw her arms around him. Mason enfolded her in an embrace and closed his eyes as he held her close. They stayed there for a long minute, locked together.

She was the first to pull away. Rowen looked up at him and brought his head down to hers. Their lips met, and heat curled through his body. The kiss was slow and languid, filled with desire and need. And tinged with regret.

For what they had shared.

For what could have been.

For what would never be.

Then she stepped out of his arms, the moment over as quickly as it had begun.

"You don't have to do this," he called. "It's not too late to change your mind."

She backed up another step, her hand on the doorhandle. "I have to do this. As you said, the plan is solid, and you have my back."

"Always."

Rowen offered him one more fleeting smile, and then she was

gone. He reached the door as it closed behind her, his hands on the wood, fighting the need, the *demand*, to follow her. He pressed his head to the door and squeezed his eyes shut, the knot in his stomach tightening painfully.

"You'd better come back to me," he whispered.

If Edie hurt her, Mason would rip her apart painfully, dragging out the agony until she begged for death.

Somehow, he found the strength to straighten and place the call. "She's in play."

"Everyone is ready. Balladyn is veiled nearby, watching everything," Carlyle said.

"If anything happens to her—"

"It won't," Carlyle said over him. "We know what to do. Trust us."

Mason clenched his jaw. "I am. Otherwise, I would've talked her out of it."

CHAPTER FORTY-TWO

SKYE DRUIDS

With every step Rowen took, moving away from the cottage, away from Mason, it felt as if the land beneath her rumbled like a drum, dark and perilous. She clung to the last traces of his warmth, but the cold, greedy air stole it the moment she crossed the threshold.

Just as it did her courage.

Inside, she was a ball of nerves, ready to crumple at any second. Maybe she'd draw Edie out. That was the plan. Bait the trap. Lure the enemy. But then what? What good would a couple of battle moves she'd only just begun to master do her when the real fight started? Could she hold her own?

Against an average Druid most certainly. But Edie wasn't average. She was something darker, stronger. Rowen had sensed the undercurrent of violence and power when they spoke, and she had no illusions about what Edie could do to her.

Yet, she was still willing to face her and whatever else showed up. It had to be her. They had singled her out. Fear churned in her gut, but it did something else.

It lit the fuse.

The gusts of wind grew wilder, howling around her like an omen and whipping the ends of her hair about her head. She shivered, wishing she had thought to grab a jacket. Above her the sky was a gloomy, woeful gray. The kind of weather that made some people cranky while others waited excitedly for rain.

She didn't walk in the same direction as last time. Instead, she followed the rock wall away from the cottage. A few nearby sheep raised their heads at her approach, but their curiosity was fleeting. She wrapped her arms around her middle and held back another shiver.

"Where are you, Edie?" she whispered as she scanned the land for the blond.

That same probing from the gravesite came again, sharper, stronger. Angrier. Her temples throbbed in response. Something was trying to get in. For the barest of seconds, she contemplated returning to the cottage and Mason's waiting arms. She didn't want to be some *chosen one*. Just as she hadn't wanted to be the one to go to London. Her aunt had assured that she was on that plane. Had Aunt Maelin knew what would happen? The moment she was able, Rowen intended to find out.

She kept her pace slow. The others were out there somewhere, but they hadn't told her where they would be so she wouldn't look in their direction. But she really wished she could see one of them right about now.

The prodding in her head happened a third time like a fist through glass. Pain detonated in her skull. She gasped, doubling over as agony bloomed behind her eyes like a bomb. The ground swayed, her knees threatening to buckle beneath the force of it.

It was like her mind had been ripped open. A hot, jagged pulse stabbed through her temples sharp enough to steal her breath. She clutched her head, trying to hold it all in—trying not to scream. But the agony spread like wildfire.

Her vision blurred, her stomach turned. She squeezed her eyes closed as tears fell. All she could hear was the sound of her blood racing in her ears. Then, in an instant, the pain was gone. Evaporated as if it had never been there.

She opened her eyes and lowered her hands as she looked around expecting to see Edie. Somehow, she was still on her feet, still in the same spot—and still alone. Slowly, she straightened and rubbed her fingers in a circle at her temples. Unable to help herself, she glanced over her shoulder to the cottage, half-expecting to find Mason running towards her, but there was no sign of him. Or any of the others.

That was good. She didn't want anything ruining this meeting. Doing it once was stupid. Being the bait a second time was insane.

The wind held an icy note now that penetrated straight to her bones. She curled her hands into fists and continued walking. She imagined that one of her ancestors, eons ago, once walked this very stretch of land. Had she looked out over the beauty and sighed with pleasure? What had caused that ancestor to leave Skye and travel to America? Had it been done for love? Or had they followed a wanderer's heart? Rowen hoped they hadn't been forced out.

If every Druid could trace their roots to Skye, then every Druid should stand together to fight for the isle. Her life might end that very day, but at least she could look back at her life with satisfaction. Because she had stood with the light, with the worthy, with others fighting for their lives.

"*Rowen.*"

Her steps faltered as her thoughts scattered. Had she just heard her name? It hadn't been shouted. It had come as a whisper, as if someone were next to her. She knew Balladyn was nearby, but he wouldn't get too close.

The wind whistled past her, not quite a roar, not quite a scream. Her cheeks burned and her lips were chapped. Her body trembled from the chill. On the other side of the fence a couple of lambs played, unaware or uncaring about anything.

"Let me...in."

Rowen jerked to a halt. There was no denying what she heard this time. The feminine voice wasn't inside her head, but around her. *All* around her. "What do you want?"

"You."

She swallowed nervously. "Too damn bad. I've made my choice, I've picked my side. And in case you didn't get that, I don't choose you."

The laughter was hushed, bitter. Hostile. And it cut through Rowen like the sharpest blade. *"You misunderstand, child. You don't have a choice. You're already mine."*

CHAPTER FORTY-THREE

SKYE DRUIDS

"Why the fuck won't she wake up?" Mason bellowed and gave Rowen another shake.

But her eyes remained closed.

He could still hear her cry of pain, see her face twisted in agony. The world had slowed to a crawl as he yanked open the door and bolted from the cottage. He had slid on the damp grass beside her, his arms going around her just before her face hit the ground.

Seconds later, Ferne, Theo, and Balladyn were beside him. Instead of springing into action, they stared frozen and silent, visibly shaken, their gazes locked on Rowen. His heart pounded as he looked from one to the next, silently begging them to do something, say something—*anything*. It was the worry in the Reaper's eyes that hit Mason the hardest

"What do we do?" Mason demanded, his panic rising with every second. He needed some kind of answers before he went mad with worry.

Theo dropped to his knees and checked Rowen's pulse. "Her heartbeat is steady. She doesn't appear to be in pain."

"You don't know that." Mason gently cradled her head with shaking hands, silently willing her eyes to open. "Rowen? Can you hear me?"

Balladyn squatted next to him. "We should get her to the manor. She isn't safe here."

She hadn't been safe from the moment she left her home, Mason realized. First London had been after her, and now this bloody thing calling itself the Ancients. He had promised Rowen he would protect her, and he had failed. *Again*. He should've listened to his intuition. It had warned him that her acting as bait had been a terrible idea. She hadn't fainted. Something more had happened, something dark and malicious.

Pain no longer etched her face or twisted her body. It could almost make him believe that she was merely asleep. Except, in his soul, he knew she was in danger. He touched her cheek and felt her cold skin before pressing her closer.

He thought he'd be standing beside her in battle, that he would be able to see anything coming toward her. How he hated this powerless, weak feeling. He'd sworn never to experience it again after his parents. Yet, here he was.

And, somehow, this was so much worse.

"She grabbed her head before she cried out," Balladyn said.

The Reaper's voice was calm in the storm of panic and fear swirling around Mason. He slid his gaze to Balladyn. "Something tried to get into her mind at the cemetery earlier."

"Did something speak to her?" Ferne asked.

Mason shook his head. "She said it spoke, but she couldn't make out the words."

"Could she have lied?" Theo questioned.

Mason shot him a furious glare. "She has no reason to lie. She would've told me."

Fast-approaching footsteps pounded on the ground. It wasn't long before Carlyle stopped before them, out of breath. "There's no sign of Edie."

"We need to go," Balladyn urged Mason.

Mason nodded to the Reaper. The next second, they were in a room in the manor.

"I know Rowen doesn't like the second floor. We're on the third," Balladyn said.

Mason climbed to his feet and carried Rowen to the bed as Balladyn yanked the comforter aside. Then Mason was alone with her. He put his forehead against hers and fought back a scream of frustration. It felt as if someone had torn open his chest and ripped out his heart, leaving him raw, exposed. Afraid.

His promise to be there for her rang hollow in his head. He should've run faster. No, he should've been with her. He should've talked her out of her plan. Everyone had been there—even Balladyn—yet something had still gotten to her.

He dragged in a ragged breath and cupped her face as he looked down at her. "I don't know where you are, or what has been done to you, but you're a fighter, Rowen. So, I need you to fight. I'd be there with you if I could. Do whatever you have to on your end. I'll take care of things here. Just…come back to me. Please."

The door to the room burst open as the others rushed in. The minute they saw him, they slowed. Mason straightened but kept a hold of Rowen's hand while they took their places around the bed. For a long minute, everyone simply stared at Rowen. Then Ferne gently removed Rowen's shoes.

"The Healers are on their way," Rhona said from beside him.

Mason briefly met her green eyes. "I didn't find any injuries on her, but it's better to know for certain."

"Once we have that answer, we'll know what to do next," Carlyle said.

They were trying to make him feel better, maybe even attempting to make themselves feel less shaken by what had occurred as they all looked on. It had happened so quickly. One moment, Rowen was walking. And then next, she was falling.

"Has anyone had eyes on Edie?" Filip asked.

Song answered, "Nothing."

"None of the cameras around the isle have picked her up on facial recognition either," Kurt said.

Three Druids entered, led by a woman whose presence was commanding and comforting. Her skin was a rich, sun-warmed brown. Short, black coils framed an angular face while her dark eyes were direct and piercing. She was dressed in jeans, a blue and white striped tee, and a navy cardigan. There was strength in her stillness—a depth of magic Mason had a vague memory of.

The conversation died as the rest of the room became aware of the newcomers. The woman nodded to Rhona before returning her gaze to him. "It's nice to see you on your feet, Mason. I'm Lucy."

This must have been the Healer who had seen to his wounds at the tea shop. "Thank you for what you did for me. Can you help Rowen?"

"We will certainly try. I need you to step away from the bed," Lucy instructed while motioning to the two who had accompanied her.

Mason grudgingly released Rowen's hand, but he didn't move away. He lifted his chin, daring Lucy to force him to move, but she was no longer looking at him. Her attention was fixated on Rowen.

The Healers took their places around the bed, as everyone but Mason backed away to give them space. The Healers held out their hands over Rowen, palms down. Lucy began chanting first, then the other two joined her.

He clasped his hands together, digging his fingers into his skin in a desperate attempt to anchor himself. Every ragged breath tasted of powerlessness and his inability to protect those he loved. Watching the Healers hover over Rowen's limp form had him drowning in a storm of guilt and fury.

Magic sparked just beneath his skin, volatile and hungry, eager to be unleashed upon the one responsible for hurting Rowen. He could make Edie pay for what had happened to Rowen, but he couldn't leave Rowen. Not yet.

He watched her face for any signs of life. She lay perfectly still, not even an eyelid twitching. He couldn't see the Healers' magic, but he could feel it. Potent. Weighty. Compelling. It filled every corner of the room and swirled around the Healers and into Rowen. The longer they chanted, the more prevalent the magic became.

Their magic slid over him, winding around his face until his hands relaxed their grip. For the first time since he'd run to Rowen, he could take a deep breath. Air filled his lungs before he slowly released it. His eyes closed of their own accord, and the tightness in his body gradually unraveled. He had no idea how long he stayed like that before prying his eyes open to look at Rowen. There was no change, no matter how hard he searched.

The Healers lowered their arms in unison as their chanting stopped. The sudden silence in the room was deafening. Before

Mason could ask why they had stopped, Lucy turned to Rhona. "There's nothing to heal."

"Try again," Mason demanded.

Rhona cut him a look. "If Rowen were wounded, Lucy would've discovered it by now."

Lucy turned and offered him a sad smile. "She's in perfect health."

"Then why did she collapse? And why won't she wake?" Ferne asked.

Unease whispered its way over Lucy's face, tightening the corners of her mouth. "Her body is strong, but her mind…" She hesitated, searching for the right words. "It's like a door has been closed. We tried to reach her, but something—or someone—is keeping us out."

"What does that mean?" Elias asked sharply.

Mason saw Rhona and Balladyn share a worried look.

Lucy looked around the room. "It means we can't tell if her mind is injured or simply elsewhere. It doesn't feel as if she's lost. More like she's…locked away."

"Thank you," Rhona said before anyone else could comment. "Balladyn will see the three of you home."

The moment they were gone, Mason asked, "What was that look between you and Balladyn?"

Rhona's lips were tight as she met his gaze. "A group of Fae channeled their magic into their leader, who claimed to be an Ancient, and she took over my mind once as I slept."

"But you came out of it. You're here. That means Rowen will be okay." He kept waiting for her to smile and nod, but she didn't. "Wait. You said Fae."

"I did. Those Fae wanted to kill the Reapers, and they intended to use me to do it."

Mason reached for Rowen's hand again. "How did you get free?"

"Balladyn. To this day, neither of us knows exactly how. It nearly killed him."

The Reaper had done that for the woman he loved. Would he do it for someone he barely knew? Mason rubbed his thumb over the back of Rowen's hand. "Do you think it's the Fae who have Rowen now?"

"I don't," Rhona said with a shake of her head.

"It is suspicious that what happened to you and Rowen is so similar," Ferne said.

Rhona pressed her lips together. "I know. I always thought those Fae were working alone, but now I wonder if they had help."

"You mean from the evil we're fighting?" Elias asked.

"I do," Rhona.

Mason wasn't a violent man, but the acute need to bellow and smash a fist into something was strong. "None of that helps Rowen. I promised her we'd have her back, and I don't know how to do that if she's in her own head."

"We'll figure it out," Carlyle said.

Mason slid his gaze to his friend, not holding back his fury. "Really? How are we going to do that? We don't know what's happening. She's facing things alone! Without anyone to help."

"We'll figure out a way," Ferne repeated softly as she came up beside him, touching his arm. "We always do. We don't give up. We keep trying until we succeed."

Mason shook his head, tired and more scared than he had ever been. He didn't want to hear anything else. He just needed Rowen. And she was too far away for him to reach. He had her body, but not her mind. That was somewhere else. Had she let in the false Ancients? Or had the evil shoved its way in? Was it turning her against them?

Would it kill her if she didn't bend to its will?

"Sit."

The voice startled him out of his musings. He looked over to find the room empty except for Song. She raised a brow and pointed to a chair behind him that he hadn't seen before. Mason lowered himself into it while still keeping a hold of Rowen's hand.

Song pulled the covers over Rowen before moving to the foot of the bed. "It's difficult to trust those here. I know just how hard it can be. I was in your shoes not so long ago."

"I trust Ferne and Carlyle."

Her grin was fleeting. "Perhaps you do. Perhaps you don't. You've heard the stories, and you believe them because your sister and Carlyle experienced them. But you don't *really* believe."

"I do." Mason sighed, not bothering to hide his irritation.

"If you truly believed, you'd understand that every one of us—and I do mean *everyone*—will do whatever is needed to reach Rowen and get her back."

Song's words were direct, sincere, and candid. He studied her. "Why tell me this?"

"Like I said, I was in your shoes. We both come from the London Druids, and we've both experienced disillusionment there. We saw the corruption before meeting someone who changed..." She paused and shrugged. "Everything. Give us a chance. Work *with* us. Because we're fighting for Rowen."

He dropped his gaze to the bed, his throat swelling with emotion. "I'd give my life for hers." He swung his head to Song. "What do you need from me?"

"Every detail you saw today, from the moment you woke until Rowen fell."

CHAPTER FORTY-FOUR

Rowen's breath snagged in her throat as panic slammed into her. Her pulse stuttered once, then became a frantic, thunderous rhythm as dread surged in her chest. She spun, her boots ripping grass from the earth as she sprinted toward the cottage, every instinct wailing for her to run faster. The world narrowed to the pounding of her feet and the mounting roar in her ears.

She waited to see Mason throw open the door, to step out and ask what was wrong. There was no sign of his face in the windows, no indication that he had been watching. She called to her magic. It flooded her veins and pooled in her palm as she lifted her hand. With just a thought, magic shot forward and into the door. It wrenched open with such force that it banged against the wall and bounced back. She shoved her shoulder into it as she rushed inside.

"Mason! MASON!"

Rowen dashed about the cottage, her anxiety rising with each empty room she found. She stumbled into the kitchen, hysterical and terrified.

"Maaaasooooooooon!"

Even as she screamed for him, she knew he wasn't there. She was alone. The very thing she had dreaded. Her knees knocked together as her legs went weak. She gripped the table, knocking one of the chairs over with her frenzied, wild grab. Yet somehow, she stayed on her feet.

No kept repeating in her head. As if refusing to believe what was all around her would somehow change the outcome. A shaking breath filled her lungs, the air more like shards of glass than any kind of relief. She looked down at her hands. She couldn't feel them. Everything was numb. This had knocked her on her ass.

She had believed she was clever, offering to be bait. Oh, how Edie and the evil must have laughed. But how had they known the plan? Unless... She shook her head, unable to reconcile the truth. She didn't want to believe that someone in the group—someone she trusted—had leaked the information. But how else would they know? How else would her enemy have known?

Rowen righted the fallen chair and straightened. Then, she slowly made her way to the back door. It hung open, only a three-inch gap, but enough for her to look out as she approached. There was no sign of any of the others. Balladyn hadn't shown himself either. It appeared as if she really was on her own in this battle. And it *was* battle.

There was no denying the stakes at hand. It wasn't just her life on the line—it was a firmer foothold on Skye.

She opened the door wide and stood in the entrance, scanning the area. Clouds moved lazily while sheep continued to graze. There were no signs of cars or the roars of engines, but the cottage was set far enough from the road that she had never heard any of that to begin with.

"Did you find what you were looking for?"

Once more, the voice sounded all around her. It began on one side of her head and finished on the other. But it wasn't inside her mind. She recalled how the evil had asked her to let it in. It hadn't been able to get inside her before, and it still couldn't. It was a small win, but one Rowen would gladly take.

Rhona had spoken about Kerry mentioning how the false Ancients had spoken to her. Rowen would bet her meager savings that it had gotten into Kerry's head just as it was in Edie's. But not hers. Not now.

Not ever.

"What did you do with Mason?" Rowen demanded.

The offensive laugh sounded around her again. *"We didn't do anything to him. Or your other friends."*

"Then where is he?"

"Perhaps you should instead inquire about where you *are."*

An icy hand of panic reached for Rowen again. It would be so easy to fall back to that emotion, to let it sweep her up and away. But she would be right back where she had been before. The only way she would get through this was by taking emotion out of it.

How many times had her aunts told her cousins that when they were learning how to control their magic? That Thornevale adage was on a plaque in her mom's house. It was sage advice, but knowing what to do and actually following through were very different things. Besides, learning magic was one thing. Confronting a nameless, faceless malevolence out for her soul was another.

Rowen stepped out of the cottage. Was her foe right? Were the others somewhere else? Or was this another trick? It couldn't get into her mind, so how would it make her believe she was somewhere else?

If she were to survive this, she had to focus on herself first. Once she was victorious, she could worry about Mason and the others.

The wind continued to howl about her, its frosty bite chafing her cheeks. She didn't know if she was still on Skye, but the soil felt real enough. Just as the damp air felt tangible. The Ancients might have been silenced, but nothing could erase the fact that Skye had held hundreds of thousands of Druids throughout time.

She didn't need to hear or see them to feel their magic. From the very first moment she had arrived, she had sensed the power of the isle. It was all around her, waiting to be recognized, yearning to be used. It was there for any who dared to imagine its existence—Druid or not.

The evil needed her scared. It wanted her to believe she was alone. But she wasn't alone when her ancestors stood beside her. That didn't slow her racing pulse, however.

A tight ball of fear coiled in her stomach, a reminder of what was at stake. Nothing about this fight would be easy or quick. This wasn't about physical prowess on the battlefield. It was about wits and cunning. It was about the strength of her mind as well as her magic. The only way to win was to outsmart whatever held her.

"We have no wish to harm you. If we wished for that, we could've done it at any time. We've been trying to reach out to you, but your mind is strong. You wouldn't let us in."

Rowen turned in a slow circle, searching for the owner of the voice. "Show yourself."

"Soon. Now isn't the time."

"What do you want from me?"

"We're righting the course of our kind, as Edie already explained. We wish you to join us and find your rightful place in the new era that will soon unfold."

Bile surged in Rowen's throat. "And if I reject your offer?"

"Refusal isn't an option."

"I've already chosen my side."

"You chose wrong. We're giving you a chance to switch sides."

Rowen walked farther from the cottage, unsure of where she was going, but following her intuition. Or maybe her ancestors were leading her. "You've killed Druids."

"There are always casualties in war. The weak and the obsolete must be removed to make room for the new generation."

"You act as if you're going to create new Druids."

There was a brief pause, followed by a low chuckle. *"Something like that."*

"Explain it to me," Rowen urged as she hopped over the stone wall and continued walking.

"Druids are weak. That has to change."

"What about the Fae?"

"You needn't worry about them. They will be dealt with."

Rowen balled up her hands and pulled the sleeves of her sweater over them in a bid to keep her fingers warm. "The Fae have more magic than we do. Even the strongest Druids can't compete with them."

"Once you join us, nothing will stop us from rewriting history. The Fae will be removed, as will the Dragon Kings."

"You want this to be a world for humans only?"

"It will be a world of Druids only."

Her heart clutched. "Are you telling me you're going to kill anyone without magic?"

"*We won't,*" it replied shrewdly.

"Meaning, your new Druids will."

"*Do you have any idea what we can do together? How powerful we can become?*"

Rowen headed toward the loch. "If there was ever a time for just Druids, it is long gone. You have no right to rewrite the world."

"*We're the Ancients. We've lived through the past and witnessed everything. This is the only way before the Druids die out.*"

"Then maybe it's what needs to happen."

"*We won't allow that.*"

The longer Rowen spoke to the voice, the clearer it became that it wouldn't change its mind. The plan was already in motion. That it could so easily justify the annihilation of millions turned her blood to ice.

"Do you honestly expect me to join you after what you've just told me?"

"*It's the right thing for you to do. It's the* only *thing to do.*"

Rowen barked a laugh, outraged by its conclusion. "Right? You think this is right?"

"*We're protecting the magic.*"

"You aren't the Ancients. And even if you were, I'd still say you're wrong. Once more, I've made my choice. Nothing you say will change my mind."

"*Don't be so sure of that,*" it replied in a deadly, soft tone.

She suppressed the chill that ran down her spine. "Go ahead. Deliver your threats. Is this when you tell me Mason's life is in your hands? Or Ferne's?"

"*How about your mother's?*"

Perhaps Rowen should've expected that comeback, but it hit

her square in the chest, snatching her breath. Then she remembered who her family was.

This thing might not be the Ancients, but it *was* formidable. She'd told the others she wasn't a fighter, and that she would only get in the way in battle, but right now, she wanted to hurt the evil taunting her. Hit it over and over again until it lay bloodied and dead at her feet.

"Good luck with my mom—or any of my family, for that matter. They won't be taken easily," she proclaimed as she stopped on the loch's shore.

The voice issued a low, knowing laugh, its amusement unmistakable. *"Why haven't you asked why we chose you?"*

Because she was afraid to know the answer, petrified it might see something inside her she didn't want to admit. "I don't care."

"Liar."

The word was drawn out, laced with delight and excitement. Rowen gazed at the rippling water as the sky and surrounding mountains reflected upon its surface.

"You have a gift rarely given to Druids. A talent so formidable that it makes you shine as bright and vibrant as the moon in the night sky. An ability that will change the course of not just this realm, but many others, as well."

It was just as Rowen feared. Merely hearing the words made her want to vomit. She shook her head, denying the evil's words. "You're wrong. I know what I can do, and it isn't that special or potent."

"Oh, child. You've barely tapped into your magic. Let me show you what you can do."

The Scottish landscape blurred and shifted before her eyes until she looked down at Earth, the continents laid out before her. And amid it all were glowing lines, dissecting the world. She recognized the invisible sacred energy channels—or ley lines, as they were called.

She stared at them for a long time before she became aware of a figure beside her. Rowen glanced over, only to see herself with her arms outstretched. Each time she moved one of her hands, a ley line would shift, sometimes cutting off its power while amplifying it in other places across entire regions.

Shock reverberated through her, but before she could resolve any of that, the scene distorted once more. When it cleared, she stood in a murky, gloomy place. She knew without asking that she stood in The Grey. On either side of her were tall walls, papery and indistinct like membranes.

Once more, she saw herself, but this time, she was opening a rift between the dimensions with just a wave of her hand—a permanent doorway.

CHAPTER FORTY-FIVE

SKYE DRUIDS

Mason paced in front of the bed, feeling like a caged animal. His gaze kept returning to Rowen—hoping, praying, begging for the slightest twitch, a flutter of lashes. *Anything*. The longer she lay there, still as stone, the more his fear grew. Dread gnawed at him, and his thoughts spiraled into dark places he couldn't bear to stay in.

"I don't like this," he ground out, voice rough with a terror he could no longer contain. "I don't bloody like this one bit."

Ferne stood beside Rowen, wringing her hands. "Maybe I can try and reach out to her through my mind."

Mason stopped in his tracks, hope exploding through him like a fireworks display on New Year's. "Do you think it's possible?"

"I won't know until I try."

Concern made him falter. He refused to put Ferne in harm's way just to save Rowen. "What are the repercussions?"

Ferne turned her head to him and shrugged. "I won't know

until I try. I can't guarantee I'll be able to reach her, but I'm willing to attempt it."

Mason wanted to contact Rowen more than anything, but they had no idea what they were dealing with. There was a good chance that something could happen to his sister in the process, and that was unthinkable. "I can't ask it of you."

"You're not. I offered."

He shook his head. "Forget it. I won't take the chance that you'll get hurt. Rowen is already out of my reach. I can't have something happen to you, too."

"You love her, don't you?"

Mason walked to the foot of the bed and released a sigh. "Yes."

"Does she know?"

"It wouldn't matter. There can be nothing between us."

Ferne turned to face him, frowning. "Don't you dare say that. If you love her, then you'll find a way to be together. Who cares about London or this war? Look at me and Theo and all the others who are in relationships."

"I'm not the one pushing her away, sis."

"Oh," Ferne said softly, realization dawning across her face.

His lips twisted ruefully. "She told me we could only have one night, and I accepted that."

"She cares for you. I've seen it."

"You can't force someone to be in a relationship. It doesn't matter how much I love her if she doesn't want to be with me."

Ferne walked to him and took his hand. "I'm sorry."

"I'm not. I found my soulmate. She saved my life and kept me safe, and I got to have one amazing night with her. That's more than most people ever get."

"You should have it all, Mas. The happily ever after and everything that goes with it."

He shrugged. "My love life doesn't mean anything right now. Getting Rowen back is what's important."

"Then I'm going to try and reach her. And I don't need your permission," she stated firmly when he tried talking over her.

"Maybe you don't, but I think you owe it to Theo to let him know what you intend to do."

Ferne returned to the chair next to the bed and sat. "Then you'd better find him quick."

Mason raced out of the room and down the hall, yelling for Theo. Within seconds, Theo came bounding up the steps with Carlyle and Song on his heels. Mason explained what Ferne intended as they walked back to the bedroom.

Theo was the first through the door. Mason watched him lean down and whisper something in Ferne's ear. She smiled up at him and nodded, love shining in her eyes. Theo placed a kiss on her forehead and moved behind her, his hands on her shoulders. Ferne shot Mason one last look before taking a deep breath and closing her eyes.

"No. Absolutely not," Rowen stated resolutely. She refused to believe she had the power to do what she had been shown.

"Deny it all you want, but it's true."

"I would know if I could do those things. My magic is gentle. It doesn't destroy."

"You may think your magic is soft, that it hears and blends with

nature, but those were just the tendrils of something vast and sleeping, waiting to wake."

She slashed her hand through the air, and just like that, she was standing before the loch again. "Enough! I'm done with this. With you."

"Don't you want to know where that power comes from?"

"You're lying. About all of it."

"A small part of your mind knows I'm telling the truth. You've felt the potency of your magic before, but you've never dared to reach for it fully."

Rowen was finished with this game. She had moved past fearful to enraged. "If you know so much, then show yourself. Show me who you really are, instead of just talking to me."

Something caught at the edge of her vision. She turned her head as the air flickered with wavy lines. A form gradually began to take shape, as if molecules were being pieced together. When the vision cleared, Rowen was stunned at the being before her. They were beautiful, but in a way that felt entirely wrong.

Not masculine. Not feminine. Not quite human. Their face was a study in symmetry with high cheekbones, wide, full lips, and eyes of molten amber, their pupils vertical and unnerving like those of a predator unmasked. Skin untouched by time or sunlight shone like polished marble, making them appear carved from stone, rather than born. Silvery blond hair flowed fine as mist to their shoulders in soft waves, neither styled nor wild.

Layers of clothing—robes, or perhaps a coat—in shades of deep charcoal and dull pewter draped fluidly across their frame, concealing their shape. Every edge was sharp, the folds deliberate. There were no buttons, fastenings, or even seams. Just fabric that moved like smoke.

"Is this what you want? Does this form make this seem more real?" the being asked.

The voice that had once sounded feminine now defied category. It wasn't high nor low, soft nor loud. It hummed with an unnatural resonance that made Rowen want to run away. "There is nothing about *any* of this that is real."

"On the contrary, I've shown you what you're capable of."

"And why you want to use me."

The being's lips curled in a creepy smile. "Come now. You've seen the decline in Druids. Even those around you back home have had their magic wane. You can fix that."

"You're really trying to put all of this on me. How very... human of you."

"You help people. Look what you did for Mason. He would've died without you."

The more the being spoke, the more incensed Rowen became. "Stop talking as if you care about any of us. I see you for what you are. I see your actions for what you're after."

"I've never hidden my intentions. I told Kerry and Edie everything up front, just as I am with you."

"You fucking preyed on vulnerable people."

The being smirked and lifted one shoulder an inch before lowering it. "I saw *women* who had been bullied, betrayed, and overlooked. I saw Druids who held something special inside them that just needed a bit of nourishing."

"You turned Kerry into a killer."

A single finger lifted in response. "I do not turn anyone into anything. I see into their soul to their deepest, darkest desires and give them the means to become the people they've always wanted to be. For Kerry, it meant taking out decades of anger on others.

For Edie, it was getting rid of a cheating husband and breaking free of unpleasant, ungrateful children."

"And me?" Rowen demanded. "What would you be doing for me?"

"You would be the biggest prize of all, my dear. A nexus of origin, if you will. You aren't just any Druid. You're the reincarnation of one of the first Druids. A figure so powerful that you were once worshipped as a goddess. You're a primal force born when humans and magic were raw and untamed. Your return has woken dormant magic. We can't forget that you're also a living conduit between realms, where magic flows. You are both a bridge and a source, a convergence point. And a rebirth. Your presence alone keeps the fabric between worlds stable."

She gave a firm shake of her head. "This is all a dream. I hit my head or something. None of this can be real."

"If you wish to travel to another world, all you have to do is open yourself fully. You can channel energy from *any* realm. It's the kind of power others kill for. With one wave of your hand, you can be worshipped again."

"I don't want to be worshipped. I want this—*you*—to end."

The resolve that crossed the being's face was spine-chilling. "You can't stop what's happening. Even if the Skye Druids find the third pillar, it wouldn't prevent the great battle. Our time is now. Join us, and I'll spare your family. I'll even grant you Mason as your lover."

"No." Rowen put every ounce of energy, anger, and fortitude she had into the word. She didn't want the thing she spoke with to have any doubts regarding her response.

"How…pedestrian of you. I expected more from you. *Of* you."

"I don't care."

The atmosphere suddenly shifted, turning lethal and dangerous. She sensed the killer within the unholy body rising, altering. Growing. The mask of their once serene expression slid away as the air around them thickened and became charged. Whatever kindness had been in their eyes vanished, leaving behind twin pools of molten amber—hot and unforgiving.

"I want you to remember that I tried to be nice," the being stated as it took a step forward.

Its movements were predatory, like a snake ready to strike. For a heartbeat, terror froze Rowen in her tracks. Then she realized that if she were dead, the being couldn't use her or force her hand. It was the perfect strategy.

The individual began to laugh, softly at first, the sound growing the longer it continued. Finally, it dragged in a deep breath. "Did you really think I would go after you? That would be too easy. Who should it be first? Your mother? Or maybe Mason. I wonder how much he would beg to see you one last time."

Magic pooled in Rowen's hands without thought. She had never been so infuriated, had never felt such hatred. Her power felt different this time. It was stronger, thicker. Heavier. She sensed the unadulterated, raw potency of it. She lurched away from it in fear, but only for a moment. This was her magic. There was nothing to be afraid of.

Then she reached for more of it, calling to the ancient magic that coursed through her blood, through her soul.

"You really shouldn't have threatened them," Rowen said as she raised her arms and turned the full force of her wrath on the being.

CHAPTER FORTY-SIX

SKYE DRUIDS

Finn found himself in the hall outside the room again. He didn't want to be there, didn't want to think about how the mist had come out of the crack in the wall and branded his legs. But here he was.

Each night, he woke up covered in sweat, reliving that moment again and again. There had been no voice, no words—nothing that gave him any hint as to why he had been marked. He hadn't been the only one in the room. It was as if it had beelined straight for him, ignoring everyone else. The worst part was waiting for the other shoe to drop. Because it would.

Every hour, every day, they drew closer to the big showdown. And with each passing moment, the certainty rooted itself deeper in his bones: he wouldn't make it out alive. It was like a shadow stretching toward him, steady and inescapable.

It wasn't that he was afraid to leave this world… Okay, that might be a bit of a stretch. He was scared. Losing the only family he had ever known—that had ever loved him—sent him into a spiraling panic. What if he went down just when he could've saved Sabryn or one of the others? He couldn't fail them, and the idea of disappointing them was too much to even consider.

Finn ran a hand down his face as he spun away from the closed door. It was time to check on Rowen. But he had only taken one step when the door rattled ominously. A visceral dread slammed into him, numbing thought as his head snapped to the side. All he could do was stare helplessly as the door shook forcefully, as if something were trying to get out.

A ferocious roar came from the other side of the door—the kind he'd heard in The Grey. Terror rooted him to the spot, the world tilting sideways. Panic thundered in his chest, clawing its way up his throat while his mind refused to catch-up.

Finn could feel the monster's presence like a foul breath against his skin, thick and oppressive. It waited just beyond the door. A flimsy barrier of wood was all that stood between him and whatever horror it would unleash. His heart thundered a warning, but his body betrayed him. To his dismay, he looked down to find his hand moving slowly, deliberately, as if puppeted by a force not his own. His fingers brushed the cold metal of the knob. Clutched it.

"FINN!"

One moment, there was nothing but a buzzing sound. The next, Finn was on the ground, thunderous noise coming at him from everywhere—footsteps pounding on the floor, doors slamming, people yelling.

"Bloody fucking hell, Finn. Answer me!"

Finn was caught off guard by the terrified bellow. He swiveled his head to find Elias standing over him, his lips pressed together as worry clouded his eyes. Finn glanced around in confusion as he pushed up on his hand, unsure of why he was on the floor. "I'm here."

"About damn time. Get your arse up," Elias demanded as he yanked at Finn's arm.

Somehow, Finn found his feet again. He looked from his hand to the bedroom door, but it wasn't moving as it had been. "Did you see that?"

"See what?" Elias was already walking away.

Had he imagined it? Finn shook his head before following his friend. "What happened?"

"Did you no' hear the house shudder?"

Had he mistaken the door shaking for that? No, that wasn't possible. He knew what he had seen—what he had *felt*. "Yeah," he lied.

Elias cut him a look, those piercing blue eyes probing as he looked Finn over. "When this is over, you're going to tell me what happened back there."

"There's nothing to say."

"Doona try that shite with me, brother. I know you too well." Elias said no more as they reached the stairs and ran up to the next floor.

There were others ahead of them, all funneling into Rowen's room. Finn barely made it two steps inside before the crowd stopped him cold. He craned his neck, peered between others, and caught a glimpse of the bed. Rowen's skin shimmered faintly, like sunlight filtering through mist.

"Someone tell me what's happening," Mason's voice rose, frantic and desperate.

Ferne shook her head. "I don't know."

"This is a first." Balladyn lifted one of Rowen's arms for a closer look at the faint golden veins.

Mason raked his hands through his hair, his expression raw—a man on the brink of unraveling. "What can we do?" he asked hopelessly.

"We're Druids," Rhona said as she walked to the bed. "We do what we always do in times like these. We use our magic."

She held out her hands and waited until, one by one, each of them linked together to encircle the bed. Balladyn stood near the door, cautious and vigilant. Rhona's voice was clear and strong as she began the chant. Magic rose from each of them before surging into one thick coil that wound through them, between them, and filled the room.

Finn put his worries aside and focused every ounce of his power on Rowen.

Rowen's first shot of magic smacked the being's shoulder, twisting it halfway around. She immediately called for more and prepared for a second strike.

The being sneered, the action cold and terrifying as they slowly straightened. "Nice try, but you won't win against me."

"I think it's time we find out."

Rowen reared back both hands and lobbed magic with a grunt. The being moved its hand, causing one volley to go wide while the other hit the earth. She didn't hesitate to let her palms fill with more as the ground beneath her feet trembled, and a growing roar filled the air.

The next thing she knew, an enormous rift tore open in the earth between her feet. Rowen spun to the side as the ground gave way, narrowly missing being dragged into the yawning crater. Something struck her in the chest just as she regained her footing, throwing her backward and snatching her breath.

A groan fell from Rowen's lips as she struck the ground hard and rolled several times, moving on instinct alone. Magic surged in her hands as she rose up on one knee and lobbed a strike at the being. The volley crashed into her foe's knee, knocking them to the ground.

There was no time to celebrate. The battle was far from over. Rowen jumped to her feet, her body moving with disturbing familiarity—a muscle memory that wasn't hers yet somehow lived in her bones. Fear struck cold in her chest as her power poured from her in deadly bursts, instinct guiding every movement.

But it was the anger that simmered just beneath the surface that pushed her: anger at the fight, but also at the truth that she could no longer deny. A truth she hadn't wanted to believe. She was all the being had shown her—and more.

Now, she had no choice but to draw upon the magic she never asked for and wield it to survive.

She barely recognized the woman fighting. It was almost as if she were floating above the scene, watching the fight playing out like a movie. But she felt every lick of magic as it moved through her, every flex of muscle as she moved.

She was Rowen.

And yet, she was this other, unnamed woman, as well.

Siofra.

The past and the present converged, creating a maelstrom of magic and defiance. Her earlier apprehension vanished with every blow she landed. The being retreated, holding their hands up in an effort to block her strikes. Whatever threat it had dared to show her had faded to panic.

Yet, she didn't relent. Not for a second. Rowen relentlessly sent barrage after barrage, becoming stronger and surer with each assault. And with it, her magic expanded and swelled, shifting to be more potent and fearsome. She felt the threads of the cosmos in her fingers and detected magic, not just from Earth, but also from other realms as it reached out to her.

"Please!"

She paused and looked down at the being on its knees, its clothing in tatters. Their hands still shielded their face. And in that hesitation, Rowen debated whether to take its life. Then she thought of all those it had already harmed, the lives it had ruined, and the deaths it was responsible for. Rowen drew back her hand, but her indecision had given it the time it needed to vanish.

"No!" The word ripped from her throat, animalistic and visceral, as the air around her collapsed inward.

Her vision began to warp, colors bled, and light twisted painfully until everything flickered and then fell into total obscurity. There were several seconds of nothingness, and she could no longer tell if she was still near the loch or if she was someplace else altogether.

Unexpectedly, the weight of something soft and comforting settled over her. Her finger moved, and she felt the softness of crisp, cool sheets against her skin and a mattress beneath her. She couldn't see because her eyes were closed. Was this some kind of trick, something to get her to let her guard down? She remained calm and prepared herself for the worst. Then, she opened her eyes.

"Rowen?"

She blinked and turned toward the husky voice tinged with hope. Her gaze collided with stormy gray eyes. Elation bloomed as she reached for Mason. Then she hesitated. This could be another trick by the being—one that had the potential to rip her to shreds.

The gray of Mason's eyes darkened with worry. "Rowen? What is it?"

"I'm not sure it's really you," she said.

He sat on the edge of the mattress. "I promise. It's really me."

She wanted to trust him, but she couldn't. Not after everything she had seen and experienced. She sat up, pushing down the covers as she examined his face.

"It's me," he whispered and rested his hand palm up on her leg, waiting for her to take it.

He sat still and patient as she inspected his face before returning her attention to his eyes. It was there that she saw the subtle but telling flash of desire, the craving to hold her, kiss her. To love her until she was too satiated to move.

And that's when she knew she had bested her foe. Her face crumpled as she buried her head in her hands. Mason enveloped her, bringing her into the safe and steady shelter of his arms. He said nothing, merely held her as she finally lowered her defenses. She wound her arms around him, clinging to him, her face in his neck as she let the reality of what she had endured sweep through her.

She wished they could return to the night they had shared together. It hadn't just been the pleasure she had experienced. It had been the time with him: his touch, the warm press of his lips, the look in his eyes when he gazed at her. His smile, in turns sweet and incomparably seductive. He had demanded nothing but the total surrender of her body. How was she to know that he would reach a part of her she had always believed she had been born without?

Tears streamed down her face. The harder she cried, the tighter he held her. He didn't ask for specifics, didn't demand answers. It was as if he knew she needed his touch more than anything else at that moment.

Rowen opened her eyes and saw their friends standing around, quietly watching the scene unfold. Reluctantly, she pulled out of Mason's arms, embarrassed to be caught breaking down so dramatically. She sniffed and wiped at her face. "It's good to be back. I wasn't sure I'd ever make it."

"What happened?" Ferne asked softly.

Rowen found her gaze drawn back to Mason's. There was an unreadable expression on his face. His fingers laced with hers, his hold firm but gentle. Just as she was about to answer Ferne, Rowen felt a thread of something sinister running through the house. The manor was fighting against it. Had been battling it for some time. And while the structure was holding, it was only a matter of time before it became too weak to fight back.

As if the evil sensed her, there was a loud bang below them. And she knew exactly where it was coming from. The others ran from the room toward the sound. The only one who stayed behind with her was Mason. She shoved the covers away and swung her legs over the side of the bed. He rose at the same time she did and followed her from the room.

Rowen made her way to the floor below. As she stepped off the last stair, she saw the others grouped around the second-to-last door on the left. Fear tried to take her, but she turned to her newfound magic and brought it around.

Mason kept in step beside her. She half-expected him to ask what she was doing. The question was there in his eyes each time she looked at him, but the words never passed his lips.

She reached the others and gently wove through them until she stood before the door. There, she paused and swung her head to the right, where Finn stood. He was pale, his body stiff, and his eyes glued to the door. The fear she sensed didn't only come from him, though. It was time to end this reign of terror.

Rowen gripped the door and readied to turn the handle when Mason touched her arm. She looked over and saw him. His trepidation wasn't for what might await in the room. It was for her. There wasn't time to tell him that she, of all people, would be safe. Instead, she gave him a small smile, hoping it would be enough. He dipped his chin and let his hand fall away. Then she opened the door and stepped into the empty room.

The crack in the wall pulsed with a glittering energy, alive and dangerous. She sensed the monster on the other side, struggling to get through. It wanted her to help it, to open a doorway so he could climb through. It *expected* her to do just that.

"Not in this lifetime, asshole," she murmured. "Not in *any* lifetime."

Rowen walked to the far wall. It stood—literally and figuratively—between the two worlds. Each time her friends had gone through to the other side, it had weakened the spot. Callum had repaired it, but it wouldn't hold for much longer. She had once been scared of this room and what it represented, but not any longer.

The being had attempted to coax her and then frighten her to its side, but all it had done was reveal her true power—and purpose. So much of her life now made sense.

Rowen looked over her shoulder to Mason standing in the doorway, his muscles bunched, ready to come for her if she asked—the kind of man who would always be there. What a fool she had been to only give herself one night with him.

CHAPTER FORTY-SEVEN

Mason's heart lodged in his throat as he met Rowen's pale blue gaze. The gold in her veins had dimmed when she woke, but it glowed brightly beneath her skin once more. He didn't know what she was doing, but he didn't want her in that room, especially after hearing the sounds. Yet he recognized the resolve in her eyes and had grudgingly relented. However, he intended to stay close. Just in case.

She faced the wall once more as the crack burned brighter. He blinked and rubbed his eyes when he thought he saw Rowen begin to fade out of sight.

"What the hell?" Scott asked behind him.

It wasn't just him. The others saw her vanishing, too. Mason lunged forward, only to have hands grip him, keeping him back. "ROWEN!"

But it was too late. She was gone.

He yanked at the hands holding him and slipped free to rush to the spot she had been. He waved his arms around, hoping it was just some trick of the light and she was still there. But she was really gone. And this time, it wasn't just her mind that had been taken.

"Where is she?" he demanded as he turned in a circle. He spun to the others. "Where the fuck is she?" he bellowed.

Silence met his question as the group stared at him, too shocked to speak.

Then, Finn said in a soft voice, "She's on the other side."

"How do you know that?" Mason asked. When Finn didn't immediately reply, he strode to the Irishman and gripped him by the front of his shirt. With his nose pressed to Finn's, he demanded, "How do you fucking know that?"

Suddenly, there were hands on Mason again, this time attempting to pull him away from Finn while others held the Irishman, though he never once tried to defend himself against Mason.

"I feel it," Finn finally replied.

Everyone stilled at his words, the room going deathly quiet. Mason stared at him for a long moment before releasing him. It wasn't Finn's fault that Rowen had vanished. Mason dragged in a shuddering breath and glanced at the wall. He had just gotten her back. How could she be gone again?

He swallowed against the growing ache in his chest and asked Finn, "Is she...hurt?"

"Nay," Finn answered with a shake of his head.

"How can you be sure?" Rhona asked.

Finn shrugged. "I...I'm not sure. I just am."

"I want to go after her," Mason stated.

Finn's brows snapped together. "You can't."

"Watch me." Mason stalked to the wall and began tearing at the crack like a crazed person.

He knew it was delusional to think he could reach Rowen, but he had to try. He had sat idly by her bed and waited. He couldn't do that again.

A sliver of wood punctured his finger, sending pain shooting up his arm, but he didn't slow. He kept ripping wood away, and when that became too difficult, he punched it. Over and over again. Mason heard his name being shouted and felt hands trying to stop him, but he fought against all of it.

Until he found himself pinned to the floor on his back.

Through all the shouting, he heard her voice calling his name softly. Mason stilled and looked through the bodies on top of him to see Rowen. There wasn't a scratch on her. She gently touched Scott and then Killian, both of whom released him and moved away. Then she put her hand on Elias, Finn, and Theo. Once they backed up, Mason realized that someone was beneath him, their arms wrapped around his neck.

"I suppose I can let go now," Carlyle murmured.

Mason rolled to his feet when his friend loosened his hold. After he helped Carlyle stand, Mason turned to Rowen and raked his eyes over her. She looked normal. No longer did her veins glow. She reached for his hand and gave it a squeeze.

He drew in a shuddering breath. "Where did you go?"

"I'll explain all of it," she said before looking around the room. "No one has to worry about anything getting through again."

"You killed the monster?" Kirsi asked hopefully.

Rowen gave a small shake of her head. "I shored up the wall. As long as we don't open it again, we'll be safe."

"I'm eager to hear how you did that," Balladyn said.

Mason couldn't stop looking at her. Her touch was strong, but she was pale. "You need to eat something."

"I am hungry," Rowen admitted with a wan smile.

Carlyle headed out of the room. "I can take care of that."

Once in the kitchen, Mason sat next to her at the table. Bronwyn put water and a glass of whisky before Rowen. To his surprise, Rowen tossed back the liquor. Her face puckered as she swallowed.

Carlyle moved about the kitchen, putting together different plates of food from the fridge and placing them on the table to be shared. Except for Rowen. He made her her own plate, piled with food. She took a few bites and, after a deep breath, began her story.

For the next half hour, the room was steeped in silence as Rowen spoke. Every word painted the being in sharper detail, and with each revelation, the unease thickened. Mason sat frozen, his jaw tight, his feelings alternating between fury on her behalf and pride at her strength.

Carlyle silently refilled Rowen's plate twice, and each time, she devoured the food with a kind of desperation that only someone who had come too close to death could understand. Her voice never wavered, even when her hands shook. When she finally finished, the weight of what she had seen lingered over them.

"I must say, it's impressive that you fought that thing alone," Elodie said.

Filip twisted his lips. "Are we sure Rowen is who she says she is? What if she joined the evil and is here to deceive us?"

"I'm not," Rowen said calmly.

Scott shrugged. "It's a valid question. It did have you, and it sounds exactly like something it would do."

Mason looked around to see everyone's reaction. He didn't like the doubt he saw reflected back at him.

"You should question me," Rowen replied. "I've come face-to-face with the evil, and I can tell you that it will use every trick it knows. The only thing I knew for certain was the being itself. I didn't trust anything else. And none of you should, either."

Theo tapped a finger on the table. "Then how do you suggest proving to us that you're on our side?"

Rowen's smile was fleeting. "Trust is a tenuous thing. It isn't something to be given. It's something that's earned. I stood in battle, but it wasn't beside any of you. This fight was done on my own. I know in my heart where I stand, and I intend to prove that to you." She looked around the table. "To all of you."

"Tell us about the being," Rhona urged.

Rowen took a deep breath. "It didn't lie to me. It laid out everything and even showed me what I could do. I don't think it gave Kerry or Edie false promises either. It was almost…kind," she said with a wrinkle of her nose. "At least, at first. It believed that showing me the power I could wield would be enough to turn me."

"It did with Kerry," Balladyn said.

Rowen glanced at the table. "It acknowledged that. It said that it sees the thing we want most and gives it to us."

"And yours isn't the power you've discovered?" Carlyle asked.

Mason shot him a dark look, even as he admitted that it was a valid question.

"No," Rowen answered. "It isn't. It couldn't get into my head as it did with Kerry and Edie, and I don't think it was able to see what I really want."

Song asked, "And what might that be?"

"Peace. Happiness." Rowen briefly met his gaze. "Affection. Once the being realized I had no interest in any kind of power or authority it offered, the threats began. It went for the jugular, to the thing that would hurt me the most."

Killian shifted in his chair. "And you didn't cave?"

"I attacked," Rowen replied. Then her gaze slid away as she bit her bottom lip. "I had the opportunity to kill it, but I hesitated a second too long. It escaped, and the next thing I knew, I was in the room upstairs."

Jasper leaned forward, his face blazing with anger. "Why would you hesitate? Do you no' know what this thing is? It could've stopped all of this."

"I don't think it could've," Bronwyn said.

Elodie shook her head. "I don't either."

"Still, it would've been nice to have it gone," Willa said.

Remorse colored Rowen's face. "I know. I'm sorry."

"It was your first battle. You made it back to us with information. That's something to celebrate," Balladyn said.

Ariah asked, "Is the magic really yours, then? Or is it from the being, like it gave to Kerry and Edie?"

"It's mine, though I can't prove it," Rowen replied. "But I believe it's recruiting others."

"From Skye?" Rhona asked worriedly.

Rowen shrugged. "From Skye and elsewhere. They wanted me, and I wouldn't put it past them to have finagled a way to get me here."

"This is all kinds of fekked up," Finn murmured.

Rowen turned the glass of water on the table with her fingers. "They said I was afraid to reach for the full depth of my magic. And they were right."

"What changed?" Filip asked.

"They issued a threat." Rowen's head swiveled, and she looked straight at Mason.

His breath left him in a rush. His lips parted, but the words lodged in his throat. Disbelief warred with a flicker of something dangerously close to hope. Could she really care for him? The thought alone made his heart stumble, a raw ache surging in his chest. He dared not hold on to the possibility too tightly in case it shattered and wrecked him completely.

Rowen sighed and continued. "I didn't believe them at first about being reincarnated, but I do now."

"Did they give you a name of this Druid you're supposedly reincarnated from?" Balladyn asked.

Rowen shook her head. "No, but the name came to me later, when I was fighting them. Siofra."

The Reaper's eyes widened in shock as his face went slack. "Siofra? Are you sure?" he questioned insistently.

"I am," Rowen replied.

Mason frowned at this turn of events. He looked between the usually unflappable Reaper who wore a fierce expression of foreboding and Rowen, who sat serenely, only a small furrow marring her brow.

Rhona turned to her husband. "Do you know that name?"

Balladyn never took his eyes from Rowen as he said, "I've heard of it. I never met Siofra, but I know someone who has."

"Who?" Mason asked.

It was Rhona who guessed, "Erith."

Balladyn nodded and finally slid his gaze to his wife. "She would know. I'll go speak to her."

And then he was gone.

"Who is Erith?" Mason asked.

Carlyle stretched out his legs and crossed his ankles. "Oh, just the leader of the Reapers. She's also known as Death."

Sabryn rolled her eyes at Carlyle. "She doesn't pay much attention to humans. It's the Fae Erith focuses on."

"Balladyn and others like him reap Fae souls," Rhona explained. "Erith is judge and jury, and the Reapers carry out her orders."

Mason rubbed the back of his neck. "Is Erith some kind of deity?"

"She's the closest thing to it," Elias said.

Rhona twisted her lips. "Actually, her race is called the Star People. They can travel anywhere in the universe, and their power is unmatched. So, yeah, they're what most would call gods and goddesses. Erith, while formidable, is a good person."

"I take it there are those who aren't," Rowen said.

"Without a doubt," came a new voice.

Mason jerked upright in his chair and looked toward the back of the kitchen, where Balladyn stood next to a petite woman with wavy, midnight hair hanging to her waist and lavender eyes. She was so beautiful that Mason could barely look at her. Without a doubt, he knew he was looking at the leader of the Reapers.

CHAPTER FORTY-EIGHT

SKYE DRUIDS

Rowen eyed the stunning woman dressed in black from head to toe. Erith's unusual eyes moved from the others to her. Rowen fought against the urge to fidget under the weight of the goddess's piercing gaze.

"Once, a very, very long time ago, Druids and Light Fae walked Skye together," Erith said. "The friendship ran deep, but it wasn't one-sided. The Druids had as much to offer the Fae as the Fae did them." She paused and swallowed. "The magic that ran through the Druids was strong, and at times, too raw to control. But there was one who brandished magic as easily as breathing."

As she spoke, blurred images flashed in Rowen's head, gone too quickly for her to make out anything. Yet she felt like she was being swept away to another time—another body. There were faint voices, the words an indistinct jumble.

"This Druid was a natural leader," Erith continued. "Someone who saw the world in a way that few others could. The good. The bad. And the expanse between. A Druid who understood that the magic given to them had the power to turn the tides of any war."

Erith stretched out her arm, palm down. Rowen stared at it while her heart began to beat quicker and harder against her ribs. The goddess then twisted her fingers as she rotated her palm upward. Unable to help herself, Rowen rose to her feet, her own hand outstretched to Erith. And along her arms, Rowen saw the glint of a golden glow running beneath her skin.

Her magic swirled through her, rushing through her body so quickly that she swayed with it. Someone grabbed her to keep her upright. She recognized Mason's strong hands, but she couldn't look at him. She couldn't look anywhere but at her fingers, nearly touching Erith's.

The glimmering beneath her skin intensified as the room faded, and she once more looked down upon Earth, the ley lines glowing in that same golden hue. Then she lifted her gaze and saw hundreds of other planets shining with their own ley lines.

"Not even my kind can see them as you can."

Erith's voice came from beside her. Rowen met her gaze as they stood in the darkness of space together. "Why me?"

"Why are any of us chosen? It's an answer I cannot give you."

"This power is…" She hesitated, struggling to find the right word.

Erith lifted a perfectly arched black brow. "Weighty? Burdensome? Intense?"

"Yes. And so much more."

"You managed it before. You can again."

Rowen rubbed her temples as her head began to ache. "How many times have I returned?"

"As far as I'm aware, this is the first. I believe you've returned because you were needed the most."

"It's terrifying knowing that a single decision I make could change things."

Erith chuckled. "I hate to burst your bubble, but that goes for anyone and everyone. Don't take on more than needed."

"I just can't understand why the being told me what I am? Didn't they realize I could choose to stand against them?"

"I can't tell you what they were thinking. It isn't a move I would've made."

Rowen turned to face Erith and tried not to focus on the darkness around her and the bright lights of the stars. "Are we really in space?"

"In a manner of speaking," she replied with a grin. "Don't think too hard about it."

That was proving difficult. "I have another question. Have you seen this battle waged against Skye before?"

Erith slowly shook her head. "I've not. I believe it's something the Skye Druids have dealt with on their own, for whatever reason. Fae may have been involved once upon a time, but they are long dead and can't give us any answers."

"I was afraid you were going to say that." Rowen looked down at her arms, but the golden light was gone.

"You have a choice, you know. You can pick a side and fight, or you can return home to Orcas Island and forget all about this."

Rowen shook her head as her thoughts turned to Mason. "I can't do that. Even if I hadn't come here, even if the Skye Druids hadn't welcomed me, I'd still fight for them."

"That's exactly something Siofra would've said."

"You were friends?" Rowen asked hopefully.

"I knew of her. I observed her, but I never spoke to her. I wish I had now."

A wave of emotion filled her throat, and Rowen blinked back a wave of tears. "Thank you for this."

"It is I who should be thanking you. You showed me a glimpse of the universe that I've never witnessed before."

"I'll bring you back anytime."

Erith laughed. "I'm going to take you up on that."

"You'd better," Rowen said with a wide smile.

"One thing," Erith cautioned. "Be careful. You've seen how the evil works, and the nearer it comes to the time of the ultimate battle, the more it will spin its machinations. Its only goal is to defeat the Skye Druids, and it will do, say, and use whoever in order to achieve that."

Rowen hated that the goddess was right. "I can't lose focus on the London Druids either."

"There is usually always more than one enemy at the gate. Now. We'd best get back before Mason loses his mind."

Hearing his name made Rowen recall the feel of his hands holding her upright, and just like that, she was back in the kitchen, her arm outstretched, and her fingers meeting Erith's. The goddess grinned as she lowered her arm. A slow smile spread over Rowen's face. That private time with Erith had grounded her more firmly in her convictions. And somehow, she knew it was the start of a beautiful friendship.

"I don't know what that was, but it was something amazing to behold," Sabryn said into the silence.

Rowen lowered her gaze to Mason. The furrows on his brow eased as he searched her face. Then, he loosened his hold and let his hands drop as he sat back in his chair. Rowen instantly missed his touch. Everything in her life had been turned upside down. She wasn't the same person she had been when she left home, or even the woman who had spent the most wonderful night of her life with Mason.

There was one thing she wanted: more. More time, more kisses, more everything with Mason

"Rowen is indeed Siofra," Erith announced. "You've found a powerful player in this deadly game. Good luck to all of you." She gave Balladyn a meaningful look and disappeared.

"Well," Bronwyn said brightly. "We might not have the water pillar, but we have Rowen."

A round of clapping and loud whistles filled the kitchen. Rowen smiled as she sank into her chair, but she couldn't shake Erith's warning. The war had taken a turn. And none of them knew in quite what direction yet. Only time would tell them that. The one thing she knew for sure was that she was staying on the isle.

She turned her head toward Mason. Everything always came back to him. Every thought, every action…he was on her mind. Stormy gray eyes met hers. So much was unspoken between them, so many things left unsaid during their night of passion—things that had drifted through her mind that she dared not give voice to. Now, they all suddenly wanted to fly from her lips.

CHAPTER FORTY-NINE

SKYE DRUIDS

The only light in the library was the candle flame that slowly wavered from the center of the coffee table. Mason sat, his arms resting on the curved arms of the chair, a glass of untouched whisky dangling from his fingers. He could hear a voice across the entryway in the other room. There was laughter and loud meows from the kitchen. No doubt Carlyle was making more cat treats.

The conversation in the kitchen had lasted for hours. Rhona and Rowen had gone off together for a private conversation, while Kurt had pulled Mason aside to review some footage from the cameras placed throughout his estate. It was during that time that Billings had called Mason from the secure mobile with some good news. He had narrowed down the spies to six individuals.

That, in conjunction with the video Kurt had captured, alleviated some of Mason's worry. But not all of it. He should be there, protecting his home and staff. It was difficult to accept that his presence could actually cause more harm than good. Billings would keep the house running, and Mason could manage the estate from Skye.

That wasn't why he was sitting in the dark library alone, though. His bags sat packed by the door, but he hadn't made a move toward them. Remaining at the manor with Rowen so close was a special kind of hell. But so was returning to the cottage without her.

He would be wrapped in pain either way. There was no way he could cut her out of his life. She was too important to him. The only way he could function was if he found a way to put some emotional distance between them. Staying somewhere else, making sure not to sit beside her, not riding in the same vehicle… They were all small steps that seemed simple enough, but he knew they would be impossible to carry out because he was drawn to her like the tides to the moon.

Their lives were intertwined on so many levels, in so many ways, that he would never be able to disentangle himself from her. And he didn't want to. It felt good to be with her. Even if it was just walking beside her. He found it easier to smile when she was around. Her mere presence brought him joy.

And the passion. He drew in a long breath. It wouldn't matter how much his body ached for release. He would never find the kind of contentment and satisfaction he had in her arms. He loved her. Absolutely. Completely. Unreservedly.

He had been gifted one spectacular night that had ruined him for all others, but it had been worth it. He might not get the happily ever after he craved, but he'd touched and held the kind of passion that many so rarely found.

It was Rowen for him, or no other. He wouldn't do himself or another woman a disservice by trying to build a life together.

Mason was okay with that, too. He had found love, and he knew Rowen cared about him. Maybe in another life, they could've been together. Or perhaps in a previous life. People didn't have the kind of connection they did and have their souls *not* recognize each other.

That gave him hope that he would find her again in another life, and there, they could spend years together laughing and loving. Perhaps even have children. He would hold on to that dream and his memories to get him through the rest of his life.

He sighed and looked at the ceiling. Then he leaned forward, placed his glass on the table, and pushed to his feet. At the library doors, he paused and grabbed the handles of both bags. He had left a note for Ferne so she'd know where he had gone. He walked to the front door and tried to open it, but it wouldn't budge.

Mason made sure it was unlocked and tried again, but it still wouldn't move. He released one bag and put his hand on the wood as it finally dawned on him that the house was keeping him there. After a long minute, the door clicked open.

As he reached to grab the handle of his luggage, he glanced behind him and saw Carlyle holding open the swinging door of the kitchen, watching him. Mason dipped his head to his friend and slipped out of the house.

CHAPTER FIFTY

SKYE DRUIDS

Rowen drank in the blush pink and lavender sunrise that announced a new day. She had given up on sleep hours ago and instead took up residence next to the window, her mind turning over recent events—a common occurrence since arriving on Skye.

Yet, as scary and exciting as her new magic—and her link to history—was, it was Mason who occupied most of her thoughts. She had almost gone to him when she couldn't sleep, but she wouldn't be there to talk—and they really needed to talk. Getting the words out, however, would be a trial of its own.

She sighed, wishing she were snuggled against Mason's body right then, her head resting on his chest, his heartbeat in her ear. His arm holding her. The last time she had seen him was when she followed Rhona out of the kitchen. Rowen had caught a glimpse of him right before the door swung closed behind her.

The next several hours had been spent with Rhona, going over every single detail of her interaction with the evil, time and time again, until Rowen was ready to pull her hair out. Then there had been the call with her mom. Next came the family discussion with her aunts—specifically Aunt Maelin, who only confessed that she had seen Rowen on Skye in someone's dream.

By the time Rowen sought out Mason, it was after one in the morning, and he was nowhere to be found. That's when she decided to get some sleep and seek him out in the morning. Except she hadn't been able to shut off her mind. All she had wanted was Mason. She longed to hear his thoughts and get his opinion. He would tell her the truth of things, even if it was hard to hear. She trusted him completely. The only other people she could say that about were her family.

Rowen surged out of the chair and stalked from her room. She didn't care if he was asleep. She had things to say. Things he needed to hear.

The thump of her bare feet as she half-walked, half-jogged was swallowed by the rug. She didn't know what it would mean if she climbed into Mason's bed again. Maybe it would turn into something. They could also fizzle out quickly. But she'd never forgive herself for not finding out.

The apprehension that had kept her holding him at arm's length now seemed laughably trivial—an echo of fear drowned beneath the weight of everything they had faced together. What had once been safety and security now felt like a barrier to something real, something she no longer had the strength to deny. The thought of standing beside him and not leaning against him or reaching for him wasn't just inconceivable, it was unbearable.

She came to a halt before his door, breathing heavily, her front pressed against it as she knocked softly. Excitement and anticipation coursed through her. She couldn't wait to tell him that she wasn't going to ignore her feelings anymore, that she wanted more than just one night with him.

She rapped her knuckles against the door again, louder. Harder. A smile curved her lips. What a fool she had been, telling him there couldn't be anything between them. Had she dared to give them a chance, she could've been lying in his arms all night, cocooned in his warmth.

Her leg began to bounce as a niggle of worry slid into her mind. Perhaps he was sleeping heavily. She knocked a third time, her smile slipping. Still, he didn't answer. Her enthusiasm twisted into trepidation—a knot of foreboding she couldn't shake.

Rowen put her hand on the knob, debating for only a second, and turned. The door swung open soundlessly, revealing the morning sunlight streaking through the parted curtains to illuminate the empty bed.

She took an uncertain step into the room. Maybe she had missed him somehow in her search before she went to bed. He could've been with Carlyle or Ferne. Or, her mind grasped frantically, he might be waiting for her below now.

Yet the longer she looked around the room, the clearer it became that Mason was gone. She turned to the closet, clinging to one last hope, but it was dashed the moment she opened the door and saw it empty. She stumbled back, unable and unwilling to believe what she saw. He wouldn't go. He wouldn't leave.

Rowen backed out of the room and shut the door as the hard truth of reality settled around her. Mason had left. Whether he had gone to the cottage or returned to England remained to be seen. She lifted her chin, spine straightening with newfound resolve.

She was going to find out.

She spun and ran down the stairs to the main floor, briefly

pausing beside the table that held all the car keys and fumbling them in her hands as she tried to grab a set. Taking someone's car without asking was beyond rude, but she would beg for forgiveness later. She couldn't let another second go by without seeing Mason.

A small thought at the back of her mind said she could call him, but that wasn't what she wanted—or needed. She had to stand in front of him. Needed to see his face so she could…well, she wasn't sure what she would do, but it was imperative that she be close enough to touch him.

She raced to the front door and threw it open. Not even the pebbles digging into her feet slowed her as she clicked the key fob in her hand to see which keys she had taken. The lights of a black Range Rover flashed, and she hurried toward it. Within seconds, she had the SUV peeling out of the drive, spraying gravel as every fiber of her being urged her to find Mason, that if she didn't, she would lose him forever.

Thankfully, the roads were empty that early in the morning. Every second felt like an eternity, as if someone or something were purposefully keeping them apart. She pressed the gas pedal, and the vehicle lunged forward in response. The curves came fast and tight. She took one so recklessly that she nearly wrecked.

But not even that slowed her. Her entire being had one decree: find Mason.

A swell of relief came when she saw the road to the cottage approaching. She was almost there, almost to Mason. A smile tugged at her lips as she laughed at her feverish actions. Mason would have a good chuckle when she told him. Rowen slowed and adjusted in her seat. There was no need to drive so recklessly now.

She spotted a car driving up to the stop sign as she neared. Instantly, she recognized the Focus. She could only stare in shock as Mason's car pulled out, heading *away* from her. If he had been going to the manor, he would've come toward her. Why could he be heading in the other direction?

And then, she knew. He was heading to the Skye Bridge.

"No," she murmured and slammed her foot down on the accelerator.

The engine roared, and the SUV shot forward as she raced to catch up with him. The winding roads kept him at an almost unavoidable distance. She increased her speed on the straightaways but had to slow down on the curves to avoid crashing. Mile after mile, the bridge grew ever closer.

Panic-stricken and seeing her future slipping from her fingers, Rowen floored it again on the last stretch of the road to the bridge. The Rover once more answered her need for speed and surged forward, quickly gaining ground. She had to pass him before he reached the village. It was the only way to stop him.

"Come on, come on," she urged the vehicle.

She sped toward Mason, moving over to the opposite lane and blowing past him. The moment she was clear of his car, she turned the wheel, angling the SUV across both lanes as she came to a screeching halt. Rowen fumbled with the seat belt release, her hands shaking as she tried to exit at the same time. Once the door finally opened, she spilled out onto the pavement as he stepped out of his car.

Fury and disbelief mottled his handsome face. "Have you lost your bloody mind? You could've been killed!" he yelled.

Rowen ignored his words and strode to him. He could yell at her all he wanted, but he was going to listen to her. As she neared, she saw his anger shift to uncertainty. He watched her warily as she stopped before him. Then she grasped his face and pressed her lips to his.

He jerked back, stormy gray eyes studying her, as if he didn't know what to make of her. She held his gaze and smiled. The next thing she knew, he jerked her against him and swept his tongue into her mouth. Her soul sang, her heart swelled. This was where she belonged. With this incredible, kind, handsome man who felt like coming home. A man fiery in his respect, fierce in his loyalty, and ferocious in his love.

She could've stood there kissing him forever, but he slowed the kiss and eventually lifted his head. He stared down at her, his breathing as ragged as hers, as he gently cupped her face. The wind cut through her thin pajamas, but she barely felt it next to him.

"Don't go," she begged.

His brow wrinkled in confusion. "I'm not leaving."

"You were headed to the bridge."

"I was going to get breakfast," he replied with a grin.

She tightened her grip on his shirt. "I was sure you were headed home."

"I thought about it."

Her heart shuddered at his confession, but she waited, hopeful after that kiss.

He moved a strand of hair from her eyelashes. "But it seems I can't leave. You're still here."

"I went to your room this morning. When I found you gone…" Rowen swallowed, the emotions too raw to put into words. "I-I panicked and took someone's keys. Then I saw you pull out."

His gaze dropped to her mouth for a long moment. "Is that when you decided to run me off the road?"

"That's when I decided I'd do whatever it took to keep you off that bridge so I could tell you that I was an idiot. I thought I'd give you one night and it would be enough, but it turns out I was wrong. You were all I could think about before that night, and now, you consume my thoughts. Even when I should be thinking about this reincarnation thing, all I wanted, all I thought about, was you."

Something tender, scorching, flickered in his gaze. "I love you. You may not believe me, but I know what I feel. I think I've always loved you. Even before I knew you."

The words eased the final knot of fear in her chest. If he had said those words a week ago, they would've sent her running. Now, his declaration made her want to shout it to the world. She could barely contain her exuberance as she brought his head to hers, stopping short of kissing him. "I believe it. I believe it, because I love you."

He kissed her again, a kiss burned with promise and passion, one laced with pleasure and steeped in love. It wasn't gentle. It was consuming. A claiming of two hearts that had finally found their places.

The world narrowed to the heat between them, and for one breathless moment, magic wrapped around them—fierce, eternal, and unbreakable.

The moment was broken by shouts, whistles, and clapping. Rowen lifted her head in surprise to find people standing outside their cars in either lane, watching them. Rowen laughed as she looked up at Mason.

"You're in your pajamas. And barefoot," he said, grinning.

She shrugged. "I couldn't let you go."

"You don't ever have to. I plan to be by your side forever."

EPILOGUE

SKYE DRUIDS

Two days later at Ferne's bookshop…

Rowen loved him. Mason could hardly believe it. He had hoped, prayed, but he hadn't actually believed it would happen. Yet it had. She had chosen him out of everyone. He would spend the rest of their life together, cherishing her as she deserved.

He watched her in discussion with his sister about a book. A few days earlier, things had been so dire that he thought he'd lose everything. Instead, he'd ended up with the greatest gift of all.

"I was there no' too long ago," Theo said as he walked up beside him.

Mason shelved the book he had in his hand and tore his gaze from Rowen. "It almost doesn't feel real."

"It still doesna for me sometimes." Theo looked over at Ferne and winked. "I'm one lucky bastard."

Mason grunted and found himself searching for Rowen again. "Me, too."

"What are your plans for London?"

He swung his head to Theo and searched his gaze. "What do you mean?"

"You know exactly what I mean. Your parents need justice. I want that for Ferne as much as you want it for yourself. You might be on Skye, but you're no' giving up on taking London down."

"My plan is to take Thomas down," Mason corrected him. He sighed and glanced at Rowen. "She thinks I should be the one to head the movement to change London."

"Why no'? I think you'd be a great candidate for that."

"It wasn't anything I ever wanted."

Theo chuckled as he pressed a shoulder against a half-filled bookcase. "Sometimes, we doona know what it is we need until it's before us."

"Maybe," Mason hedged. "But right now, my place is on Skye."

Arms came around him from behind as Rowen asked, "What are you two talking about?"

"Just talking," Theo said.

Ferne pulled a face as she came up beside Theo. "Right. What were you really discussing?"

"London," Mason answered.

Rowen moved to his side, and he wrapped an arm around her. "They need to be dealt with."

"They will undoubtedly show themselves here soon," Ferne warned.

A muscle jumped in Theo's jaw. "Let them."

Rowen turned her face up to Mason. "The next time you go home, I'm going with you. No arguments."

"Only if it's safe."

"If it's safe for you, then it's safe for me," she argued.

Ferne smiled as she watched the exchange. "You might as well agree. Ro won't give up."

"Nope. I fight for what I want," Rowen replied as she smiled up at him.

Mason pulled her close and pressed his lips to hers. "You sure do."

"No, none of that," Ferne said as she dragged Rowen out of his arms. "We have work to do, and if you two start kissing, you'll disappear like you did all of yesterday."

Theo grabbed Ferne's hips from behind and dragged her back to him. "Or we could disappear."

"I was supposed to open a week ago. Look at this place. It's a mess," Ferne said, playfully batting at Theo's chest.

Mason grabbed a box of books that Rowen tried to lift as their laughter filled the store. He walked with Rowen to the opposite side and set the box on a table. She touched his arm, drawing his attention. He looked down to find her watching him with a serene smile.

"I told you that Ferne would forgive you."

Mason grinned. "So you did. I think we can list seer on your resume, now."

"Oh, no," Rowen said with a chuckle. "I have quite enough to handle. Let's not add anything else."

He pulled her close again. "You know, whenever you get homesick, just say the word. You left home expecting to return a few days after."

"I will go back. I want to show you the islands and introduce you to my family, but that's for later. When everything here is settled."

"That might not be for weeks or months."

She shrugged, linking her hands behind him. "Then that's what it is."

"I just don't want you to start to resent—"

Rowen put a finger over his lips, silencing him. "I'm a grown woman, and I have no problem letting you or anyone else know if there's something I need."

"You're right. Again." He shot her a crooked smile.

"You keep looking at me like that, and we won't get any work done."

He gave her a quick, hard kiss. "Then let's hurry. I have something planned for us later."

"What's that?" she asked.

Mason shook his head as he began to sort books. "It has something to do with a picnic, and a secret cove Carlyle told me about."

"Let's hurry," Rowen whispered and tore open another box.

Somewhere in Scotland...

Beth looked out the passenger window at the scenery beyond.

"Are you sure about this?" Madeline asked.

Beth clutched the book in her lap, but she didn't look at it. She didn't tell Madeline about her uncertainty. She barely admitted it to herself. Was she making her own decisions, or was the book making them for her? She wasn't sure anymore.

"Beth?" Madeline prodded.

She met her bodyguard's dark gaze and nodded once. "I am."

"All right, then."

Beth's future was ambiguous. The book wanted her to open it and find out, but she was too scared now—scared to know if she died. And terrified to know if she didn't.

The hidden cottage…

"Edie."

She sat up on the bed. "Has Rowen come?"

"She won't be joining us."

"Skye claimed another one, then? I should've done more to convince her," she replied, ashamed that she had failed.

"You did exactly as asked. Rowen was never meant to join us."

Edie frowned. "I don't understand. You said—"

"We needed you to believe it so Rowen would believe it."

"Then…why seek her out?"

"For a twist they'll never see coming."

A pub in Oban…

She leaned over and lined up her shot on the pool table, gently tapping the end of the cue stick to the ball. Five thousand pounds was on the line. She didn't need the money. She played for the fun of it.

Just as she took the shot, she heard the voice in her head.

"It's time."

Slowly, she straightened, watching the ball roll across the table and sink into the corner pocket, winning her the game. She grabbed the money and shoved it into her cleavage as she winked at her opponent.

"Another game," the biker demanded.

"Another time, sugar. I have somewhere to be."

The man stepped in front of her. "I want a chance to win my money back."

She smiled as she ran a long, red nail down his chest. "I'd suggest getting out of my way."

"And I suggest we have another game."

If that's how he wanted it… She flung her hand to the side and watched him crash into tables and people as pandemonium erupted. She threw open the pub door and made her way to her motorcycle.

Thank you for reading **KISS OF SKYE**. I hope you enjoyed the ending to Rowan and Mason's story as much as I loved writing it.

If you want more Skye Druids, then you're in luck! Up next is **BETWEEN TWILIGHT**.

BUY BETWEEN TWILIGHT NOW
at www.DonnaGrant.com

* * *

And don't miss out on the Elven Kingdoms series. The next book set in Dark Universe, is **BURNING SEA**...

BUY BURNING SEA NOW
at www.DonnaGrant.com

* * *

To find out when new books release
SIGN UP FOR MY NEWSLETTER today at
https://www.tinyurl.com/DonnaGrantNews

* * *

Join my Facebook group, Donna Grant Groupies, for exclusive giveaways and sneak peeks of future books.
https://bit.ly/DGGroupies

* * *

Keep reading for a glimpse at BURNING SEA...

GLIMPSE AT THE NEXT DARK UNIVERSE BOOK

BURNING SEA, ELVEN KINGDOMS SERIES BOOK 5

Desire runs deeper than the ocean...

I was never meant to descend into the world beneath the waves—

never meant to fall into the orbit of a Sea Elf whose power could shatter oceans.

He is danger wrapped in control.

Cold. Commanding. Untouchable.

His city is beauty honed into a weapon. His restraint is legendary. And yet the way his gaze lingers tells me he wants me as much as he fears what I awaken in him.

I don't belong in his realm of tides and shadows, where ancient magic stirs and secrets are buried deep. But every step closer pulls me under—desire tightening, temptation burning hotter than the sea itself.

The truth I uncover could ignite a war.

Loving him could destroy us both.

Leaving may already be impossible.

Because when the ocean begins to rise and everything he's sworn to protect is threatened, I understand one dangerous truth—

The sea isn't the only thing capable of burning.

And I'm done resisting the fire between us.

New York Times **and** ***USA Today*** **bestselling author Donna Grant weaves a captivating story of forbidden desire, dangerous secrets, and impossible choices in this seductive installment of her acclaimed Elven Kingdoms series.**

BUY BURNING SEA NOW
at www.DonnaGrant.com

ABOUT THE AUTHOR

New York Times and *USA Today* bestselling author Donna Grant® has been praised for her "totally addictive" and "unique and sensual" stories.

She's written more than one hundred novels spanning multiple genres of romance including the bestselling Dragon Kings® series that features a thrilling combination of Druids, Fae, and immortal Highlanders who are dark, dangerous, and irresistible. She lives in Texas with her dog and a cat.

www.DonnaGrant.com
www.MotherofDragonsBooks.com

facebook.com/AuthorDonnaGrant
instagram.com/dgauthor
tiktok.com/@donnagrant_author
bookbub.com/authors/donna-grant
goodreads.com/donna_grant
pinterest.com/donnagrant1

www.ingramcontent.com/pod-product-compliance
Lightning Source LLC
LaVergne TN
LVHW032003070526
838202LV00058B/6278